Blood Under Candlelight

Ryan Coull

Table Of Contents

Dedication

To the guys I grew up with; they know who they are.

About The Author

Ryan Coull lives in Inverness, Scotland. He has published stories in The New Writer, Storgy magazine, Firstwriter, and Scribble magazine.

Baptism Of Fire

Adam Longley was finishing a fried breakfast in his second-floor apartment when his mobile started playing John Carpenter's spooky piano number from *Halloween*.

'Got a job just come in,' said Leonard Hayward. 'For later today.'

Adam mopped his plate with folded bread, looking at the clock. It was 8:30 a.m. 'Short notice, isn't it?'

'It just came on the books. You want it or not?'

'Sure, sure, I'll take it. What's the deal?'

'Big house called Laburnum, about, um, ten miles or so north of Banchory.'

Adam frowned. 'Banchory? Bit far afield, isn't it?'

'Contract's through a solicitors' firm in Aberdeen,' his boss told him. 'Some old duck's popped her clogs—spinster type, from what I understand. Snuffed it and lay in there two months before anyone found her.'

'I hope they opened windows,' Adam said, only half kidding.

'Yeah, they reckon it's been aired out. She hadn't any family or friends to bequeath her belongings to, and the solicitors want the house emptied on the quick. Old lady accrued a lot of debt. She was up to her peepers with credit companies, so the place'll be sold as well as any assets to clear her arrears.'

'How much stuff?'

'Quite a bit, apparently. They've supplied a rough inventory—' Adam heard Hayward rummaging through paperwork '—and it seems she hoarded stuff, antiques, furniture, ancient dolls, all sorts of weird crap. She hired some fancy-arse artist last year to paint her portrait and couldn't even pay the guy in the end. Something of a hermit too, and possessive, she didn't take kindly to anyone being inside her property. So anyway, bottom line, the solicitors don't know how much the stuff's worth, so we've to shift everything out before they catalogue it for probate. Probably just as well, 'cause I don't reckon we'd get a skip lorry up there.'

'Sounds like a lot of gear for one trip.'

'Proctor will meet you at the house with the Merc van. Sometime after midday, I'd imagine. You'll arrive with the box truck before him, so just go ahead and make a start. If it takes another trip, so be it, we'll get you both out there again tomorrow.'

Adam closed his eyes, groaning inwardly. Proctor was a clumsy loudmouth arsehole, and he hated working alongside him. But his boss never changed his mind without good reason. God, he hated Monday mornings.

'Old girl was somewhat eccentric,' Hayward was saying. 'They're the solicitor's words, not mine. Into a few strange practices, by all accounts.'

Adam crossed the studio apartment in his boxers and socks. He lit a cigarette and laid his breakfast plate at the sink. 'Like what?'

More paper rustling. 'Hmm. A ton of dated books in the study: hypnotism, psychology, the afterlife… that sort of thing.'

'Suze used to say I should try it to quit smoking,' Adam told him. 'I never really believed in it.'

'In what?'

'Hypnosis.'

Hayward laughed. 'Oh, it's genuine enough. Saw this show at the Albert Hall last year, me'n the wife, where this joker had folk running around the stage—grown men—flapping elbows and making chicken noises with their trousers down. Take my advice, Adam, don't ever raise your hand at one of them damned shows.'

'Reckon he could hypnotise Proctor to get his finger out?'

Hayward chuckled again. 'Maybe, maybe. Anyway, these volumes, they might be valuable. She was something of a stickler with everything she bought. Chances are her belongings will be in pretty good nick, so be careful with them.' Hayward cleared his throat. 'When we're through, Pest Control will give the joint a once-over. Any questions?'

Adam looked out the window at the August sun breaching a bank of clouds. 'Will Sat-nav find her house?'

'I doubt it. Listen, I've got to go out of town today, some damned gala thing the wife's roped me into. I'll text you through the biddy's name and address—this Laburnum place—and when you collect the keys from the office, grab the Android phone, okay? I'll leave it out for you, it has Telemap with online navigation, and you'll need your Internet connection. The postcode covers a square mile, or thereabouts, so enter it on the seeker, and you'll get a display list of addresses. Laburnum will be on it.'

*****

Hayward's text identified the deceased woman as Meredith Rycroft. After leaving the office and programming the Android phone—which did indeed have Laburnum listed—Adam stopped for petrol and also topped up the emergency canister kept in the back. En route, the potted rural roads were rife with turns and twists, most not signposted and many forested on either side. Furthermore, the scenic journey climbed and fell rather alarmingly, and he was constantly dropping through gears to compensate. Once, he was halted altogether when a flock of noisy, dye-spotted sheep jammed the roadway. Fortunately, Telemap guided him without any trouble. And Hayward had been dead right about getting a skip lorry out here: would've been a waking nightmare for the driver.

As he travelled, Adam smoked L&Bs and wished again that Hayward had assigned him someone else to work with. Proctor was a pain: loud, lazy, always chasing reasons for a wacky-baccy break. Adam knew from excruciating experience he would end up doing the lion's share. There would be weighty and awkward items he needed help with, of course, and Proctor *was* built like a Sherman tank—but here, the imbecile's attributes ceased. Another bugbear was how much the man talked. He never shut up, jabbering about topics Adam had no interest in, such as homebrew beer, American football (he was unfathomably obsessed with a local team called the Aberdeen Roughnecks), or whatever Hollywood skirt he was currently infatuated by, all the while polluting the atmosphere with marijuana smoke.

Adam slowed and took a left, steering below the steel lattice of a transmission tower, where countless blackbirds perched the length of its cables. He drove past some manner of roadkill, bedraggled carrion and pelt spilled across the way, pressed into the tarmac.

He had been in the employ of Hayward's House Clearing Services for three years, following a couple of cash-in-hand runs for Lenny Hayward while between jobs. Since then, Adam's fiancée had left him (a money issue, though Suze assured him otherwise), and it seemed he was destined to empty properties all his days. Doing grunt work while others prospered from his sweat struck him as a bleak outlook. To worsen matters, his two older brothers' careers—both in

Information Technology—went annually from strength to strength. Just wasn't much else available for a thirty-five-year-old guy with limited qualifications and questionable ambition. Adam didn't hate the job—not quite—but neither did he like it much. In truth, it could be bearable when he wasn't paired beside lacklustre individuals like Proctor. Somehow, he still hoped to land a better paying gig and perhaps win Suze back (although he was aware this leant more towards daydreams than reality).

The Android announced his arrival a few minutes after eleven. He was halted on the rise by tall wrought-iron gates, secured by padlock and chain, their paintwork blistered and rusty. Adam produced the keys and looked for a likely fit. A paper nametag was attached to the bunch—M. Rycroft—courtesy of Hayward's office. The second Yale key he tried slotted snugly into the lock, and a moment's perseverance had it open.

The gates flung wide, he popped the handbrake and accelerated up the grade until he found the residence tucked away in a clearing, among bramble plants and prickly shrubs, as if constructed with concealment in mind. A sandblasted plate, weatherworn though legible, spelled LABURNUM across the pediment above the front door. Adam vaguely recognised the word—some sort of toxic plant or tree, he thought but wasn't sure.

No sign of the slothful Proctor yet, which wasn't any surprise. He poured himself a capful of strong flask coffee and sipped delicately, watching a colourful butterfly lift and dip around the brambles. He switched on the radio and found Barry White crooning one of his seductive feel-good numbers. Then Adam reverse parked the 16ft Ford E-Series, got out, and wedged his Pearl Jam cap on his head. Birdlife called in the treetops. He lit another smoke with his Zippo (an engraved birthday gift from Suze during happier times) and stood there studying the house, wondering who would choose to set up shop here, squirrelled away in the boondocks. But Hayward did say—

'She'd been a hermit…' Adam murmured.

Snuffed it and lay in there two months.

The sandstone building was certainly too spacious by far for one spinster. Its front elevation comprised many windows: rotting frames, chipped paint, cracked glass, and raggedy curtains. No UPVC or double glazing for Meredith Rycroft. A rusted cat-shaped weathervane rose above moss-laden roof slates. Adam noticed lots of what he thought were wasps teeming by a fissure in the upper stonework; then, closer scrutiny revealed they were actually mortar bees, non-aggressive insects that make nests in masonry and harmless enough. Probably what Pest Control was for, he assumed.

He rotated gradually and looked all about. He knew he was alone out here—but he didn't quite *feel* alone.

His mobile jingled with the *Halloween* theme again: Hayward.

'You find the place, okay?'

'I'm here, five minutes ago.' Adam turned back towards the truck, still looking around. 'Just about to open up and head inside.'

'You made good time. Proctor's on his way, should be with you in a while.'

'Great.'

'Gimme a break, Adam. There was nobody else available. I warned Proctor there's no room for slacking, yeah—and to make sure he doesn't damage anything. Listen, I'll give you a buzz tonight; see how you got on.'

'Okay. Later.'

On the ring were two larger keys, for the front and the rear. He unlocked the front door and entered a gloomy vestibule area; the floors faded hardwood, the doors enriched by stained glass, ruby reds, and royal blues mostly. Bric-a-brac was positioned everywhere, pots, figurines, and ornaments, the air musty with what smelled like mildew or mould (or maybe the last traces of Lady Meredith). A broad wooden staircase and banister rose before him, the uprights and handrail shaped from a lathe, Adam guessed.

He wondered if she had any items of choice jewellery stashed up there, perhaps a lucrative gem or necklace he could appropriate for himself. Who would miss it? Judging by the circling creditors, however, Adam found it doubtful. Still, who knew with a hoarder? Maybe he could have a sniff around before Proctor showed his face. He flicked his smoke outside, then made a left beneath an archway and mounted stag head into what appeared to be the study.

Here, a dusty chandelier hung from a plaster rosette on the roof. Numerous shelves contained more books than Adam had ever seen. He read a few of the spines: *The Art of Hypnosis*; *Human Behaviour and Psychotherapy*; *Dark Psychology and Mind Control*; *Mastering the Subconscious*. Adam envisioned Hayward watching the show where people were being humiliated on stage and so wondered how any participant could perform such actions unawares. Some folk must simply be willing and receptive. Or was it suggestible? He smiled, took three paces, and inspected a few more titles: *Death and the Afterlife: A Chronological Journey, from Cremation to Quantum Resurrection; The Supernatural Guide to the Other Side; Communicate with Spirits*.

Adam softly whistled. Seems the solicitors were right: old Meredith had been into some pretty weird pastimes. Not much wonder she had been on her Jack Jones; hardly the life and soul, by the sounds of things. From the study, he entered the next room—the living area, homely as a funeral parlour, all dark woods, and faded drapes. A smattering of expired mortar bees littered the floor, which indicated they had made their way in somewhere, probably from their nest in the apex outside. He saw a shrivelled mouse too. For a moment, he was struck by an unsettling and inexplicable notion: anything that found its way inside these walls would perish.

Two bay windows allowed in shafts of sunlight, which combated the prevailing gloom. The carpet was old and hideous, bald in places, a geometric splatter of orange and brown. A jade chaise longue was given over to white-faced dolls in satiny black dresses, each of which seemed to peer intently at him. Many had curly blonde hair, some dark; others wore frilly hats and bonnets. All lined up like children of the damned. He passed a table supporting an ancient Singer sewing machine with a treadle and reams of that black sheeny fabric. In the corner was a large storage trunk with brass or copper clasps. A fireplace and ceramic surround occupied the far wall—and when Adam looked there, he did a double-take.

'Holy shit.'

Atop the fireplace mantel, to one side, was a wooden round-faced clock (stopped) with a motionless gold pendulum. To the other side was what he believed to be…a withered, upright Hand of Glory. It looked like candelabra from the pits of hell. He had seen something similar in the graphic horror comics he had bought as a kid but struggled to recall its purpose. Didn't it supposedly have…incapacitating effects?

And presiding above all this, in pride of place, a huge filigree-bordered portrait—six feet by four, Adam estimated—of what must be the lady of the manor herself. The oil picture appeared dated, the sort of artwork in which you would expect to see, perhaps, a nobleman in neck ruff. Frowning down, terribly lifelike, sporting a Maggie Thatcher barnet, she posed from a wing-chair wearing a black, body-length frock, like a woe-addled Victorian mourner. Again, her attire appeared tailored from the same lustrous material in which the dolls were clad. She looked, Adam thought, as if her mug would split apart if she dared to chance a smile. He absently wondered how she had died and decided it made little difference when you lie undiscovered for two months. She hadn't ruptured her corseted sides through laughter; he would bet on that.

'Just your garden-variety fruitcake,' he whispered, turning away from the picture and checking his watch. He sincerely hoped they could complete the job today because he didn't want to come here again nor spend another afternoon in the scintillating company of Proctor.

He began moving the manageable stuff outside. When Proctor arrived, they would systematically pack the vehicles together. He commenced with a set of ornate wooden chairs, antique most likely, followed by smaller tables, brass lamps, and various ornaments he could box and shift without help. The day was delightfully bright, the summer sun high and unchallenged, and Adam found himself perspiring feverishly. During each trip, he intentionally bypassed the moonfaced dolls, unwilling to touch those creepy little freaks until Proctor got here, though he would never admit as much to his colleague.

Scared of a bunch of old dolls, Adam?

When he returned to the living room for another load, he stopped dead in the doorway, his heart dropping a beat.

The Hand's five candle-tipped fingers were burning. He regarded the arrayed dolls. Guttering light glowed menacingly in each and every pair of synthetic eyes, injecting a grave imitation of life into these inanimate creatures, so much so he half expected them to move.

Adam raised his eyes to the portrait of Rycroft and found her embittered gaze penetrating his. If he didn't know better, he would have sworn her expression betrayed more annoyance now than it had ten minutes prior. He wanted to look away—indeed, he tried—but found he couldn't avert his eyes from her squinting, malevolent glare.

How dare you touch my belongings? her stare seemed to warn. It seized his attention, demanded it, and he could not turn his head.

Suddenly the clock's pendulum began swinging below the portrait. Adam made a concerted effort to flee, to back into the study; only his legs were fixed, leaden beneath his body. Conscious of nothing but the woman's hostile eyes and the metronomic pendulum, he felt his will dissolve a little further after each passing second. He felt sleepy. And then, through the power of the mind, as his eyelids grew heavy, the old woman in the picture began communicating with him. *Instructing* him.

Adam didn't know how long he remained standing there—his sense of time had become skewed and unfamiliar—but eventually, his state of inertia was shattered by the rumble of a diesel engine drawing up outside, followed by the *pip-pip* of a horn.

At last, he veered his attention, overcome by a floaty sensation of utter calm and relaxation. When he looked back, the clock's pendulum had ceased. The ghoulish finger-candlewicks were extinguished, though still emitting wisps of rising smoke. His sweaty T-shirt now stuck clammily against his skin. He tried to recall what had just taken place (*you will hear my voice and only my voice*) and could not.

'Hey, Adam!'

Proctor…

Adam breathed heavily, in and out. He crossed to the storage trunk in the corner, opened the clasps, and raised the lid. Inside was crammed with assorted tools, but what he sought—what he had somehow been directed to—sat right atop everything else. He reached in and curled his fingers around the claw hammer's long handle; then, he stood, concealing the implement behind his back. He felt an ugly rage in his heart, black rage born of every job he had attended where Proctor failed to pull his weight.

'Yo, Adam, you around?'

Outside, the big man's bulk leant against the high Merc van. The vehicle's panels had *Hayward's House Clearances* arced across in purple letters. Typically, he was puffing reefer and jabbing at his mobile phone. He wore combat trousers and Doc Marten boots. His T-shirt, Adam saw, was printed with the words: YES I'VE GOT A DRINK PROBLEM. I ONLY HAVE ONE MOUTH.

'There you are,' Proctor mumbled, still engrossed in the mobile. 'Almost gave up trying to find this joint. Double backing all the time. Shit, looks just like the Munsters' place, don't it?' He giggled. 'Talk about the middle of nowhere. Sweatin' like a damned pig all the way here. You had a gander inside? I see you've made a start. So how much stuff we gotta shift?'

Adam approached through the boxes and furniture he had already positioned outside. When close enough, he brought the hammer down in a violent arc on Proctor's forehead. There was a sharp splitting sound followed by the big man faltering back and toppling, his mobile and conical reefer hitting the ground—then Adam was on him, swinging the hammer in a demented fury of blows.

'You can't take her things! *How dare you touch her things?* She's doing her own clearance right now! Don't you see!' Adam punctuated each word with a devastating strike of the weapon: 'She-wants-us-off!'

He delivered the hammer furiously until Proctor became unrecognisable, until the man's boots quit juddering. Adam stood up, his face and front slick in warm blood, drawing laboured breaths of the humid afternoon air, fingers gleaming red.

He stepped away from Proctor's ruined form and discarded the hammer, then crossed to the Ford, where he opened the rear doors and dragged Proctor's corpse by the legs, leaving a bloody streak in the gravel, the big man's T-shirt hitching up to expose a fuzzy potbelly.

Entering first, Adam hauled him roughly inside and then grabbed the petrol container. He unscrewed the canister's top and doused Proctor, sloshing fuel across his colleague's body before turning it on himself. He removed his peaked cap and emptied the fluid over his own head, his eyes stinging as the truck's interior filled with potent fumes. Adam retrieved the Zippo from his jeans and opened its casing, his saturated fingers taking three concentrated attempts to light it. Only when flames erupted and engulfed both himself and Proctor's remains did grim realisation find him.

He stumbled from the box truck's open doors like a human firework, a figure of sheer agony, hollering and flailing in a world of unimaginable pain. He heard ferocious, hungry flames through seared ears and felt his nerves screaming beneath melting flesh as he thrashed his arms, trying ineffectually to extinguish the blaze. He spun in aimless circles, careering amidst the wooden chairs, crying out loud enough to startle roosting birds into flight.

Before dropping to his knees and collapsing on his face, the last thought Adam Longley had was of a stage full of people working their elbows and making clucking sounds. And the last thing he saw was the house's heavy front door swinging slowly closed.

Balancing The Books

I

On Wednesday October fifth 1988, ten-year-old Tobias Calcott was gazing through the four-panelled window of Primrose Hill Primary School in north London, aware the dismissal bell would ring shortly and his troubles would begin again. He no longer remembered not feeling scared and nervous, and although his particular problem had been active for just shy of a month, Toby had learned that four weeks could be a terribly lengthy time. For no apparent reason, the bully across the hall—an oaf named Jeremy Mullen—had taken to pushing him around after school every day.

Mullen had begun his campaign by making Toby's life hell in PE class, roughing him up during sports when the teacher wasn't looking. He had ridiculed him in front of his classmates, stealing Toby's lunch and taunting him, before tipping his sandwiches and apple out over the canteen floor. He had pushed Toby's face in a dirty puddle and dumped his schoolbooks into a waste bin. Perhaps Toby's glasses gave him a sense of vulnerability. Perhaps his slight build gave Mullen the courage to pick on him. Maybe Mullen's brain was just wired up wrong, what Toby's mother referred to as a bad streak.

Outside, a double-decker bus rolled by the schoolyard, stirring fallen yellow leaves. After it had passed, a woman in dark glasses, wearing a heavy coat and headscarf, began crossing the road, guided by a Golden Retriever. The dog's white harness, Toby saw, had fluorescent strips.

'—out there, Toby?'

'Sorry, sir?'

Mr Burnside—the Burnmeister, as he was known—scowled from behind his desk, peering over square-rimmed lenses. 'I said, is there something interesting out there?'

Toby adjusted his own glasses and sat up. 'No, sir.'

'Then why not try paying attention?'

Toby feigned interest in his arithmetic workbook; then, he lifted his gaze to ensure the Burnmeister wasn't still staring. Inevitably, the dread returned.

Initially, he had decided the best strategy was to let the situation run its course. With any luck, Mullen would tire and find somebody else to victimise. Not much of a strategy, but at least it didn't involve requesting help, something Toby wanted desperately to avoid. It was degrading enough having your arse kicked every day. He was still contemplating this when the home-time bell wailed in the hall, jerking him up straight in his chair.

Outside, Toby barely made it through the schoolyard gates before Jeremy Mullen spotted him. A crowd of gawping pupils had amassed, clad in skirts, trousers, stripy ties, and knee socks, all eager not to miss this daily spectacle. A tieless, open-collared Mullen lumbered towards Toby with a paunchy swagger, a strut that made him appear more adult than a schoolboy.

'Trying to sneak off again, you four-eyed little geek?'

Toby stopped. The schoolkids encroached.

'Can't you see without those dumb specs?' Mullen demanded, his cheeks flushed and sweaty, his hair a mass of brown curls. 'Always wincing like a stupid mole. You're such a geeky little twat, Calcott.'

'I know,' Toby said.

Mullen frowned. 'What?'

'I am a geek. I know you're bigger than me. I know you hate me. Isn't that enough?'

This seemed to scramble the larger boy's programme, causing his sweaty face to form a confused frown. Then the bad streak trumped reason again, and he lashed out at Toby, shoving him over with a lunging thrust of the arms. Toby tumbled back and landed hard, the fall partially cushioned by his schoolbag, skinning his elbow across the tarmac.

The graze stung, but relief filled Toby's heart when Mullen, surrounded by his minions, turned about and swaggered away. Today was an easy let-off, for sure. Prudence kept Toby down for a moment; then, he struggled to his feet and removed his jacket. Blood had stained the arm of his white shirt, for which he would need a befitting excuse to give his mother. Carrying his schoolbag and jacket, he shuffled off in the usual manner: alone, head bowed, wondering how much longer this situation would continue.

A few minutes later, under the purple maple trees, Toby looked up to see an elderly man occupying a wrought-iron bench by the stream. He was dressed in a black suit and white shirt, and his grey hair sleeked back. A black hat was sat on the bench beside him, a couple of pigeons strutting by his crossed legs as he watched the water. Toby had almost passed when the man spoke.

'How are you today, young Tobias?'

Toby spun around. The old gent grinned, drumming fingernails on the bench seat. He adjusted a scarlet cravat with his other hand.

'How d'you know my name?'

'Oh, I know the names of a great many boys.'

This triggered an alarm in Toby. Last month, his class had viewed an educational video concerning the dangers of talking to strangers: cars pulling up, men asking kids would they like to see some puppies? Toby found it odd that the video hadn't revealed what the men wanted—which was obviously to molest and murder children. If it had, he reckoned kids would probably pay much closer attention.

'You have nothing to fear from me, my boy,' the man said. 'I have no wish to…violate you in any way.'

Toby wondered how this person knew what he had been thinking. Had he read his mind, or was it just coincidence?

'Tell me, Tobias,' he said, uncrossing his legs. 'The undesirable who hurts you after school, how do you feel about him?'

'I don't like him.'

The man laughed, his dark eyes narrowing beneath black brows. 'I admire your restraint, Master Toby. Tell me, would you welcome a little retribution on this boy?' He indicated Toby's skinned elbow. 'Drawing blood without reason is a serious infraction.'

'I'm not s'posed to talk to strangers.'

'A wise standpoint, Tobias.' He raised a finger. 'Very wise indeed. Let me repeat myself: I have no interest in doing you harm. I wish to assist you, to help you…level the score, if you will. Would you like to do that?'

Toby glanced at the man's sharply pleated trousers and polished black shoes. He looked like the undertaker who buried Uncle Freddie last year. 'Why'd you want to help me?'

'Well, let me see. Chiefly, I abhor bullies, Toby. They're individuals even I cannot stand—and believe me, when I say, were we better acquainted, you'd appreciate the relevance of such a statement.

The Mullen boy, he has made your life decidedly unpleasant for much too long, am I right?'

'My mother says people like him have a bad streak.'

This seemed to tickle the old man, who twitched his head in appreciation. 'I think your mother is directly on the money, Master Toby.'

'You know about Jeremy Mullen?'

'Oh, I know all about him. Not much of a prospect, I fear. No Pulitzers written in that boy's future. Hardly surprising. Father's a drunk. And the mother, she spends her Thursdays performing some rather seedy deeds with the mechanic neighbour, while her husband festers at the White Lion, drinking away their pittance. Still, these parental drawbacks, these shortcomings, cannot excuse his behaviour, can they?'

Toby shrugged. 'Don't know, sir.'

'Why, what a polite soul you are. No, no. His domestic situation cannot justify his actions; trust me there. After all, he inflicts pain on you willingly. His father's taste for nectar surely cannot be blamed. And his mother's recreational habits? Well, the boy isn't even aware of her degrading exploits with the grease monkey next door, so we cannot very well allow this as any manner of defence. Agreed?'

Toby nodded. It made sense. Sort of.

'Excellent.' He rubbed his palms together, making a rough sound like sandpaper on wood. 'Now, I have something here of which I think you could make good use.' He delved into his suit pocket and, pinched between two knobbly fingers, withdrew what looked like a large silver coin. 'This artefact will grant you one wish, Toby. One and one alone. You understand?'

Toby rubbed his wounded elbow. 'A wish?'

'There is, however, a caveat—a warning, if you like. You cannot employ it for anything except revenge against this Mullen character. Is that quite clear? Should you try to pull a sly one—ask for, let's say, a million pounds—then nothing will happen, and your wish will be forfeit. You may retain the coin as long as you want and use it whenever you want, but solely for retribution against your tormentor.'

Toby recalled the video of strangers offering things to children—enticing things—and deduced that accepting the coin was likely a bad idea. But he wanted it, wanted it more than anything. He considered his recent state of constant fear and fantasised how much a wish could tip the balance. The possibilities seemed limitless…

'Interested, Toby?'

Toby lowered his hot-dot-covered schoolbag to the ground. 'Maybe.'

'Very good.' He offered the coin, then sharply withdrew it. 'In return for my help, however, there is a condition.'

Toby stared. Here it comes: the old man wasn't using sweets or puppies but the lure of a wish. He *was* going to snatch him. Yet how could he abduct someone without a car? *All the creeps in the class video had been in a car.*

'I'll be happy to give you this, Toby. But someday, I may need *your* help. A favour performed, a favour repaid. Would you be willing to assist me in return?'

Toby knew the deal was too good to be true, that there must be something iffy in what his father called the small print. Still, he wanted the coin; he had to have it now.

'What'll I need to do?'

'Honestly, I do not know, Toby.' He shrugged nonchalantly. The wind licked a wisp of his oily hair. 'Perhaps nothing. However, should I ask, you must comply.'

Toby sensed he would have to be careful. 'I don't want to hurt anyone if that's what you mean.'

'In which case, I will make a rare exception, Toby. I shall guarantee you will never be complicit in anything which may cause pain to another—our rotund friend excepted, of course.' He offered the coin again. 'How does that sound?'

Toby took the coin in his small hand and felt a brief shivery sensation flit through him, something more than mere excitement. The disc was large and weighty, dented, like something dug up from a bygone time, one side exhibiting a five-pointed star, and on the reverse, what appeared to be a faded animal head with horns. He waited until a woman walking a small Dachshund had passed by and asked, 'How's it work? What do I do?'

'Simplicity itself. Hold it in your hand, and make your wish out loud. Always out loud. Think you can handle this, young man?'

Toby nodded and picked up his schoolbag.

'Then off you go, Tobias, away with you, my boy, and lose your heavy heart. You've got some serious thinking to do, I imagine. Remember, this Mullen boy regards you as fair game, so it's only fitting you do likewise.'

Toby set off hesitantly along the bank, studying the coin. Already he had doubts. But if he didn't have to hurt anyone—other than Mullen—how bad could it be? When he had walked maybe twenty paces, Toby stopped and turned around. The bench was empty, and he heard only the slow progress of the stream and the wind stirring the trees.

That night, after the house fell quiet, Toby struggled to sleep. Surrounded by posters of Sly Stallone as Rocky Balboa and Lou Ferrigno as the Incredible Hulk, he played his Astro Wars electronic game a while, but he was side-tracked by his streamside encounter with the old man. He lay in bed, *Star Wars* lamp on, studying the coin and pondering its possibilities.

What if it was just a normal coin? What if the man was making a fool of him like Mullen always did?

This would certainly make sense. Magic wishes weren't real, so it could be the old man *was* a pervert. Still, Toby didn't quite believe it. He had had no car, for one, and hadn't acted as if he had wanted to hurt him. And also, the old man had looked too frail to abduct anyone in broad daylight. As for the coin, Toby found that he *wanted* to believe in its power and wondered if he would ever be bold enough to use it.

Somehow, he knew he would be.

As the obscure old man had hinted, Jeremy Mullen was a bully and deserved whatever was coming. Jeremy was *fair game*. Suddenly, Toby felt much brighter about the situation, as if the defining advantages had shifted from physical to mental and were now therefore tipped in his favour. Yes, the situation felt more like a kind of chess tactic, and he was holding the only queen. Yet, even at the age of ten, Toby considered himself a reasonable person. He would give Jeremy a chance to leave him alone. If Jeremy did, Toby wouldn't use the coin. And if he didn't use it, he would be free from any future obligation.

He eventually drifted off to sleep, the dented coin clutched in his hand.

In class the next day, Toby was full of newfound courage, a

strange sensation that took some getting used to. The coin—his queen—was safely zipped in his jacket pocket, ready and primed, and he had faith in it, albeit faith he didn't quite understand. He fantasised how bizarre it would be if Mullen didn't bother him again, then realised it would never happen. Stranger still, he hadn't yet decided just how to use the coin.

You've got some serious thinking to do, the old man had said.

Last night he had fancied all sorts of outlandish punishments to inflict on Mullen, but none had seemed right. Perhaps something would inspire him in the heat of the moment, Toby thought. In the act of battle.

Mullen was waiting for him again after school, entourage in tow.

'Four-Eyes!' he called, swaggering toward Toby, all stomach, sweaty cheeks, and flapping arms. 'Can you actually *see* without those binoculars on your face?'

'Leave me alone,' Toby said. 'I'm warning you.'

A startled gasp from the minions.

'What you say, you little freak? You warning me, are you?' Mullen snatched off Toby's glasses in a surprisingly fluid movement. Now Toby could see only distorted blurs—and was scared again, properly afraid. He wouldn't be able to retrieve his glasses from Mullen, no way, and being severely farsighted, he couldn't function without them.

'You want these, Geek Boy?'

'Please, I need them.'

Toby heard something crack and pop, followed by giggles and surprised laughs. Mullen had stomped on them. The glasses were thrown at his chest and fell to the ground. Then Toby made out the fuzzy crowd dispersing and felt grateful his torment was over for another day.

He squatted and searched blindly at his feet, finding the crushed specs twisted and smashed. He unzipped his jacket pocket and withdrew the coin, his heart surging with the sweet anticipation of revenge. Far off to his left, far enough for Toby to decipher pretty clearly, the woman with the dark glasses came steadily along the road, guided by her Golden Retriever. In that instant, he knew he would regret his actions, but this couldn't stop him from closing his trembling fingers around the coin and voicing his wish.

II

Over following years, Toby left Highgate Wood Secondary School with exemplary grades and completed a qualifying law degree at Cambridge University. He negotiated a vocational Legal Practice Course before acquiring a training contract with a law firm called Lovell & Dodson, a business that put him through a Professional Skills Course, which he passed before applying for admission to the roll of solicitors.

Amid these achievements, he met his future wife, a petite blonde named Leila Green, during a friend's party on August thirtieth 1997, a Saturday. Toby always remembered this date because the following day, the Princess of Wales was killed in a road tunnel accident in Paris. Toby and Leila married on Saturday June seventh 2008, at the Stonehouse Hotel in Stroud, Gloucestershire, which was Leila's hometown and where they had bought their first property. James Eric Calcott was born on November first 2012. Ellie Calcott arrived on August sixth 2015, when Toby was thirty-seven. Fulfilled with his life, he hadn't thought about Jeremy Mullen or the old man in better than ten years.

III

Wednesday April tenth 2019, Toby was reading through a dossier in his Gloucestershire office. Driving rain pelted the ancient, painted-shut windows as his secretary buzzed the intercom.

'A gentleman to see you, Mr Calcott.'

Toby closed the file. 'He has a name?'

'He says it's a surprise. He claims to be an old friend of yours?'

Toby frowned.

'Mr Calcott ...?'

'Okay, send him in, Lisa.'

When the office door opened, Toby adjusted his glasses, positive he was hallucinating.

'Afternoon, Tobias,' the old man greeted, doffing his hat. 'My, haven't you sprouted since our last discussion.' He crossed the carpet to a vacant chair, his attention roaming the office. 'Remarkable.'

Toby made a calculation: thirty years. Thirty damned years, and this man, who really should be dust and bones, hadn't changed one iota. The cravat was not red but royal blue, with little white squares, although everything else appeared the same. Teeming rain blurred the windowpanes, yet this individual, with neither coat nor brolly, was dry.

'You seem somewhat surprised, Toby.'

'That's one way of putting it.'

'We have unfinished business.'

'You can't be serious.'

'Oh, one never japes about business, Toby.'

'Look, mister, I don't know—'

'Before we commence, might I comment on the impressive disposal of your childhood aggressor. Quite inspired.'

Toby tried to grasp how this man could be sitting in front of him. Impossible, yet here he was. 'It was a mistake. I… I wanted to take it back.'

'I'm afraid revenge is rarely so accommodating.'

'I did a terrible thing…'

'You blinded the boy.'

Toby looked at his desk, ashamed. He remembered the stories, the eyewitness accounts of Mullen screaming and groping hysterically, hands outstretched, falling over himself, begging for help. 'The coin,' Toby said, 'It disappeared after I used it. I couldn't find it. I tried to retract what I had done.'

'Do not upset yourself, Toby. You've made a fine life for you and your family, far superior to anything Mr Mullen would have achieved, visually impaired or otherwise.'

'He didn't deserve what I did to him.'

The old man crossed his legs. 'Then perhaps it's a mercy he's no longer with us.'

'Not with us?'

'Well, let me tell you. Mr Mullen had numerous carers throughout the course of his handicap, Toby. Never did take to fending for himself. One summer evening, some eight years ago, he was left on his own for a short while and decided to take advantage of the opportunity. Nasty thoughts had haunted him for some time, I'm afraid, bleak thoughts I imagine would be all the more distressing to a blind individual. Anyway, this particular evening, clicking along there with his white cane, he listened for the Number Eleven bus to come by. He knew the routes in the area, you see, had used them from time to time. I can only suppose he didn't trust a regular vehicle to complete the job.'

'He committed suicide?'

'Admirably. No cry for help from your former nemesis, no. He managed, by chance, I imagine, to position his head under one of the big old Routemaster's front wheels.' He grimaced. 'Messy, Tobias. Popped his skull like a grape. But you mustn't feel downhearted. He was a bad element, and you had the good grace to offer a truce, which he declined.'

Toby took a moment to envisage this and closed his eyes. 'How the hell did you find me?'

The old man raised a brow. 'Whatever makes you think I lost you?'

Toby's heart sank. Had he known deep down that this day would eventually come? Had he merely blocked out the deal he had cut with the old man in the blind hope he would never hear of it again?

'Who the hell *are* you? What do you want?'

'I have numerous names, none of which is important, Tobias. As for what I *want*, there is a debt outstanding.'

'I'm a solicitor, I can't participate in anything…'

'Toby, Toby. You will not participate in hurting another—your specific condition, which, you'll recall, I accepted without quibble.'

'I can't break the law…I have a position here.'

'And said esteemed position will be instrumental in clearing your debt. It is exactly the commodity we need to utilise.'

Toby shook his head. 'This is madness.'

'A delicate line exists between madness and sanity, wouldn't you say?' The old man leant in, as if to share a confidence. 'You accepted the deal—and I always balance the books.'

'Jesus, I was ten.'

'Old enough to blind someone.'

Toby slotted his fingers together, and tapped his thumbs. 'And if I refuse?'

The man chuckled, genuinely amused. 'Must we travel that road? You have so much going for you. And an equal amount to lose.'

'Meaning?'

The old man's penetrating eyes found the framed photograph on Toby's desk: his family at Staffordshire's Alton Towers last year. It had rained that day, and James and Ellie grinned from under raised hoods. 'You're a sophisticated fellow. We don't really need to have that conversation, do we?'

'Are you threatening my family?'

'This needn't be painful; why make it so? You should bear in mind, Toby, that I *could* task you with burying an abusive husband in the woods, an unfortunate chap who still has a potato peeler in his temple, courtesy of a spouse who had reached her tolerance of beatings. Or what about smuggling contraband onto an airliner?'

Toby felt the hairs on his neck rise. He was in a jam here. This guy was a fruitcake. Worse, Toby was beginning to accept what he had been trying to deny since the office door opened: the man wasn't human. Somehow, he wasn't *human*.

'What do I have to do?'

'I have an acquaintance, a gentleman by the name of Wesley Blair, who is a person of interest in a recent jewellery store robbery. Summarily, there is no real evidence, Toby, nothing *binding*. Mr Blair performed his smash and grab from behind a balaclava and left no prints there at the scene. The authorities suspect him, however, on account of his having done this manner of thing before. Leopards and spots, you understand.'

Toby waited. He had read about the robbery in the newspapers, seen reports on television.

'One respectable witness placing him elsewhere would sufficiently dismantle the case against Mr Blair.'

'I can't do that.'

The old man looked again at the Alton Towers photograph.

'I can't lie for him. I don't even know the guy.'

'On the day in question, you frequented a bar called the Gin Parlour, a couple of blocks from here. If you say you encountered Mr Blair there, exchanged a few pleasantries, a few quiet words, this will suffice. Mr Blair could not be present in both places at once, Toby. Too great a distance involved, you see.'

'Have you been following me?'

The old man looked darkly impatient. 'If that's what you prefer to believe.'

'It won't work. What about CCTV in the bar? On the streets outside?'

'No cameras inside the public house, Toby. And the Gin Parlour, well, it's a bustling establishment where clientele come and go throughout the day. It rained heavily that Saturday, you'll likely recall. The townsfolk were running here and there, arriving in groups, arriving alone, leaving as couples and trios, cowering beneath brollies, trussed in jackets and hats. Considering the foul weather, any CCTV footage will not conclusively prove or disprove anything in a court of law. A simple statement conveying you spoke with Mr Blair that afternoon will be sufficient to clear your debt.'

'Spoke about what, for Christ's sake?'

'The Dow Jones Index. Hollywood movies. The Brexit fiasco. The specifics and fine-tuning you can concoct with Mr Blair.' He slid a piece of paper across the rosewood desk, on which was printed a phone number. 'I'm sure together you can produce something perfectly convincing, Tobias.'

Toby regarded the piece of paper. He felt boxed in. 'What about the owner of the store? He was ripped off, lost his stock, thousands of pounds' worth.'

'What of him? The gentleman is adequately insured; not your concern. Neither are his shiny little stones.'

'So, I perjure myself, get this Blair character off the hook…and he owes you a favour, right?'

The old man's expression brightened, like a teacher impressed by a pupil. 'Why, yes, how astute of you, Toby. And I'm quite sure Mr Blair will repay that favour without any pre-set conditions.'

Toby picked up the piece of paper with the phone number on it. 'How many of these—these scams are you running?'

'I have more plates spinning than you've had days on this planet. Extremely busy, yes. Later this very afternoon, I'm visiting with a wheat farmer in Pryor, Oklahoma, who owes me for keeping the bank from foreclosing on his land.'

'Oh yeah? And what will *he* have to do for you?'

'Set fire to a general store, as it happens, the owner of which wishes to benefit from a rather substantial insurance policy.'

Toby took a moment, trying to digest what he was being told. 'Any of your swindles have a positive outcome?'

'Of course. Your own personal experience should demonstrate that.'

'You call diving under a bus positive?'

'From your perspective, absolutely. Action and reaction. Positive and negative. Yin and Yang. The fat boy wouldn't leave you alone and wouldn't be warned. Had he reacted differently, they wouldn't have had to pluck his eyeballs from the treads of a bus tyre.'

'And, of course, my being a victim made me a prime target for you.'

The old man stood and fixed his cravat. 'When you converse with Mr Blair, please ensure the details withstand scrutiny. And if you entertain any further doubts about honouring our agreement, remember how the obnoxious Mr Mullen came to an end.' He popped his hat on, slightly cocked, and flicked the brim with his finger. 'Good day, Tobias.'

Toby watched him leave the office and sat there stunned. Then he moved to the window overlooking the rain-washed street, directly above the building's sole entrance. Minutes ticked by, but the old man in the black suit never appeared down there.

Toby studied the pedestrians as they hurried through the rain, wondering if any of them might be in debt to the dark stranger or perhaps destined to deal with him in the near future. He glanced at the picture of his family on the desk, mentally cursed, then whipped his suit jacket from the back of the chair and left the office. Against his better judgment, against every intuition in his body, he had to source a new mobile phone. He couldn't afford anyone knowing he had placed a call to Wesley Blair, jewellery thief.

Requiem In Blackett

Lafferty cast his gaze over the Thames as he crossed Westminster Bridge. At the far side, bathed in brassy sunlight, a middle-aged lady in sunglasses sat outside a bar. In a charcoal grey suit, she stared at the sweeping water as the tension cables and passenger capsules of the London Eye crept around behind her.

'Linda Hatfield?'

She removed her large sunglasses, revealing squinting eyes and thin brows. 'Yes. Mr Lafferty?'

From the bridge, he had placed her in her forties, but up close, she appeared a little older. Her black, pinned-back hair was streaked with grey, and small crow's feet marred the skin around her eyes. Lafferty found her quite attractive.

'Your message implied you might want to hire me,' he said, sitting down at her table.

Linda Hatfield lit a thin brown cigarette, blowing smoke into the breeze. 'A friend tells me you once did some good work for her.'

'I do my best,' Lafferty said.

She drew on the cigarette again, glancing around. 'This friend also mentioned you have some kind of…psychic ability.' She looked at him doubtfully. 'Is that so?'

Lafferty considered the question. 'I sometimes receive flashes—images, I suppose you could say—in particular locations where violence or death has occurred. Maybe even extreme anguish. It can be triggered by something I touch or by simply being in a certain place. It isn't a reliable resource, though.'

'Really? How so?'

'The images, they aren't always easy to interpret. And I can't control when or where they occur. The truth is they rarely help me.'

'But they have done?'

'Yes, they have.'

'I've never really believed in that sort of thing,' she said.

'I never ask anyone to.'

Lafferty got the impression her hard exterior was the result of many months of heartache, that she was all cried out. Just an impression, but one he thought was accurate. A gentler nature was probably concealed beneath the surface, he imagined.

She squinted. 'Did you hear about my daughter on the news last year?'

'Your daughter?' Lafferty was about to shake his head. 'I don't think—wait a minute. Hatfield? She's not Susan Hatfield?'

'Yes.'

'Susan was your—?' Lafferty paused, realising he had used the past tense. He raised a hand. 'Sorry, I didn't mean to imply anything.'

She waved it away. 'Most people believe my daughter is dead. Why else wouldn't we have heard from her? Even the police think the worst. In my heart, I believe she's gone, too.' She placed her cigarette in a metal ashtray and lowered her gaze, looking heartsick by the admission. 'I still have to know what happened to her.'

Lafferty thought about this. He had handled similar cases before and knew the hurt an absent child caused a parent. 'She went missing up in Scotland?' he asked.

'September fourteenth, last year.'

'It must be difficult for you,' he said.

'Susan was a carefree person. She loved going to new places and meeting new people. Quite the free spirit, not at all like her father or me. I didn't want her going away up there on her own, travelling around. But she was twenty-five, so we couldn't stop her.'

'Does her father know you're here?'

She shook her head. 'We separated a few months after Susan went missing. The strain of such an ordeal is incredibly hard to bear, Mr Lafferty.' She crushed out the cigarette and leaned back in her chair. 'Susan called us the night she disappeared; did you know that?'

'I think that rings a bell, yeah. I heard it on the news at the time.'

'She was very upbeat, enjoying her little adventure. She'd been all over the place, Glasgow, Edinburgh, all over. She was set to head farther north, wanting to travel to the Highlands, to the top of the country, before turning back. That night, she told us she was planning to stay in a small village called Blackett.'

Lafferty nodded in remembrance. 'The villagers there said they never saw Susan if I recall right. They seemed sure she never arrived.'

She sniffed and looked off as if she had considered this point many times. 'What if she did get there?'

'What makes you say that?'

Linda Hatfield shifted in her chair. 'A feeling, a suspicion, I don't know. She'd been using the trains and buses, but I suspect she was probably hitchhiking, as well. She'd done so before, against our wishes. If she was hitching...'

'You think this is when she might have run into trouble?' Lafferty considered this. 'Well, she may've come across a nasty customer on the roads. It would explain why no one reported giving Susan a lift and why the villagers in Blackett never laid eyes on her.'

Linda slipped on the large sunglasses. A woman with a pushchair strolled past. 'What if she did make it to the village? It was getting dark when Susan called from her mobile. She told us she was only a few miles outside Blackett. Isn't it conceivable she made it there?'

'But nobody saw her.'

'Perhaps something happened upon her arrival before many locals had a chance to see her.' She looked away, across at the Houses of Parliament. 'Or perhaps they're lying about not seeing her.'

'Why would they lie?'

'That's your department, isn't it?'

Lafferty titled his head, still feeling somewhat confused. 'What is it exactly you expect from me?'

Her face suddenly assumed seriousness. But it softened again as quickly. 'I want you to go up there, to Blackett, to see if there is anything to find. Perhaps your…intuition can uncover something the authorities have not. Money isn't a problem, Mr Lafferty. Just tell me what it'll cost and when you can go.'

*****

Lafferty planned to leave on Monday morning, although he had explained to Linda the likelihood of discovering anything worthwhile wasn't high. By the time their meeting was over, he had decided he liked the woman, or perhaps it was pity he felt; sometimes, it was hard to tell the difference. He then did some brushing up at the library using the Internet and old newspaper articles on microform.

Last year, after Susan disappeared, the police conducted a thorough investigation in Blackett and the towns and villages within a twenty-mile radius. Plenty of people had remembered Susan: waitresses in restaurants; passengers on a bus ride or train journey. A young woman who had queued with Susan outside a cinema described her as friendly and fun. The trail had indeed led to the point when she called her parents, claiming to be headed for the village of Blackett. Shortly afterwards, something significant had happened. Susan had vanished, and the police could locate no signal from her mobile.

Many thousands of people went missing in Britain every year, he had warned Linda, and many were never found. Nonetheless, she was adamant that Lafferty try. It was her money; she had pointed out decidedly. Maybe someone in Blackett would remember something overlooked during the investigation. Perhaps a villager would inadvertently let something slip. She had accepted the chances were slight but felt she wouldn't be doing her motherly duty should she not try something.

He wasn't convinced she had any faith in what she called his 'intuition'. But that wasn't unusual. Most people Lafferty dealt with were justifiably sceptical. His ability had grown stronger as he aged and understood it more, but he had been just ten years old when he first realised he was different.

A local child, a boy with learning problems named Donny McCauley, last seen using a tree swing in the woods behind his home, had been abducted at the end of summer. Days had passed with the police making no progress. Filled with the adventurous curiosity of youth, ten-year-old Lafferty had sneaked into the woods to that exact spot, planning to swing out over the stream a few times, more for bragging rights that he had been there than anything else. But when he had grabbed that frayed, sundried rope, an image of Donny being taken away filled his head, upsetting his balance so much he had to sit down on the grass. In this vision, a man—someone the young Lafferty couldn't decipher—dragged Donny towards a light-brown boxlike vehicle parked beneath a canopy of trees. Two weeks later, when the police made an arrest, the perpetrator was driving what they described as a beige VW van. Lafferty hadn't gotten involved (what could he have said, and who would've believed him?), but because Donny had eventually turned up dead, the incident remained fixed in his memory.

Lafferty programmed his Satnav on Monday morning and set off at eight a.m. BMW under cruise control, he headed north, the weather constantly wavering between drizzle and sunshine. At Belle Isle, to the south of Leeds, he took the road linking the M1 with the A1 at Hook Moor, to the east of Leeds.

He listened to the radio as the hours ticked by, coming across tailbacks more than once. The journey had a soporific effect on him, and twice he stopped to stretch his legs. When he crossed the border, he ate bacon and eggs with coffee at a roadside café, served by a polite red-haired woman who reminded him a little of his ex-wife. Lafferty stared through the large window, watching vehicles and lorries whip past. He looked at families and couples seated around him, wondering if he would ever marry again. He questioned the ethics of accepting this job, knowing there was very little to go on. And he wondered about Susan Hatfield and what might have happened to her.

Back behind the wheel, north through more intermittent rain, admiring the picturesque views of Scotland's east coast. Mile after mile of pasturelands rolled far and wide, dotted with animals cropping the grass.

Several hours later, he was motoring up the A9, crossing the Moray Firth, rolling steadily onward. By now, he had been going for better than twelve hours, but one mile at a time, he got there.

The village was as dreary as he recalled from news reports last year. Driving along the rain-washed main street, Lafferty took in the small houses and flowery gardens. A homely pub—the Bracken Leaf—sat atop a rise to his right, a burgundy-painted wagon wheel mounted on the mortared sandstone. An old church with tall, stained-glass windows appeared around the next bend, the building adjoining a cemetery with lichen-stained stones from a long-ago time. An elderly gentleman in a Barbour jacket stood on the path, one hand clutching a pipe to his whiskery mouth, the other holding a small collie's leash. The dog barked, its muzzle going up and down. Lafferty raised a hand in greeting, but the man only watched the car drift by.

His psychic sense offered nothing specific—nor had he expected it to. Yet he was picking up on something vague… It was unusual to receive anything at all without being in a specific room or spot, but he definitely had a vibe.

There's something wrong with this place.

He stopped at a small establishment—the Shoppe—his spine cracking as he got out and stretched. He went inside, a bell tinkling above the door, and was faced with a petite white-haired old woman standing by the till.

'Evening,' he said. 'You still open?'

The woman eyed him warily as she placed her hands on the counter, the loose skin beaded with brown spots. 'I'm about to close. What do you need?'

'Just some information,' he replied, throwing in a smile for good measure. 'Is there someone around here who could put me up for the night?'

The short woman squinted mistrustfully through her spectacles. 'You want to stay here?'

'I'm an investor,' Lafferty announced as easily as if it were true. 'Travelling north to view some property. I've had a dog of a day, and I'd rather not go any farther tonight.' He smiled at her again. 'Tiredness and driving don't mix.'

'Two rooms up at the Bracken Leaf,' she told him, shifting tubs of sweets on the counter. 'They're usually both free.'

'That's the pub I passed on the way in, the place on the hill?'

'It's the only pub.'

'Right.' Lafferty thanked her, trying to recall when he had last encountered such a hostile pensioner.

Outside, the cloud-heavy sky was darkening. Lafferty slumped into his Beamer and sighed. When he glanced out at the shop window, the old woman was standing, watching him.

Inside the Bracken Leaf, patrons in plaid shirts and caps sat playing cards and nursing ales. Despite the summer season, welcoming tongues of fire crackled below a stone mantel. Lafferty was aware of furtive glances, watching eyes, making him feel as if he had just entered a saloon in an old Western movie. He approached the tall man behind the counter, who was drying glasses with a towel, his face angular and vulpine, like a fox's.

'Old girl at the shop said you might have a room.'

The bartender was bald, wearing a white shirt beneath a suede waistcoat. He looked a genteel fellow, though Lafferty had long since stopped taking anything for granted.

'Twenty-two pounds a night,' he said. He set down a glass with long, pale fingers and began drying another. 'We'll toss in some breakfast if you make the dining room before eight.'

'Sounds ideal,' Lafferty said, trying his best to act like a brainless tourist.

'Get you a drink?'

Lafferty eyed the arrayed bottles and optics. He craved a whisky, but drink had eroded his marriage, and he had been teetotal for ages. Still, he found himself within an ace of having something: he had had a long trip, and good malt would hit the spot.

'I'll take a Diet Coke.'

The bartender popped open a chilled bottle and poured its contents into a glass as if conducting an experiment. A large taxidermy pike was mounted on the wall behind him.

'Isn't this the place featured on the news last year?' Lafferty asked, as off-the-cuff as possible. 'A missing woman, or something, was it?'

With tongs, the bartender added ice. The drink fizzed and popped. 'Far as I recall, nobody around here saw her.'

Lafferty nodded. 'Strange, though, wasn't it?'

'What brings you to the village?'

'Viewing some property farther north,' Lafferty told him and left it there. He drank his Coke, and effervescence shot up his nose, drawing a cough. 'Whoa, think that went down a wrong tube,' he said heartily.

The barman plucked a key from the board behind him. 'I'll show you the room.'

The accommodation had groaning joists and was musty and furnished only with the basics. Lafferty plonked his overnight bag on the single bed and stood by the window, looking down at the village, wondering if anything untoward was going on here. A muffled hubbub drifted up from the bar below. Turning from the window, he looked from the upper reaches of the wooden rafters to the camber of the floorboards, wondering when the room was last occupied. Had Susan Hatfield stood here?

Doubtful.

He extracted from his wallet a small picture of Susan and a fine gold necklace which had belonged to her, both of which had been supplied by Linda. Personal effects and pictures marginally increased the chances of a psychic connection but guaranteed nothing, especially if they hadn't been worn or carried by the victim at the time. As he had precious little else to work with, he deemed it worth a try.

The photograph had been taken almost a year before her disappearance. Hands on her waist, hair drawn back, Susan stood before an open garage in an orange vest and white shorts. Smiling, she was flushed as if she had been exercising and snapped without warning, the picture capturing an element of her bounce and vitality. Bright sunlight brought her into relief against the garage's dark interior. There was a likeness to her mother, though not striking. Lafferty couldn't help feeling an almost paternal empathy towards her.

Concentrating intently as he held the items, one in each hand, he closed his eyes and waited. Nothing came. He then touched the room's papered walls but again received nothing. He sat on the bed and eventually sighed and placed the items aside.

Atop the nightstand was a little TV on a brocaded cloth, a sorry-looking aerial hanging from its side. Rain whispered at the window as he tugged the curtains over the darkness. When Lafferty flipped open his mobile, the screen lit up, and he scrolled to Linda Hatfield's number. It rang four times before being answered.

'Hello?'

'Hi, Linda, it's Lafferty. I'm here, safe and sound.'

'You're in Blackett?'

'I just arrived.'

She was silent and then asked, 'What's the place like?'

'Well, it's a quiet village. The people seem a bit, I don't know, weird. They're probably just not used to strange faces.'

'Have you…experienced anything?' She sounded as if the question was difficult to ask as if she hadn't yet accepted Lafferty could do what he claimed. 'Have you felt anything?'

'I've nothing to report yet, Linda.'

There's something wrong with this place.

'Okay.'

'I'll take a squint around tonight, once everyone turns in, see if there's anything I can pick up. And I'll ask some questions tomorrow.'

'Hmm.'

'Listen, I've got a good nose, Linda. I trust my instincts. If these people are lying about Susan having been here, I'll know it.'

She didn't speak for a moment. Lafferty looked at the snap of Susan in her orange vest. Then Linda said, 'Thank you for doing this for me, Mr Lafferty.'

He found himself smiling. 'Hey, you're paying me, remember?'

*****

After midnight, Lafferty stuffed pillows under the bedsheets, shaping and fluffing them so a glance would hopefully see him sleeping there. He paced back to the door to gauge the deception. Then he slipped on his running shoes and parted the curtains. The sash window rose grudgingly, letting him slip out and descend the drainpipe.

The Bracken Leaf had closed for the night, and streetlights throughout the village were few. Under a brilliant full moon, he set off, peering studiously at the small homes lining the road. With Susan's picture and necklace in his pocket, he drew his hands over wrought-iron gates and rough dikes like a blind man trying to find his way home. He waited for something to come to him…but nothing did.

The village was calm as a pond. A bird passed overhead. Lafferty heard something hoot in the trees. He found himself in the regard of a doorstep cat, its eyes flashing supernaturally as if powered from inside.

He crossed the way to a play park, where he touched the cold metal of rain-beaded swings and climbing frames. When he rounded a bend, a limestone church loomed above him, its high steeple ominously silhouetted against the star-spangled night sky. He followed the road down, and the closer he came to the old building, the more he experienced that portentous sensation.

There's something wrong with this place.

He glanced at the graveyard, which was partially lit under the streetlight. An ancient cherub and seraphim stood among the weathered markers. Lafferty placed his fingertips against the church's cold stonework—and the vision struck him immediately, its ferocity so overpowering he had to grip shut his eyes.

She's on her back, naked and screaming, bound to a stone slab. The figures gathered around her are dressed in dark hooded gowns, each face concealed inside a cowl. She is writhing, tugging against the restraints which fetter her arms and legs. One black-clad figure produces a long blade, the firelight flashing in the steel, and she is screaming again—

Lafferty recoiled from the church wall as if scalded. 'Son of a bitch,' he whispered, touching his forehead, taking a minute to compose himself. He drew deep breaths. The night remained silent and still until a dog whined mournfully somewhere.

He climbed the church steps and checked once behind him. There was nobody out there, yet he felt watched. Beneath the arched entranceway, he tested the heavy oak door, which yielded and gave on an altar and pews, the interior softly lit by dying candlelight.

Lafferty walked slowly down the nave, shoes quiet on the wooden floor, fingertips brushing pews. He found it strange that a candle was burning and wondered how recently somebody else had been here. He touched the pulpit, the carved lectern, and the surface of the altar, prepared for another vision, but none came.

He picked up the burning candle. Looking above him at the clerestory, he stepped carefully over the low rail into the sanctuary, where he came upon a darkened doorway. He eased through it and found himself in the sacristy, where vestments hung from wall hooks. Moving the candle around, its flame faltering, he found the space housed a multitude of hymn books and an old pipe organ. There was, however, a small wooden door in the corner which drew his eye.

He tried the handle and found it locked.

After setting down the candle, he withdrew a wallet of picks from his jacket, selected one, and began working, slowly, expertly.

Minutes later, the lock gave with a satisfying click. The door groaned open, scraping against the floor, loud enough to draw a grimace from him. Lafferty raised the candle, revealing stone steps spiralling down into pitch darkness. A fusty smell swept out past him, teasing the flame, his hands trembling as they once had from the DTs.

Foreboding consumed him, for he felt sure that the answer to Susan's disappearance was down there.

*****

Underneath the church, Lafferty's candlelight revealed several empty sconces protruding from cavernous walls. Between them were pentagrams painted inside large circles: a sign, Lafferty knew, often used in magic. Shadows capered everywhere. He heard water dripping. He also turned his light on ankh symbols—cruciform shapes where the top section was a loop—which he vaguely remembered had some relevance in paganism. The gloomy chamber's centre housed a stone altar; both it and the floor were stained in dark maroon, like dried blood.

He approached, candle aloft, and scratched at the wide stain with a fingernail. He then brought the flame close, examining the scrapings, convinced they were blood. He had seen enough of it in his time to be all but sure. This was the place from his vision, and though his visions were sometimes hard to read, they were never wrong.

They had taken her down here and killed her, in what Lafferty could only conclude was some sort of…deranged ritual.

Jesus, do these things really happen? he thought.

He flinched as a run of melted wax burned his thumb.

Despite a deep-seated urge to flee, he set aside the candle and took a small envelope from his jacket. He commenced scratching off more flakes of blood, aiming them inside the envelope. He didn't know if DNA tests could determine the source of samples this old, but it was sure as hell worth a try. He slipped the evidence away and took out his small digital camera, and as he began snapping pictures, each flash illuminating the surroundings with eerie starkness, Lafferty couldn't shake the feeling he was being watched.

He felt disinclined to return to the Bracken Leaf. He had left nothing valuable there, and the notion of being indoors with these lunatics revolted him. He felt sick and wanted only to get in the Beamer and make tracks, putting as much distance between him and Blackett as possible. His priority was to call Linda Hatfield—he found himself almost impatient to impart what he had discovered. The best idea, therefore, was to get the car now and head south.

Lafferty hurried up the puddly incline towards the Bracken Leaf and his BMW, unlocking the car with his key fob. As he was getting in, the silhouette of a person appeared by the pub, their shadow elongated against the gable wall. Lafferty quickly ducked inside the car, keyed the ignition, and hit the lights.

Before he could do anything else, more bodies emerged from the darkness, closing around him. The headlamps revealed several faces, ghostly and malevolent in the bright beams. Here was the elderly woman from the store; beside her lurked the old whiskery man, the dog walker, whom Lafferty had acknowledged when he arrived earlier. The bartender appeared at the driver's-side door, staring blankly from those shadow-streaked, vulpine eyes, and now Lafferty noticed many others he had seen inside the pub.

He depressed the clutch and crunched into reverse, backing away. As he braked and found first gear, something smashed against his rear window, fracturing the laminated glass like a spider web. He frantically hit the interior switch, locking the entire vehicle. Within seconds they were yanking at door handles, splayed fingers pressed against windows. One of them scaled the car, footsteps thumping across the roof, buckling the metal. Lafferty felt his pulse rising off the chart as the BMW was rocked in the commotion. The spike of a pickaxe punched through the windscreen, its steel point ceasing inches from his nose, sprinkling his face and lap with glass.

'Son of a bitch—'

With a loud scraping and crunching, the pickaxe was worked free, and before its wielder could mount another attack, Lafferty stamped on the accelerator. Wheels spun, and the car finally bolted forward. He heard the assailant on the roof lose his footing and tumble away.

Further villagers impeded his escape as Lafferty squinted through the ruined windshield and bucketed straight into them. Heavy impacts sounded as he ran headlong through the crowd, his lights finding one individual after another like an outdoor ghost train. They leapt from his path, and all at once, the way was blessedly clear. Canted in his seat to see past the windscreen damage, Lafferty followed the road from the village, nervously checking the rearview mirror but seeing only more devastated glass. The seatbelt's warning sound pinged repeatedly.

'Holy shit,' he said.

He cracked the window an inch, regardless of the cold air streaming in through the windshield. He yelled out loud, simply in a bid to expend the tension inside him. Then he took a long, steadying breath and palmed the steering wheel, trying to determine his next move. He fumbled the seatbelt buckle home, silencing the warning noise. He felt a sting on his cheek and picked away a sliver of glass, finding it red with blood.

Jesus, could he use a drink.

When he reached the next town, he would locate the police station and make them listen to what he had to say. Damned right. Pressing the accelerator, still buzzing like a tuning fork, Lafferty scarcely believed it himself as he hit the open road, the car's backend fishtailing.

Through the trashed windshield, he studied the centreline

disappearing beneath the car. When far enough away and seeing only darkness in the mirrors, he fumbled out his phone and called Linda's number. His heart battered as the connection was made. The BMW's headlights cleaved the night.

He closed his eyes briefly when she answered. 'It's me,' he said.

'Did you…find anything?'

'I think you better brace yourself.'

At that moment, headlights flashed in his mirror like two Christmas Stars, and Lafferty put his foot down.

The Shorebridge Children

Jane Armistead was thinking about the missing kids when a sign for Shorebridge finally glinted in her headlights. She had driven all night, crossing the border into Scotland, only stopping when necessary to rest her eyes. The folded-open map on her thighs assured her she was close, a red ink mark encircling her destination.

She abandoned the main road for the right-hand turnoff and was soon hemmed in by hedgerows and lines of gorse bush. In the distance, angry waves lashed inshore from a choppy ocean. A huge black tanker sat out there, eerily motionless in the pre-dawn light. Her husband had said she was mad to drive up here on a whim, but Jane wanted this story for her new book, a collection of real-life incidents which would be entitled: 'Britain's Paranormal Activity'.

Snow patches peppered the fields and open land that flanked her descent into Shorebridge. She steered the BMW past a tumbledown barn, and gradually, as she neared the sea, the town revealed itself at intervals: a rooftop here, a church spire there.

She drove through Shorebridge's main street, past a pub and butcher shop, before the road snaked down parallel to the shore. The North Sea lunged over craggy rocks with each swell of the tide, rising into the atmosphere. Despite the heaters blowing flat out, Jane shivered.

Shortly, the harbour materialised. Two- and three-mast vessels bobbed and rocked in their moorings, equipped with nets and safety rings. The quayside walls were gargantuan, divided by a single opening through which fishermen would come and go. She parked in a vacant berth and lowered the window, inhaling brine and assorted sea smells. By the war memorial, as gulls soared above, an elderly man with a candyfloss beard and rubber boots stood contemplating the tide.

Jane scrolled through her mobile for Rupert Mannford's number, wondering why any parent would deem 'Rupert' a fair start in life. It rang four times before being answered.

'Aye?'

'Rupert Mannford? This is Jane Armistead. We spoke briefly last week, do you remember? I called about interviewing you?'

'I remember.'

'Great. I'm here in Shorebridge, right now.'

'You're here?'

'Yes, sir. Been driving all night. You're still willing to see me, I hope?'

'You mentioned money last time.'

Jane almost grinned at the man's candour. 'I have your money, Mr Mannford. So, shall we meet?'

'You said this is for a book you're writing?'

'That's right. I plan to complete it with the Shorebridge story—your story.'

'…My name'll be in this book?'

'I'm afraid that's unavoidable if the chapter's to have any credibility. That's why I'm willing to pay you. Mr Mannford.' She waited, looking at the diving gulls. 'Are we still on?'

'Aye, we're still on.'

'Fantastic. Where do I find you?'

*****

More snow began before she found Mannford's place. He was waiting with his front door open, a tank of a figure with bright ginger hair and a full beard, at least a whole head taller than Jane. In a plaid shirt and jeans, he assumed the alpha-male stance: feet set apart, back straight, hands on hips, like one of the superheroes from the DC comics she bought as a kid. Not what she had expected at all.

'Good morning,' Jane said, shrugging into her leather jacket and clutching her handbag from the car. 'Hope this isn't too early.'

'Been up hours,' Mannford said, snowflakes dancing around him. Stooping, he led Jane beneath a low lintel into a kitchen, where a small linen-covered table sat against one wall. The unmistakable scent of fried bacon hung in the air. A blond Labrador was curled in the corner, looking up at her with sad eyes.

Mannford withdrew a chair. 'So, where've you come from?'

'East London,' Jane said and sat down.

'Quite a ways. You really that interested in what I have to say?'

'Yes, I am. Those events have always been…well, muddy. Nobody seems to know what went on that autumn, even after all these years.'

Mannford seemed darkly amused, though he didn't smile. 'I told them what happened, but nobody wanted to hear it.'

'From what I understand, your account was widely discredited. You were only ten at the time, is that right?'

'You think ten's too young to know what I saw?'

Jane produced a sealed brown envelope from her bag. 'If I did, I wouldn't be here.'

Mannford glanced at it. 'Why you so interested in all this stuff?'

'Like I said, it's for a book. And also, well, I've always been curious about this kind of thing since I was a young girl.'

'You've come a long way, Mrs Armistead. I best offer you something to drink.'

'I could murder a coffee. Black, if it's no trouble.'

As Mannford busied himself, Jane's gaze went slyly around the kitchen. A range of whisky labels was visible through a glass-fronted cupboard. Beside her, a silver crucifix adorned the dated wallpaper.

'You live alone?' she asked.

'She took off last year,' Mannford said, pouring hot water. 'It'd been brewing for a while. I think we just outgrew each other; that happens sometimes.' He placed the coffees down. 'So, what about this book?'

'Well, it's a work recounting inexplicable occurrences in Britain over the last fifty years, covering a whole range of topics. I simply want to hear everything you know about what happened that autumn. Everything you saw. In return, you get your money, and I shouldn't have to bother you again.' Jane placed a Dictaphone between them.

Mannford's pale eyes, set beneath orange brows, stared at it. 'You gonna tape me?'

'More practical than taking notes. I need your account verbatim so there's nothing misconstrued. It's better this way, believe me.'

Jane clicked the Dictaphone on and waited. She feared Mannford had changed his mind because he merely regarded the machine. Perhaps he now thought better of sharing the details she wanted to hear.

Then he began to talk.

'Started in October 1991,' he said cautiously. 'Cold autumn. I was ten years old, in the last year of primary school. One night my father calls me into the kitchen, over to the window. I looked out, and these…weird lights were in the sky, strange glowing lights. Greenish they were—lasted about an hour. Everybody in town saw them. Well, it was the very next morning when things began happening.

'Abby Kingston was a classmate. Pretty little thing, she was; had pigtails and a space in her teeth, and always smiling. You probably saw her pictures in those old newspapers, right? Well, that next morning, she wasn't in school. Nobody took much notice at first. But as time went on, everybody was talking about her. Rumour was she hadn't come home the night before. Her mum and dad didn't know where she was. She'd been walking back from a friend's place—her parents knew this 'cause the friend's mother saw Abby out the door. It was about eight o'clock and dark by that time, just before the lights appeared in the sky.'

Mannford adjusted himself and cleared his throat.

'Days passed. She never turned up again. Police went knocking on doors, asking their questions. They even talked to us, the kids. Nobody'd seen her, though. Was like she'd fallen through a hole in the earth. I expect they were waiting for a body to turn up, but it didn't happen. Well, people were worried. Parents weren't letting kids outta their sight. Something had happened to Abby, though nobody knew what.

'Eight days later, it happened again. Little Norman Roderick. Not in my class at school but the one across the hall. Small for his age. Knew him to see him, you know? His old man worked the shipyards with my father. Walking home from Boys' Brigade he was, and gone, just the same as Abby.

'More police arrived. For all the use they were, would've been as well not there. There's nothing much between the old Boys' Brigade hall and the Roderick house. Norman only had to walk about four streets, wouldn't take more'n a few minutes. It was night again when he went missing, but the roads were well lit.'

Jane's mobile began braying in her pocket. Swiftly she turned it off. 'Sorry about that,' she said, watching the Lab trot out of the kitchen.

'Police drew another blank. I wasn't allowed outside. Never saw a kid play around the streets all the time it was going on. Pictures of Abby and Norman aired over the news, again and again, bulletins and the rest of it, and still, the police couldn't get a start. They were criticised for it too. They searched everywhere, but it was no good.

'Folks were about climbing the walls when it happened a third time. Wendy Gallagher was a year younger than me and Norman. Lived with her mother. Her parents had separated. Father was a drinker, I heard. A bit handy with his fists. Her mother fell asleep on the sofa one night in late October. Wendy was watching TV. When the mother woke up, Wendy was gone.' Mannford clicked his stubby fingers. 'Gone while her mother slept on the couch.'

'People thought she'd left the house of her own accord, didn't they?'

'Wendy's shoes were gone, and her coat, too. Looked like she'd left to go to the shop or something. Could be the lass was tired of being cooped up indoors—I sure was. Well, specialist detectives arrived after that. By now, everybody was demanding to know what the hell was going down, why there weren't results, you know. I suppose you can't blame the police, poor buggers were hunting night and day, round the clock. Townsfolk were scouring the fields and woods.

'It was a few days into November, evening time. The phone rang, and my mother picked it up. She called me, said it was a friend from school. I took the phone from her and said hello. "It's Norman Roderick," the voice says. "Don't say anything to your parents," he tells me. He didn't sound scared or hurt or nothing. I knew the voice was Norman's—knew it well enough. My folks were in the sitting room, so I quietly asked Norman what was going on. Did he know half the world was looking for him and the two girls?

' "You have to come and see," he said to me. "It's amazing, Rupert." I asked him what's he talking about, but he wouldn't say.' Mannford wrung his hands a little. 'Kept telling me I had to see for myself, that I couldn't tell anyone, especially my parents. By this time, I was really curious—and kind of uneasy too.'

'I can imagine.'

'He said to come meet him, that he had something to show me. "It's a huge secret. The most unbelievable thing I'd ever see," he said. I asked where he was, and Norm said to meet him behind the church. Then he hangs up the phone. I thought I was the butt of a joke, maybe. But if it was a jape, it was a bloody serious one. The police and everyone were scouring the place for them.'

Mannford looked at her, perhaps for any signs of scepticism.

'Please, continue,' Jane urged.

'I was worried, mind. But I was ten, and here was a chance to find out what was going on. I suppose I felt important or something. So, I sneaked open the cupboard under the stairs, got ma boots and coat, and off I went, easing the back door shut behind me. Being outside after dark was a thrill 'cause it was forbidden. My father'd leather me for it when he found out, but it was exciting anyhow.

'It didn't take long to reach the church. I leaped the railing, made my way through the headstones, then round back, where Norman said he'd be. And there he stood, big as life, still dressed as he was the night he vanished after Boys' Brigade. I knew the clothes because their descriptions had been on TV all the time. Well, Norman leads me away by the arm, saying, "You gotta see this, Rupert. You gotta experience it." I asked where he'd been, if he knew where the girls were, and he told me they were waiting for us.

'He led me to this corrugated-iron shed, old beat-up place the owners used for storage and such. Ain't there no more, though; flattened about ten years ago. I'd heard the police had already searched in it, and obviously, they'd never found anything. Anyway, Norman tugged open the door and beckoned me inside.

'The two girls were in there, just like he said, both wearing the same clothes they'd vanished in, same as Norman. Abby and Wendy smiled at me. I asked what was going on. "It's fantastic," the girls said together like they were sharing the same mind or something. They looked strange. The same girls but...different. And they sounded different too, programmed-like. They pointed to the back of the shed at a big wooden crate. Something was glowing in there...same vibrant green colour as the lights in the sky that first night. The shed was dark otherwise. The green light shone on the kids, and it showed something bad on their faces. They looked sort of older, their eyes all...socketed. It showed they weren't the same kids that'd gone missing.

'They kept urging me, "Go on. Go on, Rupert, it's fantastic." I looked over at that long box, at the shining light, and I'd be lying if I said I wasn't scared. But I was curious too. They kept urging, so I took a couple of steps over there towards it.' Mannford paused; his tongue moistened his lips. 'Before I reached it, I glanced behind me at those three kids ...

'The three of them had moved around, blocking the door. It was then I knew they weren't gonna let me outta there, could see as much in their eyes. They weren't smiling anymore, either. I knew if I went any closer to that green light, I'd end up just like them—a slot on the Ten o'Clock News. I was scared now. "Go on," they said. "Experience it, Rupert."

'There were wooden planks and lumber stored all up the side of that shed. I scrambled up those lengths of wood and kicked out the big window. I could've been hurt much worse than I was. Tore my arm up, blood everywhere, but I started running for home. Never ran that fast before or since, I'll tell you, Mrs Armistead. Didn't look behind me once and just kept moving, putting distance between me and them. I was bleeding badly, but I wouldn't stop for anything.

'At home, my dad was breathing fire, as I knew he would be. My mother was crying. Thought I'd been taken, I suppose. They saw all the blood, but I was so beat I couldn't even tell them what I'd seen. When I eventually got my breath, I spilled out everything. I knew they wouldn't believe me, but I was terrified, and I suppose they'd no choice other than to listen.

'My father put me in the car, told me to direct him right back out there. I didn't want to go, but Dad wasn't a patient man and he didn't listen to anybody much. The two of us were driving along the coast by the shoreline in silence, and that's when we saw it.'

Jane waited.

'This big, smooth thing—a craft, I suppose you'd call it—emerged from the sea, just came right up outta the water. Must've been one hundred feet long, at least. Wasn't that far from shore, either; just out past the rocks, deep enough to be concealed by the waves. It hung there, suspended in the air, giving my father and me a chance to see it proper. He'd stopped the car by this point, and we were both gawking at the thing. Saltwater was pouring down from its sides like waterfalls, back into the sea. The underside was bright green, blazing with lights. And then it just sort of took off diagonally, like a bullet, straight for the heavens. It really was that fast. One moment it was there, the next it was gone.'

Jane sat back and let out a breath.

'There was nothing in that shed, Mrs Armistead. The window was smashed, just like I'd said, but no sign of those kids. No wooden crate, no green light, nothing. I went through it all with the police that same night, right from the phone call I'd received. They didn't believe a word of it, even after my father telling them about that craft poppin' up from the ocean and disappearing into the heavens. They said someone else would've witnessed that; although it happened in a flash, really, it did. In the end, they said we were unreliable. My father had a few minor marks on his record—misdemeanours from his youth—so the authorities used them to discredit him. And it was dark too, they pointed out—meaning it was easy to mistake what we saw. More likely, the children had been snatched by some weirdo, they reckoned. We told them what we witnessed, Mrs Armistead, and they didn't wanna know.

'Police kept hunting for those kids,' he said, finally looking up at Jane with rheumy eyes. 'Pictures of 'em were posted in stores and on lampposts for long enough, but I knew they'd never be found. After seeing that craft disappear from the earth, I knew those kids weren't ever coming back.'

*****

Later, following rudimentary directions from Mannford, Jane located the spot where the corrugated shed had once stood. As Mannford said, it was no longer there; nothing except a crescent-shaped swathe of overgrown grass. Jane snapped a few photographs with her Kodak digital camera, anyway. She looked out to sea, trying to imagine an alien craft emerging from the waves.

Did she believe Mannford's strange account? He struck her as honest, and if he had the motivation to lie, she couldn't see it. Granted, she had paid handsomely for the story—but Mannford had remained faithful to his version of events for many years, long before Jane's interest and lucrative offer. And even if he was lying, factors remained that she couldn't explain away: those initial lights in the sky, for instance. Many people had witnessed the phenomena, yet none knew the source.

Jane regarded the dreary sky and remembered those hypnotic green glows.

She remembered, though her memory was tenuous, like her memory of the town itself—more a heightened feeling of déjà vu than a recollection. Following the trouble, her parents couldn't stay here, and Jane had always understood why they had moved away. Mannford hadn't recognised her, but that was no surprise. It had all been so long ago.

She stowed the small camera in her jacket and opened her handbag. From it, she plucked out a tattered old flier, a picture of Abby Kingston. Dressed in a white frock, Abby was squinting, her hair in pigtails, a space in her teeth. Below her image was the simple word: 'MISSING.'

Jane held the picture as she looked seaward once more. It fluttered in the wind. 'Maybe I'll see you again in the next life, little sister,' she said and turned back to the car.

Innocent Blood

He stands down the road from the ornately decorated cathedral, distant enough that nobody will give him a second glance, should they look his way. A silver hearse waits outside on the cobbled street, a modified Rolls, winter sunlight winking along its lines. From inside the old Gothic building come high choral voices—'In the sweet by and by, we will meet on that beautiful shore'—and there is something truly touching about the sound, the words, something earthy and uplifting that rouses emotion in him. Clusters of onlookers have gathered across from the cathedral, handkerchiefs on their faces, heads resting on the shoulders of friends and family. He watches the building's exterior until its great doors open, and the congregation appears: distraught parents and relatives, confused expressions, mourners embracing, drawing comfort and support from one another. Before long, the white coffin is borne down the steps and slid into the hearse, and as always in this dream, he cannot bear how small that casket looks…

*****

Andrei Dascalu awoke in the wan light of early morning, buck naked, a chill soaking into his bones through a stone floor, curled in a foetal position, mustering in his groin and armpits as much body heat as possible. Remnants of the dream—the one he was prone to more than any other—faded as he tried to get his bearings. God, his mouth was parched and vile with that bitter aftertaste. He felt pain embedded in his upper thigh, and when he brought a hand there, below the hip, he found the skin open around a ragged hole. His fingertips came away tacky with blood.

Facing him was an old blackened fireplace set into the wall's rough stonework. He had no idea where he was, but this didn't unnerve, for he had experienced similar predicaments more times than he could number. A gale whistled and whined around the structure, rain pummelled the roof—and something else, another, distant sound beneath those predominant: he thought he could hear the tide.

He blinked against dawn's grey light, aware of the familiar and overpowering metallic scent prevalent within these close confines. Dascalu knew too well the distinct aroma of blood; it was unmistakable. He leaned up on an elbow, peering at the semi-dark interior of what he now identified as a shelter, a bothy, knowing to some extent what he was about to see.

And sure enough, he saw it. *Oh, Jesus,* he saw.

He touched his forehead, breast, left shoulder, then right. He averted his eyes and got unsteadily to his feet, glancing into the dark recess of the roof space. The bothy appeared to be a ruin restored for basic sanctuary. Dascalu hobbled to the sole window, leg injury throbbing, his muscles typically stiff after the night's exertions. Rainwater washed the pane, sounding like harling chips thrown against the glass. Beyond was a rugged, bleak landscape of mountainous terrain, wind-tossed heather, and dangerous-looking rocks. And far below the headland, as suspected, the roiling, inhospitable mass of the sea. How far had he come last night? How many miles had he covered? He simply did not know. Sometimes it was farther than he believed possible.

Wind battered the bothy's exterior, rattling its old window and wooden door violently in their frames as if trying to uproot it from its very foundations. A spider in the window's corner shifted in its dusting of the web, a false widow, and Dascalu studied the arachnid momentarily. *Didn't most living things kill to survive?*

You do not kill to survive, his inner voice replied. *No, you kill because of what you are.*

He blew into his fingers and worked the heat of friction into his arms, his breath crystallising. His head hurt—his whole skull ached as if a steamroller had backed over it—a constant by-product of the Change. Typically, his recollection of last night was vague, snippets, images, fragments of memory. A deserted industrial estate. An oil drum with flames licking inside. A derelict with fingerless gloves warming his hands. Elsewhere, a woman in a black cocktail dress and heels, leaving a gathering of partygoers, walking a pathway through trees before fleeing for her life, hair streaming behind her.

He had taken them both.

'Iartă-mă,' he said: forgive me.

Following the bloodshed, a blur of endless terrain: gullies and brooks, fields and pastures, fences and trees, climbing and descending, loping beneath the bright moon and black starlit sky, muscles burning, ducking passing headlights, putting distance between himself—it—and the devastation left behind, a heightened sense of smell scenting every residual trace from animals which had passed that way. And he recalled a farmstead, a tractor, and a cow barn, a shouted warning in the dark, followed by what sounded like the double crack of rifle shots.

Dascalu inspected his agonising thigh injury incurred in his hindquarters. No exit wound, which meant the slug was still in there. Certainly, felt like it. He knew how dangerous bullet injuries could be, especially if the slug ricochets or fragments, rupturing veins and arteries.

And, of course, he retained vague memory of what had taken place right here, the frenzied attack resulting in this awful mess.

Screams. Flailing defensive arms. Ripping claws and snapping muzzle, champing, tearing.

The last solid memory he had the morning after was, in essence, always much the same: moonrise, heart racing, skin on his forearms bubbling like fat reaching the boil, limbs and spine stretching, calves rising like hydraulic lifts, fingers and nails elongating, painful muscle and facial distortion, flesh becoming lost beneath a new pelt. Then the inevitable receding of his inner self, like disappearing into a long dark tunnel, giving place to something else, something powerful and quite unstoppable. And finally, down on all fours, vitality coursing throughout his being, the vast night was alive in every way, vivid and thriving with colours, tastes, textures, smells, and sounds.

Dascalu stood at the bothy's window. Swollen clouds scudded across the dirty November sky. Daybreak struggled to life in the east. He judged the time as somewhere between 7:30 and 8:00 a.m., perhaps a little later; the gloominess made it hard to guess. He watched high combers on the ocean, then turned from the window, swallowing, ready to confront what he had to confront.

About him was carnage—a slaughterhouse. There were two of them, a man and a woman. Each wore hiking boots with striped laces, still attached to what remained of legs and torsos. The bodies were rent open, all ribs and blood, partially devoured insides flung around the little shelter. A pair of hefty rucksacks, trekking poles, and rolled sleeping bags were scattered the length of the room. An upturned camping stove and firelighters lay on the ground beside an open can of Heinz beans. Four wooden three-legged stools had been toppled in the commotion. Even the low walls were liberally splattered in arterial gore. *You kill because of what you are.*

A grim sense of irony touched him: they had come here in search of refuge but would've been safer out there in the storm.

Dascalu's nakedness absorbed the frigid atmosphere; it seeped into him. He felt oddly exposed before the two hikers, despite their having long departed this life for realms unknown. Still, he felt on display and therefore disrespectful. It was unusual—unheard of—for him to remain in such close proximity to his victims so long after the incident.

Incident! *Call it what it is,* he chided himself. *Brutal murder fits a little better, yes?*

At any rate, if not for the barren location and wild weather, he would not have stayed here overnight, although he doubted there was further shelter close by.

He went through their strewn rucksacks, finding a pair of jeans and boots in one—not the hiking variety, though sturdy enough—and a woollen roll-neck sweater in the other. When he'd struggled into the denims, awkward with his injured leg, they hung a touch wide on his wiry frame. The scratchy sweater retained a hint of sweet perfume. The boots pressed at his toes, but in this situation, anything always beat nothing, no exceptions. Binoculars. A folded map. Swiss Army knife. More beans. A modest first-aid kit. He came across a canteen and gulped his fill, the gloriously cool water underlining just how dehydrated he was—dehydrated, yes, but not hungry.

He discovered a smartphone, which revealed the time was indeed a little after eight a.m. The screen illuminated a selfie of two grinning faces, cheek to cheek, the dead man and his significant other presumably, probably the same couple shredded in front of him (it was difficult to tell). He found an iPod and headphones, a deck of cards, and vaping paraphernalia, all of which he set aside before ashamedly searching the blood-sodden quilted jackets of the victims, where he scored a pack of traditional cigarettes and a plastic lighter. He lit one and righted a stool and sat shivering amid hazy threads of smoke.

His eye caught a dull shine among the entrails on the ground, and he leaned to retrieve what he saw was a watch—a man's watch—its red-flecked silver strap of links broken away from the face. He turned the dial over and found an inscription on the reverse. Holding it towards the window, he squinted, reading, *To Garry. Lots of love, Ginny.* Was Ginny short for something? He wasn't sure. *Virginia perhaps.*

Rain poured without respite. Wind rattled the window frame, its fearsome breath breaching the bothy through each structural imperfection. The door latch trembled.

Dascalu looked from the watch to its owner. The male had tousled black hair, half his face missing, observing him placidly with his remaining eye as if to say *thanks very much, mate. I had a partner and a life until your lunar rampage took it all away.* He lay on his back, spread-eagled as if making an angel in the snow. The torn skin exposed rows of teeth along the jawline, like those novelty sets in joke shops. He wore a gold ring on a bloodied wedding finger, as did the ash-blonde with the Ziggy Stardust furrows across her face. She lay awkwardly, limbs twisted like a discarded marionette. He had savaged this poor couple. He had fed on them, warmed himself with their clothes, hydrated from their water, and was smoking their cigarettes.

And guilt consumed him. It had done so some time now, ever since he had lurked nearby that cathedral two years ago, watching them load what was left of the little girl and depart for the cemetery. Through the hearse window, a synthetic flower display spelled EMILIANA, baby blue silk around each letter. Sometimes when he woke, he could still hear that hymn in his head, hear those combined voices and the accompanying high notes of the organ. He tried to imagine her in a better life, an afterlife, in some faraway land where she would always be happy and doing the things she loved. His spiritual side often wondered if it was possible, he would see her again, in that other time and place.

In the sweet by and by…

Now he was tired, sick of skulking, hiding, feeling like the plague of society. This had to stop. It had to. He must sever the bloodline, end it once and for all. The time had come to cease considering, to take action. The body count was simply unacceptable.

The affliction had been handed down to him like a hereditary disease, as it had his lineage, tracing back, he believed, some four centuries to a Romanian ancestor cursed by a witch, or so the legend went. And it was a curse in every sense—*a pacoste*—because he had spent his nomadic existence peering over his shoulder, undoubtedly like his forefathers, never at rest.

He set down the watch and took a long pull on his cigarette.

He had expected the authorities would have caught up with him by now, those forever close behind, like Interpol, chasing at his fleeing heels. But he had been lucky and careful. He existed below the radar as far as possible, having always been meticulous about doing so—increasingly challenging in today's technological world. Lately, though, he had begun questioning this fight for survival, unsure just where his rootless life was headed.

Dascalu blew another line of smoke into the lurking haze, where it shifted and hung like the formless ghosts of two dead hikers. He knew the world was a worse place, a darker place, for his being in it, which made it doubly hard to keep finding reasons to run.

An anonymous thirty-year-old, he moved around a great deal, on foot, hitchhiking, using buses and trains. He landed odd jobs wherever possible: kitchen work, labouring, washing cars and windows, mopping floors, digging graves (which actually instilled in him a curious sense of moral balance). Oftentimes, when earning, he ate and slept in boarding houses, but also, he had adapted to surviving outdoors, mainly in warmer months, with only a sleeping bag and the heat of a small fire.

Occasionally he took a lover, not through any misguided idea of future contentment, but because it was refreshing to feel like, and be with, a human being. Sometimes, in the arms of another, he could briefly forget what he was and glimpse life through the filter of a normal person. He could not become emotionally attached, however, by virtue of a simple truth: the more he cared for particular people, the farther from them he had to get.

His first language was Romanian, naturally, although with time, effort, phrasebooks, and a good ear, he had become fluent in English, passable in French, and struggled by in one or two others. In the last couple of years alone, before crossing the Channel several weeks ago, he had lived three months in a tiny Italian town called Ingria in Turin; five months in Rattenberg, Austria; and half a year in Colmar, France, a beautiful location known as Little Venice due to attractive canals and candy-coloured houses, somewhere he could have happily stayed forever. He enjoyed waking to the clamour of church bells and strolling among the town's early Renaissance buildings. He enjoyed the wine and festivals and the mild climate. But always, he had to move on eventually, the lonely man, such was the nature of the beast.

'Nicio pedeapsă intentionată,' he whispered darkly: no pun intended.

His movements over time had become intentionally erratic, instinctive, which explained possibly why he had remained at large, an all-important step ahead of newscasts and bulletins. And all the running and evasion had brought him here, the dire wastelands of coastal Scotland. Well, it had gone on long enough. This gruesome scene had decided him. He wouldn't get far on foot anyway, not out there, and he certainly couldn't stay here. Besides, there would be another moon tonight, an inevitability that was forcing his hand. He only wished he had had the backbone to do it sooner.

It stopped today.

He stamped out the smoke, limped to the door, unlatched it—and immediately, the wind snatched it from his grasp, slamming it against the bothy's stonework. The downfall was driven sideways. He started out into the squall, advancing against the gale, the awesome force of nature, ignoring every impulse to retreat inside and shut the door. He was buffeted this way and that, swiped off-balance, struggling to breathe in the teeth of the oncoming skirling wind, its rawness penetrating the woollen sweater as if he wore nothing above the waist. This desolate land offered no cover, the elements hindering every step as if aware of and opposed to his intent. The punishing rainstorm lashed his face as he fought forward over hummocks and boggy ground, sinking and rising, arms extended in a hopeless attempt to steady himself. The gunshot injury screamed protest against each laboured movement, yet he refused to falter, bearing down, powering on until nearing the edge of the bluff, overlooking the cove and angry ocean better than a hundred feet below.

Dascalu stopped here, shivering uncontrollably, squinting, clad in ill-fitting clothes pilfered from his last victims. Not his latest, his last. The icy November rain stinging his cheeks was thickening to sleet. His numb hands had turned prawn-pink with cold, devoid of feeling. Breakers thundered against the inlet rocks, frothy saltwater rising up the cliff face. It was a long way down.

Thankfully he didn't require anything as elaborate as silver bullets or swords. Folklore and legend were stuffed with all sorts of bullshit. He shuffled closer until his snug boots met the lip of the cliff, and as he regarded the raging sea, a welcome resignation overcame him, a peacefulness he hadn't experienced in such a long time. This was the Day of Judgment. Although he had nothing to excuse his deeds—besides being what he had been made—he felt assured of taking the right course, the honourable path. Countless innocent people would live on account of his action, so there really was no other choice.

Dascalu turned and glanced at the distant bothy, in some manner of reverence to the atrocity inside. He thought of Emiliana's white coffin descending the cathedral steps, unbearably small, her name fashioned in artificial flowers; then he faced the ocean's immensity and closed his eyes and stepped off the cliff, down towards that beautiful shore.

As The Storm Raged

Pete Lumsden stepped into Deano's feeling like a condemned man and looking like a drowned rat. He brought an unsteady hand to his face and found his nose had finally stopped bleeding. It was midweek, midwinter, chucking it down outside as if the floodgates of Heaven had bust open. Almost ten p.m., and the place was dead. Two guys drinking in a booth. A blonde in leather trousers and a boob tube feeding coins into the jukebox by the men's room. Another stick-thin woman with blue hair sitting by the pool table, swiping away at her mobile.

Presuming this would be as busy as Deano's would get tonight, Pete shook the rain from his coat and approached his usual stool by the bar. Johnny Cash broke the silence with 'Folsom Prison Blues' as the jukebox blonde strutted away and joined her bony companion. The pub's owner, Frank Deans, appeared suddenly from the back.

'Hey—evening, Pedro.'

Pete gave a courteous nod, removing his sopping coat. 'Frank.'

'Cats and dogs tonight, huh?' The barman set his hands on the counter. 'Don't usually see you in here on a weeknight.'

'Had to get out of the house.'

Frank narrowed his eyes. 'Say, you're pale as a ghost. You feeling okay?'

Pete sat down. 'I've had better days.'

'You need a towel there?'

'Sure, thanks.' He accepted it and wiped his face down, and behind his neck.

Frank looked to the big window, where neon-tinged darkness and rainwater were all that could be seen. 'Weather's enough to depress a man, huh?'

Pete followed his gaze and said, 'You know, every time there's a storm, I get to thinking about Tommy. I can't help it.'

'Yeah, I know what you mean, mate.' Frank looked suitably sombre and then pointed at him. 'When spring comes in, maybe we'll get the rods out again.'

Pete knew this wouldn't happen, and something had died inside him at that moment.

'All right, what'll it be?'

He glanced at the bottles, extracting his wallet. 'I'll take a Scotch. Better make it a double.'

'Hey, man,' Frank said, frowning, 'you got spots of blood there on your shirt collar.'

Pete touched his nose again but saw no fresh traces on his fingers. 'It's nothing,' he said.

Frank shrugged and took a glass from the shelf. 'So, how's the bistro doing?'

Pete was still staring at his fingers. 'What?'

'The bistro?'

'Oh ... right. Could be better,' he told him distractedly. 'Especially this time of year. You know how it is.'

'Certainly do. This joint sure isn't drawing them in like it used to. Rates are slowly crippling me too. Business doesn't improve, this place will go the same way as every other pub in town—swirling right down the crapper.' Frank glanced at him as he poured the whiskey.

'How's Harriet doing?'

Pete was now studying Jane Austen's image on his ten-pound note, fighting to conceal the tremble in his hands. Frank set down the dram on a Guinness mat, looking into his face. 'Hey, Earth to Pete. Anybody home?'

'Huh?'

'I asked how Harriet is. You sure you're okay?'

Pete flattened his money on the scuffed counter, stared off at the rain. 'She's ... she's been messing around, Frank.'

'You're kidding?'

'Quite proud of herself too, let me tell you.' Pete shook his head. 'You know, I'm in that bistro thirteen-fourteen bloody hours a day—most weekends too—making money for her to burn on whatever takes her fancy.'

Frank stared, looking half-ready to smile as if unsure whether his friend was having him on. He fluently poured himself a shot of something from the optics, barely averting his eyes. The two guys from the booth got up and left. Frank bade them a brief goodnight, the open door letting in the splattering sound of blocked drainpipes.

The barman knocked back his drink. 'Who the hell's she been messing around with?'

'You want this money or not, Frank?'

Frank looked at the ten-pound note. 'Ah, no, put it away, mate.'

Pete found his miserable reflection in the glass behind the bar. Frank was right—he did look pale, haunted. 'You know Davie Gunn, runs a garage out by the industrial estate?'

'Sure,' Frank said. 'Changed the fan belt in my motor last month.'

Then he frowned as if the equation didn't quite compute.

Pete understood his confusion: Davie Gunn had a gammy leg, ran at least fifty pounds overweight, and had more hair on his shoulders than on his head, sprouted around the wife-beater vests he invariably wore.

'Harriet and *Davie Gunn*?'

Pete tasted his Scotch. 'His son's home from the Army. That's who she's been seeing behind my back—Jake Gunn. Bloody squaddie. Kid's fifteen years younger than her, Frank. What the hell d'you make of that? Been going on since earlier this year—so she said.'

'Damn, I can't believe it. How'd you find out?'

Cash had finished on the jukebox. Hendrix had taken over with 'Hey Joe.' Pete knew he shouldn't say any more but felt on the verge of spilling it all out regardless.

'She comes waltzing in this evening, tells me she's been out drinking with one of her friends—one of her *female* friends—but I knew otherwise.' He took another drink, wiped the damp hair from his eyes. 'It was only by chance, mind you. Still, I knew she was lying.'

*****

As usual, Pete had spent today in the Blue Orchard Bistro as general manager. He hadn't needed to help out but preferred pitching in during winter months to paying unnecessary wages. At any rate, the business had been dead all day. Later, big Bob Marshall, local councilman, arrived with his wife Claire—an old friend of Harriet's—and their young daughter, who was about the age Tommy had been when he died.

'What do you say, Pete?' Bob Marshall approached with an open hand. 'Thought we'd drop in, sample your fine cuisine. Listen, you'll be glad to know I've got the wheels turning on that stretch of road outside your property—no pun intended.'

Pete had recently discussed with Marshall the issue of potholes along the road adjoining his driveway, and but a week had passed since they had last spoken.

'Nice to hear,' Pete replied, shaking hands, and meant it. He turned to Marshall's wife. 'How are you, Claire?'

'Good,' the stout blonde said. 'And Harriet?'

'She's fine.'

'I'll have to give her a buzz.' Claire made a thumb-and-pinkie phone and wrinkled her nose. 'We haven't been out for a natter in ages.'

'And we all know how long that takes, right?' Marshall gave him a wink.

'Okay,' Pete said, smiling at their daughter, who was regarding him rigidly, clearly well drilled in the ways of good behaviour. 'Let's get you all seated.'

'Shouldn't be a problem tonight, huh?' Marshall scanned the Orchard's deserted interior and boomed a laugh. 'Not exactly Valentine's Day, is it?'

Pete waited on the Marshalls himself (feeling like he was earning that road repair) and knocked off around eight-fifteen p.m., soon after they had left, leaving his assistant to cash up. As he drove home, wipers swinging full pelt, sheet lightning flashed, and thunder roared. The driving wind had scattered waste-bin rubbish, and brittle tree branches littered the roads like skeletal limbs.

He made it back by eight-thirty, negotiating in the dark the minefield of potholes peppering Lodge Road. Lightning flashed again, which made him pause and lament over his son. He lowered the visor and plucked out the creased picture of Tommy. Straddling his first bike, he grinned at the camera, brimming with life. In a bizarre prescient omen, his son was wearing a black T-shirt with a yellow lightning bolt across his thin chest. Pete looked at the photo until he felt the squeeze on his heart, then replaced it in the visor.

After unlocking the front door, he stepped into the house's unwelcoming darkness. Harriet wasn't around, of course. She was hardly ever home of an evening. He absently wondered where she might be. Wherever it was, she'd no doubt have a wineglass in her grip. Disappointed, he hit the lights.

It'd been this way for years. Tommy's death had left distance between them, to put it kindly. They never discussed the loss, which Pete was sure would return to haunt them if it hadn't already. On a July evening, under amassing thunderheads, seven-year-old Tommy had been playing football with friends when their ball had bounced onto the road. Tommy had run out after it and been struck by lightning—zap, as the random hand of fate had landed him in the crosshairs. He hadn't been killed outright: their son had clung on for twelve hours until going into cardiac arrest. Ninety per cent of lightning strike victims survived, but their boy had died, as Pete and Harriet had been warned he might. And, perhaps inevitably, a sizeable part of their marriage had died too.

After Tommy's death, Harriet had begun polishing off more wine than was healthy. She didn't work (perish the thought) and was out most of the time to God knows where ('just with friends' was all he ever got), often dolled to the nines as if she were young, free and single. Pete once suggested consulting a marriage counsellor about their situation, but Harriet, in her typically blunt manner, had gunned the idea down as quickly as he raised it. There was nothing wrong, she claimed. She wasn't going to any shrink or counsellor; the idea was absurd. And Tommy was mentioned less and less as the seasons, and the calendars changed. Harriet lived her life, and he lived his, and so their limbo of subsistence continued.

In the kitchen, Pete looked at the chair where Tommy had sat eating Frosties each morning. Would he ever get used to not seeing him there? Then he noticed one of Harriet's little yellow Post-it notes on the cupboard door: FIX THE LEAKING TAP. IT'S DRIVING ME CRAZY.

That woman and her bloody notes. Capitals, too, if you don't mind. Talking patently wasn't her favoured mode of communication. He scrunched up the Post-it and dropped it in the pedal bin. Her unwashed breakfast plate and leavings had been placed by the sink, making him consider composing a few written directives of his own.

He studied the dripping tap—washer needed changing, he reckoned. He might as well tackle it now. 'Never put off till tomorrow what can be done today,' he quipped, well aware it had started leaking over a week ago.

He removed his suit jacket and tie and doubled up his shirtsleeves before extracting the meagre toolbox from the staircase cupboard. He turned off the water, drained the tap, dismantled it with the adjustable, replaced the washer, and reassembled it all when the front door opened.

Behold, he thought. The wanderer returns.

'Jeez, it's absolutely pissing down out there,' Harriet complained, shaking her brolly and standing it in the corner. She removed her long coat, revealing a gold sequined top and little black suede skirt. She stood looking at him. 'What are you doing?'

'Fixing the tap, like you said. Just needed a new washer.' He laid the heavy spanner down on the drainer. He spun the tap on and off. Hey presto: no drip. 'You had a good day?' he enquired, wondering if there was much point in asking any more.

She laid aside her handbag, took a wineglass from the cupboard, and poured liberally from the bottle of red on the counter.

'Claire and I had a few drinks, talking the hours away.'

Pete leaned against the sink front, bracing himself. 'Claire Marshall?'

'Of *course*, Claire Marshall,' she said impatiently. 'We've only been friends for ten years, Pete.'

'You've just left her?'

'You know how it is,' she said, waving a bejewelled hand. 'Time runs off when you're catching up. Anyway, I fancy some Indian food...'

'You left her just now?'

Harriet looked at him, her face revealing the briefest trace of concern. 'Yeah, she got a taxi home. What's with the third degree, Inspector Morse?'

He began putting his tools in the box. He didn't want to look at her.

'Come on,' she pressed. 'Something's eating you, clearly.'

'Claire came into the restaurant tonight with Bob.' Pete looked at her flatly. 'She had the lasagne.'

She turned away from him, set down the glass.

'What's going on, Harriet? Are you seeing someone else?'

'Yes.'

Pete slotted his hands in his trouser pockets, unprepared for the blunt reply. But, like politeness, subtlety had never been her strong suit. 'Who is it?'

'Doesn't matter.'

'It matters.'

She drained her glass and poured more wine. 'Leave it, Peter ...'

'Just tell me his name, for God's sake!'

His outburst made her flinch before she looked to the floor tiles and then up at the ceiling. 'You know Davie Gunn?'

Pete frowned, much the way Frank Deans would frown later upon hearing the name. He almost laughed, convinced she was pulling his leg. 'That fat mechanic on the north side? You can't be serious ...'

'Not *him*, for God's sake.' She looked away. 'His son.'

'His son?' Pete frowned again. 'You don't mean that—that kid who went off to the Army?'

'He's not a kid, Peter.'

'Are you serious?'

'He's twenty-five, if you must know.'

Pete drew a hand across his face as thunder sounded overhead. 'How long?'

'Since ... before he left town, last year.'

'What the hell are you thinking?'

She snorted and angled a hip, her tried-and-tested posture for a potential fight. Pete suspected she was better prepared for this conversation than he'd thought. 'Well,' she said, 'there are forty-year-old boys and twenty-year-old men, aren't there?'

'What's that supposed to mean?'

'Work it out, Sherlock; you seem to know everything.'

Pete opened his mouth, then shut it. A newfound disgust—no, full-bore hatred—for this woman he'd been married to for twelve years consumed him all at once, almost to the point of speechlessness. Had he seen this coming?

'*Why*, Harriet?'

'Because.' She rolled her eyes dramatically. 'I don't know. You bore the hell out of me, *darling*.'

There it was: the gloves were off.

He brought a fist down on the counter. 'I practically live at that damned bistro, so you can have whatever you want.'

'Well, I've got what I want, no thanks to you. There's more to life than scurrying around serving Joe Public.'

He should quit now, he thought. This was pointless, but it had to be said all the same.

'Wow. You think that kid—that moronic squaddie—gives a hoot about you? Christ, open your eyes, woman. A year ago, the police were charging him with being drunk and incapable. He's probably been bragging in the barracks how he's nailing some old cougar.'

'Jake loves me.'

'Oh, course he does. They're the magic words, huh? That how he gets you to open your legs?'

She folded her arms and out went the hip again. 'At least he knows what to do in there,' she returned snidely as if aware she'd scored a point.

'You think you're going to ride off into the sunset together?'

'You were the only obstacle. Anyway, now it's all been said, hasn't it? Jake's time in the Army is almost up, then we're going to be together.'

'Be where, exactly?'

'Anywhere. So long as I don't have to listen to your damned whining any more.' Harriet hiccupped, which often kicked in after she'd drunk too much. 'I mean, I tell you I'm having an affair—uh, hello?—and you—*Hic*—you just stand there with a dumb look on your face.'

'I don't care if you leave; believe me, I don't, but you must know he's not going to make you happy either. He's taking what he can from you—without much trouble, by the sounds of it. He's probably laughing his ass off with the old man. That grease monkey's probably slapping his boy on the back.'

'I'm an attractive woman. You take me for granted, and that's the truth. *Hic*.'

'Attractive? Harriet, look at you. Look at the way you dress, for Christ's sake. Skirts up to your ass, tits pushed out. Foundation laid on with a trowel. You're mutton done up as lamb, frankly, and that—that idiot you're humping thinks it's Christmas.'

Her eyes flared as if he'd found an exposed nerve. The slap hit his face like a striking snake—bang—her open hand catching him before he saw it coming. A rush of burning anger rose from his gut. Stunned, he felt a trickle of nostril blood touch his lip as she flounced away to the bottle.

'We don't give a *shhhit* what you think,' she hissed, slopping more wine into her glass. '*Hic.*'

That 'we' did it.

Before he could weigh the pros and cons—sometimes rage just can't be reasoned with—Pete found himself with the cool metal of the big adjustable in his hand. *There are forty-year-old boys and twenty-year-old men* ... The words seemed to pulse within his mind like a warning notice as he pictured her and Jake Gunn going at it. As she lifted the glass to her mouth, he raised the spanner behind her and brought it down plumb on her skull. The wineglass fell, clattering the counter with a *ting* but staying intact. Harriet dropped like a bag of gravel.

Pete shuffled back as she collapsed at his feet. He'd thought striking her would make him feel better, but it didn't. He felt worse as he set the spanner down, the hot-blooded wrath already rechannelling to something nearer panic. More blood trickled over his lip, so he titled his head and wedged some paper towel in his nostril.

Harriet's arms had finished outstretched. The spangled top revealed her pierced naval—a little red jewel—and the roll of fat she was forever trying to lose. Her swatch of skirt had risen up, uncovering the mole on her inner thigh. Spilt wine had splattered the floor and was soaking into her black hair extensions. Her eyes remained closed, the artificial lashes motionless. Her rich perfume wafted up to his vacant nostril. At that moment, he saw nothing of the woman he had married: she'd never looked less appealing.

Jesus, what had he done?

'Harriet?'

You made a mistake here, Pete. You made a big-ass mistake.

He swallowed, wringing his hands. He knelt, fumbling for a pulse in her arm and neck. There had to be a pulse, right? There just had to be. But he felt nothing beneath her warm skin. Thunder rumbled, and the lights dimmed ... flickered ... came back on.

As he knelt there, his mind kicked into overdrive. Should he split? Where could he go? What could he do? Spend the rest of his life running? Hardly. What about hiding her body? It wasn't even plausible. He had a cheating wife. He was a spurned husband, unfortunately lumbering him with the oldest motive around. It would all leak out the way such scandals do. God, he thought, ten minutes ago, his biggest worry had been a dripping tap.

Why don't you run on down to Deano's for a drink, Pete? He heard these words in Harriet's snippy voice, imagined her peering up at him. *Might be your last chance for a long time, huh? Last chance before you're some tattooed maniac's bitch in prison. Go on; the condemned man always gets one last wish, right?*

As it happened, this didn't strike him as an entirely irrational idea. In fact, it bore the uncomfortable ring of truth. He had a stocked drinks cabinet in the other room, true, but he needed to be somewhere else. Perhaps anywhere else.

Pete stood and grabbed his raincoat. His hands were trembling. There was no coming back from this. Thunder cracked, sounding closer now. Harriet's iPhone emitted a short tune from her bag on the counter. A text coming in from Jake Gunn?

More than likely.

He walked through the house and out into the rain.

*****

Led Zep's 'Gallows Pole' blared from the jukebox. What was the deal with these bloody songs? Pete wondered glumly. The two women knocked pool balls around with stabby, unskilled strokes, jigging to the sounds. He envied their freedom, an entirely new sensation.

Frank just stared at him. 'You sure she's dead?'

He pouted his lips. 'I'm sure.'

'Then, what're you ... I mean, why are you in here?'

'Figured this would be my last chance to have a drink for a while, so I might as well take it. Don't fret over calling the cops, Frank. I'll have this and go tell them what's happened.'

'So you just ... left her there?'

'I know how it sounds,' he said, drinking his third double. He nodded slightly, still trying to convince himself this had all taken place. He looked at the old photo behind the bar: him and Frank by the riverbank during one of their fishing expeditions, each in sunglasses and hoisting rainbow trout. Better times that now felt permanently beyond reach. He felt a little like a landed fish himself now, flailing without hope of safety.

'She kept needling me,' he explained, 'like she wanted to see if I'd snap or something.'

Lightning flashed, turning the heavens white-pink, brightening the big window. If thunder followed, he couldn't hear it above the music.

Frank poured himself another drink, knocked it back. 'Pete, it's gonna look bad. If you'd called an ambulance or the cops, things might've gone your way ...'

'My way?'

'Or no. I just mean she told you she'd been cheating, right?' Frank pointed at him. 'And you did say she hit you first.'

'She slapped me, Frank. I *killed* her with a spanner. Things ain't goin' my way. Not unless it's that final curtain Sinatra sings about. I'm up shit creek.'

'But it wasn't planned,' Frank told him eagerly, almost desperately. 'That'll help, right? And they'll give time off for good behaviour, yeah?'

Pete drained his Scotch, the alcohol lighting him up inside.

'You want one more in there, Pete? One for the road?'

He gave it serious thought but shook his head. 'If I stay any longer, I'll never do this. Thanks for the drinks, Frankie, and thanks for listening. It helped to air it out, get it all straight. Kind of like a dry run, huh?'

'I'm so sorry,' the barman said with candid pity.

Pete stared into the empty glass. 'I'm scared, Frank.'

'I wish ... God, I wish there was something I could do, mate.'

'Me too.'

Pete considered what had happened tonight. He'd known serious problems existed in his marriage, known how wrong it was to ignore them. He'd heard the alarm bells along the way and knew he probably should've left Harriet. The deterioration of his marriage, he believed, could be easily traced back to that cloud-darkened July evening when Tommy had defied the odds and found himself in the rare path of lightning. Hell, maybe even traced back to the random bounce of a ball. Shockwaves had reached steadily through the years, swelling wider and wider and culminating here, tonight. Perhaps their effect wasn't even finished yet.

Pete slid off his stool and pulled his damp coat back on, feeling lonelier than he'd ever felt before. He made towards the door, where he glanced back at Frank, who gave him a half-hearted salute as if he were heading off to the frontline, never to return. He actually seems to understand, Pete thought. Or maybe he just sympathises with the condemned man. Perhaps they were the same thing.

He nodded at Frank, a gesture he hoped conveyed thanks and friendship; then, he set out into the storm, collar raised, to tell his story one more time this night. At the very least.

Dana

The wee hours of Sunday morning, November 2nd. You lie awake, listening to the rain, listening for the sounds of Dana coming home. She is eighteen, a grown woman, but has never stayed out till this time before. Looking up at the plaster ceiling, you consider ringing her mobile, but it is very late—or early, depending on one's viewpoint—and you don't want your daughter to think her mother is spying. You were young once, too, after all, and not so long ago.

The hours drag, and you imagine the worst, grim thoughts playing out in your mind's eye, each scenario doing nothing to temper the unease. You consider calling your ex-husband, who lives across the city with his new squeeze, but refrain on the grounds his only advice will be to give Dana some space. Chill out, he'll say, for that's his answer to everything.

You draw a hand across the cool half of the mattress. The empty half. Mark has been gone for years, but still, the loneliness can surprise, sneaking in with the darkness and settling like a shroud. Perhaps you should have taken a pill tonight, just the one.

Turning sideways, your concern returns to Dana's whereabouts.

She may have found herself a lad somewhere. She's an attractive girl, and although shy and currently single—as far as you know—she's bound to meet somebody. Such is the way of the world. Still, it's difficult to accept that Dana would stay out with someone she's just met; she isn't that type of girl.

A car's beams wander the bedroom ceiling like a searchlight. Stragglers shout from somewhere, meandering home from the clubs.

Is Dana in their company?

Last night, before leaving for the birthday do, she blow-dried her blonde hair and painted her toenails red, and when you saw her in the snug black dress and open-toed shoes, you were secretly choked by how beautiful she looked. Your little girl all grown up already. Of course, every parent claims their kids grow up fast, but clichés are moulded from the truth.

The hours tick away. The rain grows heavier. Digital minutes elapse on the alarm clock. Your position at the bakery is Monday to Friday, so at least you don't have work to contend with today, although a lie-in certainly isn't on the cards, either. By six a.m., you're up and wandering the house with Dana's Jack Russell, Barney, scrambling around at your feet.

Daybreak at seven-thirty touches the house with wan light. By eight, she still isn't home. You shower and dress in jeans and a woollen cardigan and enter Dana's room: as ever, it's a lesson in orderliness, nothing messy or underfoot. Barney scampers up onto the creaseless duvet, collar tinkling, where he stretches his jaws and gives himself a scratch.

Above the headboard is a framed image of an ocean sunset and palm fronds, with a quote from John 11:25-26. *Jesus said to her, I am the resurrection and the life. He who believes in me will live, even though he dies, and whoever lives and believes in me will never die.*

By the window, Dana's poetry books line the shelf, collections by the greats: Byron, Shelley, Coleridge, Blake. You pass her computer and anglepoise lamp. Near the bedside is her King James Bible, from which Dana has studied Scriptures since her days at Sunday school. Cain and Abel. The three kings from the East. Lazarus of Bethany raised from the dead.

In the kitchen, you light the wood-burning stove. On the counter is a dish of nuts and candies left over from Halloween. You call Dana's mobile, and it rings until you're invited to leave a message, which you do, endeavouring to sound calmer than you feel:

'Give me a wee call. Let your old mum know you're okay.' You send a similarly worded text off into the ether, hoping it'll find its way to her at some point. Dana's cerise chiffon scarf is draped on the back of the chair, and you touch its thin silk gently.

At eleven o'clock, you call Dana's friends. Unsurprisingly, most are still in bed. According to the parents, the girls are 'hung-over' and 'still buried beneath the covers'. But Alexandra, the birthday girl, comes to the phone and chirpily explains Dana had gone home early the previous night. The news lands on you like an anvil.

'She had a headache, Connie,' Alexandra imparts in her breezy, carefree voice. 'She wasn't feeling great. I offered to go with her to the taxi rank, mind, but you know Dana. She said no, it was my birthday, and everyone should stay and enjoy themselves.'

'I see.' There is a dull gnawing in your gut. 'And what time was this, would you say?'

'Hmm. A little after ten, I reckon.' She is silent a moment. 'Hasn't she come home?'

'Thank you, Alexandra. Everything's fine.' Then you hang up.

Hasn't she come home? *No, Alexandra, she hasn't. You let her go off by herself, and she hasn't come home.*

If this isn't enough to get Dana's father involved, what is? No doubt he'll take exception to be bothered, but that's tough. You call him, and the line rings and rings, and you're ready to hang up when he finally answers.

'She's not a child any more, Con,' he says, sounding groggy and irascible. 'Look, maybe she found a party someplace. You can still remember being a teenager, can't you?'

So can you, Mark. You chose Budweiser and Jim Beam over our marriage, remember?

'She told her friends she was going home. She had a headache. Do you think Dana would be off partying while suffering one of those migraines, Mark?'

He sighs. 'Okay, listen. Try her mobile again. I'll, uh, grab a shower and take a drive over there. Give me a half hour.'

'You sure it's okay with her highness?' It's a cheap shot, but what the hell.

'Don't start, Con.'

You call Dana's mobile once more and hear the same recited spiel: *You have reached the voicemail for ...*

At ten before midday, you sit in the kitchen with Barney, preparing to contact the police. You lift the phone—and the doorbell sounds, splintering your concentration, so much so that you emit a little cry. The Jack Russell bolts to the hallway. Finally, Dana is home. Forgotten her keys, most likely, but what does it matter? With Barney underfoot, you pelt down the hallway runner and fumble open the front door, only to be faced with a solemn red-haired gentleman in a long coat. He has a smattering of freckles and a ginger goatee and stands hunched against the rain.

'Good morning, Miss,' he says, producing a wallet with ID. 'My name's DI Wilson.'

*****

You and Mark identify Dana together. He insisted he do this alone,

89

but you wouldn't hear it. Standing in the morgue, somewhere in the bowels of the hospital, your hands are gripped into fists as a man in surgical garb unveils Dana's peaceful face. Terribly pale.   The world suddenly becomes unsteady, tilting on its axis. You close your eyes and sob. This is wrong—this pallid, lifeless husk can't be your vibrant daughter. Dana studied poetry in college, said her prayers, and played in the park with Barney. You baked cupcakes together. This cannot be her.

'Is this your daughter?' Detective Wilson asks respectfully.

You feel Mark nodding gently, the admission unbearable.

'It's Dana,' he says. 'Oh God, it's her ...'

You touch her flaxen hair, brushing it aside from her face ... and frown. Adjusting her locks has revealed something odd, something strange. You wipe your eyes and glance at Mark, whose brow is also knitted in a frown.

'What the hell is that?' he asks.

*****

In a cramped room, you listen vacantly, cheeks tacky with tears. Mark grips your hand. November rain batters the roof, never-ending. A drinks machine in the corner hums. Dana, the detective explains, was found in the short black dress she'd left home in, her body discovered beneath a metal staircase in a cul-de-sac car park, hidden among the bins.

'A young trainee chef called Rory Grimes was discarding some rubbish around eight-thirty this morning,' Wilson says. 'He saw what he thought was a foot protruding from the garbage bags. After taking a closer look, Grimes found your daughter, then ran back to the restaurant and called us. We located Dana's shoulder bag not far from

90

her body. Her mobile and personal effects were still in it, and that's how we identified her and contacted you. I'm sorry to have to tell you this; I really am.'

You wonder what you were doing at eight-thirty when Dana was found among the garbage. Wasn't it about the time you sent a text to her phone?

'What are those two holes in her throat?' you ask.

Detective Wilson rakes a hand through his reddish hair. He removes his tie and pops open his shirt. 'Dana has two severe puncture wounds at the carotid artery—that's one of the arteries which supply blood to the head. She lost a lot of it, several pints, in fact. Preliminary tests suggest they're teeth marks. At the moment, I can't offer you much more information on this, but we have specialist people inspecting the wounds.'

'Did they cause her death?' you ask.

'It's a possibility, certainly a contributing factor. We'll have to wait for the autopsy results before we know for sure. I don't want to tell you anything misleading.'

'Misleading?' Mark snaps.

The detective interlocks his slender fingers, shakes his head.

'Truthfully, we don't know quite what to make of this, not yet.'

'It's your damned job to understand it,' Mark tells him, fidgeting uneasily. 'Teeth marks? I mean, if—if some arsehole's running around killing people, pretending he's Dracula, then it's your job to find him.'

Wilson nods. 'I know how you feel. Unfortunately, there are a lot of sick people out there. Why don't you get off home? I promise I'll be in touch as soon as there's something to tell you.'

✳✳✳✳✳

Driving through the rain, neither you nor Mark finds anything to say. The heaters blow warm air, and you think about Dana, cold and alone. Will they open her up? Cut her down the middle like an animal and peer inside? It's painful to leave her in that terrible, sterile place; it reminds you of her first day at school, when she cried, clutching her little lunchbox.

This unlocks the floodgates to further memories: Dana in the garden with her friends, skylarking, scooting in and out of her playhouse with those trainers she loved, the pair with flashing pink lights in the heels. The summer air was alive with shrieks and calls, heady with barbeque smells. A good time when all was well, long before the rift occasioned by Mark's drinking—before his problem was unmasked, at any rate, following which, things deteriorated quickly. You recall the day Dana cut her head after tumbling from a climbing frame, how she howled, and you soothed her and magically made it better with kisses.

You steal a look across as Mark drives the car, wanting to blame him for everything. His profile is cast in weak light and heavy shadow. How many times had he promised to stop drinking, to invest more effort in holding the family together? How many times did you believe him, trust him, only to find his promises dried up quicker than a puddle in the summer sun? Even the AA meetings you organised for him had quickly gone by the board, confirmation of his inability to persevere with anything.

You face the side window and the inclement night beyond. Shop fronts and tall buildings, shadowy figures stealing through the streets. You consider the marks on Dana's neck. This is surely something you should be discussing—both of you—but still, there are no words.

*****

It's after five p.m. when Wilson has something to share.

'We have a potential witness,' he explains over the phone. 'A bouncer from Flannigan's on Baron Street. He recalls seeing a young blonde woman in a black dress around ten-fifteen last night, standing by the mouth of the car park. He identified Dana from a photograph we showed him.'

'What was she doing?' you ask.

'He says the girl he saw was with a man.'

You glance at Mark. 'A man?'

'It was dark,' Wilson goes on. 'And he didn't get much of a look at the other guy. Tall, dressed in black. Had his collar turned high. It was all a little odd, he recalls. The young woman was just standing there staring up at the guy—that's what the bouncer told us. He said she appeared to be in a trance as if she was a bit stoned.'

'And then?'

'Well, he was called into the bar. When he came back outside a few minutes later, she was gone. They both were.'

*****

Mark stays until almost eleven. The kitchen's log-burning stove crackles quietly. You wait in silence, with Mark occasionally saying, 'I still can't believe it.' He offers to stay the night, but you refuse. He probably expects a drink—death's a drinking occasion, isn't it?—but you won't offer one. Anyway, there's only red wine, and it's earmarked.

'Thanks for being there today,' you concede, staring at the ribbons of flame. 'But I need some time. I need to be by myself for a while.'

93

You fetch the Coca-Cola brolly from the kitchen cupboard. Mark stands and shrugs on his battered leather jacket. He pecks your cheek with an ungainly kiss and stalks out into the darkness, driving rain thrumming the umbrella.

Barney laps water from his dish. The stove pops and spits, shadows cavorting around the far reaches of the kitchen walls. You lock the back door and sit with a photograph of Dana: six years old, button nose, hair in a braid. You lift her chiffon scarf from the chair, press it against your cheek, smelling the Black Orchid perfume there. How could God allow this to happen? How can you go on without her?

You pour a glass of red, its deep hue alive in the firelight. The wine's for cooking, for the most part, but tonight everything is different. Down it goes. You pour another. And another. You consider the pills in the cupboard, prescribed medication for those nights that draw out interminably.

A half hour goes by. Pouring a fourth glass, you hear the phone braying, which makes you start. You long to ignore its insistent shrill, but it's probably Mark asking after you, and he'll only keep trying. But it could also be the police, and that spurs you to answer it.

'Miss Broadbent?'

'Yes?'

'It's Detective Wilson. Are you sitting down?'

'Actually, I am.'

'Okay. Now, don't overreact. We aren't sure exactly what's happened yet.'

You sit forward. 'What is it?'

'Don't be alarmed; there's obviously some explanation ...'

'Tell me.'

'It's really too early to be sure, you know, to have any clear–'

'Would you say it, for heaven's sake?'

'It's Dana.' His voice is scarcely more than a whisper. 'Her body's gone from the morgue.'

'Gone? What do you mean?'

'I mean, she's gone. Her body isn't there.'

'How could—?'

Someone is trying the back door's brass handle: it dips down and up, down and up. Two clear thumps sound on the wood.

You shoot to your feet, scraping the chair across the stone floor. Detective Wilson is still talking as you place down the phone. Barney is alert, alarmed more by your reaction than by the knock at the door. You listen, heart pumping rapidly.

'Who is it?' You don't breathe. 'I said, who is it?'

'Please let me in, Mother.'

You cover your mouth with a hand.

Of course. She's alive. The whole thing's a mistake. Dana had woken up and did not know where she was. She isn't dead—it's a horrid misunderstanding. You're heartened by this notion, but can you really believe it? The alternative is much too dark to contemplate.

You turn the key and pull open the door—and backpedal a few steps. Absurdly, you're reminded of the trick-or-treaters who came knocking only a few nights ago.

Whatever this thing is, it isn't your daughter.

Soaked through, its long hair hangs in dripping tails. A saturated hospital gown clings to the body, translucent, revealing two small breasts and pink centres, and below this, the light thatch of pubic hair. The feet are fish-belly white, flecked in muck and rain and tiny sodden leaves; the toenails bear chipped scarlet varnish. The arms are outstretched beseechingly as it crosses the threshold, tracking wet footprints on the tiles. The eyes are red, lambent rubies, and the tongue constantly works, writhing and glistening behind two catlike teeth.

Barney scampers away, whimpering, little legs drumming a retreat.

'I'm so hungry, Mother,' it says, coming closer. 'I'm so cold and hungry ...'

'Dear God, Dana.'

'So hungry.'

Your primal urge is flight, but the pull in those hypnotic ruby eyes is telling you this abomination is still your daughter, the one who sought nourishment from your body as an infant—as she seeks it now. She's hungry, and what mother would shun her hungry child? You can be together again, mother and daughter, as before. She's come back to you, back to life, like Lazarus in the New Testament.

You kneel and nervously finger aside your long hair. She wears an expression of childish delight and doesn't hesitate, setting chill hands upon your shoulders, her body odorous of the outdoors, odorous of the night. Her face is there, on your left side, and from it comes the wet smacking of lips. You close your eyes and breathe as she breaches the skin with cautious insistence, almost as if she doesn't wish to hurt you. And gently, but pleasurably, she draws.

The Longest Night Of The Year

Harry sits in the armchair with Lucy's drawing in his hand. The picture is creased and lined, buckled by her crayons' heavy application, curled in at the edges. *Best dad in the world,* she had written in bold blue letters, with a vibrant depiction of him, her father, washing the car. He has a long body and a too-large head filled with smiling piano-key teeth, like a cartoon character.

'Did you cry out for me?' he asks the empty room, trying to block the unbearable images that flood his mind. 'Did you cry out for your dad to keep you safe?'

He remembers the moment she handed him the picture. Was it her first week at school? Possibly, though he cannot say with any real certainty. He reads the printed words for what may be the thousandth time. *Best dad in the world.* He follows them with a fingertip, tracing around the smooth, waxy letters as if reading Braille.

He walks to the kitchen and regards the container of sleeping pills and the bourbon bottle set out there on the table. Will tonight be the night? It may well be. It's the longest night of the year, after all. He looks to the old Bible atop the shelf and wonders what he's done to deserve this fate he's been given.

He flinches when the doorbell rings. The sound still unnerves him, has done since the November morning the superintendent came to the house; the morning everything fell apart. He and Elizabeth had feared the worst, of course, because by then, Lucy had been gone for more than a week.

He sets aside Lucy's drawing and trudges down the hall, clutching a pre-prepared bowl of nuts and candy. A glance through the fish-eye lens, and then he opens the door.

'Trick or treat!' cried the two boys on the front step. The hallway casts them in light against the backdrop of darkness.

He feigns a smile and mock surprise. The neighbours leave him alone these days, for the most part, but some still make an effort, even on this night.

'My, aren't you two a picture?' he says.

One child is dressed in a skeleton suit and plastic skull mask, the overall effect diluted by white Adidas trainers. The other child is some sort of zombie—at least, this is Harry's best guess. This boy's eyes are blackened with makeup, his clothes in tatters. Towering behind the children is their father, Jim. None of the kids go unaccompanied at Halloween, not any more, not since Lucy. Jim makes eye contact with him, and Harry sees pity on his face, recognisable at a glance.

'Hope you don't mind us calling round,' Jim says, setting hands on the boys' shoulders. 'These two guys just charge ahead, you know?'

There is sudden silence as if something awkward has been said.

'And miss the opportunity to see two such frightening costumes?' Harry says, filling the void. 'Not a chance.' He drops nuts and sweets into the boys' waiting bags, struck by the absurdity of the ritual.

The costumed boys make claws with their fingers and offer up their best menacing growls. Harry smiles at them and their father, unable to play along as much as he'd like.

'You keeping all right, Harry?' asks Jim.

Harry nods, having heard this question more often than he can remember. 'Keeping fine.' He has no idea what the platitude means, only that it's a lie. How could he be expected to keep fine?

'You're always welcome to come by the house, you know,' Jim

tells him. He slots his hands into his leather jacket. 'Anytime you feel like it, that is.'

Harry nods again, knowing he will never call. His preference is to be alone, though he has trouble communicating this to others without sounding ungrateful.

He lingers on the threshold as Jim and his boys head off into the darkness. It's a cold night, but not quite cold enough to fog his breath. Jim, who lives three doors down, looks back and raises his hand in sympathetic farewell.

Harry closes the door. He discards the bowl on the telephone table, spilling a few nuts on the carpet.

He can still picture Lucy in her witch's costume, standing in this very spot, grinning in her kinked pointy hat and warty nose, her black wig, like crimped crow feathers. He should have escorted her around the housing scheme that night, but it wasn't as if she'd been alone— her friends had accompanied her, and he had never imagined she'd come to any harm.

The house is a mausoleum since Elizabeth left. Silent and barren of family life. The strain of their daughter's disappearance that Halloween, the dismalness of her subsequent discovery, had proved too much for her. The loss had gradually fretted their relationship and steadily drove them apart.

He doesn't know Elizabeth's whereabouts now. For a time, they kept in touch, for the sake of their years together, until the increasingly brief phone calls stopped altogether. Eventually, they came to accept the marriage was finished, that to prolong the inevitable was doing more harm than good. Harry often wonders where she is. He pictures her alone with her thoughts, not unlike himself, her days perhaps still blurred by prescription meds. The truth is he still loves her, and he knows there will be nobody to replace her. But he couldn't navigate them through the sea of loss they were adrift in.

Statements from Lucy's friends had proved fruitless. Sometime during that October evening three years ago, she'd raced ahead of the others, rushing to the next street by herself. When her friends eventually caught up, they found no sign of Lucy, other than her bag of sweets partially spilt there on the road. At the close of that frantic night, despite Harry and the neighbours and police combing the area, Lucy was gone.

Upstairs he switches on her Donald Duck bedroom light, and emotion catches in his throat. The room has not been altered. Her furry toys still sit against the headboard, welcoming him with open arms. He eases down on her bed and draws a hand over the rose-pink duvet.

Lucy had loved pink. She'd selected the room's colour herself and helped him decorate the walls, though he'd had to tidy most of her contributions.

'Look, Daddy!' she had cried, busying herself beneath the windowsill with her own small brush. 'Look how much I've done!' She'd been standing there with her weight on one foot, two flecks of paint colouring her cheek like a little mischievous Indian. This is always the image he conjures when in her room.

Eight days after her disappearance, Lucy was discovered near a small brook on the outskirts of town. When the superintendent called that morning, Harry had known in his gut that this was the news they'd been dreading. She'd been gone for so long.

'A farmer found her a couple of hours ago,' the superintendent told them. 'I'm so terribly sorry.' And that was that. A few earth-shattering words from the policeman and everything was over. Everything had changed. Their lives torn down the middle, never to be repaired.

Nothing in Lucy's room has changed, though, and this, too, had contributed to the breakdown of the marriage. He couldn't bear to alter the room; Elizabeth couldn't bear to keep it as a shrine. Not a deciding factor in and of itself, but yet another indication that their grief could not really be shared. Grief is personal, Harry knows now, and finds its own way of debilitating a person.

'It's as if you expect her to come back,' Elizabeth had whimpered through the tears, looking around at their daughter's world, her playthings, her soft tieback curtains, the colouring books she had used to while away the hours. 'She's ... she's gone, for God's sake. That maniac took her from us.'

Elizabeth conceived late in life. Lucy was their only child, and the chances of them having another were less than fair had they wanted to. Harry can still remember his elation upon hearing news of her pregnancy. Both of them had long resigned themselves to the prospect their life together would be childless. Then expectation was turned on its head, and suddenly their future was blessed with a child, with direction, with the anticipation of new happiness.

None of it was destined to last. Life had teased them with the promise of contentment, only to snatch it away in the cruellest manner. To continue together without Lucy was never going to work, and on this account, the loss wearied them day after day.

To worsen matters further, the police never found the deviant responsible, a failing for which Harry was offered profound apologies. Trace evidence was lifted from Lucy's body but matched nothing stored in their vast databases. Without a viable suspect, they couldn't employ the evidence to produce a guilty party. Harry isn't sure if having the culprit incarcerated would make a difference, anyway. He suspects it would change nothing. The damage has been done.

'We'll keep on it,' the superintendent assured him as if this were some consolation. 'The case won't be closed.'

'What are the chances of a result?' Harry asked.

'We have his DNA. That's very strong evidence, Harry. It'll link him to Lucy without any trouble.'

'But only if he makes himself known,' Harry finished. 'For instance, if he does it to someone else's child.'

Harry often thinks about this unknown individual. Does he sit at home the way Harry does? Has he friends, a wife, kids, God forbid? Is he troubled by what he's done? Is he haunted daily, reliving the crime until it draws the spirit from him as it sucks the life from Harry? Has this man the slightest notion of what he has robbed from him?

The whole nightmare has taken everything, stripped away even the smallest pleasures Harry took for granted. He had been popular at the sawmill, one of the guys, and never would he have suspected how quickly such closeness could be lost. But his workmates treat him differently—and Harry knows he cannot apportion blame for this. They are careful in what they discuss in his company, for fear that something slips out which is inappropriate or rips open wounds which have ceased bleeding but never heal. Conversations tone down upon his arrival. A man who has lost what Harry has is easily hurt, they think. Ironically, he wishes they would forsake such caution, though he knows the camaraderie will never again be as it was. He has been made an outsider through no fault of his own and no fault of theirs.

At the local store, he receives guarded glances and prepared smiles. He believes he is the subject of gossip as soon as his back is shown, that townsfolk discuss his appearance, how he is coping, how he has borne himself since losing Elizabeth and Lucy, secretly grateful that life has not afflicted them with such a fate. To Harry, it is all a matter of bad luck. It had randomly singled him out; the locals would do well to remember this. How many of *their* kids had walked along the street that night? How many of *their* children could have been brutally murdered in Lucy's place?

At his daughter's bedroom window, he pulls back the white curtain and peers at night. He dreads this time of year. Within touching distance of November, the nights are long and the days brief. He feels the world drawing in. The relief of spring seems a long way off, far as the stars out there in the interstellar darkness. Next along will be Christmas, which of course, brings its own misery. Christmastime was Lucy's time. Her restless anticipation was their anticipation. Her joy was their joy. Her innocent wonder had fostered the magic of the celebration.

Costumed kids drift by under streetlight down there, accompanied by an elder. Always accompanied now. One child in a flowing white sheet stands out starkly, arms waving in mock-spooky effect. A girl in a witch hat and hoop-patterned tights dashes by, and this is enough to make him let the curtain fall back.

The phone begins ringing downstairs in the kitchen. Harry ignores it.

'I don't think it's a good idea for your wife to see Lucy before the funeral,' the superintendent had told him that day while Elizabeth was beyond earshot.

'She'll never accept that,' Harry replied.

'I understand, but I know these situations. In my opinion—in my experience—seeing Lucy would devastate her.'

'I'll talk to her,' Harry said, feeling his heart plummet. He had known the advice was sound. Witnessing the damage done to Lucy—

the manifold cuts and contusions—would have haunted Elizabeth as it haunts him. It would have obliterated her memories of their happy girl, replaced them with something foul and bleak. Memories were all she had left, so the least he could do was allow her to retain them. But she blamed him during the time after the funeral, which was always a possibility, blamed him for robbing her of the chance to see Lucy one last time.

During the aftermath, Elizabeth had cried incessantly and existed with daily help from Diazepam. Friends and family sent sympathy cards and visited as often as possible without becoming intrusive, but nothing had helped his wife; nothing had tempered her pain. She abandoned her Facebook and Twitter accounts, social forums for which Harry has never found any use. Lucy's death had revealed to Elizabeth the reality of the world, the ugly reality that dwelled beneath the surface. And Harry couldn't answer her constant questions. *What kind of maniac would do that to a little girl? Why did it happen to us, Harry? Why?*

What could he tell her? She was asking questions which had taken root in his own mind, as they had surely done with every parent who'd endured a similar loss. In truth, there were no answers. Ultimately, he could only put his arms around her, embrace her with the fullness of his own inadequacy.

Harry switches on the yellow fairy lights around her headboard, watches them twinkle softly.

He should have been with Lucy that night. Elizabeth had argued their daughter was too young to be out after dark, even in the company of others, and he had assured her differently. Now he must shoulder the guilt that encumbers him each day, the guilt he cannot come to terms with. He fears part of him doesn't really want to. To do so would be tantamount to letting Lucy go, and he isn't ready to do that. Maybe he never will be. Lucy had been too beautiful to forget. She had been his flesh and blood. To retain his grief was, in a way, to retain the last remaining part of her.

He snaps out the fairy lights and her Donald Duck lamp and leaves, easing shut the door, his final glance falling upon Bear, the teddy Lucy had drifted off to sleep with.

Downstairs the doorbell sounds again. He peers through the fish-eye lens like a frightened pensioner. A quartet of children waits out there, their forms stretched and distorted through the glass: two ghouls and a scarlet devil with a trident fork and something else he cannot decipher.

Harry moves away and returns to the kitchen. Facing another party of children in Halloween dresses is more than he can do. He looks at the sleeping pills and bourbon bottle on the table before pouring a finger and sloshing it over in one. It burns within pleasingly, settling his nerves to a degree. He sets down the cut-crystal glass and picks up the pills, again glancing at the Bible on the shelf.

'Forgive me, Lord,' he says, 'for what I'm about to do.' He works off the safety cap and gives the contents a gentle shake as the phone rings again.

He looks at it a moment, vacillating before he answers.

'Hello?'

'Harry?'

His heartbeats quicken. 'Elizabeth?'

'Yes.'

'How ... how are you?'

'I'm okay,' she says, and there is something present in her voice, something of the old Elizabeth, unclouded by medication. 'It's still the longest night of the year.'

Harry drops into a chair. 'Yes, it is.'

'Can we meet?'

'Of course,' he says, slightly choked, looking slowly from the pills in his hand to the old Bible on the shelf. 'I'd ... like that. I'd like that a great deal.'

Wheels Of Fortune

He hears its approaching power before he sees it, sending a shiver the length of his body. The huge multi-wheeler careers down the road before disappearing from view, gone in a rush of passing red might. From his booth, he gazes through the window at the November snow, at the afternoon traffic bucketing along. He cups his palms around his steaming coffee mug, turning his attention to the wine-coloured upholstery of the vacant seat opposite him. Simone's seat. How many days had they sat here together, looking out over this very view?

'Hi there, Dave,' the waitress says, stopping by him with a pad and pen. She's pretty, with nicely pencilled brows and an understanding smile. Some five years younger than himself, perhaps.

'Hey, Trudy. How's it going?'

'Pretty good.' She clicks the pen top with her thumb, holding it like a dagger. 'After anything to eat?'

'Coffee's fine for the minute,' he replies, touching the mug. 'Maybe later.'

'Still teaching over at the academy?'

'I'm still there.'

She makes to move away and hesitates. 'I hope you don't mind me saying, Dave, I know you're coming in here by yourself now, but, well, I just wanted to let you know it's good to see you.'

He nods. 'I guess it beats sitting home alone, right?'

'It was such a terrible thing.' Trudy's gaze goes to her slip-on shoes like a bashful schoolgirl. She drops her notepad into her apron.

'You and Simone, you always made such a nice couple. Anyway, if you ever need someone to talk to about it ...'

'Thanks,' he says. 'That means a lot.'

She proceeds dutifully to the next table. The café isn't busy, only a smattering of clientele. The way Trudy moves catches his notice. The snug uniform. Hair in a tail. The feminine grace of her neck. Not so unlike Simone, really. Outside, as if on cue, another haulage rig tools past. As its grimy red taillights round the bend, falling flakes spiral and churn wildly in its slipstream. His mobile is on the table top; he activates the screen, and there is Simone.

He had been efficient—perhaps too efficient—in removing her effects from the house. Living among her things, day in and day out had proved overly difficult, harrowing, each garment or belonging provoking its own particular memory, each remembrance in turn linking itself to a specific day or conversation. The house had been invested with too many reminders. He'd seen no option but to remove them all, drive them to the charity shops load by sorrowful load, or offer them to her family, even at the risk of appearing callous.

A Land Rover pulls into the lot out there, manoeuvring carefully in the snow. A family gets out—mum, dad and a little girl in a pom-pom and scarlet jacket. They trudge towards the café and mount the steps, the child staring up raptly into the snowflakes. He thinks about Simone and the family they might have one day had.

Although he has been assured that harbouring such ideas is irrational, he feels partial responsibility for her death. And he knows it is irrational—technically, he has no responsibility for her death. None whatsoever. Yet, the undeniable truth is that the five-day trip had been his idea. He had purchased the airline seats and hotel reservation as a Christmas surprise—without his actions, notwithstanding the intention behind them, Simone would still be alive today. This truth is hard to live with, and doing so remains a work in progress.

Trudy shadows the family to a table by the kitchen. The little girl stomps snow from her shoes in a comical march. She wants the window and scoots along the booth seat in eager anticipation. Trudy provides menus before taking away the fourth set of cutlery. The little girl snatches off her hat, unfurling a cascade of chestnut curls.

Before they had met, Simone had toured various other European cities over the years but had always wanted to visit Germany, Berlin especially. She'd been thirty-two when they were introduced at a party six years ago, and since then, she'd regaled him with many tales of her extensive travels. So, the idea to combine a winter holiday and marriage proposal had struck him as a sound one. Why wouldn't it? They'd been a couple long enough, and he believed she wanted him to propose, though this discernment didn't temper his nervousness during preparations. He'd procured a ring with the assistance of a friendly saleslady, a sparkler he felt sure Simone would love, and planned to present it on the final day of their trip, perhaps over a candlelit meal or romantic setting. He welcomed the idea that the moment wasn't preordained, that room existed for spontaneity, possibly affording him a sliver of the elation he hoped she would experience.

He drinks his coffee, good and strong. Snow drifts from the whitened heavens. A colourful artistic rendering of John Lennon adorns the wall. He thinks absently of the renowned line about life and other plans. He sees, too, the parallels between the musician's death and what befell Simone: the innocence of the victim, the needlessness of the act.

*****

Their first day, December 19th, Simone had wanted to visit Breitscheidplatz, a major public square in Berlin. It was an attraction she'd been reading up on during the flight while working her way through miniature bags of Quavers. There was a Christmas market by the Kaiser Wilhelm Memorial Church. Simone had always loved Christmas, a time which brought out the young girl in her. They'd held hands as they wandered slowly through the brightly lit festivities, a premature apprehension idling in his stomach at the prospect of the proposal. But it had been good apprehension, curiously comforting, almost as if it were necessary.

'Isn't it beautiful?' she'd said, looking at their surroundings, performing a movement close to a pirouette.

'Sure is,' he told her, catching a pleasingly fleeting glimpse of that youthful girl again. He had been tempted to produce the ring there and then. If it hadn't been their first day, maybe he would have.

'I'm so glad we came here, Dave,' she said. 'It's the best Christmas present I've ever had.' She raised her gloved hands, showing him the palms, letting him read the words there.

Before they continued any farther, he had slipped off for a minute to use a nearby public toilet. It was a little before eight p.m. They'd had a couple of drinks not long before, and he really had to go. She'd stood there smiling at him, her long hair tucked beneath an orange woollen hat, gloved hands in her jacket pockets, her face coloured a gentle pink from the cold: this is the last living memory he has of her.

He was washing his hands. An elderly gentleman with a long beard used the washbasin next to him. He spun off the tap. Both he and the old man heard the commotion from outside. Screams and raised voices, unmistakable. Initially, he considered the reactions may be enthusiastic responses to some sort of breathtaking festive display—a hope soon shattered when he stepped back out to the street.

Crowds of people yelled and hollered, running this way and that; others stood dumbstruck, hands to their faces or pointing farther down the way. Bodies lay on the ground, unmoving. A small boy stood screaming. Simone was gone. He studied the carnage, the spilt blood, the battered stalls, wondering what the hell had happened, a wary voice in his mind telling him what he didn't want to hear. A queasy sensation filled his gut like the feeling incurred crossing a humpback bridge in a car.

*****

He looks beyond the café window and closes his eyes. Opens them. His ducts stir, trying to form tears. Outside, a dainty seasonal bird lights on the roof of a parked car. It hops forward, performs a brief look around, fluffs its wings, and takes to the air again. He turns his head. Trudy's talking to the little girl who came in with her parents. The waitress is bent at the waist, palms on knees, bringing herself to the child's eye level.

He hopes in his heart that Simone didn't suffer, but even this small mercy proves hard to reconcile with any credibility. Her last moments, her last thoughts, must surely have been composed of fear and shock; this is what he has the greatest trouble living with. She didn't deserve to leave the world like that. He supposes none of the victims did.

He sets his empty mug aside, conjuring unbidden images of the aftermath. He doesn't want to think about them, but his brain replays these images nonetheless. Ruined Christmas trees and glass strewn across the market grounds. Bullet holes in the lorry's windscreen. Grief-addled families and friends, searching in vain for a reason where only madness dwelled. The juggernaut's original driver, still there in the passenger seat, shot dead. He's tried to forget the terrorist's name,

111

to simply let it go as one might a helium balloon, but like the rest of it, he cannot get it out of his head. A failed asylum seeker and a desultory act with the direst of consequences. It tumbles round and round his mind like washing in a drum.

How rapidly life can switch from a positive track to complete derailment. They had been holidaying, preparing for Christmas, soon to be engaged. In the blink of an eye, it had all gone away. In the time taken to use the toilet, to wash his hands, his future was swept up and disposed of like the glass shards littering the Breitscheidplatz Street.

Trudy delivers a bowl of strawberry-drizzled ice cream to the little girl. The child, all dimples and happiness, spoon in hand, beams at her. The innate ease Trudy has with children isn't lost on him. She would make a good mother.

*****

Coming home had been a profoundly affecting time, which he recalls only as an out-of-body experience. They had left together, and he had returned alone, pushing forty, facing a tinsel-draped house that was filled with an unusual and worrying silence. He had climbed the stairs, entered their bedroom, trying to accept she wouldn't be coming back. He looked at her Kindle atop the bureau. He opened the closet, brushed her blouses with his fingers. He sat on their bed, took the velvety box from his jacket, and raised its lid. In a sudden bout of unaccustomed anxiety, he had wept for better than an hour, struggling to process manifold emotions; the most prominent was the feeling of protectiveness he retained towards her. How does one channel such a feeling for someone no longer alive?

*****

Trudy is situated at the counter. He watches her tallying a bill for a hefty guy with a baseball cap. She smiles at the man as he leaves,

112

flashing pearly whites, and then her eyes catch his. He quickly looks away.

He wonders what would've happened had he been there with her. If he had, say, used the toilet before they'd left the bar. Would he be dead now besides? Would he have managed to somehow steer her to safety? Could he have sensed danger a split second earlier, in time to save Simone? Had she been struck because of where she was standing, waiting for him? They had planned to visit Berlin Cathedral, the Potsdamer Platz. Why hadn't they been elsewhere on that fateful day? A million possible variations.

These things he will never know, will never be able to stop asking himself. It is scant comfort that he isn't alone in his grief, in his wonderings. For this manner of groundless brutality is spreading throughout the world like a virulent disease of the mind, leaving a growing number of friends and relatives with only memories and a surplus of unanswered questions.

Yet he will get over this. There is no choice but to. People are built to endure—a truism no amount of deluded martyrs will ever change. Little by little, bit by bit, he'll leave his old life behind, carve a different way, forge a path ahead without her. For these are the cards fate's indifferent hand has dealt him. Simone is gone—gone in the worst of circumstances—but her memory sustains through the weeks and months right alongside him, like an unseen shadow, as if she were there in spirit if not body.

A plump waitress passes, skilfully laden with balanced plates, trailing scents of home cooking. He contemplates ordering more coffee when his mobile comes to life beside him. The caller display reveals Kenny. Reluctantly, he answers.

'Hey, Kenny.'

'How's it going, man? Long time, no see.'

'How are you?'

'Not bad, Dave, not bad. Listen, me and Yvonne are planning a little get-together at the weekend. Our place. Nothing much, just a few laughs and some cold ones. You up for it?'

Outside, light is dying. Passing cars have headlights on, their beams highlighting the snowfall. 'I don't think so, Ken. I don't much feel like it.'

'You gotta start getting out again, Dave.'

'I don't fancy it. Thanks anyway.'

'Aw, you're tearing me up here, man. Tell you what. I'll hit you with a joke. If you don't laugh, you don't have to come. If you do laugh, you show up.'

'I've never laughed at your jokes, Kenny.'

'You ain't even heard it yet.'

'Go on, then.'

'Good man. Okay. This gorilla walks into a bar and asks for a drink, right? Well, the barman doesn't know what to do, so he goes and tells the owner what's happening. The owner he's a bit unsure too. He doesn't want to serve the gorilla in case his bar becomes a hangout for other gorillas. But he doesn't wanna refuse the gorilla either, in case he gets mad and trashes the place, right? So the owner tells the barman, "Give him his drink, but charge him twenty bucks, and maybe he won't come back." So the barman returns to the gorilla, takes his twenty, and gives him his drink. Then the barman says, "We don't get many gorillas in here." And the gorilla says, "I'm not surprised, the prices you charge".'

There is silence. He smiles, although the laugh's a long way off. 'It's better than your usual efforts.'

'Hey, come on, you're holding it in, and that's cheating.'

'You got me.'

'Seriously, Dave. We'd all love to see you, man. How about it, just for a few hours like?'

He considers, aware it's a good idea, whether he wants to go or not. How would he feel turning up alone without Simone? How would he look? 'Let me mull it over. I'll let you know before the weekend.'

'I really need to know the numbers now, Dave. Can I count you in?'

He shakes his head. The little girl guzzles her ice cream, still transfixed by the weather. 'All right. Count me in.'

'Atta boy. And listen, Dave. Don't take this the wrong way, but ...'

'What?'

'Well, if you wanna bring someone along, you know, that'd be okay. I mean ... it's up to you, obviously.'

After the call, he studies the world disappearing beneath the fall. Perhaps it *is* time he started getting out again. It's what Simone would've wanted. He removes the orange woollen gloves from his pocket. The right is bloodied at the wrist, the one with *Live Life* weaved into the palm in white letters. He turns over the left glove, which has *To the Fullest* knitted into it.

'Like something else then, Dave?'

Trudy is suddenly there beside him, feet together, notepad poised, attendant as ever. She cocks her head sympathetically.

He slips away the gloves. 'I think it's time I was heading off.'

She nods and smiles softly, touching her hair. 'Okay.'

'A few friends are having a bit of a party at the weekend,' he ventures, unsure what he's doing, feeling oddly exposed. 'Would you, uh, like to come along?'

Her initial warm reaction tells him she's pleased. Or flattered, maybe. Perhaps both. Could be she pities him.

'I'd like that a lot, Dave.' She rises slightly on the balls of her feet. 'Are you sure about this?'

'I think so,' he tells her, sounding genuinely unsure. Blood warms his cheeks.

She bites her bottom lip, scribbles on her pad, and tears off the sheet. Her number is there in bubbly digits when she places the paper on the table. He folds the number into his pocket, feeling equal measures of guilt and confusion.

Outside, he descends the wooden steps. The air is crisp. He fixes his scarf, his breath visible in plumes. His boot treads compress the snow. Trudy passes by the expansive window and pauses, raising a hand to him. He reciprocates, wondering once more is he doing the right thing. Then again, perhaps there is no right or wrong thing, but only actions, period. The wheel is in motion, and that is that.

Live life to the fullest.

The afternoon light quickly wanes as if a celestial shroud has been drawn across the world. The snow becomes heavier as the day darkens, obscuring parked cars and the stand of nearby evergreens. She would have loved to look at it coming down like this. He is mildly hypnotised by the soundless, cathartic beauty as he sets off for home with Trudy's number in his pocket. For a moment, if he tries, he can almost shut out the tainted memories and concentrate on the good. He can feel her gloved hand in his; hear the excited timbre of her voice as they enter Breitscheidplatz Christmas Market, where, for a short time, the future is as bright as the lights around them.

After Debbie

It's been awhile since he made the trip up to Morland House. The track there is long, peaceful, with spokes of summer sunlight breaking through the trees like overhead searchlights. John observes from the side window as the car steadily climbs, studying the dense woodland where he and Debbie often walked after purchasing the house. They would take morning strolls among the birches and evergreens, picking through dew-damp scrub and bracken, discussing future plans for their life together. Occasionally they spotted deer, whose tendency on sensing company was to lope off in the opposite direction, always drawing an excited cry from Debbie. As he drives by, John is surprised to find that his memories of walking these acres, on the whole, remain fond ones.

The winding track eventually opens out to a gravelled clearing before the expansive front of the old house, the home that was once everything to him and Debbie. Confronted by it now, he is struck by a profound sense of sadness: this place feels symbolic of everything in his life which did not reach fruition; a bricks-and-mortar reminder that the best-laid plans can fail as surely as the whim.

Debbie had come across it first. A friend of hers, who'd been selling her own home, knew they were in the market, and brought it to Debbie's notice after flipping through a property publication. John had suspected, even before the initial viewing, that the enthusiasm the house excited in her was prospective of future ownership. He had always found her enthusiasm catching; therefore, he too developed a genuine interest in the place, seeing the house as a chance at lasting happiness. But he subsequently learned that life seldom stays the same for long and that happiness is short-lived at best.

John parks the blue Peugeot and gets out, absorbing the

strangeness that dwells here now, that sense of abandonment. He takes in the bay windows, the upper casements, the dormers high above, and the Victorian stonework, which is mostly lost beneath clinging ivy.

The lawns remain overgrown, the nearby trees and neglected bird-shaped topiary, once so carefully tended, have spread wild, effecting the impression the property is being slowly devoured, integrating with nature itself. The FOR SALE sign stands in the ground by the front door, canted by recent winds.

He recalls the day he and Debbie first stood here. The house had been attractive, in so much better repair than it is now. He doesn't expect the place to sell, for there's been barely a ripple of interest— from potential buyers, that is—despite it languishing considerably below market value. John knows people won't invest or live in a house whose rooms have recently been tainted by murder.

He starts towards the front door, his shadow sharply defined on the ground. A sparrow takes to the air above the treeline as he sifts through his keys and opens up. Inside, the house is fusty, something Debbie wouldn't abide by while she was alive. Throughout spring and summer, she typically had windows flung open and the wide sills decorated with marigolds and dahlias.

He steps inside the living room. There's a picture there on the coffee table of Debbie and him on their wedding day. She wore white lace, her coal-black hair twisted into ringlets, her fingernails enamelled in flamingo pink varnish.

The silence that prevails here is striking. There's a canvas of the Golden Gate Bridge on the wall above the sofa, which Debbie painted last year and was inwardly proud of. He would always know when she'd created something that really pleased and satisfied her: it buoyed her and lightened her mood for a time.

John studies the painting, its rich colours, the blends and tonality, the bold swirl and sweep of the brush. She had loved to create and had been so talented. Even now, her easel stands in the small turret room at the back of the house. He had promised to one day take her to San Francisco on holiday; it's somewhere she always wanted to go and now somewhere she never will.

He was away the night she died; his work in construction necessitates he spends a great deal of time out of town. Debbie, likely awoken from light sleep, heard the burglar from her bedroom and proceeded downstairs to investigate. She'd called the police from upstairs, which surely would have been action enough for most women. But his wife had been proud and protective of their property and disinclined to let anyone walk away with it. She wasn't genetically programmed to allow someone to steal from them, to let fear hold sway in her life. This inner strength, this confidence, was one of the virtues he'd loved about her.

Morland House was alarmed, but the police gave him to understand that the intruder used a suction cup and glass cutter to gain entry through a back window, thus bypassing the alarming section of the property. Once confronted, the faceless stranger stabbed Debbie twice in the ribs and absconded with her jewellery and some valuable ornaments.

By the time the police arrived, she was dead there on the kitchen floor, gazing blankly at the ceiling. Dead at twenty-nine years old.

John looks around the room and hunches his shoulders. The stagnant air is humid, yet he feels a chill steal beneath his shirt.

He knows that she's still here.

Her body is buried a half-mile from Morland House by a drystone wall in the cold ground of the village cemetery. But the other part of her, the part destined for the hereafter, still lingers. It was this knowledge, in fact, which had driven him from the house. Once, he'd wakened in the dead of night to a long-haired womanly silhouette in a nightgown, and now, as he leaves the room where she died and ascends the stairs, he vividly recalls the fright instilled when he'd snapped on the lights and found nothing there, the atmosphere redolent with the faintest trace of perfume—her perfume—before it dispersed like a half-remembered dream.

He gently opens the bedroom door. Their hand-carved bed is there, the white rug, the walnut bureau, the three-mirrored vanity table where Debbie would sit and train a brush through her black hair. The air is musty here now, uninviting, like someone else's room. He closes his eyes and can hear her in his mind.

Pass me that brush, John.

He looks towards the phone on the nightstand, where she called for help. Upon request, he once heard the recording of what was said that November night, though he tries not to think of her whispered words.

'There's someone in my house downstairs.'

'Where are you, miss?'

'In my bedroom. I'm at Morland House, on Woodlands Park Road.'

'Can you stay in your room and lock yourself in?'

Hearing that conversation had hit him hard, creating a compound sensation of sadness, loss, heartbreak, and regret.

He crosses to the bedroom's casement window, which is draped in a dusting of cobwebs. Distantly, over the trees, the church steeple towers like a giant marker: where he and Debbie were married on a clear July afternoon. Where her remains lie today. Happiness and loss. Life and death. He peers down at the untidy, overgrown lawns below. In past times, he often saw Debbie stand right here and regard the freshly cut greens.

'I sometimes imagine our children playing down there, John,' she once said. 'One day it'll be a reality ...'

She then touched the pane of glass with her slender fingers.

'I think about that, too,' he'd replied, gently massaging her shoulders through her silk gown. And he did. He would picture their kids careering around on the lawn, perhaps with him playing among them. An expectation that never became a reality.

Now there's only the grass and weeds, the memory of a past conversation.

He steps away into the bathroom.

Debbie's effects are still here, her bath potions and conditioners, her bottles of nail polish gathered on the counter. He selects the one labelled 'flamingo pink' and runs his fingertips over the glass and smooth black handle. This was her favourite, the shade she wore most often. The shade she applied the day they married. She wore it the night she lay bleeding on the kitchen floor, surely praying that help would arrive before it was too late. Somehow, to John, that detail seems terribly wrong, inappropriate, though he cannot grasp exactly why he feels this. Some things elude explanation, like why Debbie's ethereal form roams here when nobody else is around, as if her confused spirit cannot understand that it no longer belongs.

Soon he'll return here and box up her things. It's something he must attend to, though the prospect fills him with foreboding. He moves out to the landing and sets off back downstairs. He reaches the kitchen doorway and glances sidelong in that direction. No clear indication remains of what came to pass in there, although the floorboards still bear the slightest discolouration if one knows where to look.

He imagines her pottering by the sink, cutting vegetables, or sorting those marigolds, as she loved to do. In this reverie, she is wearing jeans and an off-the-shoulder white top. It takes a moment before he realises this was what she was wearing the last time he saw her.

Outside, he feels glad to be free of those walls. The summer air is close and warm, its heat fine on his face. Cool sweat adheres his shirt to his back. Birds are cawing and calling from unseen perches, just as they had the day he and Debbie first viewed Morland House.

There's another vehicle parked by his Peugeot now—a gleaming silver Mercedes, its windscreen a reflected mosaic of leaves and branches. A tall man steps from the car, barrel-chested, with close-cut grey hair and faded denims. An A4 brown envelope is clutched in his large gloved hand.

'This will be the last time we talk,' John tells him.

The man nods once, looks up at the house.

John produces a small package from his jacket, bound by elastic, and hands it to him. 'It's all there, what we agreed.'

The man takes it and looks around at the high trees, at the house again. He makes a cursory glance inside the package. 'What'll I do with the jewellery? The ornaments?'

'Make them disappear,' says John. 'Don't try to sell them.' The man smiles a little, wryly, as if the very suggestion is ridiculous. 'You have the rest of the pictures?' John asks.

He hands John the envelope. 'Negatives are in there too.' John watches him get back in the car. The Merc reverses and moves off down the track through the trees, sunlight playing and flashing across its polished panels. He thumbs open the envelope and slips out the glossy pictures: Debbie and her lover in a parked car. Debbie and her lover in a hotel doorway. He sifts the photos like playing cards. Debbie and her lover. Debbie and her lover.

He remembers the day his suspicions were confirmed, the wall of denial he'd thrown up, the last resort against an unwanted reality. He recalls the pain, actual physical *pain*, when contemplating what she had done, how easily she had destroyed him, unmanned him. He remembers fruitlessly self-searching for what had driven her away, making himself sick through contemplation of the nature of his failings, whether they were financial or of the flesh or perhaps some more subtle imperfection he hasn't yet identified. Maybe he had unknowingly become ground down in routine, thus subjecting her to a life of increasing repetition, even monotony. The only thing he knows for sure is that he will never know. This is possibly a blessing, though it feels anything but.

He paces to the Peugeot and instinct commands him to glance back at the property, at what might've been. A blackbird perches on the angled FOR SALE sign, preening itself with its beak, eyes like obsidian. All at once, another movement from above draws his attention. He looks up there, up at the bedroom window, where he stood minutes earlier.

The afternoon sun reflects intensely against the pane, but he distantly sees the outline of dark hair, the pallor of her skin. He shades his eyes and squints, and there is the hand on the glass, the palm, and splayed fingers. He cannot tell from here if she's watching him or the neglected lawns where their children will never play. It doesn't make much difference in the great scheme of things.

He drives away, back down through the sunlit woods, leaving her and that house far behind. As he goes, glancing now and then in the rear-view mirror, he can't help thinking of those fingers pressed against the window. He wonders if they're still painted in flamingo pink.

Lifting The Lid

'This is really your first trip back here? Since you were a kid?'

'Since the tender age of thirteen.' Jack steered the car through town. The streets remained familiar, even after all the time elapsed. It seemed he'd been gone but a few days rather than fifteen long years.

Leanne ate her crisps, brushing crumbs from her dress and globular stomach. 'So why come back now?'

He took in the corner newsagent, where he bought sweets and lemonade when growing up. The name was different—Harper's back then—although the paintwork and stripy awning looked unchanged. 'It's something I have to do, so I can finally put this place behind me. I guess part of me wants you to see it too. You always grill me about my childhood ...'

'And you always tell me practically zilch,' she finished. Winston, their Collie, appeared from the backseat, muzzle jutting. Leanne fed him a crisp. 'I mean, I know you had a troubled time here, but you never fill in any of the gaps.'

'Maybe I can today.'

She brushed more crumbs. 'Amen to that.'

'I never tried to be evasive. It all just ... my life became such a mess here.'

They passed the White Hart pub, outside which a few patrons lurked, smoking cigarettes. Sallow faces tainted by excessive drinking turned to watch as they drove by. Jack indicated on to Main Street:

Thompson's Bakery. The electrical store. The Coffee Pot, where his mother once waitressed part-time. To the right the Sea Breezes Funeral Home, a single-storey detached brick building. Beneath the name were a phone number and the words, *Always caring*. He decelerated, taking a look, wondering who ran the place now. A long hearse occupied the parking bay, black panels gleaming like a beetle's shell. Jack passed St Peter's tall mosaic windows, remembering the vigil outside its sturdy doors. Farther down was the Salvation Army property on the corner and across the way, the Kingdom Hall of Jehovah's Witnesses.

He turned off, ascended Lovat Brae in low gear, drawing to the top of the bluff where the road terminated in a grand viewpoint. He popped his seatbelt and arched his back. From this vantage, one witnessed the ocean for miles unto the horizon. Below were the town's residential areas: fishing cottages and houses; men unloading trawlers by the wharf; a network of narrow roads; an inlet of beach marred by a sewage pipe; slippery rocks and tide pools where he played as a youngster.

Leanne twisted her empty crisp bag into a bowtie. 'Quite a view.'

'This is where guys would take their dates at the weekends,' Jack said. 'They'd drive up here after dark with a few beers and smooch.' He indicated a peninsula of a distant land, maybe a mile away, the farthest spot visible from where they were parked. 'That's Angler's Point,' he said. 'Right out at the end there, see?'

Leanne plucked a wet wipe from the glove. 'The *Angler*—wasn't that the name of your father's boat?'

'Yeah. The accident happened two weeks before his forty-ninth birthday. They overturned in heavy seas between Shetland and Orkney. There was an all-night search—offshore helicopter, seven or eight vessels, including lifeboats and coastguard, even commercial ships. The whole works. The men were never recovered, though. A commemorative monument was erected out there. The site became known as Angler's Point.'

'Must've been awful for them. You were only a child when it happened?'

'Five.'

She squeezed his leg.

'I'd go out there all the time. You can't drive to the Point; you have to walk or cycle. My mother didn't want me going there on my own, but I went anyway. I suppose it made me feel closer to my dad. It's kind of peaceful too, a place you can sit and think.' He looked across at Leanne. 'You really want the gory details?'

'Really, Jack, I do. It'd do you good to get it off your chest. Closure, you know?'

He contemplated this. She was probably right. Closure sounded pretty good, and if he spoke to anyone of it, it should be Leanne. She was his future, was carrying their future inside her. It felt somehow wrong to withhold things.

'Back then, my best pal was a kid called Henry. His father was the local undertaker, Marius Lundberg. He owned the Sea Breezes Funeral Home, that place I slowed at when we drove in? Well, Marius was long divorced, and he and my mother eventually met through my friendship with Henry. They hit it off, so to speak, and after a few years, they married. Henry and I became stepbrothers, which was fine with us because neither of us had siblings. So Mum and I moved into Lundberg's place, much grander than where we were living. She quit waitressing and doing hair. She and Henry got on well; she treated him just the same as she treated me.' He looked at the reach of ocean.

'I suppose Marius would've been considered a catch, at least financially. He had business savvy and clearly employed it to make money—directorship at the funeral home, municipal bonds, various holdings. Wasn't short of a quid or two.'

Leanne laced fingers across her stomach.

'Everything was fine at the start, mostly. Marius was an order freak—coasters and labels and the like. OCD, they'd call it these days. He was a bit straight, never laughed or enjoyed himself much. Stereotypical funeral director, right? But my mother, she never struck me as completely happy either. With her, I think it was something in her nature, a natural worrier. I don't know; she always seemed preoccupied about something, even before she met Marius.

'When Henry and I were thirteen, a young girl called Lily Melrose went missing in October that year. She was nine, and she'd been gone roughly a week before they found her.' Jack stared out at the grassy hill by the smokehouses overlooking the harbour. 'I remember sitting over there with Henry while it was going on.'

*****

'What you reckon happened?'

They sit on the grassy rise, supping Cokes, their bikes on the ground beside them. Among the narrow streets below, police cars and uniformed officers stir. A Volkswagen van pulls up down there, from which crew-bearing microphones and television cameras disembark.

'Henry?'

'What?'

'What you reckon happened to Lily Melrose?'

'I dunno, Jack.'

128

Below, the search party congregates by the harbour. Jack has never seen so many people roaming around town. From up here, it looks like a busy ant-colony.

'My dad's out helping search,' says Henry, releasing a gassy burp. 'I don't see him down there. Do you?'

Jack shakes his head, says, 'You ever been in his funeral place?'

'Coupla times.' Henry crumples his empty Coke can. 'He once showed me some of the stuff he uses. He's got all these weird tools and this big machine that flushes all the blood from a body. Pretty gross. Like Frankenstein or something.'

'Really?'

'Sure. I seen it.'

'Ever see any of the bodies?'

'Nah.'

Jack watches a trawler way out on the water.

'Suppose we better get home,' Henry says, raising his Woodworm bike from the grass. 'Coming?'

Jack watches a moment longer. Just then, cutting across his eye line, the beating rotors of a searching police helicopter slice the air. Henry is already cycling away when Jack mounts his Muddyfox and pedals after him.

*****

'Next day after school, I cycled out to the Point,' Jack said. 'I'd go out there for a sneaky cigarette, usually pinched from my mother's pack— she smoked like a fire, my mother. It was a few days before the October holiday. I didn't much feel like going home because I knew I wouldn't be allowed out again. Lily's disappearance was causing a big stir, and parents wouldn't let their kids out after dark. My mother and Marius weren't getting along, which put a strain on Henry and me too. Anyway, I didn't want to go home, so I cycled out there. Henry had stayed behind for football training; otherwise, he would've probably come with me.'

*****

Breathing sea air, Jack follows the ragged trail. The sky is overcast. Pedalling, he glances at the sheer cliff faces to his right, favourably anticipating a quiet cigarette. He soon fetches up at the Point and drops his schoolbag. He leans his Muddyfox against rocks pooled with saltwater. There are two wooden benches where folk can sit and enjoy the view. Seagulls drift overhead. A granite monument has been erected here, six feet tall, smooth as glass, each of the trawlermen's names inscribed in gold. The Point's main attraction, though, for Jack at least, is its isolation. Finding someone here is rare, especially during these colder months; therefore, he can sit and enjoy his smoke without fretting about prying eyes.

Ankles crossed, he clicks his jaw, expelling rings lazily heavenwards. The sky is darkening. Sat there before the sea, he contemplates his late father, picturing vague images he retains of the man. He wonders upon what must've gone through their minds as the vessel sank, how they had reacted to tragedy. How long had they stayed alive? He wonders what it'd be like to experience tragedy firsthand, how he himself would cope if he had to.

*****

Leanne's eyes met his, her expression one of empathy. She knew how this story ended—broadly—but this was the first time he'd pieced it together for her in relative detail.

'Go on, Jack,' she said. Winston appeared again, and Leanne

130

ruffled the fur under his jaw. 'All right, boy.'

Jack stared at gulls in the air. Their gulping, repetitive cries reminded him of engines struggling to start. 'When I came home that day, I felt something was wrong. Not sure how exactly. It was— sometimes you get a sense, you know? Anyway, I felt something wasn't right.'

*****

His mother has been down a great deal. Occasionally, if he asks her anything, she doesn't reply, as if she's zoned out. Jack sometimes wonders if she'd open up to him if he were older. Maybe even confide in him. She often comes across as burdened by some manner of problem, past or present: the death of his father, the worries of being a parent, making another life with Lundberg. In Jack's opinion, it drags her down. He longs to tell her he understands, that things will right themselves and they'll be happy again. But, for all his age, he doesn't really believe it. Life isn't like that. He might be young, even a bit naïve, but he's old enough to know problems don't always get better and rarely just go away.

Henry's Woodworm isn't there when Jack returns to the house, meaning his stepbrother hasn't yet finished training. It's too early for Marius to be home, so the undertaker's drive is empty. Setting down his bike, Jack looks at the garden statuary, the regency urns. Water spills from a winged-angel, pooling at its base. He opens the front door to the stale smell of cigarette smoke and shoulders of his schoolbag. No washer running. No TV, no radio. And his mother isn't moving around, either, not that he can hear.

She isn't in the living room. On the coffee table is an ashtray crammed with butts. The TV is actually on, silenced. The screen shows a wildlife programme, a stealthy lion closing on prey. It strikes

131

Jack as a bad omen.

He returns to the hall, wondering if his mother has gone out. Maybe she put on her coat and left, possibly with the intention of never coming home again. He sometimes believes she wishes she could do this, that it's among the possibilities she weighs when zoned out.

He hesitates by the kitchen, his gut yet insisting this is a bad situation. He swallows, taking another step towards the doorway.

Inside, she occupies one of the table's four chairs.

With her back and tangled hair facing him, she is slumped over the tabletop, her right arm extended, the left folded at the elbow. Next to her hand is a pill bottle, a little brown container with a label. A second bottle and some white pills are scattered among coloured capsules. A smattering has fallen down by her purple slippers. And there's a bottle of booze standing on the tabletop, barely an inch of liquid remaining.

Jack moves around and braves a look at his mother's bloated face. She's peaceful, eyes closed, lips parted with a glisten of saliva on her chin. He touches her arm and shakes her gently.

*****

'While Henry and I were at school, the police had interviewed Marius about the Melrose girl's disappearance. Lily was last seen at the other side of town, and someone had remembered a car—the model and colour Marius drove—cruising around the place the same day. So, the police spoke to him that afternoon, and they must've grown suspicious—they've got body language experts and all sorts, haven't they? Anyway, long story short, he eventually came clean. Lily's body was hidden in one of the caskets at the Sea Breezes, some old guy due to be buried the next day. She'd been interfered with ... and suffocated.'

Leanne touched her lips, staring at him.

'Marius Lundberg. My stepfather. Henry's dad.' He gripped the wheel. 'When my mother found out, it was the last straw, I guess. She'd already ... well, she'd been on different meds for depression. Couldn't take any more, I suppose.

'I called an ambulance, explained what had happened the best I could. Henry got back minutes before it arrived. I didn't know what to say to him, didn't yet know what had caused my mother to do this. Later we learned what Lundberg had done. I couldn't believe it, Lea. It was his fault my mother was dead—that Lily Melrose was dead. But I couldn't help thinking it was *my* friendship with Henry that brought my mother and Marius together. In a way, I'd invited him into our lives. I suppose ... I've always felt partially to blame.'

'That's crazy.'

'In such a situation, a million crazy things go through your head, especially when you're thirteen. How could I sit there and eat meals with someone like that and—and not know?'

'You were only a boy, hon.'

'If I'd gone straight home from school, maybe she'd still be alive. Maybe it would've made the difference.'

'You couldn't have known anything about it.'

'No.'

'Did your mother leave you anything? A letter, anything to explain?'

'No, nothing.'

This seemed to warrant a moment's silence. Then Leanne asked,

'What became of Henry?'

'Went to live with his mother. Down near Newcastle somewhere. I left after my mother was cremated. Her ashes were scattered from this viewpoint, right over there. She just disappeared into the wind. Uncle Tom ... my father's brother ... he and his wife looked after me up north till I was seventeen when I went out on my own. I lost touch with Henry. The friendship never would've survived what happened.'

Regarding the horizon, Jack wondered if Leanne was trying to process what he'd told her. He knew now that the reason he had not spoken of these occurrences to her was owed to the fact she might think less of him; he realised he'd been foolish to believe this. It was an ugly story, sure, but he wasn't the villain of the piece.

'He was planning to bury her with someone else.' Jack shook his head as if still struggling with the idea, even now. 'It's sacrilege. He'd have let her family suffer, wondering where she was, what'd happened to her. What kind of person would do that?'

Darkness encroached. Saltwater broke against the rocks, sending up spindrift. A tabby cat slunk by and disappeared in the long grass. The ocean's expanse made Jack feel inconsequential.

Leanne fixed her hair in a tail and smiled sympathetically. 'Have you seen enough? Do you want to go?'

He nodded. He had more to say but didn't know if he could express himself adequately. He loved his wife, could not imagine himself without her, although often he contemplated the direction his life had taken, how he'd met her. Had the tragedies of his youth steered him towards Leanne? Without those happenings, without him abandoning this town, he'd never have laid eyes on her. He pondered such concepts often: fate and karma, chance and randomness, how none could really be explored or identified one way or another, not to any satisfying end. He wondered if Henry ever processed such thoughts and where his old friend might be today. What had Henry learned to live with in the intervening years? Jack weighed these issues, but they remained too unfinished to give Leanne a fitting gist of what he meant.

'Thanks for coming back with me.' He started the engine. 'And thanks for listening.'

'I'm your wife, Jack.' She caressed her belly. 'Better or worse, remember? It's you, me, and Junior here—and you too, Winston, baby.' Winston barked, and Leanne smiled. 'No stopping us,' she said.

Her assertions filled him with profound gladness that he was the person with whom she had chosen to share her life. He had more baggage than Heathrow, but here she was, still by his side. He hoped he could match her courage and optimism, make her proud in coming years. He wanted to explain, and again words proved elusive, but he knew there would be many days to discuss such feelings.

He manoeuvred the car down the brae, followed the road out of town, casting one last look at the Sea Breezes before leaving Main Street. He activated the headlights at the outer limits. Fir trees lined the roadsides. Leanne found his thigh again in the descending dark, assuring him she was there for him, that she always would be. As the town receded in the rearview, he considered the nature and ripple effect of tragedy, how in life it is unavoidable, how everyone must face and overcome it eventually. He considered his impending role as a father and felt lighter and freer than he had in years—physically, mentally, perhaps even spiritually—as if a colossal nameless weight had been displaced from his shoulders for the first time since he was a child.

Taking Care Of Business

Through the café window, Scott Dawson watched the private investigator's VW Estate swing into the car park. Craning his neck, Hobbs reversed competently into a berth and got out, six-two of solid ex-Royal Marine, before starting across the tarmac, his regimented motions ingrained through years in the forces: ramrod posture, eyes front, arms swinging in time. In his fifties, Hobbs remained strong and toned, and Dawson didn't doubt he could still shift across tough terrain with a casualty slung over his shoulder. The investigator held the café door for a woman exiting, then entered and peered around, moving only his tree-trunk neck, finding Dawson in the corner.

'Scotty,' he said, approaching the table.

Dawson nodded, straightening up.

As Hobbs lowered his immense bulk into the chair opposite, a young waitress in a lime-green uniform tottered over, smiling.

'Uh, coffee, please,' Dawson said. He glanced at Hobbs, who ordered orange juice with ice.

'Menu's on the blackboard, okay?'

'The drinks will be all,' Dawson told her. When she left, he shuffled his chair in and put his palms on the table. 'So, you find him?'

'Yeah, I found him.'

'How long's he been out?'

'Almost a week,' Hobbs reported. 'His sentence was trimmed for good behaviour.'

Dawson snorted, shook his head. He glanced across the café at an orange-mouthed baby in a highchair, then looked out at the steely cloudscape above East London.

'He's labouring on a construction site,' Hobbs said. 'I poked about, and it turns out the job foreman's his brother.'

'Construction?'

Hobbs shrugged. 'He was struck off for manslaughter, medical negligence. His scalpel-wielding days are over, I'd imagine.' He laid down a page of notepaper, tapped it twice. 'I've listed the builders' company and its business address, though I doubt they'll be much use to you. At the bottom, that's the apartment where Turner is staying.'

Dawson raised his brows. 'He's not in Knightsbridge any more?'

The investigator leaned back, pushing out his broad chest. 'Far as I can tell, things between him and the wife took a nosedive after he was incarcerated. She's still there in the big house with the teenage daughter, but word is she's chasing a divorce. When the GMC dropped Turner from the register that would've caused problems. But hubby serving time? That obviously made her want to duck out. So much for vows, hey?'

Dawson studied the scratchy handwriting. 'This address; where is it?'

'Apartment block behind Beech Park. Not the sort of digs the former doctor would be used to.'

'No?'

'No rosebushes and parasols, if you get my drift.'

'Better than prison,' Dawson suggested.

Hobbs tilted his head, as if this was debatable. 'He's usually there in the evening, after six-thirty or thereabouts.'

The waitress brought their drinks, still all smiles. Dawson peeled open a miniature milk container while Hobbs drained half his juice.

'What about the ... the other matter?' Dawson prompted, still looking at the notepaper.

Hobbs waited until Dawson met his eye again. 'Sure you want to go ahead with this, Scotty?'

'I'm sure.'

'Listen, I know how you feel about Turner. God, I understand.' Hobbs rattled the cubes around in his glass. 'But trust me, the type of man who can pull off what you're planning? It ain't you.'

'You're wrong.'

Hobbs grinned, but it was humourless. 'You think you've figured out what it takes? How to do it without making mistakes?'

'I've had lots of time to consider since Laura left.'

Hobbs was silent a moment, as if in sympathy. 'Have you heard anything from her?'

Dawson shook his head again. 'She was in Cornwall with her folks. I gather she's moved on; I don't know where.'

'You want me to look for her?'

'No. God no. She left of her own accord; she made her decision.' Dawson tried to keep the hurt from his voice but couldn't quite manage it.

'Is it worth losing everything? For him?'

'I've already lost everything ...'

Hobbs stared at him. 'You've got the hotel, a reliable business. You were dealt a shit hand, but there *is* a choice here. You might even patch things up with Laura one day.'

'Look,' Dawson said, showing a palm, 'we go back a good long way; I appreciate that. But I'm paying for information, not advice.'

Hobbs drained his orange juice, smacked his lips. 'Consider the advice a freebie, for what it's worth. I'm serious, though. Once you get this outta your system—all the anger and hatred—you'll be the one showering with your back to the wall, wishing you'd listened when you had the chance.'

Dawson tented his fingers impatiently. 'Will you help me or not?'

The investigator drew a palm over his bristly crewcut and blew out a long breath. 'Are you familiar with Marcus Aurelius?'

'Who?'

'A Roman emperor and philosopher. He said, "The best revenge is to be unlike him who performed the injury".'

'Very insightful.' Dawson stared into his coffee, stirring it thoughtfully with a small plastic spoon. 'I had to bury my little boy. You don't know what that feels like.'

'Hey, don't lecture me on loss. I lost more friends in combat than you'd believe. And let me tell you, when you take a life, you forfeit a piece of your own in the process.'

This last exchange seemed to give them both something to think about. Syrupy Muzak floated from above. The highchair baby started to wail and wave its arms. Dawson winced and sipped his bad coffee. Eventually, he asked, 'So?'

'I don't think it's a good idea.'

'Objection noted.'

'I mean it, Scott.'

'I need your help. Please ...'

'I can give you a name; that's where it ends for me. I'm not a mercenary.'

'Sure. Just, you know, point me in the right direction.'

Hobbs tapped his index finger on the tabletop. 'Genuine Army Surplus on Mile End Road, across from the church. See a guy called Zander. He runs a sideline, under-the-counter gear.'

'He'll help me?'

Hobbs shrugged his broad shoulders again. 'If he doesn't think you're a liability.'

'Maybe you could put in a word ...?'

'No, Scotty, I couldn't.' He stared coldly across the table. 'I told you, you're making a mistake. But it's your life.'

Dawson looked at the address on the notepaper, his heart pumping faster. 'Turner's the one who made a mistake.'

*****

He drove back to Islington to the four-bedroom home he hated occupying alone. In the living room, he poured a Glenlivet he didn't really want and sat by the broad brickwork fireplace. Aaron smiled from a mantel photograph, a captured moment in a vanished history. Nearby was a framed snap of Dawson and Laura at La Troza Beach Resort in Mexico, their last family holiday. Good times, when life had been on an upward curve. But the higher you climb, the farther you fall. He had learned this the hard way, and how.

The separation wasn't bitter, no raging storm. Laura hadn't even wanted to sell the house; she just needed out. He had at first been angry and hurt, surprised how she could so easily walk away as if

140

Aaron had been their only substantial link. It made him wonder if his view of their marriage was skewed, rose-tinted, or whether he'd been selectively blind to weaknesses. In the end, he had to let her go.

So, stellar Dr Turner of Royal London Hospital had taken everything; that's what Hobbs didn't seem to understand. The investigator had seen his share of death—Somalia, Bosnia, the Gulf War—but that didn't mean he knew how Dawson felt. Forty-two, struggling for direction, Dawson was now a man without love or purpose. This vendetta at least provided him the drive to right a heinous wrong, and although he accepted nothing would fill the void, he had to avenge his son.

That night, Dawson lay in bed with the scalloped lamp on. Facing him on the wall was Laura's Elvis clock, which he'd bought for her before they married. She hadn't taken it with her. The image was from the King's Hawaiian show, a garland of yellow blossoms round his neck, the infamous high collar framing those otherworldly features. He found it hard to look at the clock now: the King, who'd had everything and, like himself, still finished up in tragedy, reclusive and alone.

Dawson had first met Laura at an Elvis tribute act. By chance, they had been seated together throughout the show—the original truck-driving youngster, the '68 renaissance, the final jumpsuit period—and during each interval, they had talked and eventually exchanged numbers. Years later, when their son was born, Laura wanted to call him Aaron, after the King's middle name. Right about then, it had seemed that life was perfect and nothing could hold them back.

*****

The following day, standing in cold April drizzle on Mile End Road, despite just idling with his hands in his pockets, Dawson felt conspicuous. The establishment looked quiet, nobody going in or out. Steel mesh-protected dark windows on either side of the main entrance. A sign bearing the business's name swung in the wind from a rust-eaten bracket above the door.

He'd planned to boldly approach this Zander character, feigning confidence, but now Dawson wasn't so sure he could. These types dealt in illegal firearms—and God knows what else—lurking in an underworld he knew nothing about. It gave him food for thought and caused him unwanted hesitation. Yet this was the only lead he'd likely get, and he wasn't about to pass it up. He touched the envelope of cash in his jacket's breast pocket, waited for a break in traffic, and hurriedly crossed the road.

Inside was colourless, heavy with shadow, breached only by weak daylight through the windows. No other customers. Aisles of equipment—camouflage jackets, footwear, canteens, headgear—were displayed under weak light. A radio played Fleetwood Mac's 'Don't Stop'. Mustiness fouled the air. Suspended from the ceiling were the electric-blue bars of a rectangular light-trap for frying bugs. A tall guy with a Mohawk haircut stood at the back, reading. As Dawson approached the counter, he saw it was a glass case stocked with lethal-looking knives.

The Mohawk guy set aside his magazine. His white T-shirt revealed a well-toned chest and sinewy arms covered in Celtic-design tattoos. A metal stud glinted in his lip. Sections of his left eyebrow had been shaved away. 'What's up, man?' he said.

'Are you ... Zander?'

The guy's dark eyes narrowed with suspicion. He slipped his hands into his jeans' rear pockets. 'Who wants to know?'

'I, uh, I'd like to make a purchase.'

'What kinda purchase, man?'

Dawson licked his lips, cleared his throat. 'I need a gun.'

The guy's expression changed, falling somewhere between a grin and a sneer. 'Come on, beat it.'

'Something from your ... private stock?' Dawson touched his jacket pocket, as if taking an oath. 'I have cash.'

'Shit, what's a dude like you want with a piece?'

'Does it matter?'

The guy still appeared wary. 'Who sent you here?'

Dawson regarded the arrayed knives—long blades, big solid handles—and felt his stomach flip. 'Someone who did some personal work for me.' He glanced about himself uncomfortably. 'Look, can you help or not?'

'Hobbs, right?'

Dawson exhaled, nodded. 'He, uh ... he reckoned you were the man to talk to.'

The guy dialled down the radio and leant on the counter. Small tattoos darkened the sides of his shaved scalp.

'What sort of thing you after, man?'

'I know nothing about guns,' Dawson admitted. The sound of a frying bug sizzled in the light-trap behind him. 'Something manageable, that'll do what it's supposed to. I'm not really sure.'

Zander dealt him a measuring look, and Dawson wondered if he saw the same inadequacies Hobbs had. Perhaps this was all the reason he needed to refuse his help. But, to Dawson's infinite relief, he did not refuse:

'Come back closin' time, man,' he said and turned up the radio again.

*****

Dawson nursed dark ale in a bar called the Rusty Bike. From his window seat, watching people and traffic through the rain, he paid attention to parents with kids, which put him in mind of Aaron, imagining how his boy would've matured. How tall would he be? Would his fair hair have darkened? What would his interests be?

When he and Laura had learned their son was sick, it had been all but impossible to accept. Day-to-day life, even working and sleeping, became difficult. Why would such horror befall a young boy? Where was the fairness in that? He and Laura had been strong—what option was there?—and the situation did seem less dire after assurances that, regarding the transplant Aaron needed, outcomes were largely successful. They had embraced the statistics, reminding each other the odds were in Aaron's favour. But sometimes odds don't pay off, and life ... well, life was never fair.

Dawson drank his beverage and wondered if his need for vengeance was now a coping mechanism, a means to the end of him moving forward every day.

Back at the store, Zander locked up with keys and deadbolts.

'Follow me,' he said and led Dawson through a doorway down wooden-plank stairs.

The descent was narrow, pitch dark, the absence of light affecting Dawson with claustrophobia and a feeling of vulnerability. Below street level, Zander tugged a cord, and an unadorned bulb lit cardboard boxes and merchandise piled everywhere. The subdued sounds of footsteps and vehicles passed overhead. As Dawson blinked away darting spots of light from his vision, Zander set a small case on a

144

table.

'Gun's untraceable,' he said, ruffling his long cockscomb hair. 'But listen, you ever mention my name or this place, we'd have ourselves a real problem, dig?'

'I was never here,' Dawson said, feeling a jolt of excitement, a sense of progress.

Zander unlatched the case with long fingers and swivelled it around, revealing a black automatic pistol. Dawson just watched as Zander removed it from the foam cut-out and held it up.

'Beretta 9000. Traditional open-top slide,' he said, working the weapon. 'Self-loading chambered for 9 millimetre Parabellum rounds. Twelve to a magazine. Fixed sights. Good gun, good price.'

'Can you, uh, show me what to do with it?'

Zander raised a shaved eyebrow. 'Man, you're 'bout green as they come, huh?'

'I have a plan,' Dawson told him defensively.

'Man makes plans, and God laughs,' Zander said.

*****

Darkness had seen off daylight when Dawson drove slowly past the tower block. Its very appearance, he thought, must've mortified the good doctor upon first sight. Dawson parked his Citroen and reconnoitred the building as casually as possible, feeling anything but. The communal entrance had a buzzer/entry-phone system. One apartment had a cracked windowpane, grinning furry toys attached to the glass with little suction cups. Graffiti around the ground floor. A far cry from Knightsbridge, for sure.

Back home, he stood before his bedroom mirror, levelling the handgun like Robert De Niro in *Taxi Driver*. He held it one-handed, then both hands. It was heavier than it appeared. He shuffled his feet to a comfortable stance. He felt good, empowered, and ready to take care of business, as Elvis had said (though he'd no intention of laying waste his flat-screen TV). Somewhere deep inside, he knew his intentions were wrong, just as Hobbs had suggested. *The best revenge is to be unlike him, who performed the injury.* Yet the need was too great; he couldn't allow Turner his freedom. He had waited too long for the sonofabitch to leave prison, and now he was walking the streets. Paroled for good behaviour. It was an insult to Aaron's memory. The only justice, Dawson had long since decided, was what a man exacted for himself.

He poured a hefty Glenlivet, climbed the deep-pile carpeted stairs to Aaron's bedroom, and looked at his son's things, small yet poignant reminders. The football in the corner, with which they'd done keepy ups in the garden. He sifted through the richly coloured drawings of superheroes on the desk. Iron Man, Spiderman, the Green Lantern. He picked up the remote-control racing car Aaron used to chase around the house, crashing into everything; he looked at the PlayStation, where his son spent hours battling endless galactic enemies, despite school-night reprimands from Laura. All from the pre-sickness days, before his young life was stolen. It was easier to leave everything in place than clear it out, and Dawson had no issue with that. He looked until he felt his chest swelling with emotion, with love, and inevitably with loss.

He struggled to sleep, listening to the steady hiss of rain, rehearsing everything mentally, fearful that mere planning couldn't substitute for experience. He played out fanciful scenarios in which Turner begged for his life.

When he eventually slept, he dreamt he was walking along a

starkly white corridor, which terminated in tall double doors. Laura was seated next to them, looking into her lap, hands clasped, her face hidden beneath her straight black hair. It seemed to take a long time to reach her as if he were moving under water, and when he did, he realised he was gripping the pistol in his hand.

Laura raised her head. Teary-eyed, she looked first at him, then at the gun. 'What're you doing with *that*?'

'Takin' care of business, baby,' he said, in a slow, lazy drawl like the King's, and lovingly touched the side of her face.

He shoved open the door, finding Dr Turner standing before him in blue medical scrubs and facemask, working his hands into surgical gloves. Flexing his fingers, he regarded Dawson with expressionless eyes. Behind Turner, under the brilliance of surgical light heads, a small lifeless form lay on a trolley beneath a white sheet.

Dawson raised the automatic and opened fire, four bursts of spattering blood erupting from the doctor's front before he collapsed to the floor.

*****

'Hi, son.'

He stood at the graveside, holding cellophane-wrapped flowers. He and Laura had chosen a heart-shaped stone, a white cherub sleeping on its forearms in the cleft at the top. Dawson's mother had evidently been by with carnations and gypsophila. He poured water from a nearby canister, washing away flecks of dirt. Morning mist wreathed Manor Park's trees and monuments like a set from an old Peter Cushing flick.

'I thought I should drop by and, uh ...' He felt a lump in his throat. 'Well, I've gotta do something today. And, uh, if it goes the way I expect it to, I probably won't be able to come by as often. I just want you to know that it's not 'cause I've forgotten you, son. This is something I have to do.'

He replayed random memories of his boy, and when his mind became overcrowded with the images, Dawson finally laid his bouquet before the stone, pressed his fingers to the marble, and left.

He spent that Wednesday pacing the house, psyching himself, awaiting nightfall. He took out the Beretta several times and pointed it. He likely wouldn't get away with killing Turner—he was realistic enough to accept that—but it nevertheless struck him as a task best tackled under the cloak of darkness. Chances were that Turner would be home of an evening, as Hobbs had reported. Still, if he escaped unseen and managed to discard the gun successfully, he just might get away with it. The Crown Court required powerful evidence for murder convictions, and he'd do his damnedest not to leave any.

At eight p.m., well beyond sundown, dressed in a black jacket and trousers, Dawson drove through London's streets. The temperature had plummeted, and swirls of dense fog obscured signs of passing life. Travelling with the Beretta made him anxious enough to keep glancing in the rear-view. Should he be pulled—a routine stop, say, or faulty brake light—and the gun found, he'd be finished. No reason he should be stopped, but fate sometimes conjured surprises just when you least expected or wanted them. Dawson knew this better than most.

Man makes plans, and God laughs.

Nobody stopped him. He didn't see a police car the whole way. Amid the fog's opacity, he saw little more than murky silhouettes and blurred lights. Dawson parked the Citroen a few streets distant and walked to the tower block, a black beanie over his head, surgical gloves on his hands. At the main entrance, an old woman in a tea cosy hat was leaving, wheeling a tartan suitcase, so Dawson held the door and slipped inside with scarcely a glance from her.

Because the lift was a horror show of graffiti, he opted for the stairs, moving quietly in old running shoes, zig-zagging up the flights, trying to keep his breathing steady. His mouth was dry as sand as he passed refuse bags and an upturned mountain bike with one wheel. He heard a distressed baby, a heated quarrel, and thrash metal music which sounded to Dawson oddly like guys eating each other. The stairwell walls were a gouged confusion of swearwords, cartoon faces, and bizarre nicknames. A scrawny black cat yowled at him, leaving him wondering if superstition deemed the luck good or bad. His hands trembled as adrenaline did the rounds through his body. Keeping his head down as he ascended, he prayed he wouldn't encounter anyone. Fortunately, when he reached the right floor, he hadn't passed a soul.

Four flats here. One was Number 42, which should be the good doctor.

Dawson sidled stealthily across the landing and leant in, listening. A television on the inside. Canned laughter. He had planned to knock, then barge in when Turner opened the door ... but now a better idea presented itself. He tried the handle gently, and when he exerted a little pressure, the door swung inward without resistance.

He stepped inside and closed it behind him. Took out the Beretta.

The apartment hallway was dim, shifting blue light from a TV set playing on a wall up ahead. A pair of muddy work boots stood on the mat. Detecting a citrusy odour, like shower gel or deodorant, he began along the hall as a man appeared from a side doorway—

Turner started—'Jesus'—stepping back, raising his palms. He was bare-chested, a white flowery towel around his waist.

'Move to the living room,' Dawson said, gesturing with the handgun.

'Look, I don't have money, please—'

'Shut up. In the living room.'

His hair a towelled mess, Turner backed through the doorway like a cornered animal. Dawson followed, gripping the gun tightly, his heart motoring now.

'Shut that shit off.'

Keeping eye contact, Turner fumbled with the remote and killed the TV. The room fell silent, now lit only by a spill of hallway light. The curtains stood open on misty London. Dawson smelt something vaguely spicy and traced the scent to empty Pot Noodle tubs on the coffee table.

He motioned with the gun. 'Sit—over there.'

Turner sidestepped to an armchair, running a nervous hand through the wiry hair on his chest, frowning as he lowered into the seat. 'Don't I know you?'

'You killed my little boy.'

He closed his eyes. 'Mr Dawson.'

'He needed a transplant. You botched it because you were drunk.'

He opened his eyes again, looked at Dawson. 'Now hold on. There was more to it.'

'Aaron lost blood. He had ... tissue injuries. You did that. You were drunk.'

'He had a reaction to anaesthesia.'

'You killed him. You pleaded guilty.'

'There were complications.'

'You were a drunk, a drunk doing operations.' Dawson stepped forward. 'Your colleagues smelt it on you afterward.'

'I'd been drinking that day—but I wasn't drunk. Look, okay, I know the distinction doesn't carry much weight. I shouldn't have been anywhere near the stuff; I accept that, of course, I do.'

Dawson's trigger-finger tightened. Rage stirred within him as he aimed the gun between Turner's eyes. *So why were you?*

Turner seemed to think about this as if choosing his words with caution. His stretch in prison had corroded his once-handsome looks, Dawson noticed now. The cheekbones were more pronounced, and worry lines, doubtlessly etched over many a lonely night, were evident even in the poor light.

'My marriage had become a nightmare,' Turner finally began. 'Once my wife got a whiff of money, well, she squandered it like a drunken sailor. Didn't matter how much we had, how much she got; she always wanted more. Like a tap, you couldn't turn off. Racked up frightening debts quicker than I could earn—credit cards and loans, things I wasn't even aware of till later. Then I found out she was sleeping with other men. After this, God, she didn't even try to hide it. I had pressures of work, surgery. The booze, it just helped ... take the edge off.' He shook his head several times, as if denying the way his life had gone. 'It got a hold of me, didn't it. Before long, it was keeping me going more days than not.' His beady eyes roamed the room forlornly. 'It's no excuse. God, I know that. When I was sentenced, my usefulness to her had clearly expired. She's the one who filed divorce proceedings—how do you like that? Out doing God knows what with other guys, and *she* files for divorce. Look at me now. Look at this place. She's taken everything. I'm left with nothing.'

'Your daughter's not dead.'

'No. No, she's not.' Turner was silent, reflective, staring at his hands. Then: 'I love my Katie. Love her more than anything.' He looked at a glittery photo frame above the TV, showing a smiling teenage girl. 'I can't imagine how I'd feel if something happened to her. After I was sentenced, my wife turned my daughter against me, Mr Dawson. I wanted to tell Katie what her sanctimonious mother had been doing with other men, bring her up to speed, you know, just to put her in the picture, even the score a little. But I couldn't. I knew it'd only damage the girl more—and I'd done enough damage already. I'll never get back what I had with her.' He gripped the chair's armrests and looked Dawson in the eye. 'I'm so sorry about your boy, really I am. I'd give anything to have that day over again.'

Turner drew a hand across protruding ribs, his pupils reflecting bright points of hallway light. 'Put a bullet in me, Mr Dawson. My family's gone. My career. Go ahead, finish this if you mean to. Truth is, you'd be doing me a service.'

Dawson looked at the dark-haired teenager in the photo above the TV. Winged eyeliner, like a cat, attractive. Katie Turner had been born the same year as Aaron; Dawson remembered hearing this as Turner was sentenced. He tried to imagine how Aaron would've felt if someone shot his father dead. He swallowed and, with a sense of gradually dwindling focus, realised this wasn't going to plan, not at all.

'Go ahead,' Turner urged resignedly. 'I'm finished anyway.'

The ceiling creaked as footsteps crossed in the apartment above.

Dawson contemplated how Laura might react when she heard he'd murdered someone, even a deserving lowlife like Turner. He didn't know why this mattered. Perhaps he still expected her to one day come back. How disappointed would she be? How disappointed would Aaron have been? He recalled what Hobbs had said—that he hadn't the mettle to pull the trigger, that he couldn't carry this off without making mistakes. Had he proved it already by delaying? Maybe he had always known so himself, deep down.

He lowered the weapon.

'I went to Aaron's grave when I got out,' Turner said, bringing his bony pale feet together.

Dawson found he didn't know how to respond to that.

'I brought flowers.'

Dawson frowned, recalling the carnations and gypsophila. 'I thought ... I thought my mother brought them.'

'I hope you don't mind. I told him how sorry I am, that I'd give my life to bring him back ... if I could.'

Dawson's sight blurred a little, and he turned away. He sat on the settee, laid the pistol on the coffee table by the Pot Noodle tubs. So, Hobbs was right. He didn't have what it took after all. He looked at Turner, a pathetic individual whose wife had deserted him. Who didn't see his kid any more. They had more in common than Dawson wanted to accept. *Jesus, he probably sits staring at the walls just like I do.* He realised then that he'd blamed Turner entirely for Laura's abandonment, but in truth, if he and Laura had been solid, she wouldn't have packed up and disappeared. She wouldn't have done that.

'He asked me if everything would be all right,' Dawson said, feeling queasy now, nauseated. He pressed his gloved fingertips together and looked down at his shabby running shoes. 'He asked if the operation would make him better. And I told him, "Of course, son. The people at the hospital are there to make you well again".'

'I'm so sorry...' Turner moaned, his cheeks shining with tears.

'...What else do you tell your kid when he asks something like that? I mean, even if you know the risks? Jesus, what do you tell him?'

'You're a good man,' Turner said, his voice hitching.

Dawson felt a sudden drive to be outside these confining walls to breathe fresh air. Tears threatened, and he would not shed them in front of this man. He stood and paced to the door, Turner now sobbing inconsolably behind him, and stepped into the stairwell. He grabbed hold of the railing a moment, then bounded down the stairs in two- and three-step jumps, his vision distorted by moisture, the black cat hissing like a burst tyre as he rushed by.

Outside, he peeled off the latex gloves and stood in the road, breathing heavily, hands on his knees. He tugged the beanie off his head, his mind spinning with conflicting thoughts.

He had almost killed a man ...

Then he realised he'd left the pistol with Turner—a stab of panic straightened him up as he calculated the possible consequences. Craning, peering at the tower block, he contemplated returning for it when a single gunshot rang out high above. Dawson saw a flash up there in the misty darkness between open curtains, like someone snapping a photo.

He turned and walked away at pace, keeping his head down, trying not to acknowledge what he knew would now surely haunt him: that perhaps Turner, like everyone at some time or another, had been affected by life's relentless pressures and didn't deserve to die.

Hobbs had been right. The whole idea really was a big mistake.

Married In D Minor

Cora sipped coffee and gazed out through the open kitchen window at the rear garden. Her husband sat slumped in his deckchair, polishing off little green bottles of beer, reading his paper, the modest patch of lawn lit in brilliant July sunshine. The summer breeze teased what remained of his white hair, like static electricity, and fanned the corners of his newspaper.

She came away from the window and slipped out a postcard from beneath the fridge magnet. It depicted the lush interior grandeur of the Vienna Opera House. Cora turned over the card and skimmed the superlatives in her best friend's tidy hand again. *Wonderful time. Amazing architecture. Glorious weather.*

She walked outside carrying her coffee mug, her face pleasantly heated under the afternoon sun. 'Lovely day again, isn't it, Arthur?'

Arthur raised the beer to his lips. He scratched at his navel between an unbuttoned checked shirt, mumbling something that may have been agreement.

'Have you taken your pills?'

'Yep.'

She hesitated by the whirligig clothesline. 'We're supposed to have record temperatures over the next couple of days.' She drank her coffee, looked down at him. When he didn't answer—he seldom did—she said, 'I thought we might go for a walk.'

He blew carefully into the newspaper's pages, separating them, then screwed up his face. 'Walk where?'

'Doesn't matter, really.' She watched bumblebees and an orange butterfly flit among the lilac flowers of a shrub plant. 'Perhaps down along the water, what do you think?'

'I'm reading the paper.'

'Oh, come on, Arthur. You have to do more than sit out here every day, drinking beer.'

'I'm retired. I'm allowed to sit in my own garden.'

'I just mean ...'

He made a shooing motion. 'Give me peace, woman, go on,' he said wearily.

*****

In the room by the stairs, Cora sat at her old walnut Steinway piano, moving her fingers over the major scales. She ran off a few basic melodies from memory, the notes floating around her. As a soloist, she kept the piano top raised for improved resonance. Its keys had begun to yellow, but the soundboard was unaffected by predicable problems like climate changes or years of vibration. The room stood unfurnished except for the piano, white transparent drapes softening windows, sunlight flaring across the laminate floor. The walls displayed her various framed achievements and certificates of competence, arrayed equidistantly around a pendulum clock. She played less nowadays than in her teaching years, her fingers less nimble, but the Steinway kept alive her love of the instrument.

'I'm off down the bettin' shop,' Arthur announced, startling her. He was standing in the doorway, a grey cap on his head, newspaper under his arm.

'To give away more money?'

'I don't complain when you sit in here, tickling the ivories.'

'Tickling ivories has nothing to do with wasting our money.'

'Whatever. Why don't you just learn to look the other way instead of complaining all the time?'

He left, and the front door closed, louder than necessary. A tear formed warmly in the corner of Cora's eye. She quickly wiped it clear with a fingertip, unwilling to cry in this room, which she'd always equated with happiness and calm.

She regarded the clock, it's second-hand circling relentlessly, and felt again the uncomfortable sense of time, of life, slowly wasting. She looked at her hands, aged and slack-skinned, and marvelled how the body continued to deteriorate while the mind, for the most part, remained the same. She positioned her pale fingers and struck D minor, traditionally considered the most melancholy of keys, its sound reverberating throughout the space until it dispersed, consumed by the silence. Then she closed the varnished fallboard and vacated the room.

*****

The next day, the heatwave continued. Cora observed Arthur through the kitchen window as she positioned the lunchtime dishes in the drainer. The radio played Beethoven's *Moonlight Sonata*. Arthur was supping beer in his deckchair, perusing his paper, bare-chested now, his sagging flesh burned an unsightly red, paunch exposed in all its glory.

She dried her hands, opened a drawer, and withdrew her glossy cruise brochure. She smiled childishly as she paged through the scenic destinations—France, Bora Bora, Singapore, the Americas, the fjords of Norway—admiring both them and the great lavish ships, like floating hotels, ready to take you there. The liners provided terrific nightlife, the brochure revealed, great dance halls and Broadway-style shows, fine dinners interspersed with music, from classical to

Memphis blues. Something for everyone. She saw herself stepping out to a cabin balcony, champagne flute in hand, the setting sun flashing a million sparkling sequins across the ocean's breadth.

Since they had retired, she from teaching, Arthur from his warehouse job, she felt they were under each other's feet more than ever. It wasn't surprising, with both of them constantly kicking around the house, less like man and wife than passing lodgers. And his irritating little habits did annoy her: the way he sat out there and picked at his nose as if it didn't matter whether or not she could see it. The way his eyes darted around as he drank from those stupid green bottles, like a baby feeding at its mother's breast.

Now that she considered it, many things about him irked her, from the uncouth smacking noises he made when he ate to his stony refusal to visit her mother when she was alive. And what about his moods? He hardly smiled any more, certainly not at her.

Perhaps a good holiday would work wonders. Perhaps it could release some of her tension. A nice cruise. She took a Cornetto from the freezer, one of her limited guilty pleasures, and flipped through images of sun-splashed foreign lands as she savoured the ice cream and raspberries, the wafer cone, and finally its rich chocolatey base.

Having returned the brochure to its place, she wiped her hands and stepped outside and stood in the sunlight beside Arthur. She looked at his yellowed toenails, his sagging jowls, and the collection of bottles at his feet.

'You know what Dr Kilbride told you about drinking so much,' she said. He penned a circle on the newspaper's racing page. '... Arthur.'

'What?'

'Dr Kilbride said you shouldn't drink so much. He also advised you to lose weight. Your sugars and cholesterol aren't good.'

'Hell does he know? Them quacks, they love to dish out advice.'

'You shouldn't sit here without a shirt. You'll burn.' She stooped and collected a couple of the empties in her apron. 'I'm going to brew coffee. Would you like some?'

He circled with the pen again, batted at a fly. 'Give me peace, will you, woman. Can't you see I'm busy?'

'Busy with racehorses.'

*****

Cora prepared coffee—for one—and sat at the kitchen table, pondering her life and how it had turned out, a train of thought she found herself following more and more lately. She looked at Maryanne's postcard from Vienna, the tiered seats of the Opera House pinned to the fridge door. She contemplated another flick through her travel brochure, but the mood had passed now. What was the use in torturing herself? The situation wouldn't change. So again, she daydreamed about life's possibilities and refused to concentrate on the downsides.

She believed people's situations, their status quo, was ultimately the result of all the decisions they make. Which partner to take and whether to remain with him or her. Where to live and whether to stay there. Which career to follow and whether to stick it out. Who to avoid or befriend. Whether to travel or always put it off. Whether to turn down a date or see where it might lead. To accept injustice or fight against it. Indulge or abstain. Countless choices over many years. The biggest decision she'd made had been to stay with Arthur, probably due to an antiquated, misguided sense of loyalty. Despite her mother's reservations. Despite their never having children. Despite the nagging inner voice throughout the years assuring her the situation would not improve.

Cora drank her coffee, deep in thought.

It seemed she didn't make decisions any more; that Arthur made them, based solely on the effort the subject in question entailed. When they had married many decades ago, it'd felt like the beginning of something unique, exciting, full of possibilities. Had she been entitled to feel expectant? Or had she been young and naïve? Either way, it hurt now to reminisce, knowing as she did that the majority of those expectations had not reached fruition and perhaps were never destined to in a life of routine and repetition that, after a while, felt like marking time. Marriage wasn't a fairy tale, she knew this better than most, but that didn't stop two people from trying to make it so, did it? Contrary to an exhilarating journey, wedlock had proved a steady, single-track progression, and she wondered if others felt this way after a lifetime of marriage. Relationships were hard, and many failed, and nobody could exempt themselves from the possibility.

She had loved Arthur, at least she believed she had, back when they'd laughed and actually had fun, but was never really sure he'd felt the same. He had told her he loved her, of course, although not for a long time now and never very convincingly. Often, when considering how little he conversed, how little he did, she couldn't avoid the notion he had simply settled for her, that he was no happier trundling along this single track than she was.

*****

That night, occupying separate single beds, Arthur tackled a crossword while Cora cooled her face with a handheld fan, which whirred quietly like an oversized summer insect. A paperback copy of *Mozart: A Life in Letters* sat on her side table, but the air remained too warm for her to concentrate on reading. No breeze came from the open window. She glanced across at her husband, chewing her lip, preparing herself.

'What do you think about a cruise, Arthur?'

Arthur printed an answer, pressing against raised knees. He plucked off his thick glasses, frowning at her. 'Cruise?'

Working the fan, she smiled innocently, as if the topic were spontaneous. 'I've been looking at a brochure Maryanne gave me. We've got money tucked away; we can afford it. Imagine the journeying, the anticipation, the fresh air.'

He tapped the newspaper with his pen like a conductor with a baton. 'Can't get this last bugger. Ten letters finishes with an e,' he said. 'L in the middle. Dreary or uninspiring.'

'Arthur ...'

He shook his head. 'Why you wanna go trekkin' round them far-flung places? Can't even drink the water in half of them damned countries. What kind of endorsement's that?'

'We owe ourselves a break.'

'Cruises, they're bloody expensive, Cora. No. No, I don't think so.'

'We'll just give all our money to the betting office, shall we?'

'I worked all my days. I wanna bet, I'll bet.'

'So I gather. But being retired doesn't make gambling a worthwhile pastime.'

'Does for me.'

Cora looked at the wall and sighed. 'It's lacklustre.'

Arthur put his glasses back on. 'Call it what you want.'

'The *crossword*. The answer is "lacklustre".'

'Hey, look at that ... There it is.'

Arthur completed the grid and clicked his retractable pen. He switched off his lamp. Cora switched off her fan.

*****

In the morning, as Cora loaded the washer, her lower back twinging with decades of wear and tear, the phone rang in the kitchen. She dialled down Stravinsky's *The Rite of Spring* on the radio.

'Mary!' she said happily, drawing up the little corner chair. 'How was Vienna?'

'Fantastic,' Maryanne told her. 'You and Arthur have to get away, Cora, really, you just have to. Did you mention the brochure to him?'

'Oh, no, I haven't got around to it yet,' she lied. 'But I will. I will. Come on, more about the trip. It was an anniversary, wasn't it?'

'Forty years,' Maryanne said. 'It's hard to believe us pair have lasted so long.'

Cora smiled. 'Oh, you don't mean that.'

'No, I don't. It was so breathtaking, Cora. The Imperial palaces, St Stephen's Cathedral. Don't get me started. It was all just, well, breathtaking. You'd *love* the Opera House; it's simply divine.'

'I saw it on the postcard. It looks wonderful.'

'And what about this heat? God, it's unnatural. Oh, and guess what Doug gave me on our last night before we went to dinner ...?'

'What?'

'A beautiful bracelet, with alternating rubies and diamonds.'

'Really?' Cora regarded her own unadorned wrist. 'That's so

lovely.'

'I spent the whole evening peering at it, right through the meal and everything.' Maryanne touched on the Grand Ferdinand Hotel and its nearby restaurants, then said, 'Ooh, listen, Doug and I've pencilled in a few drinks for tomorrow evening, just to sort of finish off the holiday, you know. Why don't you and Arthur pop round? We'd love to see you both. Are you free?'

'I'll ask him,' Cora said, staring at Arthur's old colour-drained underwear in the wash basket. 'It should be fine.'

'Great. I brought you back a chic little something I think you'll love. Any time after seven.' Maryanne giggled. 'I'll look out the rum and coconut milk.'

*****

Around noon, Cora draped and pegged washing on the whirligig line, the soft lawn warm beneath her bare toes. The sky was an expanse of faraway blue, marred only by the contrails of a passing plane. The neighbours' Irish setter barked playfully, the sounds growing louder as the prancing dog would near the high perimeter fencing. She heard the distant whine of an electric saw. The air, odorous of shorn grass and creosote, felt even muggier than earlier in the week, almost unbreathable.

'The weather forecast said it might be the hottest day of the year,' she began, fluently fixing coloured pegs to the clothesline. 'It's gone above forty degrees in parts of Europe.' When he didn't respond, she separated a bedsheet from the load and said, 'Maryanne phoned.'

'Hmm. Thought I heard you gassing to somebody.'

'They've just come back from holiday. Doug gave her a ruby-and-diamond bracelet for their fortieth anniversary.'

Arthur scratched one foot with the big toe of the other. 'La-di-da.'

'They're having a few drinks at the house tomorrow.' She glanced at him. 'They've invited us round, sometime after seven?'

'They're your friends, Cora, not mine.'

'Doug's your friend, Arthur.' She pegged the sheet, smoothed it out. 'Least he tries to be. I told her we'd go along, you know, just for a little while.'

'You go if you want, I'm staying here.'

Cora stopped what she was doing. 'Please, Arthur. Only a little while.'

He drew a paisley hanky across his brow. 'Listen to him prattling on about his fancy liqueurs and conservatory? I'll pass, thanks.'

'They've just got back from Vienna; it's a nice gesture.'

'God. Be pictures an' stories an' all sorts. Look what we did. Look where we went.'

'Arthur, you can't spend your whole life sitting out here.'

Arthur drank his beer.

*****

By early evening the weather remained stifling, too close to cook anything save simple cheese omelettes and side salads. Cora, in her striped apron, chopped baby tomatoes and cucumber, and shredded lettuce. The radio played Mozart from the corner, whose compositions always instilled in her a sense of freedom, of relaxation. A fan spun cool air on the worktop. She sipped from a glass of red on the counter and topped it up at intervals. She'd set about beating eggs when she turned and absently glanced out at Arthur. And gradually, her practiced wrist-motion came to a stop.

He was standing unsteadily, bent double, clutching his left forearm with his right hand. His newspaper lay on the grass, large pages curling, trying to blow free. Cora laid down the glass bowl and fork. Arthur's eyes were gripped shut, his face pained, his lips moving as if in an attempt to communicate something. He staggered a few steps backward and collapsed over the deckchair, capsizing it.

Cora rushed across to the phone and snatched it from its mount. When she returned to the window, Arthur had worked himself onto his back, his mouth open, arms outflung, his chest rising and falling slowly. She watched a moment longer before placing the phone down on the counter.

Then she retrieved the bowl of eggs and turned from the window. She closed her eyes against tears she knew would come and went on beating as Mozart's symphony soared through the kitchen.

A Bit Of Fight

When Mr Skinner called him into the office at midday on Tuesday afternoon, Duncan James Abbot knew he was about to get fired. Regrettably, he had come to recognise the lay of the land before it happened. Truth be told, in the six months since his partner's friend had managed to swing him a start here, Duncan hadn't been cutting the mustard as a salesman.

Selling had proved more demanding than Duncan believed possible. He'd expected, in the beginning, it was simply a case of arriving at a front door, merchandise at hand: if the individual wanted what he saw, he'd buy; if he didn't, he'd politely decline or swing the door closed in your face. Unfortunately, there was much more to the selling game, which became depressingly evident with every blunt refusal he endured. Selling anything—however impressive the gear—required what Mr Skinner called The Gift, which Duncan quickly understood he didn't have.

To Duncan, The Gift represented an amalgam of traits, principally confidence, oodles of it. Confidence sustained the possibility of a sale—if a potential punter was willing to stand and listen—and was even more important if, lo and behold, you got past the doorstep. Yet, like most things in life, confidence could be feigned if you persevered enough. Another requirement was self-belief, which couldn't be so easily faked. (Duncan had never really believed in himself, not as an adult, not back in school, not ever.) The successful salesman shrugged off negativity like an old coat, something else Duncan struggled with. Every closed door smacked of personal rejection, undermining his resolve when trying the next house along. Typically he ended up wondering if people had a dislike towards *him*.

So when Mr Skinner appeared at the office doorway and asked—
'Hey, Duncan lad, you got a minute for me?'—intuition warned him
he wasn't being invited for a cosy chat.

He rose from his desk, taking gingerly glances around.

Thankfully, everyone seemed busy on the phone or computer,
nattering among themselves, all-natural as you like. Possibly they
were aware what was happening but had decided to spare his blushes
by not peering. He'd always felt he was last to know anything.

'Close the door, lad,' Mr Skinner instructed. He raised the sash
window before situating his bulk behind his cluttered desk. Pinned to
the wall was a poster that read: *Sales are contingent on the attitude of
the salesman—not the attitude of the prospect.* Mr Skinner retained a
wealth of such adages, which he drew great delight in sharing
regularly. He was, Duncan thought, a philistine whose only regard
was money.

'Sit down, sit down,' he said, motioning a hand.

Mr Skinner dressed smartly, although today he'd removed his tie
and opened his collar, clearly due to the June heat. His shirtsleeves
were rolled back, revealing freckled forearms coloured with
amateurish tattoos. He drew a hand over his bald head and scratched
his remarkably bulbous nose, which was reddened by alcohol-ruined
capillaries if office gossip was on the money. His moustache and
eyebrows were grey, threaded with white, making him appear as if
he'd been locked away in cold storage.

'You'll remember the talk we had when you started here, Duncan,
back around the beginning of the year?'

'I remember.'

'Well, we did say your position with us was sort of a ... what did
we call it?'

'A probationary period.'

'Right.' Skinner nodded and set his jaw. A car horn blared down on the street. 'We said we'd give you a run, try you out and see how it went. You just can't tell how people'll progress in this game until you give them a shot, you know? Anyways, it's been six months, give or take, and I don't reckon I'm being harsh when I say—despite the training—you're not really suited to this line of work.'

Duncan felt a peaceful relief carry through him, like a mild sedative. Never again would he have to traverse the walk to another front door, all but knowing the outcome before he rang the bell.

'I'd say that's fair.' Duncan laid his hands on his thin thighs, fidgety, unsure which posture to adopt. 'It's harder than I expected.' He didn't mention that he thought the training was a sham, tactics which amounted to little more than exacting money from people. Neither did he mention his belief that it was morally questionable to pressure individuals into buying goods they'd explicitly indicated they didn't need.

'Would that things were different, lad. But listen, it takes a certain kind of individual to sell. It's a tricky game; you need the gift of the gab. You need that ... that pushiness to your nature, and you just don't have it, Duncan.' His look of sympathy deepened into seriousness. 'I simply mean that everyone's got their own qualities, see? Their own talents. Look at Gardener out there—a case in point, ain't he? Could sell sand to the Arabs, he could. Won't leave a mark alone till he gets that sale locked down.' Skinner raised a fist to emphasise his point. 'Oh, there's more to it than being pushy, course there is—but pushy's a big part of it.'

Duncan wasn't really listening to Skinner's sermon now. He was side-tracked, wondering what Jeremy was going to say about all this.

After a short silence, he wondered if Skinner was done holding forth on the type of huckster who would forge ahead in the dodgy sphere of selling. He was about to stand when the man spoke again.

'Your partner—he's still working, right?'

Duncan nodded.

'Good, good, that'll keep the two of you afloat till you find something else. What's his name again?'

'Jeremy.'

'Jeremy, right. Drives a cab, isn't it?'

'He works at the gym.'

'Right, the gym. Well, wage is a wage, hey?'

Duncan pondered if his sexuality had any bearing on losing the job, same as he often wondered if the people he tried to sell to sensed he was gay and held this against him. Folk were pretty liberal these days, of course, but he wondered anyhow. Still, he didn't see Mr Skinner as prejudiced in that way. Duncan's sales figures *were* undeniably poor, non-existent really. Underlying concerns over how others perceived him nagged him constantly, however, possibly the biggest drawback in his life. The least tolerant treated him as if he had purposely set out to be the way he was, as if he had a choice in the matter: to blame him for his sexuality was like blaming him for having blue eyes and two arms.

'Look to the bright side, lad,' Skinner was saying, leaning into his chair. 'You're a fairly young man, Dunc. Hell, you ain't even hit your forties yet. Wiser you duck outta this game than look back in, say, twen'y years and wonder what went wrong with your life. Just remember what I said. Plenty folk waltz through this office over the years, plenty of 'em. Some aren't built for the cut and thrust of selling.

Sometimes you just got to say: I'm moving on.'

Duncan stood. 'Thanks for the opportunity, anyway, Mr Skinner ... I'm sorry I let you down.'

'Welcome, Duncan, welcome. Never let nobody down.' Skinner stood up too. 'Can I give you a last piece of advice, lad?'

'Of course,' Duncan said. People had been listing his faults his whole life. What difference would one more make?

'It's not just this game—selling like—that you need a bit of ...' Skinner set his jaw again as he sought the right word. 'A bit of *fight* for, you know? Having a bit more self-belief and self-esteem, that'll stand a man in good stead for most things in life. There's a Japanese proverb says, fall down seven times, get up eight. You catch my drift?'

'Sure,' Duncan said. 'Thanks, Mr Skinner.'

After packing his meagre possessions in his brown Lethario briefcase, he bade his colleagues farewell, receiving token hand-pumping and pseudo-consolation. As he walked out of the building for the last time, his foremost worry now was how Jeremy was going to take the news.

Their relationship had become strained, to the point where Duncan believed Jeremy didn't want him around any more. Recently, when their situation had begun to break down, Jeremy started dishing out snide remarks and parried responses; he would push Duncan and slap him, occasionally punching him in heated tirades, saying how irritating he was. Right now, Duncan's chest and shoulders were marred in ugly contusions. He'd long suspected Jeremy was utilising steroids to bolster his training regime but had never asked him directly—it wasn't a topic you could raise without risking a meltdown. Duncan knew enough about steroid abuse and its side effects to be sure it was, at least, a viable possibility.

The smart reaction would be to leave—nobody should have to endure violence—but where would he go? Duncan had ever struggled making friends and would never return home as long as his father was alive.

He had left home at sixteen, though his departure had been brewing a long time prior. His father couldn't—*wouldn't*—accept having a gay son, something he viewed as a slight on his own manhood. Duncan wouldn't hide who he was, and the situation came to a head one November night better than two decades ago. He had come home late in the evening, and his father, typically inebriated, had started making trouble.

'Where you been, Sissy Boy?' he'd said, hoisting himself from his armchair. 'Out queering it up again?'

Jaws was on television: Chief Brody perusing his book of shark attacks, the riffled pages reflected in his glasses (curious how he always recollected this detail when thinking of that night).

'Leave him alone,' his mother called from the kitchen doorway, drying her hands on a tea towel. 'Let him be, Bill.'

'Keep your snout outta this, Maggie.'

His father feigned a punch—one of his tired attempts at intimidation—and Duncan flinched.

'Jesus bloody Christ.' His father took a mouthful of Budweiser, shook his head in disgust. 'Look at him, Maggie. Damned boy can't even stand up for hisself.'

Actually, Duncan could. He wouldn't retaliate against his father's taunts, but he *would* distance himself from them. Recognising a crossroads, he went to his room and, in a dazed kind of auto-pilot, crammed his sports bag with clothes. He didn't say goodbye but left through his bedroom window, dropping to the ground and stealing like a fugitive into the night. He wrote his mother a week later but had seen neither of his parents since the day he left. How ironic: he'd escaped one bully all those years ago, and here he was living with another. Was he perhaps a born victim, always destined to be on the receiving end of somebody's intolerance?

Lost in memory, Duncan worked off his tie and crossed the street, headed back to his apartment, thinking about Mr Skinner's words. *Sometimes you just got to say: I'm moving on.*

He'd long suspected arrangements with Jeremy weren't likely to work out. Initially, Duncan had chosen to interpret Jeremy's abrasive manner as protective, a positive attribute; but lately, he'd come to admit to himself that Jeremy was just like his own father. If you loved someone, you didn't mistreat them physically and mentally, didn't take advantage of their weakness. Then again, if steroids were involved, all bets were off.

Only last night, he'd cooked Jeremy's favourite meal (fully loaded pizza) from scratch, preparing dough, cutting toppings, mixing sauce. Jeremy, however, had only eaten a slice before characteristically announcing he was going out with friends, leaving Duncan by himself.

Crossing the park, one hand in his pocket, Duncan passed a clutch of elderly ladies feeding ducks by the pond. Drakes powered through the water like little toys. A young couple threw a Frisbee, their Collie shadowing the disc back and forth. Another couple occupied a blanket with a baby between them. Duncan looked at the chubby infant's booties and round, inquisitive eyes and had to smile. Sometimes these feelings—quiet sadness and reflections over things he would never have—they drifted unexpectedly to the surface, like silt disturbed from a seabed. Farther on, a Labrador bounded into his path, cheering him instantly. He petted the dog, rubbing its sides, repaid with licks until an apologetic middle-aged woman appeared and attached a lead.

When he reached the park's exit, his trepidation returned again. Jeremy would be at the gym, so at least the apartment would be empty: Duncan would have time to straighten out his explanation. But what was there to say? He'd been fired again and that was that, right?

When he crossed to the lot outside the apartment, though, Duncan noticed Jeremy's buffed silver Mondeo gleaming there in the corner.

He stopped.

A fix of adrenaline coursed through him, priming him for trouble. He tried to think what Jeremy might be doing home at this time but couldn't imagine. He stood there, undecided, looking up at his apartment's green door.

How much longer would he be living here? he wondered absently. He felt convinced his life was set to change but couldn't imagine how. He felt strangely directionless, disconnected, a feeling he'd never really learned to leave behind.

Seated on the stairs, a little blonde girl in rainbow-striped socks was colouring with a felt pen. She lived in the apartment below his. Her front door was open slightly, a radio inside playing Peter Gabriel's 'Sledgehammer'.

'Hi, Annabel,' Duncan said.

'Hello, Dun-kin.' She squinted up from beneath an aquamarine visor, showing him her picture. 'You like my drawing?'

'That's nice, sweetheart. A pony, right?'

Annabel nodded proudly. He touched her hair as he ascended the stairs.

And he keyed open the door and stepped inside the kitchen.

Jeremy was standing there in a black tracksuit trimmed with yellow lines: the gym's colours. Sunlight through the blind cast him in bright striations. He was hunched over, winnowing through paperwork at the table, correspondence spread around.

'I thought you were working,' Duncan said, closing the door. He set down his redundant case.

'I am,' Jeremy snapped. 'My lunch hour, isn't it?'

'You don't usually come home.'

'Trying to find the sodding documents for my pension—they're adjusting it all at work again. You been moving them?' Jeremy stopped what he was doing and turned around, six inches taller than Duncan, muscular, broad.

'I haven't seen them,' Duncan said.

'What're you doing here, anyway?'

Duncan looked away.

'Hey, I asked you a question, Dummy. What you doin' here?'

He shrugged. 'I got fired.'

Jeremy exhaled theatrically. 'Are you shitting me?' He positioned his fists on his waist, the dominant-male stance. 'Oh—that's great. I help you get a start—get someone to grease the wheels with that windbag Skinner for you—and what do you do? You get fired. Can't you do anything right, you idiot?'

'I wasn't cut out for it. Mr Skinner said—'

'What *are* you cut out for?' Jeremy jabbed at Duncan's chest with his fingertips, pushing him back a step. 'Huh? What *can* you do?' He slapped Duncan's face—hard enough to make him flinch.

'I'll find something else. I'll—I'll look tomorrow.'

'You're pathetic.' Jeremy returned to his papers at the table. 'Can't do shit, can you? Can't do a damned thing. Useless.'

Look at him, Maggie. Damned boy can't even stand up for hisself.

Duncan felt his last shred of self-respect shrivel up and disappear like burning paper. He glanced at the stacked implements in the drainer and laid hold of the rolling pin—used to make pizza just yesterday. Mr Skinner's parting advice flashed into his head.

You need a bit of a fight. That'll stand a man in good stead.

He held the rolling pin in both hands, testing its heft.

'Think jobs'll magically turn up whenever you need one,' Jeremy was muttering, sifting paperwork. 'Can't do a damned thing right ...'

Duncan prepared his footing like a golfer. He took a breath and raised the rolling pin—then brought it down hard on Jeremy's skull.

Jeremy wailed with surprise as he collapsed, toppling a slew of papers, one hand going reflexively to his head. Duncan brought the rolling pin down again, bludgeoning him twice, three times. A trickle of blood ran from Jeremy's black hair through his fingers, and with a loud deflating sigh, he settled and stopped moving. Rage stirred within as Duncan loomed over his partner's motionless body. Jeremy lay there, bleeding and breathing steadily. Duncan imagined how it might feel to finish the job, to pound this man's arrogant, steroid-addled head in a frantic blur of release. To beat him until his body shook convulsively on the kitchen floor. Beat him as he had imagined beating his father until his arms ached through exertion.

But that was not who he was. And recognising this separated him from those who languished in prison cells. He would not forgo his freedom to even a score, no matter how thrilling the temptation. Duncan dropped the weapon, which struck the floor in a muted clatter.

Vaguely, down below, he heard Annabel's mother calling her inside.

He opened the drawer under the counter, removed a roll of parcel tape, and commenced winding it around Jeremy's hands and ankles, binding him good and proper. Next, he went into their bedroom and, for the second time in his life, began stuffing his sports bag with clothes, moving again under that weird auto-pilot sensation.

Back in the kitchen, as Jeremy moaned on the floor, Duncan scooped up the Mondeo keys from the counter, stepped over him, opened the door, and went outside.

He descended the sunlit stairs, where he saw Annabel in her doorway, sun-visor clutched in one hand, lollipop in the other. She pointed to his bag.

'Are you going away, Dun-kin?' she squeaked.

He looked up at his apartment's green door. 'That's right, sweetheart,' he said. The weight of the sports bag felt fine in his hand, solid, reassuring. He no longer felt directionless but simply free. 'I'm going away,' he said. 'I'm moving on.'

He started towards his ex-partner's Mondeo, unlocking its gleaming doors with a zap from the fob. 'Fall down seven times,' he said to himself. 'Get up eight.'

A Great Night For Freedom

He was woken by the yobs shouting outside. Or, at least, when he opened his eyes, the first sound he heard was their familiar racket from down near the playpark. A brief sense of anxiety found him as he listened beneath the comfort of his duvet, inevitably followed by irritation and weariness.

Had the disturbance actually wakened him? It didn't matter. Since Enid's passing six months prior, Bill Handley didn't sleep long anyway. The bed yet felt strange without Enid's warmth beside him, and he wondered if this would change over time. Hearing people's sympathies and condolences, Bill believed that many perceived the loss of a partner as a mere setback—like unemployment or illness, say—but for Bill, life had inexorably changed following Enid's death, no more likely to return to the way it was than Enid was likely to rise up from Highbridge Cemetery and come back to him. After decades together, he'd accustomed himself to having her there, someone with whom he could share his worldview. Existing without his partner, the other half of the whole was proving a humdrum affair that required a great deal of getting used to.

The yobs erupted again, a high-pitched whistle, a chorus of raised voices, juvenile laughter. One of them barked a single syllable that could only be a curse. Probably up to the eyeballs in drink, as usual, he thought. The park's mulchy ground always remained littered with bottles and tins and cigarette ends after they'd been lurking around. Several of the area's waste bins were partially blackened and melted, set alight shortly before Christmas. The yobs' very presence constantly put him on edge.

Bill turned back the duvet, sat up, and parked his long bony feet in his slippers. An attack of racking coughs took hold of him, deep at his core, whereupon he pressed a handkerchief to his mouth until it passed. He'd gone to bed early after saying goodnight to Rembrandt and saw now with a squint at the clock that it wasn't even ten p.m. He pulled on his robe from the bedroom door, knotted the sash, and shuffled through the bungalow to the bathroom, where he relieved himself, wincing in mild discomfort. Lately, the need to urinate woke him often, a niggle he'd initially accepted as another symptom of Nature's relentless ageing process, although it actually turned out to be an enlarged prostate. In his eighties, every part of him had weakened, slackened off, become less reliable; but he didn't see any percentage fretting over it. What's more, these combined lesser ailments were inconsequential in comparison to his test results from last week.

He'd be with Enid soon enough, he thought, if any veracity accompanied those biblical tales she'd spent her life reciting. Meantime, he'd just have to accept his body's gradual deterioration. Suck it up in modern parlance. *Everyone has a cross to bear*, Enid used to say. *What cannot be cured must be endured.* He smiled. She'd had a plethora of sayings and proverbs for every circumstance and situation.

More commotion rose outside, followed by the muffled crash of something smashing—a bottle, no doubt—and cries of hyena-like approval.

Bill studied his tired reflection and tugged the pull-cord, shutting off the bathroom light. He crossed to the semi-dark living room, glancing at Enid's chair, where she'd sat doing word-search and crossword puzzles and watching television. Positioned above the fireplace was her painting of the Holy Mother, depicting Mary in an azure gown, arms outstretched, surrounded by a blazing corona of light like emanating rays of the sun. The framed picture had been one of Enid's favourite possessions, acquired better than ten years ago when they'd holidayed in Florence. Bill passed the painting and positioned himself by the front window, peering through the blind at the February night. Across the scheme a ways, he saw the high-rise flats against a black sky, their many windows randomly lit. In keeping with the rest of him, his ailing peepers were failing, but he could see what he needed to:

Streetlamps highlighted the hooded yobs, like demons, down by the children's playpark, shouting, drinking, smoking. Feral bloody animals. Bill shook his head. There were half a dozen of them tonight, slumped on swings, hanging from climbing frames and the jungle gym. The tall one was present, the spindly git with spiky blond hair. From what Bill had inferred, this punk acted as the ringleader, the one who'd kicked Enid's shopping bag from her hand, sending her groceries rolling along the street before the rest of them stamped everything to a pulp.

'I'm going out there,' he'd told her when she'd arrived home, empty-handed and severely shaken. He hit the door jamb with a closed fist. 'Somebody's gotta teach those—those *bastards* how to respect their elders.'

'You'll do nothing of the kind,' Enid had warned, situating herself in front of the door and raising a palm. She'd known how violent the youths were and wouldn't let him pass. 'You'll only make it worse, Bill, so just get that out of your head. Let it be; you don't know what they're capable of.'

'Sometimes you gotta do what's right, Enid,' he said, standing with his jacket in hand, ready to take up arms.

'Oh no, you don't, William Handley.' She held up a stubby index finger. 'There's been plenty trouble enough without you stirrin' the pot.'

He had felt so helpless that night, minded as he was to storm outside and fight her corner. They'd been with each other for decades, and it wasn't right that society allowed trash like these yobs to treat anybody with such contempt. Enid had been aware she was ill at the time, bless her soul, and the thought of those idiot youths disrespecting her proved more than he could bear. Yet Enid ever strived to keep the peace; no matter what, therefore, he could do nothing but reluctantly agree. Breathing heavily, with closed fists, he'd sat down and let the matter pass.

He and Enid had spent most of their married life in this bungalow, and he found it depressing that their last years had been marred by something as avoidable as harassment. They had involved the police, of course, although the authorities eventually grew evasive and reluctant, tired of trying to keep troublesome local youths from the area. If the truth were told, the police had their work cut out: they might move the youths on, but as troublemakers, they only returned with an ingrained sense of retribution. And nobody really cared about an elderly couple and their trampled groceries. The entire situation was hopeless, and Bill sometimes found it difficult to accept life could be so unfair.

Still stationed by the window, he considered what might dispose youngsters to develop this way, if it really boiled down to nature or nurture, or if likeminded individuals just recognised and appreciated twistedness in one another.

He'd even witnessed those damned yobs stopping little kids from using the playpark. What the hell was that about? Good people are subject to threats. Mothers from the estate would venture along with children in pushchairs—in broad daylight by God—and were practically chased away, frightened off by the intimidation and filth from these degenerates. And they were a bunch of tealeaves, as well. Bill had heard numerous accounts of them filching goods both at the local supermarket and from people's gardens. They kicked wing mirrors from cars. A few months ago, they'd set about a teenage boy cycling past, leaving him bloodied and badly hurt and likely facing a future of psychological trouble, besides. Last year they killed Mrs Green's cat by forcing fireworks into it (which had distressed Enid terribly), a docile animal which rarely ventured farther than the doorstep. Again, nothing was done due to a supposed lack of witnesses. Jesus, when he considered the young men who'd given their lives in wars, so these ungrateful layabouts had the freedom to—

Bill squinted as a figure came sauntering tipsily from the cover of the trees and along the pathway, passing adjacent to the playpark. The gentleman wore a cap and walked with his head down. As the lone figure drew closer, Bill saw it was Edward Healey, a retired builder—another widower—who lived a couple of blocks behind himself. No doubt on his way home from the Lion after an evening of dominoes and a few halves of bitter. Bill had drunk with him several times. He was an affable and talkative old guy, especially when in his cups. Now, as Edward moved beneath the streetlight into clear view, the yobs spotted him and began flitting across the grass, a pack of wolves closing on a deer.

'Oh, here we go ...'

Bill slipped partially behind the curtain, though there was no chance of him being seen from such a distance. He bettered his view by lowering a slat on the blind. The tall blond yob led the pack towards Edward, and Bill could see the youth carried a bottle of beer or cider in his hand.

He didn't like this. He held his breath, fingers clutching the curtain's fabric. He watched sadly as the running yob reached Edward and clamped a hand on his shoulder. Using Edward to boost himself, the blond yob leapt into the air and doused the old man in liquid.

Bill drew a little closer to the glass.

Edward came to a halt as the adolescents hooted and bellowed; they pranced towards him and away, slapping thighs as if beckoning a dog, pointing and applauding. Edward raised his palms, inspecting the liquid running from the sides of his cap down the fur-lined collar of his jacket. The yobs levelled mobile phones, weaving in front, around, and behind him. Someone flicked a cigarette butt, its fiery tip missing Edward's face by inches. The old man removed his soiled cap and glared at it confusedly; then, he regarded the yobs laughing and filming as if he were some sort of circus freak. He brought his sleeve across his eyes, half-heartedly clearing them, and continued stiff-legged on his way, cap in hand. The yobs jeered and called as they returned to the playpark, arms triumphantly raised, the gangly blond-spiked individual again leading the way. One of them clapped.

Bill remained at the window for a time until poor Edward's beset form had passed from sight. His ticker reached a gallop—not good for a man his age, but what did it matter? What the hell did anything matter? Rage mounted inside him. He ground his teeth and drew a hand over his prickly chin, feeling the same wrath he'd quashed when they'd accosted Enid on her way back from the shops.

But Enid wasn't here any more. And she couldn't stand in the door and protest his intentions. For this, he was glad because he didn't want anything impeding him tonight. He imagined Edward arriving home to an empty house, peeling off ruined garments, washing himself, wondering if he'd done anything to warrant such abuse. Wondering if this was his reward for being a decent human being, a hard-working father and husband.

Bill turned and looked at the picture of the Holy Mother, which always triggered fond memories. He remembered their holiday in Florence, standing in the Galleria dell' Accademia, viewing Michelangelo's David sculpture, how Enid had developed such a respect for the arts, how she'd scrutinised the beauty of Botticelli's Birth of Venus in the Uffizi Gallery. He remembered breakfasting under Italy's early morning sunlight, loosely arranging plans for the coming day. And he thought about her out there in Highbridge Cemetery, how her last weeks had been needlessly blighted by thugs who didn't even know her.

Slippers flapping at his heels, Bill clumped into the kitchen and approached Rembrandt's cage in the corner. The canary bobbed its head as he tapped the thin bars with a fingernail. The bird had been Enid's, but he'd found himself glad of the little creature's company since his wife had been gone.

He turned about, leaned across the sink, and pushed open the stiff casement window. Fresh night air wafted in, finding its way beneath his robe and pyjamas. He then turned back to the cage and opened its door with two pinched fingers. The yellow songbird shifted, working its wings gently, and Bill said, 'Easy there, little fella, easy.' He reached inside and carefully cupped his hands around the feathery, warm body. 'There we are,' he whispered, removing the canary and returning to the window. 'There we are.' He gave the bird a tiny kiss on the head, feeling tremulous fluttering against closed fingers. 'It's a great night for freedom, Rembrandt,' he said, opening his hands. After a moment's hesitation and gentle encouragement, the canary was gone in a beating of wings.

He looked at the vacant cage, its open door, accepting he was now alone. He hoped no harm would find the small bird. Then he purposefully conjured an image of Rembrandt winging over rooftops, which eased his incipient sense of loss. He wondered if the creature could possibly appreciate the freedom as a man might, elated as it flew through the darkness, high above the widespread lights, where it belonged.

Bill closed the window, secured the latch, and eased a long knife from the cutting block by the microwave. The honed edge gleamed lethally in the moon's glow. They had been Enid's knives for cooking, and he seldom used them any more, but he liked that they'd belonged to her. It was rather befitting, he thought, gripping the handle—rather befitting in light of what had happened and what he was going to do.

He took an almost-finished roll of black electrical tape from the kitchen drawer and began securing the blade's wooden handle to his right hand. With his left, he wound the tape round and round, crisscrossing until only the roll's plastic core remained, which he dropped into the bin.

The weapon felt good, secure.

He slipped his bladed hand into the deep pocket of his robe and left the kitchen. Sometimes you gotta do what's right, he thought. Maybe it was up to him to give the boys in blue something to get their teeth into. Maybe he'd been keeping his powder dry long enough.

In the gloomy hall, he was seized by another burst of harsh coughs. With his free hand, Bill brought the hanky to his mouth again, leaning against the wall until the coughing fit eventually subsided. When it had, he lowered the hanky unsteadily, seeing the white material speckled with blood. He caught his poorly defined reflection in the hall's body-length mirror: an old man in a housecoat and slippers would be a sufficient lure; he felt quite positive.

Further shouts emanated from the playpark. Bill scrunched the handkerchief away and set off along the hall, pausing at the living room's threshold, where he looked wistfully upon Enid's shadowed armchair and her picture of the Holy Mother. Then he took a breath, deep as he could manage, unlatched the front door, and set out into the night.

He shuffled down there, little stones pricking his soles through the spongy slippers, winter air nipping his body. His heartbeat was fast, his wasted muscles taut with a terrible sense of finality. A siren sounded somewhere far off as if prefiguring what lay ahead. Bill could see them moving and hear them giggling, six dark demonly shapes, all in hoodies and trainers. He made his way along the footpath, playing his part as the doddery old fool.

'Hey, check out this barmy old sod!'

'—Whoa, shit, he's in a robe and slippers—'

'—Yo, Grandad, you lost your marbles?—'

'—C'mon, we gotta get a piece of this.'

They came, as he knew they would, positioning themselves around him, brimming with swagger and arrogance. And here was blondie, right in front, the head man. Bill allowed them nice and close, within arm's length, before he pulled Enid's kitchen knife and waded in, stabbing and slashing, inflicting as much damage as he could before they took him down.

Beneath The Twisted Tree

'Daaaaaaad.'

Zoe stretched the syllable, bending it in her best pleading voice, the one she saved for when she wanted something from her parents. She stood dangling the dog's lead in her hand, already wearing her blue jacket and new Nike trainers. 'It's time for Bracken's walk.'

On the floor, her father tinkered with the inside of the electric fire, his tools spread in front of him. 'Bracken's fine, sweetie. I've a bit of work to do here first.'

'But he's waiting to go out,' she complained, jangling the lead for effect.

'I'll be a little while. Be patient, okay.'

'When'll Mum be home, then?'

'Mum's out with friends, Zoe.'

Bracken clumped around them, panting with expectation.

'He wants out, Dad.'

'Scoot upstairs and play with your sister for a while; I won't be long.'

Zoe screwed up her nose at this suggestion as if the idea were sour. Sarah was playing with dolls in her room, and Zoe would much rather walk Bracken than play with silly dolls. Nine years old was too big for dolls. She looked at the dog: Bracken watched her with sad eyes, tail impatiently swishing back and forth. She smiled and waved at him and faced her father once more.

'Can I take him out, then?' Zoe tugged at the hem of her father's work shirt, which was drawn up over his bellybutton. 'Just to the end of the road ...?'

He shined his thin torch into the fireplace. 'What? No, Zoe. It's dark outside.'

'I know, but ... only to the end of the road, Dad. Can I?'

Her father rummaged blindly through his tools, finding a screwdriver.

'Dad?'

Bracken drew up beside her as if to offer moral support. Zoe ruffled his fur.

'Dad.'

'What!'

'Can I take Bracken to the end of the road? We'll be super-fast, I promise.'

'I said no, Zoe. You know you don't walk him by yourself.' His reaching fingers tried the switch a couple of times, snapping it on and off. 'Why isn't this darned thing coming on?'

She jumped up and down, jangling the lead again. 'But he knows it's time for his walk, Dad. Can't I? Please? *Please* ...'

'For God's sake, Zoe ...'

'Look at him; he wants his walkies.'

Staring into the fireplace, preoccupied, her father shook his head and sighed. 'All right.' He tried the switch: click-clack. 'No farther than the end of the road. And straight back, you hear me?'

She was already attaching Bracken's lead, grinning and triumphant. The dog panted, trying to lick at her hand, tail in overdrive.

Her father aimed the torch into the fireplace. 'Make sure you put his lead on, Zoe.'

'On, Dad.'

'I want you back in this house in ten minutes, hear?'

'I know, Dad. Come on, Bracks.'

'... And stay away from the cemetery.'

She darted from the living room with Bracken in tow, her small shoulders lifted proudly: she'd never been allowed out with the dog by herself. Especially not after dark. She left the house quickly before her father had a chance to change his mind. Minutes later, she made small steps along the gloomy stretch of Hillhead Road with Bracken panting at her side. Living a little ways from the heart of the village, they had no close neighbours. No streetlights lined Hillhead Road, but she and her parents had walked the dog this way countless times, and she knew every dip and turn. Besides, as a coastal spot, hardly any cars passed this way at night.

The community lights glowed in the distance. St Mary's spire rose against the November night sky, where Mummy often played the organ. Farther back were the wide white walls of the primary school.

She liked most things about school. In the mornings, first thing, their teacher took them through The Lord's Prayer, the verses of which Zoe now knew by heart. Then it was sums or reading or writing stories or drawing; Zoe really didn't mind what they did in class, as she could adapt to most things.

And stay away from the cemetery.

She would obey her father's warning. Daddy wasn't talking about the new cemetery on the far side of the village, where Granddaddy had been buried last year. No, he meant the old one. The old graveyard had so many dead people in it—dead people from really long ago—that it was all full up, with no room left inside. In the dark, she could barely see it there at the end of the road, close to the shore. Nobody much went near it any more. Maybe people stayed away because of what Mummy called 'The Stories'.

She sang quietly: 'Zoe and Bracken, walking by the sea ...'

As she paced, she considered texting her friend Sophie to boast she was out walking Bracken on her own. Sophie always thought herself the most mature, and this would give Zoe a chance to get one up for a change. Yet a quick pat and rummage of her pockets told her she had left her phone in her bedroom.

She glanced down at her new trainers, enjoying the bounce in their spongy soles. White with a pink stripe, they shone brightly in the dark. She didn't want to get them dirty and kept to the main road, clear of the gutters. The laces were double-knotted, so they didn't trail the ground. The bouncy soles seemed to match the spring in her step. She took a Wispa bar from her pocket—smuggled from the kitchen cupboard while Daddy was busy—and bit into it, smiling at the rush of chocolate and sugar.

Her attention went to the bay, finding only a wall of darkness. Rolling waves crashed out there. Moonlight made them look like black oil. What would it be like to work at sea, like Daddy and his men, with their nets, away for days at a time? The ocean was big and smelly and slimy, jam-packed with loads of ugly things. She and Mummy watched Blue Planet on Sundays. It was amazing, the different beasties swimming around out there. There were skinny seadragons and prickly urchins and sharks, all stripy, just like pyjamas. Luckily, fishing wasn't a job for girls. Yuck.

Bracken strained ahead now and then, tugging her into a light jog, but when she pulled the lead, he settled again to a trot. He shook himself down and sniffed at the air, sensing her chocolate. She fed him a little (just a shaving because her mother said dogs couldn't digest it properly), giggling as his wet tongue slobbered the ends of her fingers.

'Zoe and Bracken, walking by the sea ... eating chocolate, happy as can be.'

As she stared up at the pinprick stars, they soon came upon the old cemetery to the right. Usually, the graveyard didn't bother her—at least she pretended so—because Mum or Dad was with her. Tonight, however, as she glanced warily at the shadowy headstones, the first stirrings of unease took hold.

Everyone in the village knew The Stories about the wicked lady.

Somewhere in there, among the stones, was the grave of the old Rawling woman. People said she was buried under an ugly twisted tree, that her headstone had been made so long ago the weather had scrubbed away the words like an invisible rubber. Zoe's schoolmates sometimes repeated The Stories about the old woman, how she drowned her three children in the sea hundreds of years ago. Some people said she'd been a madwoman who always dressed in black. Some said she'd been a witch, trying to make a deal with the devil— whatever *that* was—and that the villagers had knocked down her cottage with big hammers while she was still inside, killing her. Zoe didn't really believe in witches. Her father explained there was no such thing, and Daddy was always, always right. He said there was no such thing as the devil, either.

Still, Dad also told her to keep clear of the cemetery, didn't he? This was probably because of The Stories. Some folk believed that the old woman could still be seen around the graveyard at night, moving between the tall stones in a long black dress. Some even believed she wanted revenge against the villagers, but Daddy said this was just make-believe, like *Rumpelstiltskin* and the tooth fairy.

Still, a ripple of cold worked through her as she thought about the jump-rope rhymes the schoolchildren sang.

Old lady Rawling wading in the bay, drowning her children till they turn grey

Old lady Rawling horrible and mean, drowning her children till they turn green

She didn't like that rhyme, not one bit. She averted her attention as she and Bracken passed by the cemetery, trying not to imagine all those dusty bones buried in the ground. Must be cold, cold, cold. She didn't like thinking of death. Death struck her as something that happened only to other people, an idea too far out to make any sense of.

'Zoe and Bracken, walking by the—'

From nowhere, a dark animal darted across their path. Zoe barely caught the lightning-quick movement—a small rabbit or cat—as it shot through the cemetery gate, disappearing into the graveyard.

Bracken barked twice, loudly. Before she could react, the dog bolted, its momentum snatching the lead sharply from her fingers. The Lab vanished through the old pillars, the lead trailing along in his wake.

'Bracken!' She stomped a foot on the ground. 'Bracken, come back here!'

Barks echoed from inside the cemetery.

A minute crawled by.

'Bracken! Come here, you silly dog!'

The Lab barked, this time sounding farther away. Zoe knew the cemetery was large. She imagined Bracks had probably chased the animal so far inside that he couldn't find his way out. She stood still, disappointment blossoming in her, rubbing her stinging fingers where the lead's handle had been yanked away. Would she have to go get Dad to find the dog? That would be bad. He would be unlikely to let her take Bracken out again. This was her chance—she'd been lucky to get it—to show she could walk him all on her own. She didn't want to mess up.

She waited, stomping her feet, but still, the dog didn't return. A wind gathered, chilling as it stole beneath her jacket. She couldn't go home without Bracken. But this meant going into the graveyard—and she wasn't sure she could. She listened over the wind for further telltale sounds from the Lab, and none came. She imagined her sister playing with her dolls, warm and cosy indoors. Suddenly dolls didn't seem so silly any more.

'Bracken!'

She stomped her foot.

The only response was the wind easing through high grass lining the roadside, sending it this way and that. The black ocean whispered to her as she looked left and right, left and right. She thought about the witchy woman drowning her children in the bay—even imagined herself glaring up into a water-rippled face as strong hands held her down, pinning her beneath the waves ...

She shivered and gripped her eyes closed, shutting the image from her mind. When she opened them, she saw the distant soft lights of the village and wondered what her mum might be doing. She turned around and looked at her house. The kitchen light shone way off in the night, so far away. She slotted her hand in her jacket pocket, finding only the empty Wispa wrapper, remembering she had left her mobile in her bedroom.

She made a few short steps towards the high pillars, zipped her jacket tight to the neck, and halted by the entrance. About to call the dog, she heard him whine, almost whimpering: a lonely and sad sound. Another chill seized her, making her hunch her shoulders and work her chin down inside her jacket collar, finding the metal zip-tab with her lips. Now the cemetery seemed an awfully big place. Awfully big and dark. She tried not to think of the evil old woman moving around between the headstones, searching for more little children ...

But they were just tales people told at Halloween—her father had said so.

Go get Daddy.

The dog whimpered again.

Bracken must be lost. Her heartbeats quickened. She chewed her lip. If she followed the sounds, she should be able to find him in a few minutes if he'd been a good dog and stuck to the pathways instead of exploring. Then Dad would never know she'd let Bracken get away, and maybe she'd be allowed to walk him again ...

Go get Daddy, the voice persisted.

She pressed a finger to her lip. Bracken suddenly began whining once more. Zoe made a similar sound of her own, a nervous noise in her throat like a kettle whistling. She couldn't run off and leave him in there. She just couldn't. With her hands still balled into fists, she inhaled a deep breath and stepped through the cemetery's entrance, ignoring the inner voice telling her to run—run and find her father.

The graveyard's pathway was overgrown and barely visible. All was quiet, like another world. It felt strange, finally being inside here for the first time, going against her father's strict instructions. Milky moonlight touched down here and there, lighting random spots. Some of the stones leaned, looking about ready to tip over. Zoe stared straight ahead as she walked, feeling the sad cherubs and looming angels studying her every move, like the eyes in spooky paintings that follow you around the room. The sensation was terribly creepy, but she assured herself they weren't real, nothing except dirty old stone. Not real. Not real. She was a big girl; that's why Daddy let her take Bracken out.

And stay away from the cemetery.

She did not have a watch and so wondered how much time had passed since leaving the house. Ten minutes? Twenty? Was Daddy watching at the window yet? Had he snatched up his car keys from the coffee table and come searching for her?

She veered left, between more dated markers, brushing her fingers through overgrown grass that stood as high as her, almost. A night bird's screech filled the air somewhere above. Still following the pathway, trying to memorise her way back, she moved yet deeper inside the graveyard. Her heartbeats picked up a little. She wanted to call to the dog but feared doing so might alert her presence to ...

To what? There's nothing in here, Zoe. Nothing but long grass and old stone people watching you pass. She liked the sentence, the way the words slotted together, and nervously repeated it to herself. *Nothing but long grass and old stone people watching you pass.*

She listened for Bracken and heard only the wind. It teased her hair as it teased the tall grass. How was she supposed to find him if she couldn't hear him? How—

She stopped.

Off to her right, something shifted in the darkness. She squinted there but found only the motionless shapes of the headstones.

'Bracks?'

She chanced a few more careful steps, little ones. A shard of glass popped beneath her trainer—and something moved over to her left this time. She turned her head and paused, bringing the finger to her mouth again. The ocean crashed inshore, pounding against the rocks.

Up ahead, positioned beneath a towering black tree with high, crooked branches, a dark form shifted in the long grass. Zoe focussed, straining her eyes. The form, whatever it was, stood upright, roughly thirty feet in front of her. It was tall as a man—tall as Daddy certainly—and seemed to be making strange noises.

Quiet cackling noises.

The more she listened, the clearer the sounds became. The silhouette was thin, spindly legs and arms poking from a long black shawl. Dark hair framed a bony face which almost shone in the darkness, bright and ugly as a mask. Long white fingers ended in nails like claws, and those fingers caressed a small black animal held in its arms.

About the same size of animal Bracken had chased.

Zoe swallowed and began to tremble. She gave forth the whistling-kettle whine again, louder this time. Felt her bottom lip going. The hissing-cackling closed on her as the presence glided across the graveyard, carried on the night breeze like a stray plastic bag. Hot tears tracked Zoe's cheeks. Her breath hitched fearfully in her chest. She wanted to bolt—run like the wind, as fast as her Nike's would take her—not stopping until she reached the safety of Daddy's arms.

But her small legs were fixed in place. Trembling, rubbery, they wouldn't budge an inch. Unsure, she gripped shut her eyes and began mouthing the words she'd learned in the classroom each morning.

'Our Father, which art in heaven, Hallowed be thy Name ...'

Something cold and ancient took her hand. And suddenly, she was being led through the long grass, the rush of breaking seawater from the bay coming gradually closer.

Astaroth

Isabella's waking nightmare began with her driving through September morning traffic on Friday the 13th, trying to convince herself she wasn't superstitious.

The streets were astir with townsfolk making their way to work. Proprietors swept shop fronts and raised corrugated shutters. Delivery trucks made drops, and men unloaded provisions. A window cleaner shook excess water from his squeegee. A motorised road-sweeping conveyance trundled by, its driver watchful like a farmer ploughing his field. She wondered whether this supposedly unlucky date could really affect any of these individuals, whether it could affect *her*. But that was silly, she thought because today was just a day, same as any other.

Left at the lights, she accelerated past the Panasonic store where Gregor worked. Last night, he had surprised her with an unexpected proposal. They'd been in the restaurant, enjoying a candlelit meal, when he produced a sparkler and asked her hand in marriage. She hadn't seen it coming and felt terrible explaining she wasn't ready. She did love him and had promised they'd tie the knot one day. She just needed some time, she'd said, cringing inwardly at the trite cliché. What was the rush, after all? Gregor's face had downturned like a little boy who'd dropped his ice cream. If they were going to do it, he reasoned, why not get on with it. In truth, she didn't know what to do for the best. Marriage was a big step. Perhaps the biggest. Didn't they have all the time in the world, as Louis Armstrong sang?

Another left, and she passed by the Four Winds Funeral Home, the sight of which managed to draw her mind from Gregor and marriage. A shiver ran through her. She remembered the day last week when Holly, her assistant, had come running into the salon uncharacteristically flustered.

'Have you heard the stories going around about that Bailey guy?' she'd blurted as she collapsed her umbrella.

Isabella had just looked at her. 'You mean Michael Bailey?'

Michael was infamous in town. His good looks and toned physique drew admiring whispers from most girls. He and his annoying buddies, one of whom was Holly's brother, had a fondness for practical jokes and a reputation for taking nothing seriously. They drove past her salon in noisy, souped-up cars with those racy spoiler-things, ruining the ambience. She had even reported Michael to the police last year. Thus there was no love lost between them.

'He's dropped dead!' Holly had said. 'He and his goofy mates were doing one of those—those séance things with a ... what d'you call those wooden board things?'

'Ouija boards?'

'Yeah, one of those.' Holly placed a hand on her breastbone, allowing herself a deep breath, the better to impart her gossip. 'They were drinking in Michael's house—his parents are away—and they were messing around with this Ouija thing, and the shot glass they were using started twitching back and forth. Then it started spelling out a name ...'

Isabella raised a sceptical brow. 'A name?'

'It spelt out A-S-T-A-R-O-T-H. Then they said the glass was shifting across the board on its own!'

Isabella smiled, smelling a practical joke. 'Come on, Holly ...'

'No, *seriously*.' She fingered a cross over her ample chest. 'According to the other guys there, Michael began pawing at his throat like he couldn't breathe. They reckon ornaments started flying around and hitting the walls. And the room turned dead cold—cold enough to see their breath. Can you believe that, Isabella? Isn't it creepy as hell? And you know what? I looked up that name—and guess what it means?'

'I can't imagine.'

'Astaroth is a name from demonology,' Holly said, drawing out the words and holding up her hands for emphasis. 'The internet says he's a part of the evil trinity—whatever *that* is. It says Astaroth is in— wait for it—he's in the first hierarchy with Beelzebub and Lucifer ...'

Now, on her way to work, Isabella shook her head. She hadn't believed any of it, although it transpired there *was* truth to the story. Michael Bailey was indeed dead. He and his friends had indeed been messing with the Ouija board while Michael's parents were in Brussels for a long weekend. But all that other stuff his moronic mates had claimed? A load of rubbish, surely. It was an unfortunate coincidence that Michael had suffered some manner of seizure while fooling with the Ouija board. In any case, she did feel sorry for his bereaved family. For all her dislike of Michael, seventeen was no age to die.

So, at eight-fifteen a.m. Isabella pulled up at her salon—Beauty by Bella—and parked her Mini in the usual berth. Holly was standing reliably outside the front door, as usual, wrapped in a muffler and coat, a furled brolly in her hand.

Inside, Isabella shared her news about Gregor and the ring.

'He proposed to you?' Holly asked, eyes widening in overdone surprise. She had her chestnut hair pinned up, a red lollipop glistening in her hand.

Isabella hung her coat. 'Yup. There we were, having a romantic meal, and the next minute he's got this little velvet box in his hand.'

'And what'd you say?'

'That I wasn't ready. We shouldn't rush into it.' Isabella shrugged, smiling unsurely. *I told him we have all the time in the world.* 'We're still in our twenties. We've our whole lives to get married, Holly.'

Holly stuck the red orb in her mouth. It rattled and clicked against her teeth. 'Aw, I wish someone would propose to me.'

As Isabella emptied the float into the till, the phone rang, and she heard Holly calling her name. Her assistant was standing by the front desk, a nail file in one hand, telephone in the other, performing her time-honoured impression of Frankenstein's monster: arms outstretched, jaw hanging, eyes rolled into her head. Isabella smiled— Mr Lonsdale from the Four Winds Funeral Home was on the line.

'Thank you, Holly,' she said, swallowing a laugh and taking the receiver.

'Good morning, Isabella,' came the undertaker's deferential tone. 'I was wondering whether you'd be free to do some work for me later today.'

'We never turn away business, Mr Lonsdale, you know that.'

'How does four o'clock suit?'

Isabella consulted the appointment book, tracing the entries with a painted fingernail. 'Four o'clock ... shouldn't be a problem. We'll be winding down by then, anyway.'

'Excellent.'

'So, anyone I know?'

'It's the Bailey lad,' the undertaker said. 'I trust you've heard he passed away last week?'

Isabella hunched her shoulders. 'Yes, I heard. Such a shame. And so young too.'

'Quite, quite. Poor boy was only seventeen.'

'He and his mates used to roar past the salon all the time in those noisy cars.'

'His parents are devastated, naturally. A tragedy if ever there was one.'

Isabella looked at Holly. 'Do they know what happened to him yet?'

'Inexplicable cardiovascular failure.'

'Inexplicable?'

'That's what the post-mortem found, so I was told. They suspect he died of shock. A terrible thing. You never know what's round the corner, do you? Well, thank you, Isabella. I'll expect you at four.'

Isabella replaced the receiver, trying not to register the unease that had settled within like damp in her bones.

'Count Lonsdale need you over at the funeral home again?' Holly asked, arranging her brushes and combs.

Isabella nodded, glancing at the date on the calendar. 'He wants work done on Michael Bailey.'

Holly's teeth worried at her lip, a rather-you-than-me expression on her face. 'You feel okay about doing it?'

'Of course.' Isabella straightened and pushed back her shoulders. 'His money's as good as anyone else's.'

She and Holly worked through the day's appointments, cutting, styling and administering nail treatments. During her lunch hour, Isabella contemplated calling Gregor, aware he was probably still sulking on account of her response to his proposal. In the end, she decided against it, feeling she was apt to make matters worse.

It started raining when she left the salon at ten to four and drove three blocks to the funeral home. She had with her a handy cosmetics bag containing an array of makeup, brushes, and utensils. There were various shades and textures for different races, ethnicities and skin types. Occasionally, Mr Lonsdale paid her to style the deceased's hair, but more often, the undertaker's requests concerned only facial cosmetics. Although she was accustomed to this more macabre aspect of her career, the prospect of being alone with Michael Bailey made her insides wither. Holly's talk of Ouija boards and airborne ornaments had spooked her good and proper.

Part of the evil trinity ...

She parked the Mini and entered the funeral home's polarised glass doors at four exactly, aware of Lonsdale's intolerance of lateness.

The whip-thin man, clad in an immaculate black suit, wished her good afternoon, his pale fingers clutching a briefcase. His gold tiepin and cufflinks gleamed in the light. His grey hair was parted with meticulous precision, like an altar boy. 'I'm sorry I cannot remain here with you,' he said, 'but I must venture to see a client.' He made a show of checking his watch. 'Michael is in his coffin, by the embalming machine. He doesn't require much work, merely some basic concealment to hide any imperfections. Well, you know the drill, Isabella. Should you finish before my return, please use the rear exit and forward me an invoice, yes?'

'Fine,' Isabella replied. She watched Lonsdale step outside the foyer, lock the door, and strut over to his Mercedes, briefcase swinging.

Alone, she found the heavy silence oppressive.

She looked around at the dark panelling. Brass lamps emitted weak light. Portraits of dapperly dressed old men frowned at her as if unamused by her presence. Potted plants with wide leaves filled the corners. The carpet's wine nap yielded under her soles. Wingback leather chairs, antique-red and studded, were positioned here and there. Slowly she walked through the door, which let her into the brightly lit embalming room.

A cherry wood coffin was propped on a bier toward the far end, its lid leaning against the wall by a fire extinguisher. A little brass nameplate caught the light. Between her and the casket stood the electric embalming machine and its three-gallon reservoir. On her flank, a table displayed Lonsdale's tools. Stainless-steel surfaces reflected fluorescent light, everything burnished to a gleam.

Rain drummed on the roof. As always, the nauseous clinical smell made her a little woozy. Cosmetics bag clutched in her hand, she set her shoulders and paced towards the casket.

Rather you than me, Holly whispered in her head.

'You've done this plenty times before,' she assured herself, her suede boots echoing on the tiled floor.

She reached the casket and halted, eyes narrowing in confusion. At first, she assumed she had the wrong coffin—but a glance around confirmed it as the only one. The bag dropped from her hand to the floor. A finger of ice traced the nape of her neck and slowly down her spine.

The casket was empty.

No—that wasn't strictly true. Inside the silk lining was several items she'd come to recognise after picking Lonsdale's brain whenever the chance presented itself. There was a cotton filler in there, used to pack a corpse's nose and help it retain its shape. Also, she recognised the plastic eye-caps. She saw gauze, too, with which Lonsdale would fill the throat and other bodily openings, to prevent leakage. At the foot of the coffin lay two thin wires which attached to a tack on each jaw, keeping the deceased's mouth closed. Isabella glanced at the shiny plate on the upright coffin lid, which was engraved with Michael's cursive name—Michael Colin Bailey—and date of death.

The door clicked shut behind her. She whirled around and emitted a shriek.

Michael Bailey stood by the entrance. He was decked in a grey suit, grey penny-loafer shoes, and a white starched shirt. A lilac tie with a broad knot was fixed beneath his chin—a chin Lonsdale had recently shaved. He glowered at her, and her heart raced under the baleful stare. Those eyes were rheumy and brimming with a terrible wrongness.

He'd been embalmed.

Okay, this is too much.

Shocked, she watched this suave abomination drag a table across the floor, the steel-on-tile noise gratingly high-pitched. He shoved it against the door, a thundering crash reverberating around the room.

He turned and took measured steps towards her. To her astonishment, he suffered no functional encumbrance, his gait fluent and controlled, almost as if someone of a greater maturity now manifested inside the teenager.

It's not Michael! Holly screamed in her head. *It's Astaroth, Bella, it's the demon!*

One hand in his pleated trouser pocket, Michael paused by the table of tools: implements which had just been used on *him*, Isabella registered with no small degree of alarm. His colourless fingers performed a selective little dance, like a tourist shopping for a souvenir.

Oh, you gotta be kidding me.

He chose a pair of long scissors, which he raised aloft as if to gauge their suitability. They caught the light as he came for her. Isabella's mind seemed to have stalled, unable to process this bizarre turn of events. Part of her expected him to erupt in hysterical laughter, delighted with the flawless execution of such an elaborate jape. But those scissors assured her this was no jape, and Lonsdale's staid manner would never be a party to such a ploy. Suddenly she was assailed by thoughts of her parents, of her little brother, and of Gregor—loved ones she might never see again.

She backed up a step. 'Please, Michael ...'

The corpse's mouth moved as if trying to emulate her words. Yet no sound escaped those shiny, moisturised lips, as if this Lazarus was without the function of speech. Isabella's instincts implored her to run—but that heavy table blocked the only exit. And Michael, in turn, blocked the path to it.

She retreated again, her rump touching the vacant coffin.

As he drew in, his pallid face grinned, accentuating the evil in those dead, staring eyes. He was merely feet away. Desperately, she glanced to her side, where the fire extinguisher was fixed to the tile wall. She clumsily seized it, tugging its heavy casing free from the bracket, raising it in front of her.

Michael—Astaroth, whatever the hell it was—brought the scissors to bear in a clenched fist, his intention clear. Isabella pulled the pin from the nozzle and opened up on him, white foam powering into his face and midsection, sending him reeling backwards and down on his rear, like a well-rehearsed clown act. She blasted the stuff into his eyes, then discarded the extinguisher before dashing past him towards the exit. Wasting no time looking behind her, she dragged the table aside and yanked open the door.

Run! she heard Holly scream. *Run like f—*

In the hallway, she tugged the door closed as Michael crashed violently against its other side. Isabella dashed for the rear exit, the one through which Lonsdale had instructed her to leave. She could hear Michael in the hall now, his steps coming after her again. In her haste, fleeing past the frowning portrait subjects, she capsized a three-legged table and its frilly lamp and almost ran straight into a Chesterfield settee. She careered round a left turn, and her bodyweight slammed into the push-bar, the door clattered open, and she was outside.

Well done, Isabella, well done!

Rain lashed the street, driven on a blustery wind. A couple of people turned to gape at her. Everything struck her as surrealistically normal: the traffic and pedestrians appeared bizarrely *regular* while adrenaline surged through her body. A woman driver gawped through the swing of windscreen wipers. Verging on hysteria, drawing stares from umbrella-toting passers-by, Isabella bolted into the road.

She heard the door behind her slam open against the funeral-home wall. She glanced back as Michael appeared, shedding globs of white foam, still clutching the scissors. He stumbled into the road after her—and a shriek of brakes filled the air, followed by shrill screams from onlookers.

On the opposite side of the street, Isabella whirled around in time to witness a fuel tanker smash headlong into Michael's suited form. A brutal impact sounded as the long vehicle blasted him from his feet, ran over him, its undercarriage dragging his body as huge braking wheels locked on the road. Isabella heard bones crunching like so many snapping twigs. By the time the tanker drew to a halt, the arms and legs pinned beneath were motionless and twisted, as if a tailor's dummy had borne the impact and been pulled apart.

You got him, Holly yelled ecstatically in her head. *You got him.*

Isabella watched, stunned, her heart a base drum in her chest. Moans and yells and distressed calls arose from those thereabouts. They covered mouths and hid faces. A little Yorkie Terrier yapped, straining at its lead. A grey penny loafer lay on the road, and she found herself wondering if maybe, just maybe, there was still a foot inside it.

'What the devil's going on?' a grizzled old fellow in the rain slicker asked. 'You all right there, lady? Who *was* that?'

'Michael Bailey,' Isabella said, quivering in the rain.

The old man puckered his lips. 'Well, by the looks of him, I'd say he's dead.'

Isabella regarded the trail of pink embalming fluid spread along the road. The door to the Four Winds swung on its hinges.

'He was supposed to be,' she whispered, feeling so lightheaded she might faint.

*****

The detective staring at her across the desk was called DI Spears. Darkness had fallen. Isabella had been in the police station for hours, beginning to fear she was stuck in a time loop and that this nightmare would never end. She found herself hearing the *Twilight Zone* theme playing in her head. A small desk calendar sat before her, and she kept regarding the date: Friday the 13th.

Still think that date is no different from any other?

'Michael Bailey has been dead for days,' she said wearily. 'You must know. He's been through an autopsy, for God's sake.'

Spears scowled, but the expression seemed born of curiosity rather than mistrust. 'You're positive the person who came at you was Michael Bailey?'

'Yes, I'm sure. Mr Lonsdale's sat right out there—he embalmed the body today. Just ask him. I know this sounds crazy, but take a look at the remains, and you'll see it's him.'

'We have people examining the body, Isabella. That tanker did a pretty thorough job on it.'

Ask him, Isabella. Go on.

'Do you know what Michael and his friends were doing the day he died?' she asked. 'I mean, all that Ouija board stuff?'

'We have their statements,' he confirmed.

'Do you believe them? What they said about that Astaroth thing?'

'I think they were all probably spooked by what happened to Michael,' Spears said. 'And perhaps their imaginations went into overdrive.'

'But they either saw what they saw, or they didn't, right? And how could a dead person just ... just get up like that?'

'Don't worry, we'll find the answers before long,' he said. 'Once they've scrutinised the body, what's left of it, it'll fill in some of the gaps.'

She could tell by his tone that he wasn't given to flights of fancy, that he was most probably an atheist and laughed at tales about séances. She supposed it was hard to be any different in his line of work.

But we know better, Holly whispered. *Don't we?*

Spears gave her a smile, which transformed his grim demeanour. 'Okay, I think that'll do it for now. If we need anything more, I know where to find you.' He stood and cracked his interlocked knuckles. 'I'll arrange a lift home for you, okay? You look like you could use some sleep.'

This, she knew, was a polite way of saying she looked like hell on toast. Still, she was grateful to finally put this day out of its damned misery.

Isabella stands on rubbery legs as the DI opens the office door. Spears is most probably right: she must look a state, and the prospect of a warm bed right now is heavenly. But as she leaves the office, she doubts she'll manage to sleep. She wouldn't be surprised if she never gets a visit from the Sandman again. Besides, there's something she has to do first. Something important. She has to find Gregor and tell him she wants to marry him. Because if she's learned anything today, it's that Louis Armstrong had it all wrong. Life is too short. Just too damned short.

Garage 54

Jenny looked at the kitchen clock, wondering what sort of a mess her father would be in when he returned from the pub. Either he'd fall asleep in his chair, twitching and mumbling, or he'd fly into one of his rants, spouting how life hadn't worked out, how everything and everyone was against him. She saw little point going to bed; she'd get no peace until her father had fallen into his own drink-induced slumber, snoring and grunting like something from a farmyard.

She checked her mobile phone, but as usual, there were no messages. At fifteen years, Jenny was no stranger to whiling away the hours alone. She hated being an only child, which meant she was, for the most part, a lonely one too. She missed her mother, who had died years before, leaving her in the reprehensible care of her father. She had no real friends due to crippling shyness and the unshakable sense that she just didn't fit in, hindering her all her days. As if all this wasn't enough, her father treated her like a live-in maid, there only to clean up after him and prepare meals.

She laid away her supper dishes and tidied the living room, aware it was a fruitless exercise—her father would have the place reverted to a pigsty in short order. She retrieved the local newspaper from his armchair. The front page showed the smiling face of Eleanor MacDonald, a local teenager who'd gone missing last Tuesday. Jenny studied Eleanor's attractive image, wondering what had befallen her. She had beautiful feline eyes and nicely aligned teeth and the tumbling hair Jenny had always coveted. Jenny wasn't on speaking terms with Eleanor—Eleanor was one of the *popular* kids—but she passed her in school every day. Maybe Eleanor had just run off, she thought, folding the newspaper away. Jenny had certainly considered it more than once.

The back door opened, startling her, and her father ambled into the kitchen, bringing with him a breath of chill night air. His eyes were red-rimmed, his face prickly and unshaven. His grey hair sprouted wild, like Einstein on a bad day. A familiar yeasty reek emanated from him, and Jenny's heart plummeted when she saw he was clutching a carrier bag of beer.

'Shall I make some coffee, Dad?'

He dumped the beers on the counter, pulled one free, and began plucking at the ring-pull, sparking it open. 'Off to bed, Jen.'

'Don't you think you've had enough to drink?'

'You sound just like yer mother, you know that? Ain't you got homework to do or something?'

'Please, Dad. Why don't you just get some sleep? You'll feel better in the morning.'

'Shut up, Jen.' He produced a kinked cigarette and, off balance, struggled to light it. 'Quit squawking at me, girl.'

'Dad, you've had enough to drink.'

She reached to take the beer from him. Like an angry dog protecting its meat, he shrugged away and brought the back of his free hand across her face. Jenny collided with the pantry door and crumpled to the ground. Her cheek was aflame, and ... was that blood she tasted?

'I *hate* you!' she cried, scrambling to her feet.

'Jenny, listen, girl—'

But she had bolted past him, out the back door, into the night.

The midnight moon shone in a black sky. A fogbank had

descended with the February cold snap and nothing stirred. Jenny hurried across the street, probing her split lip with her tongue, her face burning from her father's blow. She never wanted to go home again— ever. Her dad didn't care a stuff about her. Sometimes she wondered if she'd be better off dead than enduring this unremittingly friendless existence. She wished her mother were still here, and as always, that thought brought about memories that plucked at the strings of her heart. She could visit her mother at the cemetery, but if there was ever a night for cemeteries, this surely wasn't it: passing headlights bled through the mist like something from a sci-fi movie.

Jenny came to a high wooden fence, slipped through a space created by a missing plank, and began along a receding length of lock-ups. Her father's garage was situated halfway down, the inside of which housed his old Toyota car and all sorts of miscellaneous junk. Sometimes Jenny came here when her father was being a pain, but of course, she never let him know that. She didn't have a key, but his garage was old and poorly maintained, and Jenny knew how to manipulate the faulty lock.

She came to her father's garage—number 54. The metal door was a mess of profane graffiti from a time out of mind. She turned the handle and pushed the door inward. It failed to budge on the first attempt, but then it always did. She repeated the manoeuvre and forced the door a little more, kicking the bottom sharply, and *voilà*: the handle turned, and the door swung open with a groan. She slipped inside and pulled it closed again.

She snapped down the light switch, and the fluorescent tube stammered and hummed before blinking on. Inside was cold and reeked of oil and damp—and something else that made her wrinkle her nose. Her father's mud-brown Toyota filled most of the space. He barely used the car these days, although it still ran. She slumped down on a large toolbox and rubbed her exposed arms, wishing she'd thought to bring a jacket with her. A beat-up electric heater occupied the corner, but it took ages to get going, and she didn't intend staying long. She walked around the car's front and noticed the Toyota's nearside headlight was smashed.

Jenny squinted at the bits of jagged plastic, like shark's teeth, and on further inspection, found the bonnet had a sizeable dent in it. She could guess what had happened immediately. Her father had lost his driving licence many years before through alcohol consumption, but heeding a lesson was never his strong point. She knew he still got behind the wheel while intoxicated, and judging by the state of the car, he'd recently ploughed into a lamppost or something.

She inched farther around the vehicle's front, straining to see in the heavy shadows. The other headlight, while undamaged, was spattered with what looked like blood. In the tight space between the car's bumper and the garage wall, Jenny wondered what poor animal he'd cut down. A deer maybe, or ...

What makes you think it's animal blood?

Of course, it was. What else could it be?

Come on, Jenny. You don't have to be Miss Marple to come up with another scenario.

She tried to control her imagination, to assure herself her father couldn't have hurt someone with the car. After all, it would've been reported, wouldn't it? And there had been no reports of a hit-and-run accident, so far as she knew.

Maybe nobody knows about it yet.

How could that be? If someone had been hit by a car, he'd need medical assistance. There'd be police and witnesses and ...

Eleanor MacDonald's image sprung into her mind, the beautiful face with feline eyes and nicely aligned teeth. Eleanor, who'd been curiously AWOL since last Tuesday.

'That's just crazy thinking,' she whispered to herself, not liking the way her words lingered in the air. Her father could barely cook chips without starting a fire—he wouldn't be able to conceal something like that.

Wouldn't he?

Jenny bit her fingernail. Okay, if he'd hit Eleanor with the car—and that was gargantuan if—where on earth was she? Could she really imagine her father hiding away a young girl's body? It was ridiculous, something from a television drama ... right?

What's that smell, then? It hit you as soon as you lifted the door, didn't it? You ever smelled anything like that in here before?

No, she hadn't. She didn't know what the hell it was. Her eyes shifted to the rear of the car. She stood stock still, her breath smoking the cold air. She slowly stepped around and touched the boot's cool metal with her open palm. This is loopy, she told herself.

She tried the boot and found it locked. A pent-up breath escaped, and her shoulders sagged. Locked. Nothing unusual there—her father always locked the car. So that was that.

What about the other key?

Yes, there was indeed another key, a spare. It was kept in the bottom drawer of the old wooden chest in the corner. She approached, squatted, and slid open the lowest drawer. It was crammed with odds-and-ends, more junk than she could shake a stick at, but the jar of keys was right there on the left. She removed it, a small spider darting out from under. After unscrewing the cap, she made tweezers with her fingers and plucked out the car key.

She studied the fob and pressed the OPEN button, whereupon the car's indicators flashed and a lock disengaged, making her start despite herself. She pressed it again because she'd seen her father using this selfsame device and knew that once opened only the driver's door, while twice unlocked the entire car.

Well done, Jenny. Top marks. Now, what about the boot?

She tried it again. It was reluctant but gave under persistent tugging. The car's boot lid rose slowly, and from inside escaped the most *awful* stench she'd ever experienced. She recoiled as if the Toyota were a mechanical beast that had yawned and engulfed her in foul breath. She dropped the key, bringing her forearm across her mouth, and peered in at the rolled-up rug crammed into the space. It was of Oriental design, bound with parcel tape and folded slightly in the middle, and maroon blood had seeped through in two or three places. Inside was a body—of that she had no doubt because the reek now pervading the garage could only be the reek of death.

Fearing she may be sick, Jenny slammed the boot and killed the light. She forced open the groaning garage door and used her weight to close it again outside, greedily drawing in the chill air, struggling to comprehend what she'd seen.

Jenny took her mobile from her jeans, and the screen lit up, revealing a picture of herself and her late mother, each smiling from a bygone time. As she stared at it, her hands shaking, it started to rain.

'What am I supposed to do, Mum?'

When she arrived home, her father was sprawled in his armchair like a grotesque puppet with its strings cut. The TV was on, turned down low. Jenny's soaked hair hung in rats' tails around her shoulders, her clothes drenched. She stared at him, trying to make sense of her conflicting emotions. She began shaking him awake, which always required considerable effort. Eventually, his legs twitched and flailed, and his lids fluttered, revealing marbled eyes, disoriented and unfocussed. The reek of old booze seeped from his pores.

'Dad?'

She felt the tears coming despite every effort to conceal them.

'Dad, there's something I have to tell you ...'

'Jenny, off to bed now,' he mumbled, squirming in the chair.

She stood looking down at him. 'Dad, I've been to the garage.'

He didn't seem to hear. His head lolled against the armchair again, and he closed his eyes. Jenny heard cars approach hurriedly outside, followed by the ratchet of a handbrake and muffled voices. Footsteps on the walkway.

'I'm sorry, Dad,' she said as the pounding started at the door.

Galloway's Darkest Hour

Derek was dreaming he was back home with his wife and child, back in England. The three of them were at the beach, as they'd been in reality only weeks before his unit left the UK. His daughter, Chloe, squatted in the sand, wearing a little yellow bathing costume, her nose and cheeks coated in protective cream, a turquoise visor shielding her young eyes from the sun. The surf fizzed up before her as she squatted contentedly, patting out upturned buckets of sand. The little girl looked over at her mother and father and called something, but in Derek's dream, he couldn't hear his daughter's words. He and Hilary lay on a blanket, enjoying the weather as sun-bronzed crowds waded around in the water.

Before long, the image began to fade, replaced by physical pain. Was it possible to dream pain, he wondered, from some dark recess between wakefulness and sleep. Minutes passed, and Derek found his discomfort was certainly not dreamt; it was real, transient pain coursing throughout his body. He became unsettlingly aware that something covered his head, a realisation manifest in the quick fluttering of his heart. He was sitting upright in a chair. As he regained a modicum of focus, he incurred an inrush of anxiety, assuring him he was in trouble ... trouble of the worst kind.

The dream had provided comfort, but now that comfort had gone, dispersed by the gradual return of reality. He blinked open his eyes to the scratchy material covering his head, saw nothing except darkness. The inside of the sack was stifling: trickles of sweat dampened his forehead and cheeks. He tried to dislodge the hood by working his neck, but it was tied and wouldn't budge. Damned thing smelled like a skunk had decomposed in it. He almost retched with each laboured breath.

He didn't know how long he'd been bound in the chair, for he had no sense of time. His limbs were a continuous ache and had already begun to seize up. He couldn't move his extremities; his hands were secured at his back, his ankles bound to the chair legs. Panic rippled within him. He feared his blood had ceased circulating in his body. Dehydration had reduced his lips to cracked sores and stings. Coarseness layered his throat, the need to drink unbearable. His left arm growled with exquisite pain below the shoulder, which was, he suspected, a shrapnel wound. An insistence pressed in his bladder, tempting him to simply let go to alleviate one of his collective discomforts. He tried to recall his last movements, and piecemeal, the images returned.

*****

Derek and his troops rumbled along in their military conveyance, bound for Camp Taji, some twenty-seven kilometres north of Baghdad. Most of the soldiers were unusually quiet, checking equipment, drinking from canteens. Daniels and Lazenbury played cards on the divide between their seats. Sanders cleared dirt from his fingernails with the tip of a knife. Davidson slept.

Derek was talking with Wilkes, a red-haired twenty-five-year-old from Birmingham, with whom he'd developed a close friendship. Wilkes called a spade a spade, a straight talker, and was the kind of upfront personality Derek had always felt comfortable around. Wilkes and his partner were expecting their first child, and Derek could determine it was weighing on the man.

'How long's she got to go?' Derek asked him, drawing from his cigarette, the heated wind carrying off drifts of smoke.

'Three months.' Wilkes smiled and shook his head as if he

couldn't envisage this moment.

'You gonna get home for the birth?'

Wilkes shrugged. He adjusted the strap on his helmet. 'I'd like to, man.' He gazed wistfully at the expanse of passing bleakness. The wreck of a fire-blackened car marred the Iraqi landscape. 'I mean, what father wouldn't wanna be there? But it's not that simple, is it? Not out here.'

'Have you asked?'

'Course, I asked.'

'And?'

'They can't promise anything.' Wilkes shifted aside his SA80 rifle. 'Which goes without saying, right?' He shook his head and spat. 'I couldn't even promise her I'll be alive for the birth, never mind back home beside her.'

Derek tossed the cigarette. 'What's her name?'

'Ellie.' Wilkes plucked a small photograph from his fatigues, tattered around the edges.

Derek accepted the picture. It showed a tanned Wilkes, bare-chested, wearing shorts and shades, standing by a dark-haired lady in a blue-and-white polka dot dress. She was smiling, as if at some immediate joke, holding a fedora hat to her head with one hand. They seemed to fit together the way some couples do, like soulmates.

'It was taken in Rome last year,' Wilkes told him. 'Outside the Coliseum. Ellie'd wanted to see it for years. The city, I mean. She's up on all that stuff, the religious buildings, the renaissance. Vatican City.'

Derek returned the picture. 'She's pretty.'

'I hope I get back to her in one piece.'

'You'll be fine.' Derek dealt Wilkes a brotherly jab on the arm above his bird tattoo. 'There's no other way to think out here. You have to focus on your hopes and dreams. You have to believe that you'll be home with her one day, that all this'll just be a bad memory.'

Wilkes didn't look so sure.

'They hate us here,' he said, taking in the arid landscape again. A mangy dog with protruding ribs cowered as it watched them pass. They went by a black-clad wizened crone drawing a shawl under her chin. The sun bore down from a clear sky as the vehicle jounced along. 'We're supposed to be helping them, you know, bringing *them* hopes and dreams. And I can dig that, I can. But despite talk of democracy and regime change, and whatever else, all I feel is—is hate from these Iraqis.' Wilkes made a vague, sweeping gesture at the open land as if it were currently peopled with accusatory souls. 'All they see are soldiers who've invaded their country. Most of us don't even know why we're here, do we? We're just pawns in the game, I reckon like the old Dylan song says.'

'We go where we're sent,' Derek told him, looking down at his boots. 'That's the job.'

They didn't say anything for a time. The Leyland four-tonne lorry dipped and rumbled on, its humming engine the only sound. 'What was it like when you had your little girl?' Wilkes asked. 'I mean, the first time you saw her?'

Derek smiled. For the briefest moment, he became lost in memory. His head and shoulders swayed slowly as the lorry rumbled over uneven terrain.

'It alters your outlook on everything. When you first hold your kid, it's something else. Chloe fitted into my hand.' Derek looked at his palm. 'I remember thinking that she was reliant on me for everything—and Hilary, of course. That's what struck me most of all. She was helpless. Helpless as it's possible to be, I suppose.'

Wilkes was considering this when they encountered the IED.

The roadside bomb exploded and flipped their vehicle like a coin, sending it tumbling, throwing them around inside. Eventually, it settled on its flank, grinding to a halt in drifting billows of opaque dust. Rapid gunfire commenced across the desiccated land as they were ambushed by insurgents. Derek's ears rang as he scrambled for cover, embattled, trying to remember the drill: find his bearings, decipher the enemy's location, familiarise himself with the positions of his men.

Incoming fire rang out like pyrotechnics, punching holes in the exposed manifold. Shots zipped by his head. A haze of smog dwelled around the overturned Leyland, hampering his ability to take control of the situation. He heard shouts and calls, flustered commands and panicked responses. He returned fire, singular bursts, shooting wild for the most part, spent cartridges accumulating by his boots. From somewhere came a second explosion, which blew him clean from his feet and onto his back.

The world suddenly muted into silence; he reached and found his rifle gone. Shrapnel had torn into his shoulder; it flared with new, searing agony. As he lay there, staring up at the finest blue sky he'd ever seen, displaced earth raining finely down on his face, Derek blacked out.

*****

A door opened, hinges groaning, snapping him back to reality. Several sets of heavy boots clumped across what sounded like a stone floor. A man spoke heatedly in Kurdish, and someone whipped the sack from his head.

Brightness assaulted Derek's vision. He winced and shied his gaze before a hand clutched his hair and yanked his head upright again.

'Open your eyes.'

The room was small with a low slanted ceiling. A filthy window admitted a ray of sunlight, in which dust drifted and spun like stirrings inside a snow globe. The walls were stone grey blocks, partially damaged and crumbling. A threadbare woven rug lay on the floor, one of its tasselled corners turned back. The single overhead bulb threw out the wan light.

A filming camera and tripod were positioned before him, a red light blinking on and off. Four men in rumpled black uniforms blocked the door, peering malevolently through eyeholes in their balaclava masks, Daewoo K2 automatic rifles in their grasp. Derek could sense their hatred, the enmity almost tangible. The acerbic reek of sweat hung heavy in the air. Fettered to the chair, he suffered pangs of trepidation under their regard. He was helpless. Helpless as a newborn.

The black-clad figure in front of Derek wielded not a rifle but a sword. Like the others, a balaclava concealed his features. The weapon's lengthy steel flashed under dust-laden sunlight. Despite the heat and clamminess, Derek's blood ran cold.

'You look, camera!' The man jabbed a finger at the tripod. His eyes were red and intense. 'You say the name and who work for! You say American and British soldiers leave Iraq! If not, you die here!'

This last threat the man emphasised by raising the sword to Derek's eye line, as if he couldn't make the connection himself. He then flounced aside as one of his counterparts lowered his rifle and activated the camera.

Derek swallowed. The effort tore at his parched throat. He pictured Hilary back home and his unbelievable daughter. Chloe would be four this year. Happy Chloe, all curls and smiles. He wondered what they were doing right now. The chances were fair he'd not touch them again. Christ, he was only twenty-eight. How had his life come to this? The situation was such a complex mess, the ineradicable hatred countries harboured for one another. Warring factions. Militants. Religious intolerance. What was the point? he wondered. What *was* the point?

Perhaps Wilkes had it just right. Maybe they were pawns in a much larger concern, a complex game they would never understand. Pawns trained and sent to their deaths by the overseers, the politicians who never left the desks from which they orchestrated the whole bloody affair.

I hope I get back to her in one piece.

He recalled Wilkes's words as the sword man encroached again, violently shoving his head with an open palm. 'Speak now!' he barked and stepped away once more.

Derek stared fathomlessly at the lens. Sweat bled from his pores and stung his lips. His eyes were heavy, and he wanted only to sleep. The thought of sleep was blissful. He couldn't feel his arms any more.

'My name is Derek Galloway,' he croaked. The words were difficult to shape in the strange dryness of his mouth. 'First Battalion ... the Queen's ... Queen's Lancashire Regiment.' He should say what he'd been instructed to—it might at least buy him some time—but he was a soldier. To overtly admit the coalition was wrong to be here was to undermine everything they were doing.

And what the hell *were* they doing? Derek didn't know any longer.

The man shifted behind him. Derek felt the honed edge of the sword against the nape of his neck. He thought about the dream of Chloe patting out her buckets of sand. He wished now that he were back in England, back on friendly ground, back on the beach with his wife and child. He thought about Wilkes and his woman smiling outside the Coliseum, and he hoped his friend had made it.

In The Room Above

I heard it playing again earlier. The music box. Never during daylight hours. Only after dark. It's still in her room at the top of the stairs. I haven't yet summoned the courage to go in there, although I intend to tonight. I simply have to know. The first time I heard it—the first time after the accident—I was passing outside her closed bedroom door, alone, about to turn in for the evening. I listened to the soft tune playing with fear in my heart. But I didn't go in. I couldn't.

*****

You and I had been trying to conceive for two years, Lesa. Married seven, desperately trying for two. With no results, eventually, you suggested we consult a doctor. We had no definite reason for concern, although when you're waiting, one year can feel like an eternity, let alone two. I suppose you thought getting help was better than pressing on with only hope in our corner. Dr Gupta advised couples to try for at least a year, as there was nothing necessarily unusual in not conceiving over this length of time. Because we'd been trying twice that duration, he was agreeable to running some tests.

'Nothing alarming about your sperm count, Mr Strickland,' he said from behind his desk, brows knitted, skimming the document in his hand. 'Your swimmers are fine, perfectly normal. Fewer than fifteen million per millilitre is considered low, but you are way above that.'

You smiled then, Lesa, only I could see worry underlying the expression: if things were kosher on my part, more likely there was an issue with you. 'Then the problem could be with me?' you asked as if

225

reading my mind.

'Various factors can prevent a woman conceiving,' Dr Gupta explained. 'The causes of female infertility are often difficult to diagnose. Menstrual cycles, for instance, which are too long or too short, can indicate a woman isn't ovulating.'

He touched briefly on polycystic ovary syndrome, hormone imbalance, premature ovarian failure, and low oestrogen. Yet, for all that, when we returned weeks later for the results, he divulged he couldn't find any irregularity with you, either.

'There is certainly nothing to suggest you won't conceive, Mrs Strickland,' he said, looking at you, then me. 'Sometimes it just takes time.'

'There's nothing to suggest I will, either, is there?' you said.

Gupta adjusted the pin on his Bart Simpson tie. 'I'm afraid biology doesn't work that way.'

In hindsight, I wonder if you had some premonition it wasn't going to happen for us. Hearing your results should have brought relief; instead, you looked downhearted, staring into your lap, as if we'd been shunted back to square one, which, of course, we had.

'The best advice is keep trying,' Gupta remarked as we were leaving. 'It's often the case that when you relax and stop worrying— that is when something happens.'

Sound counsel, if somewhat clichéd. However, as I'm sure you intuited, our time never did come. We tried for another year, our efforts dictated by your biological calendar, which became rather routine and disheartening. By this point, we were in our mid-thirties, and I witnessed your frustration, Lesa, despite your efforts to conceal it. We joined an infertility support group that sounded promising but from which we drew little inspiration. We even talked about involving a third party to try to get things moving—sperm donors and surrogacy—but later jettisoned the idea. You presented a brave face, day to day, but I saw through it. You'd done decorating work to the spare room as if the act itself could effect a result, but the room wasn't getting used. Personally, I could've accepted us as a childless couple, though I knew you didn't feel that way. You wanted to be a mother, Lesa, so much it was cutting you up inside.

*****

When I returned from court one Friday in October, approximately eighteen months after we'd last seen Dr Gupta, you had prepared risotto and uncorked wine. You were wearing a tight crimson dress and had done your black hair, tying it up with two coiled locks flanking your face. You appeared happier than I'd seen you in a long time. My first thought was that I had overlooked an anniversary or birthday. Then I assumed you simply wanted to discuss keep trying for a baby, regardless of past disappointments. You were nothing if not persistent. The candlelight and wine were, I presumed, your way of setting the scene.

'You look great,' I ventured. 'Special occasion?'

'I want to talk,' you said, fingering the heart-shaped pedant of your necklace, the one I'd given you years ago when we met.

I shucked off my suit jacket. 'Can I take a shower first?'

'Of course. We'll eat, then talk later. It's nothing bad, don't worry.'

I showered in a hurry, admittedly curious. Making small talk—my day, your day—we shared the risotto and polished off the Cabernet Sauvignon. All the while, you kept regarding me, candlelight touching your eyes. I suspected you were finally pregnant, such were your cheeky smiles and perky tone of voice, but I'd grown too cautious to

227

assume anything before I knew for sure. Besides, I doubted you would've been able to keep a lid on a joyous announcement like that.

You were turning the wine goblet by its stem and suddenly seemed focussed, indeed solemn. 'There's a lot of sorrow in the world, isn't there, Ally?'

'Sorrow?'

'You know. Heartache. Tragedy.' You looked away.

'Disappointments.'

'That's the way it is,' I said. 'Life isn't fair.'

'Maybe. Well, if we can't have a baby of our own, perhaps we should offer a home to a child already born. A child who needs a family needs a decent start in life.'

'What are you saying, Lesa?'

'I want us to adopt,' you said.

*****

I was unsettled by the prospect, by the unknown, I suppose. I'd never entertained the idea of adoption, but you had patently given it much thought. You worked on me, pointing up the positives. An adopted child would not be ours by blood, but did that mean we couldn't offer him or her a good home? And love? Of course not. In any event, you won me round, as always. Providing a youngster with a home was a good thing, the best of things. And if you fell pregnant afterwards? That possibility didn't faze us; it wouldn't matter whether we had one child or two.

We spent weeks swatting up, mainly over the Internet, researching laws and regulations. This was new ground, at once challenging and exhilarating. We talked on the phone with two helpful couples who had adopted, which answered many of our questions. We received advice on a good agency before providing references, birth certificates and a marriage license, which you prepared fastidiously. Background checks took some two months, if I remember rightly. We hoped that my being a lawyer and you a former primary-school teacher would serve in our favour.

We were introduced to a social worker named Abigail Newman, who held a degree in child psychology. She performed a home study, assessing our strengths and eligibility before presenting a report to the Adoption Panel. You told me you had a good vibe from her, and I felt that too. She explained that the agency worked with local authorities to find a suitable child, and a matching panel made the final decision. Abigail had navigated the process time and again, which assured us we were in safe hands, didn't it, Lesa?

You were all but bouncing when I came home that day at lunchtime. You were wearing your old AC/DC sweatshirt and grey joggers, your default outfit when cleaning the house.

'Abigail phoned,' you chirped, clapping your hands. 'There's a little girl named Vicki they think would be perfect for us.'

I slid the groceries onto the counter. I have to admit your excitement was contagious. Suddenly the situation was real. After several long months of red tape and preparation, they had a child for us to meet.

'How old is she?'

You were beaming, wide-eyed. '*Five.*'

I nodded, my heart ticking over quickly. 'Five, huh.'

'What d'you think?'

'I think we'd better meet her.'

You ran into my arms and wrapped your legs around my waist, and at that moment, with you clinging to me like a koala, it felt as if something had healed, that we had made a step forward at last. Holding you, I knew that adoption had been the right decision.

*****

Our first contact with Vicki was on a rainy Tuesday afternoon, with distant grumbles of thunder overhead. We met Abigail in an office on the second floor of a brick building called Bishop House, her workspace as blandly functional as the heavy brown shoes she wore.

'Remember,' she said, escorting us down the hall, 'don't have too many expectations of a first meeting. Both parties can feel awkward; it's quite natural and rarely indicative of how things will progress. Try to just go with the flow, okay?'

You squeezed my hand.

Abigail entered a room where several kids were painting and drawing, and a noticeable hush descended. One wall was decorated with a mural of clouds and rainbows, like a children's ward. Vicki, seated at the front, was working on a big sheet of paper. I recognised her immediately from the photo we'd been given. She glanced at us nervously and looked away again. Her watercolour was of an angel with yellow hair and white wings spread before a bright sky. I sometimes wonder if there was relevance in that picture, Lesa, considering what we discovered later. Vicki wore a powder blue shirt and disposable plastic apron, her blonde hair tied back from peachy skin. She studied us shyly as we stood behind Abigail, and I was struck by how vulnerable she looked.

Abigail approached the child and leaned in close. 'Vicki, this is Mr and Mrs Strickland. Remember, I told you about them?'

Vicki nodded, blinking, looking up at us.

'Well, you're all going to spend some time together, okay. Won't that be nice?'

I was overcome with doubt, unsure what to say or do. But you, always proactive, you released my hand and approached Vicki's desk, where you took a small chair and sat next to her.

'Hello, Vicki. My name's Lesa,' you said. 'Abigail thought you and I and Ally might get along together. Can I sneak a peek at your picture here? Is that okay?'

Vicki nodded, smiling a little, seeming to relax.

'Hey, wow, that's pretty impressive. He's got great wings, hasn't he?' You looked at me and smiled, and I stepped forward to join you. Quick as that, the tension lifted. For a time, at least.

*****

I can hear it now. As always, it begins after the setting sun, when I'm left with only heartache and memories. The house is silent otherwise. If I remain very still, I can just make out the soft tinkling notes from upstairs. She has opened the music box, Lesa, and I can hear it playing. Faintly.

*****

The authorities had removed Vicki from abusive parents when she was nearly four, and she'd been in foster care since. Her first home visits to us were accompanied by Abigail, which was a common procedure. Abigail was great at filtering any awkwardness and well versed in what she called 'transitional issues'.

Afterwards, Vicki made a few short stays unaccompanied. We bought her paints and a few canvases and encouraged her to feel free to use them only if she wanted to. We nestled her between us on the sofa and watched movies like *Home Alone* and *Finding Nemo*. You

231

and Vicki hung birdfeeders in the garden, and she beamed when birds eventually swooped in and clung to them, pecking away. You baked cupcakes with her, giggling as the kitchen became a bombsite of sugar, eggs, butter and flour. She was a quiet kid unless spoken to first and polite in response. We went for ice cream, frequented the amusement park and cinema, and all the while, I felt Vicki grow quietly accustomed to us. We visited the local primary school, where we'd prospectively enrol her at the end of summer, should everything develop as expected. Your parents called now and then, naturally interested, and we kept them informed.

One Saturday, travelling home from the municipal swimming pool, we passed a boot sale in the park.

'Let's have a browse in there,' you suggested. 'What do you think, Vicki?'

Vicki appeared between us from the backseat, her hair towel-damp. She nodded, so I drew the Audi in, glad for an excuse to walk in the sunshine.

Numerous families and hordes of youngsters were treating the area as a playground, wending between foldout tables, cheap merchandise disposed of everywhere. I bought us soft drinks from a nearby vendor. Vicki soon found an elderly man selling used kids' annuals, which she paged through contentedly, with an almost adult awareness that belied her years. She never struck me as a kid who'd create a scene in public, throwing tantrums or acting up to get her own way. Since living with us, she had grown less reserved but remained watchful of everything, probably with good reason. Diabolic parenting had forced her to mature quickly, robbing her of time that should have been carefree and fun.

Nearby, you had come across a music box, pink with gold trim.

'Aw, she'd love this, Ally, don't you think?'

'I'm not really sure,' I admitted, taking a closer look.

'Trust me, she will.' You regarded the seller, a paunchy man in a palm-tree shirt, asking, 'May I open it?'

'Sure thing,' he said. 'Works just like new, that one.'

A tiny, skirted ballerina figure sprang up, slowly rotating before an oval mirror as a tune played, gentle as a lullaby. The moment seemed poignant to you somehow, Lesa, perhaps kindling a childhood memory, perhaps making you mindful of the baby we hadn't yet been blessed with. You watched the little figure complete her cycle, then paid the man what he asked—you usually haggled—testimony to how much you wanted it.

I carried the gift to the Audi while you and Vicki meandered behind, hand in hand. I stored it in the boot, got into the driver's seat—and noticed something slotted beneath the window wiper, like a flyer, perhaps four inches squared. I reached to retrieve it: a piece of card with the black outline of a beetle drawn on it. Below this, SHE IS NOT YOURS was printed in black capitals.

I stared at the image: the thorax, the six legs and the long antennae. As you and Vicki got in, I tucked the card away, looking discreetly around. People milled about the car park, coming and going. One man, in particular, caught my notice, not because he was at all memorable— he looked entirely generic—but because he was staring at me from about twenty feet away. Grey-haired, fiftyish, he wore jeans and a woollen sweater, hands in his pockets. He squinted under the sunlight, expressing a vague smile as if privy to some secret.

'Everything all right?' you asked.

'Right as rain.' I pulled away and glanced in the rear-view mirror, seeing the guy still there, staring after us as we left.

When we got home, I took a walk through the grounds, looking at that strange card. What the hell did it mean—she is not yours? Who would dare claim such a thing? Was there someone out there opposed to our intentions concerning Vicki? Her parents, perhaps? And what possible relevance could there be in a beetle image?

If I'd been honest with you that day, Lesa, if I'd shown you what I found on the car, it might've set in motion an alternative chain of events, and things might've worked out differently.

*****

Vicki did love the box and gradually filled its compartments with the inexpensive jewellery that you donated to her. Sometimes, when we passed her room before going to bed, we'd hear the ballerina's tinkling tune playing as the clockwork mechanism turned. We would stand on the landing and listen, exchanging smiles. The melodic sound became full of meaning for us, indicating Vicki had accepted her life in our home.

Inevitably, I began speculating what the child might have endured and whether we should try to unearth more details of her past, the better to understand. The girl's biological parents, Abigail had informed us, would never be fit to care for her. I'd thought that claim sounded oddly definite, but after I pressed Abigail for more information, I found it was quite accurate.

'Under normal circumstances, I wouldn't share specifics about a child's past,' Abigail said during one of her post-placement visits. We were having coffee while Vicki was upstairs. The social worker ran a hand through her silver hair. 'What I mean is, I've told you Vicki had problems with her parents, I know. But if I elaborate, it may help you appreciate her situation a little better.'

You glanced at me, worried.

'Do you remember I explained that it was neighbours who initially raised the alarm, suspecting Vicki might be in trouble? They'd seen her with bruises, looking malnourished, dirty?'

We each nodded mutely.

'Well, these neighbours called social services, and I was asked to look into it. At first, I didn't involve anyone else, just kept an eye on the house, trying to get a sense of what might be happening. After a while, I noticed something of a pattern. People were coming and going from the property at all hours, men and women, even elderly folk, though I couldn't understand what they were doing there. I spoke to the neighbours—discreetly—and discovered they'd heard a young girl screaming during the night more than once. They also heard chanting, like an incantation or something. God knows. Obviously, I had no doubt Vicki was in trouble.

'One night, after dark, I waited till I saw people going into the house—I wanted to know what was happening in there, you understand. Then I approached with three police officers.' Abigail turned and faced the living-room window, raising her shoulders as if chilled. 'When we entered the property, Vicki's parents and those other people ... they were all dressed in red hooded robes. The house was full of candlelight everywhere, like a séance. I'd never seen anything like it. Most of them scattered out the back and ran into the woods, but a few were apprehended, and they fought with the officers, fought hard. Some candles were overturned in the struggle, a pair of curtains caught fire, but we managed to douse them with water from the sink. It was chaos. We radioed for help, and more officers arrived, and I, for one, was glad to see them, let me tell you.'

'And Vicki?' you asked, barely more than a gasp.

Abigail took a breath. 'I found Vicki upstairs, strapped to a bed. She didn't have anything on. The poor girl was covered in ... in strange markings.'

'Markings?' I looked at the social worker, touching my forehead.

Abigail sat down in an armchair, palming her skirt. 'Symbols,' she said, producing a handkerchief from her clutch bag. 'Occult symbols. Pentagrams. Awful-looking things. On her arms and torso. And shapes like insects. The ink wasn't permanent, but still ...'

'Dear God,' you said, taking an unsteady half-step back.

I stiffened, recalling the strange card under the window wiper.

'We don't know what it was all about, though it seemed self-evident her parents were involved in some form of sect.' Abigail hugged her sides again as if cold. 'There were books on occultism and entomology in the bedroom with Vicki, and volumes on alchemy, trying to link the metamorphosis of insects to magic and the occult. Twisted rubbish. Clearly, we'd done the right thing getting Vicki out of there. She doesn't talk of it, so we've no idea how long she'd been subjected to that kind of treatment. Her parents received custodial sentences for child abuse, which they're still serving, but they wouldn't divulge anything under questioning. None of the others was charged—apparently, there wasn't the evidence to make anything stick. Can you believe that?' Abigail regarded us both. As a devout Christian, these details obviously disturbed her. 'I just want you to have the full picture before making any definite decisions. It's only fair to you both, and to Vicki.'

I wanted to say something but couldn't find words. I was truly struggling to comprehend what the woman was telling us, Lesa.

'It wasn't appropriate to share any of this with you earlier,' Abigail said, tugging her cardigan together. 'It would've been unfair to the child; I'm sorry.'

When Abigail finally left, you sank into an armchair in shock, your face blanched.

'The occult?' I said, peering out the window, where I'd remained since Abigail's Rover disappeared down the drive. I turned around. 'Alchemy? *Insects*?'

You were fighting tears, fingers pressed to your lips. 'It doesn't change the way you feel about Vicki? Oh, Ally, please tell me it doesn't.'

'Of course not,' I said, willing myself to believe it. 'But, I mean, what the hell were they trying to *do* to her?'

You hid your face in your hands. 'What does it matter? They're obviously off their heads. You heard what Abigail said. God, that poor girl.'

'They should've told us about this.'

'Ally, they told us she'd had serious problems.'

'They should've been specific,' I snapped. 'They scrutinised *us* for long enough, didn't they? Least they could've done was have everyone on the—the same damned page.'

'It doesn't change anything. This just means Vicki needs us even more than we thought. It's *more* important we're here for her. We took her in because of her troubles, didn't we? Why would the nature of those troubles make any difference?'

'Should we mention this to Vicki?' I asked. 'That Abigail told us ... what her parents did?'

You shook your head. 'Maybe someday, not yet. She likely wants to forget it.'

Of course, you were right. My reaction had been poor, impulsive. A young girl had suffered, and now we had an opportunity to right those wrongs the best we could. We had pledged to care for Vicki. I shouldn't have lost my temper and vowed to exercise more patience in future. Meantime, I decided not to mention to you the beetle image left on the windscreen. I don't know if I did the right thing or not, Lesa, but my silence was only to protect you.

We endeavoured to make Vicki feel loved, to abate any fears she harboured around trusting adults who were supposed to care for her. You managed this effortlessly, Lesa, I must say. You and Vicki grew close, comfortable with each other, which made it easier for me to form a paternal bond with the child. We soon jelled as a family, and any lingering reservations on my part dispersed, though I still felt loathing towards anyone who'd subject a young girl to such an ordeal. It was hard not to think of her strapped down, afraid, covered in crazy symbols and insect drawings. I tried not to imagine her tormentors standing over her in red robes, how frightened she must have been. And I wondered at their depraved fascination with the metamorphosis of bugs. What it could all possibly mean, I hadn't the slightest notion.

We loved the kid and determined not to pity her, and before long, it seemed life's inequities were consigned to the past for all three of us. You hadn't fallen pregnant, but now we had a daughter of our own. Abigail told us to give it some time; then, we were free to apply to the courts to become legal parents.

The last Sunday in July, about nine p.m., I stopped at the local petrol station on the way home from the supermarket. Queueing inside to pay, I glanced at the forecourt, where a thin, pale woman was filling a white Nissan at one of the fuel islands. She was staring at me through the glass. She had long, straight, auburn hair, maybe thirty-five years old. She wore a knee-length black dress, had sunglasses propped on her head, and stared with the same peculiar half-smile as the man at the boot sale. At the counter, as I settled up, the woman paid at the pump, glancing at me with that mildly amused expression. When I stepped outside, she was pulling away, window down, still looking.

Another card was wedged beneath the Audi's wiper. It depicted what I inferred was the black outline of a butterfly but later found, through the Internet, to be a moth. Below it, again, were the chilling words: SHE IS NOT YOURS. I turned and looked for the woman's car, but it was gone, Lesa, lost in traffic. I just stood on the forecourt among the evening's long shadows, feeling terribly alone, wondering what on earth was wrong with these people.

The following Tuesday was overcast, with light rain showers. You and Vicki were baking gingerbread in the kitchen. I was drinking coffee at the front window of the living room, looking out at the drive curving away towards the main road.

A man stood by our driveway entrance with a large Alsatian on a lead. An older guy, mid-sixties, I'd say, dressed in a brown Fedora, fur-collared fawn coat, and flannels. He wore black gloves, too, attired more for winter than July. The animal sat regarding the property in the same manner as its master. They didn't look set to move on; instead, they appeared fixated, as if posing, focusing on the house. I wasn't sure if he saw me at the window, this man, but now I feel certain he did, just as I feel certain he was smiling that same knowing smile.

I was becoming uneasy concerning these occurrences; if such, they could be called. Nobody was causing us direct trouble—I hadn't even mentioned anything of the strange images to you—but the apparent surveillance, the passive hostility, was enough to unnerve. They felt like a veiled threat. I couldn't conceive of such people in society, subversive characters one could unknowingly pass on the street.

After a couple of minutes, the guy twitched the lead and moved off, the dog at heel, leaving me staring at passing traffic. I like to think I had been set to run down there and confront the man, Lesa. But what could I have accused him of?

*****

In August, two weeks before the schools resumed, you drove Vicki south to your parents' place on the Essex coast. It was Vicki's first trip to see them, and I'd have been there too if not tied up in court. I think about that all the time, Lesa, believe me.

Early that evening, your dad phoned as I heated spaghetti in the microwave. Summer rain streamed down the windows. I was aware you should have already made it there, so found it unsettling to hear from him.

'They haven't arrived,' he said. 'We've been trying her mobile, but she's not answering.'

I felt a stab of concern, the first seeds of upcoming despair. There were numerous reasons why you might have been delayed. Yet, wouldn't you have let somebody know? I was at a loss as how to reassure your father. How to reassure myself.

'I'm worried, Ally,' he said.

'Let me try'n get in touch with her,' I told him, aware he'd likely been doing just that. 'I'll ring as soon as I hear anything, okay?'

As it happened, it was he who called me back a half-hour later. It took him a moment to say anything, confirming my worst fears.

'There was an accident, Ally ...' He sounded choked, almost unable to talk.

240

He told me you were in a collision with an old woman in her eighties, driving the wrong direction on a dual carriageway. You and Vicki had died at the scene. Days later, I saw what remained of your red Fiesta, which explained why you hadn't made it out alive. It was crumpled like a tin can.

*****

Life is grim without you, Lesa. You were the other half of me, the voice of reason. Daytime can be bearable, which is about the best I can hope for now. I watch birds pecking at those feeders in the garden. I watch snow falling, finding it impossible to accept what has happened. But nights are hard; they are long and abundant with memories. At night my fears overwhelm and breach every defence. At night I sometimes tell myself it would've been better if I'd died in the car with you. Then again, if I'd been there, perhaps the accident wouldn't have happened. A minute's delay, waiting for me to use the restroom, say? Who knows what might have made the difference.

I haven't worked since you've been gone. The bottom has dropped out of any career plans. I burned those two hideous insect images in the hearth and wonder every day if I should've shown them to you. I haven't received any more, but I still catch strangers giving me looks when I venture outside. Some stare a little longer than seems normal as if intent on imparting their awareness. It has gotten to where I cannot differentiate between them and those who innocently catch my eye. There's an agenda, I'm sure, one I cannot fathom. Are they a sect, as Abigail Newman called them? A cabal? Or something far worse? These people have, so it seems, a vested interest in me, or maybe in that which has taken residence in Vicki's room upstairs.

Nearly a fortnight ago, I realised I am not alone in this house. I heard noises from above, strange drumming on the living-room ceiling as something crossed the floor of Vicki's bedroom. At first, I tried to write it off as the result of my overwrought mind. Then I heard the music box—and no words can describe how I felt, Lesa. I haven't been brave enough to open her bedroom door since.

It's late now. The music will play again soon. I've come to know the intervals. The tune is starting to drive me mad. I must be rid of the box and have to see what's up there, though I have a rough idea.

Yesterday, a little before midnight, from down here in the study, I saw Vicki.

I was typing when she flitted by the balustrade on the landing in the blink of an eye, and I heard those awful drumming sounds again as she moved. It lasted only a second. But I saw her. My god, Lesa, as surely as I've heard the soft musical notes, I saw her. Her scalp was completely bald, devoid of lustrous blonde hair. She wore not a stitch, and her back was arched like a bow as she scuttled on all fours towards her room into the darkness.

The Absent Soldier

Mary had never imagined she could lose her faith. This was an absurd notion, like the idea of her running Olympic gold in what was now her sixty-fourth year. Yet lose it she had, though she hadn't mentioned this to her husband, and she still wore her small crucifix pendant around her neck.

Throughout her life, she had been a devout churchgoer and, in adulthood, a committed disciple of the Salvation Army, helping the homeless and poor and elderly alike. But her belief in forgiveness, her capacity for it, simply wasn't there any more; it had been swept away as surely as autumn had yielded to winter.

From her armchair, Mary watched her grandson gaze up at her from the carpeted floor. Little Jamie, two years old today, waved and kicked plump arms and legs. Filaments of hair curled from his head like wisps of candyfloss. His smile was full of cheer as he clapped small fingers and bounced on his rump. Mary marvelled at the rich violet of those round eyes—the selfsame brilliant colour of his father's eyes. In an all-in-one of duck egg blue, like a windup toy, the child scooted across the room, hands and knees, before settling on his bottom again, infatuated by the decorations festooned around him.

He'll eventually love Christmas as much as his father had, Mary told herself, feeling a restriction in her throat. When he's older, of course. When he's older.

These thoughts drew her attention to the framed picture on the wall, positioned above the ornate frieze. The photograph captured Eddie in his beret and fatigues, arms folded. Her only child. Taken in summertime four years ago, in the garden behind the house, it was the last picture they had of him. In it, Eddie's smile revealed his friendly nature and, she believed, his benevolence and also the undercurrent of mischievousness that dwelled just below the surface.

Joe had taken it. Mary remembered that July day well. Eddie, then twenty-six, had arrived accompanied by Janet, sweet and delicate Janet, and it was, in fact, the first time they'd all been introduced. They'd laughed and shared barbeque food and cold drinks. She and Joe had been delighted that Eddie had met someone so ... well, so delightful.

Eddie and Janet married quickly, a church wedding, and two years ago, on a cold December afternoon, the long-awaited phone call had finally come.

'It's a boy, Ma,' Eddie had said, voice brimming with paternal pride.

'Oh, Eddie, that's fantastic,' she told him. 'All fingers and toes and everything?'

'All present and correct. He's got this little tuft of blond hair.'

'Aw, I can't wait to see him. And how's Janet?'

'She's okay—tired but doing well.'

'Have you settled on a name yet?'

'Janet likes "Jamie".'

'Baby Jamie ... I like that too. Like a little Christmas Star.'

*****

Memories of Eddie forever played in her mind, a personal montage, and by virtue of this, the yearning to see him again was an unbearable ache, enhanced by the knowledge that she never would. It required daily effort to concentrate on the positive times of Eddie's life, of which there were many, but it was an effort too not to allow his unutterable demise to taint fonder remembrances. He had lived as a soldier, a profession which had taken him to far-flung places that she herself would never see. For that, she had always been first to commend him, though she now wished she had advised him against a military career.

Mary regarded the gifts beneath the tree, wondering if the yuletide season could ever again be as it was. She thought absently about the Nativity, about the kings with their frankincense and myrrh—traditional details she had always regarded as fundamental to the time of year. But with Eddie gone, the decorated tree and arrayed gifts struck her as somewhat sterile, ineffective to a broken heart. She looked between the open curtains at the night stars. Snow had begun again as her husband stepped out for his daily constitutional. She imagined Joe trudging the pathways, broad shoulders squared, paying the weather no heed, for he took his walk during rain or shine or flurrying snow. She suspected it was when he did his deepest thinking, his own grieving, for his grief was no less substantial than hers.

Little Jamie gurgled, reaching among the coffee table's spangled cards, capsizing one with a baby deer on the face. The front door opened and closed, followed by sounds of Joe in the hallway, shucking off his duffel and unfurling his scarf. A wintry chill slunk through the living room, breathing around her calves like a malevolent spirit. She smoothed her dress and preened at her platinum hair in a bid for composure.

'I'm home,' he called in his deep timbre. That was all he said. She yearned to hear his jovial greeting from years gone, though this, like so much else, was something consigned to the past.

Man, ain't half putting down out there, Mary. Be covered over, come morning, nothing surer. We'll need huskies to make the shops, I reckon. I'm having coffee, you want coffee?

Now Joe just made the coffee, and that was that. She heard him clattering in the kitchen, cupboards and mugs, and felt better he was home. Sometimes, for a few stolen moments, she could almost forget. Things could almost seem normal again.

Her husband appeared with two mugs, set them down. Joe pinched his trousers, carefully squatting on his hunkers to brush the infant's cheek. Jamie waved his arms, ever enjoying the attention.

'What'll he make of it?' she asked, studying the child. 'When he's older, I mean?'

Joe settled into his chair and extended a splay of fingers towards the fire. His toes scrunched inside thick woollen socks. 'What can any of us make of it, Mary?' he said. 'It's the world we live in today.'

Another might have interpreted it as an offhand response, flippant even, but she knew the sentiment encapsulated his true feelings: the world is no longer the place it once was. Technology, Joe believed, had tainted modern life. Anyone could capture the most heinous atrocities on pocket devices, post them for all to see, stripping an individual's dignity, turning a macabre public display into a worldwide spectacle. Barbaric cultures performed these bloody humiliations, but technology allowed it into every household, every bedroom. Mary reasoned differently, however: technology, as far as she could see, was nothing without individuals to misuse it. Unfortunately, those individuals had become blasé of the most abject horrors.

'Do you think Janet will be better soon?' Mary asked. 'I can't stand to think of her in that place, all alone ...'

'It'll take time,' Joe told her, staring into the flames through the protective mesh. He drank his coffee, and firelight shimmered across his grey cap and wiry sideburns. 'She's shut down,' he said. 'But she'll get better. They'll help her in there, Mary. That's their job, isn't it? To make people better again. She'll come back one day, back to little Jamie.'

Mary nodded, although in her gut, in her heart, she didn't really believe Janet would ever be the same again. Sweet and inoffensive Janet. She had loved to bake and paint watercolours and loved working in the garden and had a facility for it all. But she had retreated away and locked the door. Janet was lost, adrift on a distant sea, and even the prospect of raising a healthy and dependent child couldn't cast the lifeline she required. Eddie's death had taken something from them all, of course—how could it not? But from Janet, it had taken her resolve and her fight. Wasn't it Einstein who'd once compared life to riding a bicycle? In order to retain balance, he'd said, one had to keep moving. She thought it was Einstein anyway. In any case, Janet had certainly stopped moving, and Mary's heart went to her.

'What if she doesn't improve?' Mary asked. She looked to the window and wondered if their daughter-in-law could see the snow. She wondered if militaries who acted under bully-boy terms like 'shock and awe' would ever understand—really understand—terms like 'fallout' and 'collateral damage'.

'She'll improve,' Joe said evenly as if the assuredness in his voice could make it so. 'That lass's stronger than she looks.' He regarded Jamie. 'We'll support her, give time a chance to do its thing. One day we'll hand back that little 'un to her. Until then, we have to keep him safe and well. He's our own. We always look after our own.'

'Perhaps he's better off with us.'

'Janet's his mother, Mary. She's his mother, and she'll just take her own time to get past this. God knows it's understandable.'

'If he'd died fighting, she may've been able to accept that. A soldier is always at risk, isn't he?' She looked at Eddie's picture again. 'But I don't know if she'll get over this.'

'We'll be right here for her, whatever happens.'

Mary wished she shared her husband's inner strength, his resilience. She sometimes wondered if it were entirely real or partially for her benefit.

'He was over there because that's where they were told to go,' she said. 'They didn't choose where to go.'

This was how they now spoke of the Middle East: over there and that place.

'He was doing his job,' said Joe proudly, large hands settling on the armrests. 'Our boy was doing his duty. He chose the life, and we have to respect that.'

'He only wanted to help others,' she replied. A knot of wood popped in the flames.

Again, Mary looked at the snow, teeming now, natural beauty that had always made her feel festive and snug; but tonight, the sight left her feeling strangely alone, like her absent faith. She thought about Eddie and tried to concentrate on the good times. Snapshot: here he was as a youngster, grinning from his red pedal car. And another: standing in his whorls-and-swirls cowboy outfit and Stetson, wielding his silver cap-gun. She didn't want to picture him the other way, pitiable, powerless. Yet she couldn't fend off the image of him kneeling in the sand, hair shorn, clad in those terrible orange clothes. For that image always intervened, corroding all others like a rogue malignant cell. His last moments had testified to his character, his mettle, for the need to cry out must have been overwhelming. The need to call for mercy he knew would never be granted. Was it really possible for a mother to overcome such a thing when simply washing knives in the kitchen suds was enough to trigger reminders?

The child crawled to her. Mary hoisted him, brought him close. She raised his little hood, giving him two white bear ears. A string of saliva marred his chin, and she dabbed it away. She held Jamie near and administered light-loving claps. Jamie inspected her nose with wet fingers. She savoured his small form, his newly bathed scent, his warmth. She gazed into his face as she had gazed into her son's when he was young. Eddie wasn't with them any more—but still, he existed right here in her arms, right at this moment. Perhaps as the little one grew, day by day, the pain, in turn, would subside, and she and Joe could watch their boy living again.

All at once, the child broke into a laugh, violet eyes rolling. Mary found herself also smiling, realising that, despite everything, she and Joe still had much to be thankful for—and poor Janet, of course. Janet had much to be thankful for too.

The fire popped and hissed. Joe warmed himself and drank his coffee. Mary watched the snowfall, silent and steady. Jamie's fingers found the small crucifix pendant around her neck, and he stared at it for a time as if drawing comfort from its touch.

Memories Of Murder

I suppose the safest place to start is with Brian Wylie. He was a private man in his sixties who did ancillary work at the local hospital. Nobody knew much about him, and if truth be told, nobody was much interested, either. He lived alone, had no pets anybody was aware of and kept his simple patch of garden well-tended. He'd often be seen mowing his square of lawn or kneeling on a cushion, plucking weeds from his bedding plants and turning earth. He didn't own a car and walked the half-mile back and forth to work, usually toting plastic carrier bags. He wore shabby sweatshirts and jeans mostly and worn sports shoes—I always thought the tatty trainers looked strange on someone his age. Wylie was myopic: his thick lenses rendered his eyes bulbous, which I believe made him self-conscious. The crown of his head was bald, with unruly grey clumps at the sides like a clown; this downtrodden and secretive man, however, was anything but.

'You heard about Sheena Walker?' my friend Danny asked on the way to school. It was November 5th, 1986, bright but crisp, the paths littered in golden leaves.

'What about her?' I asked, still half-asleep.

'Didn't come home from school yesterday. Police've been round to see her folks. Everyone reckons she's been taken.'

'Taken?'

'She left school, usual time, and no one's heard from her since.' Danny hitched his schoolbag onto his shoulder as we crossed the road. 'I overheard my dad talking on the phone.'

Danny's father was a plain clothes police officer, which Danny seldom let me forget. It wasn't unusual for him to listen in on the upstairs line when his old man thought he was having a private conversation.

'Overheard?' I asked.

'I only listened for a few minutes,' Danny told me, his voice laced with guilt.

'So you were eavesdropping again?'

'Maybe a bit,' he admitted with a sly smile. 'But I could tell there was something big going on.'

Sheena Walker was in the year below Danny and me. She lived with her mother, stepfather, and a younger sister on a well-to-do scheme about five minutes' walk from ours. Her mother had recently married a builder. Sheena's biological father, a fireman, had perished in a warehouse blaze several years before.

In the assembly hall, we'd seen Sheena presented with medals and prizes for front-crawl swimming and maths. Out of school, she tended to wear brightly coloured dresses, usually pinks and reds, and walked with a self-assuredness that made her seem older than her age. Sometimes when we passed on the street, she would flash me a cheeky smile and toss her hair, and I would inevitably feel flustered and awkward. She was blessed, and she knew it, and most of my peers and I had at least a slight crush on her.

'My old man said that Wylie guy on Elm Drive's got somethin' to with it,' Danny continued, grinning like the cat with the cream.

I looked at him as we reached the bus stop. Sometimes I thought Danny fancied himself as some sort of amateur sleuth. Like father like son. 'That old sod? Why do the police think he's involved?'

Danny grinned, clearly on the cusp of imparting something

important. He was full of surprises this morning.

'This was when I *knew* it was worth a bit of eavesdropping,' he said. 'Apparently, his name isn't Wylie at all. It's a fake one he's using. Get this—he abducted and killed a young girl about twenty-odd years ago. Spent *ages* in jail. When he was released, they gave him a whole new name and life—right here in Ravenshead.'

I thought about the overweight scruff who carried his possessions in a plastic bag. 'That loser? You sure?'

'Totally.'

Danny spun his yellow yo-yo and palmed it with a snap. The school bus drew up, and its doors folded open with a hiss.

I was surprised to discover that what Danny 'overhead' his father discussing turned out to be true. It later transpired from several TV and newspaper reports that Brian Wylie was actually Walter Manning and had indeed languished in jail for killing a seven-year-old girl called Elsa Willis in 1963. Manning had plucked her from the street, drove her to secluded woodland and interfered with her (I remember reading this with bug-eyed fascination). She was found strangled a day later by an elderly gentleman walking his dog in the same woodland. A farmer's wife remembered seeing a white Ford Consul Capri—Manning's car—parked in the woods around the time the girl went missing. The authorities then systematically hunted down every white Capri in the area (a fairly new model at the time), thereby hopefully effecting an arrest. Eventually, they matched fibres from Elsa's corpse to those in Walter Manning's car, and within a day, he'd divulged the whole sorry tale. Before his release many years later, Manning/Wylie underwent psychiatric evaluation and was deemed fit to re-join society. As it happened, it was our society.

But I'm getting ahead of myself.

In Ravenshead, it wasn't long before the police were thumping on Wylie's door. An officer who'd spoken to him on the street during the after-dark search for Sheena had found him fidgety and nervous and thus did some digging. Before long, Wylie's skeleton in the closet was uncovered, and the bones were rattling loudly. This soon became common knowledge, the way secrets in small towns do. On top of Sheena's disappearance, it caused further unrest, as people were outraged such a man could be here among their children, with nobody aware of his past.

That evening, some twelve hours after I heard of Sheena's vanishing, more than twenty-four hours since she'd been seen, Danny and I were on Elm Drive having a sneaky cigarette in the bus shelter (Players liberated from my mother's packet). Fireworks fizzed and popped in the night sky, their brightness raining down like brief celestial flowers. As we smoked, we saw a police car parked outside Brian Wylie's house by the cherry blossom tree.

'You reckon they'll need back-up to bring him in?' Danny asked.

'You watch too much *Starsky & Hutch*,' I said. 'Maybe he's not involved.'

'But he's one of *those*.'

Stern-faced mothers and fathers stood huddled by the kerb, shivering and stamping their feet, muttering and staring across at the house.

'Why would he do it again?' I said, crushing out my smoke underfoot. 'He's got a new identity. He spent all that time in prison. He'd have to be pretty stupid to dump on his own doorstep.'

'They have urges,' Danny said as if he dealt with such types for a living. 'They can't control themselves. They see a kid walking the street and—' he drove a fist into the palm of his hand '—and they just pounce.'

It could've been like that. But somehow, Wylie didn't strike me as a guilty man—not in the case of Sheena Walker. A rather sad, defeated figure, he didn't seem to have it in him now. Still, I was fourteen years old, so what did my amateur psychology amount to? In any case, Wylie was soon escorted from his home by two officers, subjected to bellowed insults like 'Paedophile!' and 'Lowlife!' as fireworks screamed and burst overhead. The display seemed to me like a distasteful celebration because the guilty man had been collared—and nobody appeared to care much now about Bonfire Night.

But as I lay in bed later, the fusillade of banging continued towards midnight. Rain began sheeting down, and I wondered if Sheena were out in that foul weather somewhere, whether she might be hurt or worse. Was Wylie guilty of taking her? And if so, had he revealed anything to the police?

*****

When I entered the kitchen the next morning, before school, Sheena's smiling, attractive image beamed from the little portable television on the counter. Stopped short, I listened to the newsreader recounting her last known movements. The report cut to an image of our school; then the newsreader revealed that police were questioning a local man. My mother stood watching in her housecoat and bunny slippers, a Player's cigarette smouldering between her fingers.

'Do you remember seeing her in school that day?' she asked.

I opened the fridge, looking for the orange juice. 'I think so,' I said, though I noticed Sheena *every* day.

'Jeez, what must her mother be going through?' She blew a line of smoke at the screen. 'The police took in that Wylie character last night.'

I remembered the officers putting him in the car.

'He always struck me a queer one, that Wylie,' she said.

Because Ravenshead had no police headquarters to speak of, the authorities assembled a command centre in the east wing of our school, in the gymnasium, where a task force directed the hunt for Sheena. Over those days, as suited officers busied themselves around the building, their stern presence brought home to us kids the grim reality of the situation.

Wylie's neighbours were scornful when they spoke of him, citing multiple reasons—even particular incidents—why they'd always considered him suspect and strange. They accused him of leering at them as he passed or peering secretively from his house windows, none of which, incidentally, was ever mentioned prior to the current situation.

Gossip was rife, and it was rumoured that Sheena's mother was one step removed from breaking point. The ordeal had obviously devastated her, probably worsened by a man with a history of child murder being in the frame. A police liaison officer, a woman, accompanied her at the house much of the time, and other high-ranking officers, Danny's father among them, could be seen coming and going. Sheena's stepfather put the brakes on his building work to support his wife through the trouble. But despite the fervour surrounding Brian Wylie, despite his aptness as a suspect, the authorities soon released him and the news spread like wildfire.

'They've only let him go again!' Danny announced one morning as we entered the school canteen, where we usually bought milkshakes and chocolate bars before form class. Pupils bustled everywhere.

'He was working at the hospital when Sheena disappeared,' I said, having already heard the gossip.

Danny scowled as if this didn't dovetail with his version of events. 'Nah, hospitals are busy places.' He fiddled with the spongy Walkman headphones around his neck. 'Wylie's only a cleaner there. He could've slipped out and snatched her without anyone knowing.'

'Don't you think the police would've considered that?'

'Could've happened that way,' Danny insisted sulkily. He slumped down at a table and tore open a chocolate-bar wrapper with his teeth. 'He's only a helper there, an orderly.'

'Doesn't matter if he's a head surgeon or a toilet cleaner. He's got an alibi.'

'Why you so keen to stick up for Wylie?'

'Because he couldn't have done it.'

Someone smashed Brian Wylie's house windows, every last one of them, though nobody ever found out who. His home was pelted with eggs, and police intervened more than once to stop trouble from escalating. In the eyes of the law, Wylie had served his time; all he likely wanted was a chance to live quietly. Conversely, it was unlikely someone guilty of child murder could ever enjoy a peaceful existence. Elsa Willis never had a chance at life—why on earth should her killer have one? People simply didn't want to believe that Brian Wylie hadn't harmed Sheena Walker.

Soon they didn't have a choice.

To everyone's amazement, myself included, Sheena reappeared four days after she went missing, seemingly oblivious to the current upheaval. At about two o'clock in the afternoon, a local couple driving through the streets saw her brazenly walking along in her purple and grey school uniform, whereupon the driver slammed on the brakes before staring and pointing and eventually approaching the girl. When the police finally arrived and the press caught up with the latest developments, some of the pieces began to slot into place. The details varied slightly, depending on who you spoke to, but the gist went like this:

Sheena's stepfather, who'd come into her life only recently before her disappearance, had apparently been 'inappropriate' with Sheena when her mother wasn't around. Sheena had brought this to her mother's attention, but rather than admit she had made a poor choice in her man, the mother disbelieved her daughter's claims. Sheena later revealed to police that it had all left her 'feeling alone with nowhere to turn'.

Have I mentioned Sheena's best friend, Angela?

Well, Angela had mentioned to Sheena that her parents were looking after a neighbours' house while the owners were abroad for a fortnight. This involved watering the plants and making sure they hadn't been burgled, I assume. Angela also let slip that there was a spare key secreted beneath a plant pot at the foot of the back garden. Absorbing all this, Sheena saw an opportunity to get away from home. She hid upstairs in that house during her absence, and whenever Angela's parents came by to check on the place, Sheena simply squirrelled herself out of sight. While her picture aired over the news, while police went door to door, the missing girl was holed up a few blocks from home, likely tucking in to crisps and sweets to her heart's content.

Sheena's mother was mortified, asserting how uncharacteristic her daughter's actions were. 'Sheena's well behaved,' she emphasised in a broadcast before a raft of microphones, her face still anxious and swollen from lack of sleep. She sobbed into a handkerchief. 'Running off is so ... so *unlike* her.' Curiously, there was no sign of her husband.

Nobody knew exactly what Sheena was trying to achieve. Some said she only wanted time apart from the lecherous advances of her stepfather. Others believed her disappearing stunt was partially to get back at her mother for not listening to her. At any rate, Sheena's mother separated from the stepfather about the time the police called to arrest him. Even Sheena's friendship with Angela became strained—Danny saw them having a heated argument outside the bakery—as people suspected Angela complicit in her friend's disappearance.

A fortnight after Sheena decided to show herself, I was passing the local shop when I noticed a brawl about a hundred yards away. Though it was dark, streetlight revealed what looked like several youths setting about somebody on the ground, kicking and stamping the individual mercilessly. One attacker wielded a club of some description, waiting for a chance to strike as the others performed their frenzied assault. My impulse was to hurry past, but they were really going to town on that poor bugger, and decency dictated I should do something.

I ran over there—'Hey, what're you doing?'—in time to witness the three attackers strike off towards the nearby woodland. I felt relieved to see their heels, as I had no idea what to do if they turned their wrath on me.

A man in dark clothing lay on the road, writhing on his back, blubbery midriff exposed. He wore a hood, but I could see his face was heavily bloodied. His hands were raised like a begging dog's paws.

'Are you all right?' I asked stupidly.

He groaned a long woeful sound. 'Ahhhhh.'

Cold streetlight revealed eyes rounded in shock. Even without the thick glasses, which must've been knocked loose, I recognised Brian Wylie. Nearby was a carrier bag I presumed was his; bread and milk spilt out onto the road. Beside him lay a pointed fencepost, its blunt end slickly red in the streetlamp's stark glare. He tried to say something and coughed a splatter of blood, like a plughole backing up, the liquid trickling down his neck.

I ran back to the shop and stumbled inside, where the fluorescent lights were unnaturally bright. 'Call an ambulance,' I said, breathing rapidly. 'That Brian Wylie guy's just been attacked ...'

The young woman behind the counter blanched and froze as if this was outside her sphere of duties. Then she disappeared from sight, a braided ponytail dangling at her back. When she returned, she said, 'He was just in here, ten minutes ago.'

'They must have jumped him when he went outside,' I said.

She looked to the window, which showed only our spectral reflections against the darkness. 'The ambulance is on its way.'

*****

Wylie suffered internal bleeding and a fractured skull, and his battered body gave up the fight for survival in intensive care around eleven o'clock. Part of me thinks he might have been glad to do so. The three perpetrators, each in their twenties, received custodial sentences, although I considered they were curiously lenient. In a bid to look inconspicuous, Wylie had evidently done his meagre shopping after dark, concealed in a black hooded top, but clearly, it hadn't been precaution enough. Once the locals knew what he was, what he had done, it was only a question of time before they reacted. Maybe their willingness to inflict violent justice made them no better than him.

He was buried in Green Valley Cemetery in early December, at

Ravenshead's northernmost point, which commands a view of the ocean. The affair was brief, I heard, attended only by a few of Wylie's colleagues from the hospital. The air was bitter, and it snowed lightly as his remains were laid to rest.

Danny and I were passing the dead man's house on Elm Drive about two weeks later, driven by morbid curiosity more than anything else. We'd already been nosing around outside the posh house where Sheena hid away and the spot where Wylie took his beating (the pathway still bore his blood).

'You reckon he'd still be alive if he hadn't gone out that night?' Danny asked, working his yo-yo.

'They'd have lynched him eventually,' I said. 'Probably would've hanged him from his own tree. And he hadn't even touched the girl.'

'People don't want his sort around,' Danny said.

I recalled the man lying on the street, coughing blood, and had to agree.

We regarded Wylie's house. Graffiti-scrawled plywood still covered the windows, most of which alluded to the man being a deviant child murderer. Stains from smashed eggs were dried into the stonework, like seeping pores from within the mortar. The meagre garden Wylie tended was now a mess of torn-out plants, hacked lawn, and kicked-up dirt, almost as if the property mourned his death.

*****

Today, nobody mentions Brian Wylie—or Walter Manning—or anything else that took place back then. That's not unusual, though; it was all long ago. Perhaps if you don't discuss certain things, you can pretend they never happened.

My wife and I visited the Green Valley Cemetery this morning, which got me to reliving all these buried memories. She laid carnations at her father's grave.

Leaving, she paused by Brian Wylie's stone. There were no flowers.

'I always felt a bit guilty about his death,' she said.

'There's no need,' I assured her. 'It's not as if he was a good person or did good things. He was killed because of his own actions.' I touched her arm. 'For things he did before you were even born.'

'Do you think his time in prison made up for that?' she asked me.

I shrugged. 'In the eyes of the law, maybe.'

She seemed to weigh this; then I motioned her away, out through the spear-tipped bars of the cemetery gates.

The Black Carriage

Your flight from Scotland touches down at Heathrow Airport right on schedule, and you release a breath as the plane's undercarriage meets the runway. Your first time in London, you disembark at 2:30 p.m., collect your luggage from the carousel without fuss, and follow the phalanx of bodies from the terminal out into the overcast November day. As you trundle the suitcase along the concourse, the sight of other passengers greeting and embracing friends and relatives inflicts within you a pang of loneliness.

You don't like to fly—horror stories surrounding airliners have become too commonplace lately: passenger planes downed by militant armies or blown up by fanatical terrorists. Hell, an airliner had even been ditched in the Alps by a suicidal pilot. MH370 had disappeared altogether. And who can forget the World Trade Centre and 9/11? These days, one cannot fly without at least a modicum of trepidation. It is enough to dissuade you from taking to the skies with any regularity. In this particular case, however, because your destination was not overseas and because air travel shaves considerable time from the journey, you accept that flying was the most sensible option.

You're here in west London to attend your best friend Gillian's wedding. Unfortunately, having recently divorced after a turbulent three-year marriage, you do not have a partner with whom to attend the affair. Not exactly ideal, then, but you'd much rather attend the function alone than round up some last-minute date to accompany you.

Several black hackney carriages are coming and going, moving around outside Heathrow. You flag one nearby and smile at the female driver as you climb in the back with your case.

'Hi there,' you say, looking through the clear plastic partition cordoning the front of the vehicle.

'Where to, miss?' the driver asks, her tinny voice transmitted through a speaker system. Regarding you in the rearview mirror, she's wearing a white T-shirt and has a shock of long, black, tousled hair. Her left-hand bears a small tattoo.

'I've a reservation at the Hotel Novotel,' you say, inclining forward. 'It's around Hammersmith somewhere, I think.'

'It surely is,' the driver says and sets off from the airport.

Shortly, there are signs for the M4 before the taxi joins the fast-moving traffic. You run a hand through your long chestnut hair and check your polished nails. Then you take out your mobile and begin scrolling through texts, deleting old messages and looking wistfully at pictures of you and your ex-husband. Today's news is mostly the same old headlines vying for attention: ongoing conflict in the Middle East; fears concerning antibiotics becoming ineffectual; an inmate called Charlie Marshall has escaped from the Cassel Hospital; the scandal concerning emissions-testing in Volkswagen vehicles. Nothing uplifting, as usual.

'Just arrived, then?' asks the driver. She lights a cigarette and exhales a bluish plume.

You frown at the NO SMOKING sticker on the dash. 'First time in London,' you reply. 'I'm here from Scotland. Glad to have my feet on firm ground, actually. I don't much care for flying.'

'Scotland? The land of tartan and Nessie.'

'I like to think there's a little more to us,' you say, almost brusquely.

'Which part you from, then?'

'Edinburgh. Have you ever been?'

The driver shakes her head, teasing a lock of black hair around her finger. 'I don't really get the chance to travel,' she says, exhaling more smoke. 'They don't let us out much.'

You frown again, wondering what on earth she means, but decide to let it go. Perhaps you don't *get* the London humour.

'So what brings you down here?' she asks.

'My friend's getting married tomorrow. She's—'

'I'm getting married in the morning!' the driver suddenly sings, ridiculously out of tune. 'Ding dong, the bells are gonna chime ...' She laughs, and her hazel eyes catch yours in the mirror again. 'A wedding? That's grand. Going by yourself, then?'

'I'm afraid so.'

You feel your cheeks redden a little, then chasten yourself. What is there to be embarrassed about? You aren't the only thirty-year-old divorcee in the world.

'Nowt wrong there. Bloody men're only after one thing anyhow— right? They sink a skinful, and their bloody hands'll start wandering and pawing ...'

Slightly wrongfooted by the driver's curious outbursts—are all London cabbies like this?—you look out at upcoming signs for the A4 and Hammersmith, feeling a little better. It starts to rain, fat droplets pitter-pattering rapidly at the windows, blurring the view.

Your attention returns to the phone, scrolling through the news items again.

Police are on high alert this afternoon after inmate Charlotte

Marshall—known to her carers as Charlie—escaped from the Cassel Hospital in Richmond, Surrey. Marshall, forty-two, who suffers severe disassociation and a violent personality disorder, stabbed a doctor with a pair of scissors at ten o'clock this morning before escaping in a stolen Austin TX4 black cab. The cab's driver, Mr Adam Beckett, discovered his vehicle gone when he returned from inside the hospital. The public has been advised not to approach Miss Marshall, who is extremely unpredictable and exhibits transient psychotic states. Charlotte Marshall has long black hair and a distinctive heart-design tattoo on her left hand ...

'So where're you from,' the driver is saying, her insistent voice rasping through the speaker system.

You stare at the phone a moment longer, then glance up at the woman driving the car at the pinkish heart-shaped tattoo on her hand. There are several unsightly parallel scars marring her forearm. And closer inspection reveals the driver's white T-shirt—what you can see of it—appears more like, well, more like, a hospital gown.

Surely not. It can't be. Can it?

'Where are you *from*?'

Your eyes meet again. 'What? Edinburgh, I told you.'

The driver's ID by the cab radio shows a fair-haired bearded male with the name "Adam Beckett" printed beneath. Your heart performs a giddy-up. Suddenly, you're aware of the car's increasing speed, travelling apace, doing approximately sixty miles per hour—and the traffic has stalled a mile or so up ahead.

'Let's end it all,' the driver bellows, tugging the steering wheel back and forth, weaving the taxi drunkenly over the centreline. 'Me and you, Nessie, what d'ya say? Just like Thelma and Louise ...'

The taxi is still getting faster, oncoming vehicles zipping and tooling past.

'Please, will you slow down ...?'

'Slow down? *Slow down?* No way, Nessie. We'll go faster, faster, faster.' She erupts into peals of laughter, shrieks which rattle unsettlingly through the cab's speaker, doing nothing to temper your rising unease. 'Nothing's gonna stop us—it's you and me all the way!'

You glance frantically at the door handle. The word LOCKED shines there in bright red.

'Please, *slow down.*'

Panic-born questions flow through your mind. *Why the hell did I have to pick up this taxi? There are 20,000 black cabs in London— how could I choose the bloody Mad Hatter?*

You're off the seat and up against the plastic separating the smoky front of the cab. The bumper-to-bumper tailback up ahead is disconcertingly close and getting closer by the second. The lunatic is bouncing excitedly around in her seat like a child in a go-kart. She works down the driver's window, letting in wind and rain, which tosses and lifts her long snakes of hair. She then stretches one arm out and begins waving at oncoming cars, wailing all the while.

'We're on the last ride, Nessie!'

'Charlotte, please, for God's sake, *stop the car.*'

'Charlotte? Who's *Charlotte*? I'm Wonder Woman! I'm Hillary Clinton! I'm Maid Marion! We're Thelma and Louise!'

You start screaming, able now to read the number plate on the nearest stationary car up ahead. It's a red Saab with people sitting in the rear. Your stomach rolls and a dizzying sensation swirls through your mind.

'Stop the cab!'

Life flashes before your eyes—your family, your wedding day, colleagues at the salon, the little red bike with the stabilisers on which Father taught you to ride—a quick-fire montage played out in seconds.

Charlotte Marshall unsnaps her seatbelt, which slithers away with a *clunk*.

'Oh my God ...'

There's simply no more time, no stopping distance. With the woman braying maniacal laughter behind the wheel, you reflexively raise your arms as the taxi hurls headlong towards the rear of—

Teen Poppy

I came across the troll yesterday, quite by chance. I'd been clearing the loft, and there it was at the bottom of a tattered box containing miscellany from my youth, that impudent smile I hadn't seen in many years. Finding it brought to mind a much larger troll, for want of a better word, an evil man every bit as real as you or me. I was thirteen when events that winter taught me a crucial lesson—one not covered by a classroom curriculum, that is. A life lesson, you might call it. For a moment, I just stared at the little figure; then, I retrieved it and smoothed its long hair with my hand. I found the old newspaper cutting in the same box, so I sat down on a dated ottoman and read it again. As I did, the memories soon came rolling back, strangely clear in my memory.

*****

The house across from ours, number 11, was unoccupied. The Marsdens had lived there for years with a Labrador called Bramble until Mr Marsden died from a stroke. Mrs Marsden then sold up, and the new owners decided to lease the place.

It snowed the Saturday the Burrells moved into number 11, a blast of wind-spun flakes as the light faded. In late November 1997, I watched them pull in from my friend and neighbour Nate's bedroom window. They arrived in a rust-eaten blue Vauxhall Cavalier, its back end almost scraping the ground like something ready for the scrapyard. Number 11's TO-LET sign had been removed after several months, though I can't recall exactly when. The house needed some TLC after being neglected for a time: the lawns were a mess; the windows needed a good clean and their frames a fresh lick of paint.

A well-built lofty man got out and lumbered up the walk to the front door, where he hunched down, jiggling the key, struggling with the lock. He shook his head and thumped the door with his palm, and I had the impression he was set to reduce it to kindling when it finally yielded.

'Someone's moving into number 11,' I said to Nate.

He was watching *Terminator 2* again. His whole room was a disordered den of sci-fi stuff, from the *Alien* posters on the wall to the *Interzone* and *Starblazer* magazines littering the floor. His hamster, Ripley, squeaked away inside its little wheel.

With the door open, the man stalked back down the walk to the passenger side of the car. A girl appeared from the Cavalier. She looked around my age, with shiny auburn hair, wavy like a waterslide, cascading down to her bottom. That's what I noticed first. She wore a black coat and a blue and yellow flowery dress, which seemed inappropriate for the season. The man—her father, I assumed—made a hurry-up motion, and they both went into the house.

The streetlights blinked on. When the flurry had passed, the bullish man returned to the Cavalier's rear seats for two large suitcases, which he hefted easily, and kicked the car's door shut harder than necessary, as if in frustration.

*****

The day after their arrival, a long truck rumbled up. The father and two burly movers carted chairs, sofas and beds into the house. There must have been a radio in the truck because the father kept pausing by the passenger-side window, frowning and listening. The girl, wearing a black coat over a dress with a butterfly motif, made unhurried solo trips carrying smaller bubble-wrapped items and manageable boxes. Sometimes she appeared to have a slight limp. Mr Tayburn's grey cat from number 24 slunk by, and the girl bent to pet her. Flakes of snow spun in the air again.

Peeking down from my bedroom window like a curtain twitcher, feeling somewhat snoopy, I was unable to stop watching her. Maybe it was the amazingly long hair, or that she was new in the street, or that she moved so dreamily, seemingly without a care, all of which, to me, made her intriguing. In any case, it didn't take her father and the movers long to empty the truck, and it grumbled away as he and the girl went back inside. Then the threat of snow became a reality, and it came down the rest of the day. Perhaps the cold weather explained why nobody in the street had opened a front door to say hello.

A week later, the snow had almost cleared, though the air remained cold, the streets dirty. She sat alone outside the local store on its low wall, eating jelly cola bottles. I'd been sent to collect gravy granules for my mother with an eye to bartering a bar of chocolate for my efforts. Her head was bowed, her impressive hair rippling beneath a red bobble hat. Up close, I saw her black winter jacket was decorated with an assortment of badges—ladybirds and peace symbols and the like—and underneath another flowery dress, a riot of dark blues and purples. Her pale legs were crossed above little black shoes with luminous green laces.

'Hi,' I said.

She raised her head and smiled shyly, fixing me with narrow blue eyes. Her freckled nose was round and cute. A small mark marred her bottom lip. It looked like a cut but might have been a cold sore.

'I'm Ben. I live across from you, number twenty-six.'

Twirling a lock of that fantastic hair, her mouth working on cola bottles all the while, she said, 'Poppy. Poppy Burrell.' She snapped out the syllables almost proudly, and it seemed they were all I was going to get.

'Your hair's really long,' I said, shifting my feet. 'Longest I've ever seen. Doesn't it take ages to dry after you wash it?'

She giggled at that. Maybe she thought I was dumb.

I felt an impulse to reach and touch her hair, to see if it sparked with static. 'How long did it take to grow?'

She shrugged, offering the cola bottles. 'Long time.'

I took one—fizzy, sour as hell—making my mouth ooze with spit.

'What happened to your lip?' I asked.

Her smile melted, and she looked away.

'Will you be starting school soon?' I asked. I was curious why I hadn't seen her at the academy. I also wondered about her circumstances: why she had moved here, where her mother might be. But these questions I felt were too intrusive.

She bounced her heels on the wall, popped another sweet in her mouth. 'My dad says after Christmas. New year, new start.'

'Well, if you're wondering anything—about the school, I mean— just let me know. Anyway, I gotta get some stuff for my mother ...'

She unpinned an orange-haired troll from her jacket, maybe two inches high, and handed it to me. 'A present for you, Ben.' She smiled two dimples into her cheeks. 'You rub its hair for luck.'

I looked at its comically bulbous eyes and grinning face and returned her smile. 'Don't you need luck too?' I asked.

'I've got another one at home.'

I turned towards the store and climbed the flight of steps, the troll clutched in my hand, a pleasant glow inside me.

It snowed again that night. I opened my bedroom window around eleven o'clock, watching the flakes drift by streetlights for a while, covering cars and gardens. Poised to close the window after I got a little cold, I heard shouting across the way. The sound seemed to come from number 11, which was dark save for a single light burning upstairs. The curtains were drawn, but I knew it was Poppy's room as I'd seen her passing the window, brushing her long hair. Forearms on the chilled sill, I listened through the snow's blanketing silence, and it sounded again—a man's voice, deep and scolding. I strained to hear, but the words were unintelligible. Moments later, the light winked out, and all I could decipher was the rustle of leaves from the trees on our street.

I scurried back to bed, but memories of that angry voice—it had sounded heavily impaired by alcohol, I thought—kept me awake the rest of the night.

*****

Monday morning, I headed next door to Nate's before school. The world glistened, dazzling to the eye. Across the way, Mr Burrell's Cavalier was gone, leaving a neat rectangular patch on the driveway untouched by the snowfall. Poppy, in her badge-laden jacket and navy wellies, was shovelling snow from the pathway in front of the house, her wonderful hair tumbling from the bobble hat.

'Morning,' I called over.

'Hi, Ben.'

I drifted across.

She laid the shovel aside, her cheeks ruddy. 'Dad says I have to clear the path to the door—*boring*. But I'm going to make a snowman.' She clapped her mittens twice, and I couldn't help smiling. 'Maybe he'll take me for a ride on a motorbike, like the one on TV.'

She squinted at the winter sky and spread her arms. 'Or maybe flying, right over the ocean to see all his snowmen friends—remember?'

'Of course. They show it on TV most years, don't they?'

'Off to school?' she asked.

'Yup. Just going to get my friend, Nate.' I thought about her father's incensed voice, shuffling my feet uneasily. 'Is everything all right, Poppy?'

'Half right, half left.'

'What?'

She smirked. 'Never mind.'

'I thought I heard something last night. Shouting, sort of.'

She looked away, as she had when I'd mentioned the mark on her lip. 'Sometimes he gets angry.' She picked up the shovel, which was nearly as tall as her. 'It hasn't been easy for him since my mother died.' She rubbed at her nose. 'She had ovarian cancer.'

'Oh ... I'm sorry. So ... you're okay?'

She nodded, the hat's bobble doing a slack little dance.

'Well, I better go get Nate.' I turned to walk away.

'He gambles.'

I looked back. 'Gambles? On what?'

'Mmm. Anything with legs, really.' She shrugged. 'He's trying to find work around here, but I don't think there's much going. He's started betting again, and when he loses, he gets kind of mad.'

I didn't know what to say. Wasn't gambling just one long losing streak? *Young gambler, old beggar*, the proverb stated. She resumed working, and I felt compelled to stay and help. Then I heard Nate calling behind me, coming from his house.

'Have fun at school, Ben,' she said, digging her shovel into the snow.

*****

I didn't see Poppy for a time, not at the shops or on the street, nor at her bedroom window. I kept watch for her sometimes, but her curtains were usually closed. I figured it would likely be at the academy next year before we met again. The plastic troll with its miniature denim jacket and blaze of orange hair took pride of place on my bedside table, smiling with open arms. I guess I was still happy that Poppy had felt comfortable gifting me something so soon after we'd met. *Rub its hair for luck*, she'd said, but I suspected she hadn't enjoyed much luck of her own. I felt sorry for her, as it seemed she didn't have anyone in her corner. I wasn't in that position myself, but I knew what it was to be an only child.

During early December, after school, I saw her putting out rubbish at the head of her drive. The day had been sunny but brisk and now nearing twilight. I was at my living room window. Her father's car wasn't in the driveway. She lifted the dustbin lid, peeked inside, and disposed of the black bag before turning languidly back to the house. I almost ran outside to say hello, then reasoned she'd be gone before I got there and that I'd probably appear somewhat desperate. As she turned to go back to the house, enough daylight remained to decipher what I thought was a purple-brown bruise on her cheek.

That weekend, Nate went away with his folks. Some family shindig. I held vigil from my room, waiting for Mr Burrell's car to pull out of the drive. I'd begun to think he wasn't going to leave the house that day when he appeared wearing a beanie hat, marching down the walk in a black sweater and jeans. He sported a scruffy beard and held a small radio to his ear as he got into the Cavalier, scowling as usual, and roared off, leaving behind a haze of exhaust fumes. I watched his taillights disappear over the hill. I could guess where he was going. Nate's older sister cashiered at the bookies in town, and the word was that Mr Burrell had become a regular there.

I crossed the road and pressed the doorbell. It was completely dead, so I knocked twice. The front door had a blurry glass pane. A light glowed somewhere inside, so I tried again. About to give it one last go, I heard a key turn, and the door opened an inch or two. Poppy lurked there, peeking past the jamb.

The first thing that struck me was her hair: it had been cut off—hacked by the look of it—close to her scalp. I was so taken aback that I almost missed the faint crescent of bruising under her eye. She stood barefoot in a mint-green dress.

'What happened to your hair?'

Poppy looked away and shrugged. 'My dad cut it.' She sounded as if she didn't care, as if she were resigned to this sort of treatment, which made it all the worse.

'Why?'

She opened the door a little wider, small and frail now without the streaming hair. Nate's hamster once climbed into a pail of water, and the drenching had made it appear half the size. Poppy looked similarly shrunken and defenceless.

I wanted to reach out and hold her. 'Does he ... you know ... hit you?'

'You better go. He's just gone to get tobacco.'

'But ...'

'Please, Ben, go home.'

I stared at the unsightly tufts on her head, unable to comprehend anyone doing this to her, let alone her father. 'Why'd he cut your hair?'

She leaned out and peered down the road as if wary of being overheard. 'He lost the rent money on horses. He was in a mood, said my hair looked stupid and it needed doing. Knowing him, he'll probably try to sell it and gamble the money.'

'You can't let him treat you like that, Poppy ...'

She wasn't open to discussion. She said, 'Bye, Ben,' held eye contact for a few seconds and snicked the door closed.

*****

I had to do something. I lifted the phone in my parents' bedroom, careful on the creaky floorboards, and stood staring at the rotary dial, listening to the tone. 999—that's all it'd take. But the police would want to know my name, what I'd seen. They'd question me. Probably they'd come into the house. What would my parents say? Perhaps I could call the police anonymously? Or social services? I felt beyond my depth, so I replaced the receiver, deciding to check in with my father. He knew what to do in every situation. The police and social services weren't going anywhere, I figured. Before I left the bedroom, I picked up the little troll and smoothed its long orange hair. 'I wish Poppy would be okay,' I said.

My dad spent lots of time in the garage, where he had a workbench and shaped wood with his lathe and router. He'd crafted the bed he and my mother slept in. The concrete floor was ever awash in chips and shavings, and so was he. He always warned me to keep away from his lathe when he wasn't around. Once, he told me about a guy who'd got his necktie caught up while 'turning'. Suffice it to say it didn't have a Walt Disney ending. I don't know if it was true, of course, but he made his point sure enough.

'Hey, son,' he said when I creaked open the door. Van Morrison's *Astral Weeks*, his favourite record, was playing on his portable CD player. The mystical, otherworldly sounds of 'Slim Slow Slider' filled the space as I stepped through sweet-scented pine shavings.

'Dad ...?'

'Hmmm?' He brought his thumb along a length of wood he was sanding. He wore goggles and a tatty red Highland Fabricators boiler suit and was puffing one of his roll-ups.

I dug my hands in my pockets. 'If you knew something bad was happening to somebody, should you do something to help them?'

He straightened and raised the goggles, blowing a woodchip from his mouth.

'Depends, son.'

'What on?'

'The details.' He cleared his throat. 'What situation are we talking about?'

I imagined Mr Burrell hacking Poppy's hair. 'Just someone who might need help ...'

'Uh-huh. What kind of help?'

I hesitated, letting sawdust sift through my fingers like sand in an hourglass. This was going to be harder than I expected. 'You know. If someone was being hurt by someone else.'   He puffed on his smoke, considering. 'Well, depends on the facts. For instance, if a man was hurting his wife, say, then I'd probably tell you it's down to her to do something about it.'

'Even if she had no help?'

'Even then. Adults gotta resolve these things themselves. Third parties get involved, it can backfire. Sure can. Especially these days. Can't say or do any damned thing without offending someone.' He sounded as if he were talking from experience. 'Best to mind your own business, Ben. You don't always get a second chance to make a good decision.'

'What if it was someone younger?'

He squinted at me through stagnant smoke. 'Somebody botherin' you at school?'

'No.'

'Listen, only one way to deal with *that* situation.' He made a fist and jabbed at the air. 'Pop him straight in the mug—hard enough to do some real damage. You understand?'

'No, that's not what I mean. Is it wrong to interfere with someone else's problem? To, you know, call the police or anything?'

'Calling the law's a big step, son. People don't really take to that, rubs folk up the wrong way. You're young. Few more years, you'll know what I mean.' He lowered his goggles. 'Mind your own business, son; that's the strategy. You can stick your beak in with best intentions and still wind up being the one in the wrong.'

I wanted to scream. *The girl at number 11's being hurt by her father.* But the words wouldn't make the transition from mind to mouth. Perhaps Dad was right, I thought: perhaps I should mind my own business and hope the problem would blow over.

*****

Monday, I couldn't concentrate on the lessons. Periods dragged as I stared from classroom windows, watching rainfall drench the sports field. I pondered Poppy's predicament. I considered my father's words, wondering whether such advice might be irrelevant: perhaps people's tendencies to turn away had left Poppy in her vulnerable situation—that and a psychotic old man with the world's shortest fuse.

Heading home, Nate jabbered about which film was better, Ridley Scott's *Alien* or James Cameron's sequel. He weighed each movie's merit and concluded John Hurt's chest-bursting scene swung it by the nose. I nodded distractedly, only half listening.

On our street, we heard a commotion from number 11, Burrell's raised voice, shouting—all but screaming—as if he'd finally slipped a cog.

'You hear that?' Nate asked, slowing up.

'I hear it,' I said, feeling my innards contract.

Mr Tayburn, at number 24, pretending to rake leaves, was glancing over. A couple of other neighbours lurked at the windows. Something smashed inside number 11, a windowpane or glass vase, maybe, and Nate and I started. Poppy was in deep trouble this time, of this I was deathly sure—then I heard her scream, followed by the father's outraged voice again.

I shouldered off my school bag. 'Watch that for me.'

'Where you going—?' Nate yelled as I broke into a run.

I sprinted towards the house and up the drive past Burrell's rusty Cavalier, acutely aware of how surreal the situation felt, unable to believe what I was doing, even as it was happening. My heart pumping, I barged in through the front door, which was ajar, clattering it against the inside wall.

They were in the kitchen to my right but, with all the commotion, hadn't heard me enter the house. Poppy cowed behind raised arms as Burrell loomed over her. Broken jewels of glass littered the floor. The atmosphere was thick with a stale, beery smell, like a pub cellar. Eyes wide with shock, Poppy looked too petrified to say or do anything. I crept into the kitchen warily, taut as a drum, as if entering a wild beast's domain. Burrell suddenly struck her hard with a closed fist—I heard that awful sound—sending her small body hurtling against the refrigerator.

'Poppy!'

His towering bulk rounded on me, beanie covering his head, face flushed purple like rage personified. Big veins pulsed in his neck and forehead. Terrified, I made to pass him, trying to reach Poppy—now lying motionless on the diamond linoleum—but he roared something about trespassing and lunged, seizing my jacket hood. As I turned, squirming, babbling that I just wanted to check his daughter was okay, his fist crashed plumb into my head. I had no time to bob or weave, zig or zag—and that was the end of my attempted heroism. Lights out.

I came to in a garden chair on our front lawn, my mother patting my hand. I don't know how much time had elapsed, but the light was starting to fade. My head felt like a rotten apple like I'd been hit by a truck. A dilly of a bruise closed my left eye. Neighbours peered from doorsteps, whispering. Two police cars and an ambulance were parked askew outside number 11. A young paramedic with a neat beard knelt by my side.

'Ben—can you hear me?' my mother asked, rubbing my hand. She was wearing her glossy pinny with a cartoon chef on the front. I didn't see Nate anywhere.

'*Ben*?'

'I'm okay,' I said.

'Your face is bleeding!' she wailed, high and reedy.

'It's not bad,' the medic said, tending my cut. 'Don't worry.'

Sitting up, I could see two uniformed officers were grilling Burrell by his front door. His eyes were red and swollen with tears, and he was dragging a hand through his thinning hair repeatedly, shaking his head. Two female medics appeared from the house with Poppy on a wheeled stretcher, her face lost beneath an oxygen mask, eyes closed. I stood and stepped woozily nearer the ambulance, against my mother's protests, looking at the tufts of hair on Poppy's scalp, looking at her motionless body, trying to see an indication that she was breathing.

They loaded her in and drove away siren wailing. The police firmly assisted red-faced Mr Burrell into a squad car. I wanted to find my father, to tell him this was his fault, that his shitty advice had let this tragedy happen. I knew it wasn't strictly true, however. I'd needed someone to tell me to do the right thing when I should've done it because it was the right thing to do.

My mother's consoling arm circled my shoulder, a gesture which normally fixed just about anything. But that day, it provided no comfort at all.

Word of mouth soon spread that Poppy didn't make it. She was non-responsive. Her father's blows had inflicted traumatic brain injury, and she passed away that night. When my mother told me, I went straight up to my room and wept, staring across the street at her bedroom. Still concussed and nauseated, with a swimmy headache that worsened with every movement, I felt my failure had sealed her fate. I sat on my bed and picked up the troll, looking at its plastic, joyous smile through bleary eyes. What if I'd run a little faster that day? If I hadn't hesitated inside the house? If I'd intervened before the brute had a chance to hurt her so badly?

Burrell pleaded guilty and I heard he spent time in prison. I hope it has been a long time. Perhaps someone somewhere eventually paid him in his own coin. I still have a faint scar today, below my eye, left from his finger ring, a permanent reminder of that afternoon. The neighbours in our street all talked about how his gambling debts had skyrocketed. Horses, dogs, football, whatever was happening. Anything with legs, Poppy had said.

For me, it took time to come to terms with the knowledge I should've helped her sooner—or at least shared what I knew. I now wonder if what happened to her was instrumental in my following a career in social work.

The local paper ran a three-paragraph piece with the headline: TEEN POPPY DIES AFTER FATHER'S STRIKE. The incident taught me to go with my gut, to trust my intuition. The price of inaction is far greater than the cost of making a mistake. It taught me you can't always wait around to be told to do the right thing and that sometimes in life you have to make the call yourself. That sometimes, you might be a person's only hope. That sometimes, in some situations, you simply don't get a second chance to make a good decision. I suppose my father was right about this, at least.

*****

The day after Poppy died, my dad knocked and came into my room, rubbing his palms together. He looked sheepish and awkward as he closed the door behind him.

'Son,' he said. 'I think ... I think I know now what you were trying to ask me out there in the garage.'

I didn't say anything.

He crossed to the rain-smeared window, scratching at his unshaven face, looking over towards number 11. 'I guess, uh, I wasn't really listening, was I?'

'It wasn't your fault, Dad.'

'I'm your father, Ben.' He turned away from the window. 'When you come to me for help, I gotta make sure I try to give it to you.'

'It wasn't me that needed help,' I said.

'No. But you were asking on her behalf; I see that now.' He sat on the bed beside me and put his hands on his knees. He smelt of sawdust. 'I didn't know the situation over there, you see? Me and your mother, we just didn't know anything about it. I'm sorry, son.'

'It's okay,' I said.

After a short silence, he asked, 'Did you know her well?'

I nodded because I felt I had. 'She was a nice person, Dad.'

'I heard that,' he said. 'I heard that. So, why don't you tell me about her, huh? What was she like?'

I sat there a moment, thinking about Poppy, looking at the little smiling troll on the bedside table with its arms outstretched. Then, with tears brimming in my eyes, I took a breath and I told him.

A Charnel House In Texas

G ranger stares through the windscreen of his Chevrolet Malibu at the secluded house. Directly above the property, like stage illumination, a perfect moon shines in the Texas night sky.

It stands high on a rise, the old, dilapidated house, visible via wall-mounted exterior lights, its outline lost against the starlit backdrop of the heavens. A dark-coloured vehicle, a model Granger cannot decipher from here, is parked on the summit of the steep drive. A light burns upstairs behind a curtained dormer window, but despite a second night of surveillance, he hasn't seen one definite sign of life. Yet he means to give the job at least token effort, so he waits and observes as the hour grows late. It's possibly the most preposterous affair he's been involved in—he's been tangled up in some doozies too—and still, he wonders that he agreed to any part of it. Perhaps he agreed because the Martinez woman is the mother of a deceased friend and boss of Granger's, and he feels an obligation to her, a sense of duty. And hell, she *had* struck him as convincing, despite the bizarre nature of their conversation in her big old Austin manor house two days ago. Despite her bizarre claim.

*****

She had shown him into a spacious lounge, whose leather sofas, high nautical-blue walls and glossy white French doors were lit by the westering sun. Framed russet landscapes, similar to Constable's works, were positioned all around. Granger performed a fleeting scan, more reflex than interest, his gaze finishing at a glass coffee table, whereon lay a silver serving tray and china crockery.

'Thank you for coming, Mr Granger,' she said quietly. 'I appreciate you taking the time. May I get you something? Will you join me for some tea?'

'No thanks.'

'Something stronger? Cognac? Bourbon?'

'Nothing, thank you.'

Granger had met her twice before, years ago: once at a *Houston Chronicle* fundraiser her late son had laid on and once at the man's funeral. She'd been trim back then but far from as malnourished-looking as the ghoulishly thin lady before him. Drastic weight loss had aged her, mapping the contours of her skull, rendering her grey eyes rounded and intense.

'You worked for Edward when he ran the newspaper,' she said, not a question but a statement.

Granger paced by a parlour grand piano, gazing at cabinet displays of porcelain ornaments. 'On occasion, yes.'

'You were freelance?' she asked, moving slowly behind him.

'Still am,' he said. 'Ed slid some work my way over the years, and we became good friends.' He turned about. 'You and I spoke briefly at his funeral, do you remember?'

'Yes,' she said, touching the pearl clasp holding her grey hair just so. 'I do.' Flattening her navy skirt against her legs, she sat down on a couch, indicating an armchair for Granger, then poured tea into a little white cup that appeared as brittle as her.

'I understand,' she said in a light-hearted tone, 'you sometimes took assignments that were dangerous?'

'Goes with the job,' Granger confirmed from his chair.

She nodded, sipping her tea. 'Yes, I imagine so.'

'Why don't you tell me why I'm here, Mrs Martinez.'

'Very well.' She set the cup in its saucer and angled herself to face him. 'I want you to find my granddaughter.'

He sat forward, uncrossing his legs. 'She's missing?'

'Karine is dead,' she told him, reaching for something flat and rectangular from the sofa beside her. It took Granger a moment to register it was a Ouija board, and that's about the point when things started getting weird.

'I'm afraid you'll need to elaborate,' he said, glancing at the board, wondering if maybe she wasn't firing on all cylinders. Granger had never had anything to do with Ed's family while the man was alive and hadn't seen Karine Martinez in years—since her father's funeral, in fact, when she was a young girl.

'I assume you know what this is?' she asked, extending a palm.

'Looks like a Ouija board, but séances were never my bag.'

She adjusted the heart-shaped planchette as if it was just another ornament. 'My granddaughter contacted me through this rather unsavoury device last week,' she revealed and let the statement linger in the air.

Granger wanted to tell her he didn't believe in such rubbish—he'd encountered too many horrors in real life to buy into the paranormal— but decided the best approach, for now, was to let her talk.

'Karine disappeared two months ago,' she went on. 'During the previous six months, she'd been preoccupied with a lot of Gothic nonsense, dressing as if every day were a Halloween party. Black clothes, black tights. Rings and chains. Awful boots. She practically lived on energy drinks. I don't know what her father would've thought.' She shook her head and smiled wistfully. 'Karine lost her mother in a road accident in Dallas last year, a terrible collision on the North Central Expressway. That's when she came to live with me when she started dressing in black all the time.' The elderly lady appeared aggrieved, briefly, as if a life beset by tragedy was wearing her down. Then, she asked: 'Do you have children, Mr Granger?'

'A daughter about Karine's age, as it happens.'

'We do our best for them but cannot predict how they'll develop.' She paused a moment, considering. 'I found the dark clothes and dyed hair absolutely abhorrent, I cannot lie. Yet, tell me, what can you do with a strong-willed teenager?'

Granger listened, smiling politely, but his eyes were drawn to the board's whitish wood, the alphabet displayed in two arcs of black letters, numbers zero to nine underneath, YES and NO on either side. In the corners were crescent moons and stars.

'Are you saying the only evidence you have of Karine's death is contact she made with you through this?'

'What more evidence would I need?'

He thought it prudent to let that one slide. 'Tell me about when you last saw her.'

'She left here to visit a friend in Blanco—another young girl with a penchant for black. And ... well, I'm afraid she never arrived there.'

'What did the police say?'

'They've discovered nothing. Karine is just another name. Young girls are missing all over the state, so they tell me. Fredericksburg. Wimberley. Lockhart. Right here in Austin. All over.'

Granger considered. 'Is it possible she ran away?'

'Without telling her friends? Without accessing any of those tiresome social media forums? Without using her bank account or taking any of her clothes?' She waved a dismissive hand, saying, 'No, no. I didn't approve of her dress sense, Mr Granger, but we otherwise enjoyed a good relationship. She wouldn't leave me like that, not knowing where she was or what happened to her. Especially after losing her mother the way we did. Karine wasn't heartless.'

Granger eyed the scratched old board, poised to ask where it fitted in when he made the connection. 'The board ... it belonged to your granddaughter?'

She raised wispy brows as if quietly impressed. 'Why, yes. How did you know?'

'I merely surmised,' he said, shrugging. 'More likely hers than yours.'

'Oh, I've really no idea how long she had it, or why, or from where she might have obtained such a thing.' She adjusted the gather on her navy dress. 'Another distasteful addition to the Goth persona, most probably.'

'You mentioned a message?'

Mrs Martinez closed her eyes, as if in a bid to relive events, and opened them again. 'I was tidying her room when I stumbled upon this ... contraption. I was somewhat unsettled to discover such a device, as you'll imagine. I sat on her bed with it and started moving this pointer thing around, just aimlessly. And I truly don't know what possessed me to say what I said ...'

Granger sat forward, interest piqued despite himself.

'I said, "Are you there, Karine? Are you there, sweetheart?" I felt utterly ridiculous; of course, I did. Then something stirred the curtains, even with the window closed. And this pointer—' she picked up the planchette '—it began to twitch away on the board, just barely noticeable. I was startled, my *word*, was I startled. I placed my fingers on it, as I assumed one is supposed to, and it began ... spelling out words, Mr Granger. It was Karine telling me where she is. Or where she was ...'

Granger stared at her. 'Words?'

'Two words.' Mrs Martinez produced from her navy dress a folded piece of paper. 'The name of a house,' she said slowly and handed the paper to him, pinched between two fingers. 'One letter at a time, Karine spelt the name of a house.'

*****

Slouched in his car, one eye trained on that upstairs light, giving serious thought to pulling the plug, Granger takes a nip of Wild Turkey and a second for good measure. The alcohol sets his insides aglow. As rain blurs the windscreen, he gets to thinking about Ed Martinez and the headline stories they collaborated on. Prior to the man's untimely death in the newsroom, Granger and the *Houston Chronicle's* editor enjoyed a beneficial working relationship and shared a mutual trust. A strong leader and manager, Ed had hired him occasionally when discretion was paramount or when there was a delicate angle to a potentially explosive story, and Granger had always done reliable work, just as Ed had always recompensed him fairly. Their dealings ended abruptly, however, when an aneurism felled the great newspaperman in his late forties. Poor sonofabitch had a ballooning blood vessel in his brain and hadn't known anything about it.

Granger screws the cap on Wild Turkey. He stretches his legs in the footwell, trying to ease the crick in his lower back. A drift of black cloud sails across that unflawed, bright moon like a ship on the water.

At nearly fifty, he wonders that he hasn't yet left this game behind. He's endured the devastation of two botched marriages, and both exes would swear he hadn't learned a solitary thing, which is probably a fair assessment when it came to his history with women. Covering the Waco massacre in '93, in his early days, he'd been so engrossed in the weeks-long siege that he'd forgotten his first wedding anniversary: a mere misdemeanour, he'd believed, though his then-wife deemed otherwise. Weighing it now, he accepted that the vocation and marriage, like oil and water, were never destined to mix.

The light goes out up there.

Granger straightens.

He sits waiting, the rain pattering the Chevrolet's roof. He checks his Rolex—it's a little after midnight. Probably just someone turning in, he figures. No big deal.

But a few moments later, somebody leaves the house, locking the front door. Granger doesn't worry about being seen: the headlights are off, and he's tucked among a cluster of oaks, sufficiently distant from the road.

The figure—a man, judging by build and strut—heads over to the parked car. Headlamps flare before the vehicle starts down the drive. It pauses at the bottom and performs a turn, then accelerates into the dead of night. Texas plates. Looked like a dated Buick, though Granger can't be sure as he watches those water-blurred rear lights disappear into the blackness.

He opens the glove and withdraws his Smith & Wesson .38 Snub-Nose revolver, purchased years ago after one too many close calls. Moonlight catches its perfectly shaped metal. He checks there's a cartridge in every chamber, snaps shut the cylinder, and vacates the car, wedging the gun in the back of his belt.

But he's startled by a commotion at his side as a blackbird touches down on the car's hood. It paces around on stick-like legs, opens its wings, and screeches at him. Then it lifts off and flaps away into the dark, making him step back in surprise. He collects himself for one moment before moving surefootedly through the undergrowth, abandoning the cover of the oaks and heading for the ascending driveway and property looming high above.

*****

'Why didn't you call the police?' Granger asked, studying the notepaper on which she had printed the words: HILLCREST HOUSE.

'They'd think me mad,' she replied, topping up her tea. 'We both know that.'

'But I'll take you seriously?'

'I'm telling you the truth, Mr Granger. I have nothing to convince you other than my word—though I doubt my word would've convinced the authorities, don't you? They wouldn't even react to such a claim, especially from a missing child's grandmother. They'd label me distraught, delusional, clutching at straws—and they'd be perfectly justified, I suppose. Besides, don't police require evidence to perform a search?'

'They'd need probable cause,' Granger affirmed, still staring at the piece of paper.

'I have a friend in the Postal Service. She did some checking on my behalf and told me the only location she's aware of in Texas with that particular title is approximately three miles north of Round Rock. She was helpful enough to provide an address.'

Granger thought about that. 'How can you be sure it's the same house?'

'I can't, but one has to begin somewhere. Doesn't *this* house having the same name make it a worthwhile starting point? And the fact that Round Rock is only some twenty miles from here?'

'I suppose so,' he admitted. 'Do you know who owns it?'

'I believe the sole name on the register is a Mr Dwight Salinger.'

Granger nodded. 'You've certainly been busy.'

'Having confirmed such a house exists, it seemed good policy to hand over the reins to someone ... well, somebody more experienced in these matters. Suppose I'd talked to the police, and they inadvertently gave this individual a chance to cover his tracks? The opportunity would be wasted, no? I think this approach is better. If Karine *was* taken to this place—and I know in my heart she was—I can only assume a murderer owns the house, Mr Granger. It's obviously dangerous, which is why I called you.' She set down the teacup by its delicate handle. 'Will you go there? As you can see, I'm fairly comfortable here; I'm sure I can pay you what you ask.'

'Mrs Martinez, I'm a reporter, not a private eye.'

An expression of disappointment crossed her face. Then she seemed to steel herself and said, 'I assume in your career you've occasionally deemed it necessary to ... bend the rules, dare I say? Resort to unorthodox strategy, perhaps? I'm requesting you look into this for me, just as my son might have tasked you with an assignment. And who knows, you might even land yourself a great story.'

'There's something I don't understand,' Granger told her, scratching his cheek. 'If all you've got is a house name, how do you know what Karine—if indeed it *was* your granddaughter—how do you know what she was referring to? Couldn't the name of a house mean, well, just about anything?'

'Karine disappeared, Mr Granger. And she's found a way to tell me where her remains are.' She stared at him, and in her pale grey eyes, Granger could see desperation. 'I know it,' she assured him. 'I feel it in my heart. So I'm asking you to trust me.'

Granger stood and crossed to the French doors. Beyond the terrace, on a sunlit ribbon of road, a big rig headed into the distance. Much closer, a blackbird angled graciously across the sky and found itself on a high perch, facing the house.

'If somebody abducted or killed Karine, Mrs Martinez—and I sincerely hope that isn't the case—I owe it to Ed to look into it.' He turned to her, hands in the pockets of his leather jacket. 'It sure wouldn't be a matter of money.'

*****

Keeping to the shadows, Granger slinks by small shrubs and what appears in the dark to be juniper bushes. He finds the drive's gradient more precipitous than it looks, or perhaps he's more out of shape than he thought, the exertion robbing his wind and working the dormant muscles of his calves.

The property is built of wood panelling in various stages of ill repair. Ancient paintwork has flaked and peeled from its sash frames. Glistening rainwater drips from dilapidated eaves. High exterior lighting, rather incongruous on such a neglected abode, stretches Granger's shadow across the grounds, making him feel vulnerable, despite there being nothing and nobody for miles. A rusted oval nameplate reading HILLCREST HOUSE is fixed to the wall by the weathered front door.

Granger cannot believe he's got himself involved—doesn't know what to make of the message-from-the-other-side malarkey—but acknowledges it's too late to back out. In any event, if someone here has hurt Ed's daughter, difficult as it is to accept, he owes it to his old friend to probe. Of this much, at least, he's sure.

He pulls on leather gloves and slinks around the back. No interior lights are visible on this side, either, which indicates nobody else is home. He peers in a grime-smeared window but can't see a damn thing. The rain's getting steadily heavier, so he opens his collar and moves on, staying close to the house, and soon comes to a rickety-looking door of frosted-glass panels. He sets his back to it before jabbing an elbow sharply through a pane by the handle. Broken pieces tinkle down inside. After clearing away the larger shards, he reaches in and, following a minute of blind perseverance, has the door open.

And so past the point of no return.

Inside, avoiding winking glass on the floor, Granger shuts the door behind him, letting his breathing level out.

As the downfall intensifies outside, he thumbs on his little torch, exposing a shithole kitchen. Jesus—the stink of what must be spoiled food is unbearable. Pots and pans jumbled in a sink, cereal packets everywhere. Honey Nut Cheerios. Frosted Mini-Wheats. Cocoa Pebbles. Countless tins of soda on a breakfast table. Unwashed plates and leavings. Cartons of apple juice. Milk. The worktop stops short of the corner, leaving a conspicuously empty space in which Granger imagines an appliance should be. His cone of torchlight finds a cooker and washing machine but no refrigerator. He masks his face with his sleeve as he proceeds further into the house.

He resists switching on a light: it'll make searching a whole lot simpler, but it's risky, should Salinger—or whoever the hell lives here—return unannounced.

The hallway floor is faded hardwood, sections of which are

missing, revealing the joists beneath like a wooden skeleton. He shines the circular torchlight on a tasselled runner. An empty coat-stand. The walls are damaged with sporadic raggedy holes as if someone has ventilated their frustrations on the plaster. *Or perhaps struggled or fought?* Granger thinks. As he creeps along, playing the beam into various rooms, he incurs stirrings of that primal fear, that innate uneasiness that only comes alive in the darkness.

And suddenly, a figure moves up ahead.

His heart leaps, and he goes for the gun—until he realises it's a mirror reflection.

Composure back in check then, he enters a room to his left—an old parlour—shining the torch into the farthest corners. There's a battered settee positioned against one wall, stuffing oozing out here and there. Situated immediately by the window is a wooden chair, a simple spindle-back affair, which seems a little out of place, so Granger crosses the stained carpet for a closer look.

There's a plate of bread crusts on the sill and an empty bottle of Gatorade. Evidently, someone has been stationed at this window. From his car, Granger had been concentrating on a room above, the one with the light on, and hadn't paid much heed to the other windows. He leans past the curtain and risks a cautious glance outside. The far-off glow of Round Rock shimmers distantly, but the nearby spot where Granger's Chevrolet is hidden in the trees reveals nothing except darkness.

Back in the hall, he senses that vile smell getting stronger. His spanning torch finds a skin mag on a small table, a scarlet-lipped brunette in bunny ears, cupping a breast in each hand, winking salaciously in Granger's spotlight as if finishing a burlesque routine. He pauses by an uncarpeted staircase, waiting, placing gloved fingers on the newel post, pointing his torchlight at faded risers right to the top. Then he notices another door to his left, housing a single pane of leaf-design opaque glass.

Granger steps across and carefully tests the knob, and with a dry screech, the door swings inwards, disconcertingly loud in the silence. His light finds a flight of steep stone stairs leading downwards, the terrible stink stronger yet from in there. And different too. Something with a chemical base. Granger hesitates a few seconds; then he descends, angling his feet almost sideways, so steep are the steps.

Below the ground floor, he plays the beam around and locates an old-fashioned toggle switch, flicks it up. An overhead bulb blinks rapidly, causing his eyes to do likewise, revealing the basement's interior.

'Holy Christ ...'

He sees the blood first, streaked down the outside of an ancient claw-foot bathtub near the far wall. The tub's inside is a gory mess of red splatters, as if it's been used for drainage. Beside it, two iron shackles, currently empty, are attached to ringbolts in the wall by lengths of rusted chain. A few feet away, a tall white fridge-freezer is stationed in the middle of the space, its white doors stained in bloody handprints. A filthy workbench with a metal vice attached displays a jumble of deadly implements, hatchets and hacksaws and lengthy serrated knives. And nearby stands an empty oil drum, surrounded by plastic containers of hydrochloric acid, a respirator mask, heavy-duty rubber gloves, eye goggles, and what looks like a black leathery apron. Atop another, larger table are severed human limbs—a slim white forearm, a hairless shin and a foot.

Young girls are missing all over the state, so they tell me.

Granger's stomach lurches. His stunned attention roams the

basement, falling on shelving against the side wall, ledges stocked with glass jars, all housing dismembered hands—female hands—floating grotesquely in cloudy preservative. The slender, shapely fingers are curled slightly as if beckoning him, and as he steps towards the nearest jar, peering through the colourless liquid, he notices this hand's fingernails are lacquered black, the index finger adorned with a ring bearing a little silver skull.

Granger crosses to the dirty fridge and opens its door. Inside, under stark light, are clear plastic packets, dark red with blood, containing what look like various sizes of organs—heart, kidneys, liver—all nestled in a tray of glinting ice. As the thermostat clicks on, he delves into his jacket for his cell. *Jesus, someone is harvesting organs*. He has to have pictures. He can't believe this, just can't believe—

'Havin' a good look?'

He pivots, all but losing his footing.

First, he acknowledges the shotgun barrel levelled at his chest. A 12-gauge, he'd say. He then takes in the imposing individual wielding the weapon: broad, dressed in black, his scarred face hideously ugly, bordering on deformity, wild eyes set too far apart and evincing blatant madness.

This repellent character sniggers, sounding like a strange breed of simian, revealing wide spaces between crooked teeth. His slab of a chin glistens with spittle.

'Close the fridge,' he says in a deep baritone. 'That's none of your business.'

Granger pushes closed the door, never taking his eyes from that barrel.

'Let's see the hands.' The big man twitches the shotgun. 'Come on, get 'em up.'

Granger edges a couple steps back, raising his palms. 'Take it easy with that thing, fella ...'

'Knew you musta been hanging round for a reason,' the freak says, jutting out his square chin, stepping closer.

'You saw me out there?'

'Course I saw. Dumb shit. Watching the whole time.' He takes a hairy hand from the weapon and touches the binoculars around his neck, which Granger hadn't even noticed. 'Night vision,' he says, laughing goofily as if the situation's but a game. 'For spottin' snoopy assholes in the dark.'

'You're the good Samaritan, I take it, providing organs to the needy?'

'There are folks who pay top dollar for them inside bits,' the big man confirms, grinning. 'Surely do.'

Granger frowned. 'How do you determine their blood types? To ensure the organs match?'

'Take a sample when I bring 'em here. Irons hold 'em while it's tested. Someone always needs what I got.'

'Maybe not if they knew how you got it.'

'You'll find desperate folks ain't none too picky.'

Granger stares at him. 'What's with the jars?'

The big man regards the floating hands. 'Well, hell, I keep some things for myself.' He gives Granger a horrid smile. 'Rest goes in the acid. What are you, a cop?'

'Reporter.'

'No shit. How'd a hack get wind o' this?'

'You really wouldn't believe it.'

'Don't matter none.' He snorts and motions with the barrel. 'Back up there and get in the tub. Don't wanna be moppin' your dumb ass off the floor.'

Granger's stomach leaps again as he envisions the effects of the 12-gauge. 'Hey, wait a minute. I have ... colleagues who know I'm here.'

'That was true, you wouldn't be sneakin' around on your own. Stand in the tub, mister—or I spill you right there.'

Palms up, Granger retreats another step, nearing the blood-splattered bathtub. His hip catches a small table, wobbling one of those empty glass jars. Instinctively he reaches to steady it—then splays his fingers and, in one motion, hurls the jar at his assailant and dives clear. The jar shatters against the wall as a thunderous shot blows the little table to smithereens, splinters of wood flying as Granger takes cover behind the fridge-freezer. Ears ringing, he pulls the revolver as a second blast rocks the fridge, almost toppling it, buckshot tearing ragged holes in the aluminium.

'Stick your face out, reporter, I'll make it nice'n quick.'

As the big goon emits mutant laughter, Granger drops to one knee, aiming quickly, firing two shots into his chest. The shotgun arcs wide, releasing a third blast—what should be its last, Granger vaguely registers—obliterating one of the shelved jars like a bomb detonating. But the ogre remains upright, ragged chest wounds oozing blood, eyeing Granger with a confused expression which soon morphs back into a grin. The shotgun swings from his finger by the trigger guard before clattering to the floor. He lumbers forward through lingering gun smoke, binoculars hanging, arms raised, meaty fingers curled as if set to wring the intruder's neck—so Granger sights between the big man's set-apart eyes and puts a round in his forehead.

The impact takes him blundering back, falling like a drunk against the stone steps, mouth open, pupils rolled as if trying to see the softly smoking bullet hole in his own skull.

*****

Outside, free of the sickening stench, Granger fills himself with untainted air. Hands shaking, he calls the cops from his cell, disclosing only enough information to get them here.

'Send a forensics unit,' he tells the dispatcher. '...The place is a slaughterhouse.'

He slumps down on the front step, hanging his head in the rain, the .38 still clutched in his hand. He's owned the gun a long time, but never has he taken a life. He harbours no sense of guilt, however; it was a kill or be-eviscerated-by-shotgun scenario. There's no sign of the maniac's car, he notices, meaning the sneaky sonofabitch had returned to the house on foot.

Looking at starlight above the shimmering lights and shadowed rooftops of Round Rock, Granger thinks about the grisly set-up in the basement, the floating hands, the grievous waste of life. He considers Karine Martinez's message to her grandmother and the unknowable realm from where it came. He'll think about this a great deal in days and weeks to come, he's sure. For, after all, these events will undoubtedly alter his worldview, such as it is. In fact, he feels sure his time as a reporter is finally over. He wonders with what kind of headline his old boss would have led such a horror story. 'CHARNEL HOUSE DISCOVERED OUTSIDE ROUND ROCK', perhaps. Yeah, he decides. That's about what Ed would've gone with.

He remains there until the first police cruiser ascends the drive, its light bars silently flashing.

*****

Later that day, back in the old lady's sunlit lounge.

'You were right,' Granger says, walking the room, pausing at the French doors. He hasn't slept, having been with the police, fielding questions, for hours. He gazes out and notices the blackbird is back on its perch, across the way, looking at the house again. Looking at him. 'I'd, uh, sooner not go into details,' he tells her, remembering severed hands and misappropriated organs. 'Suffice to say Karine was taken there, just as you said ... You'll no doubt hear what went on in due course.'

'I know what went on,' Mrs Martinez says.

He turns around. 'You do?'

She indicates the Ouija board and planchette on the coffee table and a page of notepaper full of neatly transcribed handwriting. 'It seems Karine can communicate easier now that it's over.'

Granger nods and finds himself smiling at her.

'She tells me she can fly,' the old woman says brightly.

'Fly?'

Her attention goes to the board. 'That's what she communicated. Anyway, it's a comfort to know she's still with me in some capacity. Will the police come here, Mr Granger? To speak with me?'

'I told them I got an anonymous tipoff. A citizen with suspicions.'

'They believed you?'

'Probably not. Hard to say at this point, but my story won't change. I think they're just glad to have a break in all those missing-person cases.'

Back outside, in the early afternoon sun, the sky is vast and bright. Approaching the car, keys in hand, he spots the blackbird on a picket fence across the road. Somehow he feels sure it's the very one he's seen from the French doors, the one that lighted on his Chevrolet's hood that night. Impossible to know, but he feels it just the same. It caws at him, an exotic one-syllable word, before extending its wings and rising into the air. Granger stands there, squinting, shielding his tired eyes against the fierce sunlight, watching its dark form work higher and higher, watching it become gradually fainter until, finally, there is only a clear blue sky.

Disappearing Act

Ian's hands trembled as he slumped into his Jaguar and eased down the electric window. He inhaled calming breaths of December night air. Drops of rain dampened his cheek. When he'd regained composure, he gunned the engine, which turned over smoothly, hit the lights, and edged from the drive. Squinting through his glasses, he accelerated up the street between denuded trees. His teeth ground together as his mind, unbidden, replayed Miriam's belligerent words.

Go on, get in your damn fancy car, do another disappearing act. Drive away like you always do. That's your answer to everything, isn't it? Go on, run away and practise your stupid magic tricks.

She called it running away; Ian called it his Time Out.

He was still shaking his head as he veered off Silverfern Road, where he and Miriam had stayed for better than eight years. On the surface, they lived an enviable life in the town's most affluent area— but their blessings went sailing over his wife's empty head. It mattered not that he'd purchased a beautiful four-bedroom house, an expensive car, five-star holidays and first-class flights, extortionate handbags and shoes that contented her only until the next design hit the shelves. All this and whatever else she dropped unsubtle hints for. Miriam took it all for granted. Her limitless sense of entitlement kept dogged pace with his earnings as if she couldn't bear that there might be something in the pot to which she hadn't yet laid claim.

Ian drew up at a set of lights. The car in front had one of those 'BABY ON BOARD' signs in the back. He shook his head. He couldn't understand the purpose of such things. How did one alter his driving to accommodate an infant in another car? It suggested people drove like maniacs unless aware of The Baby. It was almost insulting.

He looked left, where a pack of hooded youths idled outside a convenience store, the white splash from the electronic sign washing them in cold light. They swigged from bottles and called at each other, and Ian felt glad he wasn't that age any more.

The lights changed and he moved off.

Miriam wasn't the same woman he'd married, bearing scant resemblance to the easygoing blonde he'd fallen for. He didn't expect her to be some sort of trophy wife, but she could at least make an effort. Where had it all gone awry? How had they ended up poles apart? At a mere thirty-two years old, he felt aged and distanced from the man he once was, so ground down that a weary resignation had seized hold of him.

Headed towards the town's outer limits, he squinted under the blaze of oncoming headlights before activating the car's full beams. Rain thrummed on the roof. The car's interior was dark, dashboard dials and instruments illuminated in orange and red. He activated the CD player, and Dire Straits began 'Your Latest Trick.' But even music couldn't take his mind from her constant nagging.

She was always having a go about something. Lately, not for the first time, it was his lifelong hobby—performing magic. He'd always enjoyed the process, the trickery, and although it was harmless enough, she wouldn't allow him even this simple indulgence.

For his eighth birthday, his parents had presented him with a magic set, complete with a black top hat, wand, and cape. The gift had struck a chord, the interest took hold, and Ian spent hours every day rehearsing, posturing before the mirror, perfecting every flamboyant revelation until it became second nature. He had mastered those tricks, juvenile though they were, and gradually escalated his efforts to more challenging and visually impressive endeavours.

His teen sweetheart, Miriam, was the only thing Ian had worshipped more than performing tricks. When he still lived with his parents, she would spray perfume on his pillow to make him think of her in her absence. Back then, before he'd landed his lucrative line-manager's position with the pharmaceutical company—Johnson and Johnson, no less—they'd been at their happiest. Next, they had rented a one-bedroom apartment, not earning enough to be frivolous, but they'd known contentment, and life had been great, for the most part. They'd had sex regularly, laughed a great deal, and it had seemed they always would. And Miriam had been supportive of his magic—or perhaps she'd only tolerated it. Yes, tolerated, as if expectant that he'd one day mature and realise magic had no place in a marriage. But should a person abandon a lifelong interest to please another?

Following the wedding and fortnight in Hawaii, Miriam had run to seed, as if he was no longer worth the effort. This had hurt, though Ian knew better than to broach such a thorny subject. Miriam's threshold for criticism was low; her response to it was disproportional and scathing. As time passed, she ballooned by four stone. She lounged around in anything with an elastic waist—when she wasn't parading her ever-increasing designer wardrobe in clubs and swanky restaurants. Her occasional cigarette became a pack a day—a habit he'd ditched in his twenties—and the lingering stench on her and the house was—

'Awful,' he muttered, shaking his head. A lorry sped past in the opposite direction, buffeting the car. The rising tempo of drums introduced 'Money For Nothing.'

She devoured chocolate, crisps, and Indian takeaway insatiably and whiled away entire weeks watching soul-crushing soaps he couldn't abide. Failing that, it was her blog and her Twitter account.

Any common thread that existed between them had long since snapped. Their love life had suffered a slow death as if every consumed chocolate robbed her libido—and the damned stuff was called an aphrodisiac. She ignored him much of the time, which he often chose to interpret as kindness. When Miriam did bother with him, it was invariably to complain about him rehearsing tricks or when she wanted something for the house.

What shade of drapes should we get in here, Ian? We need a Persian rug for over there, wouldn't you say? There's a grand Kashan I've had my eye on. It's hand-knotted and a hundred per cent wool. And we need some new scatter cushions; I saw satin ones with 3D-effect roses. For God's sake, Ian, you could at least show some interest. I know you'd rather be pulling satin hankies from your sleeve, but you can hear me, can't you?

And so it went, on and on. Listening to her, anybody would think she earned half the money, although she did nothing more than whittle it away on needless tat, most of which they had in abundance already. Their quarrels usually ended the same way: him getting in the car and driving around to cool off. His blessed Time Out. It annoyed the hell out of her, so Ian drew pleasure in doing it all the more. Far better than wading into another no-win debate. The truth was, she no longer loved him, and vice-versa. But Miriam had accustomed herself to having everything and intimated that she'd fleece him for it all should they separate.

Some of the blame stopped with him, of course.

Marital problems are rarely one-sided. He'd given her everything she'd asked for, after all. Easier to buy the damned Kashan rug and scatter cushions and whatever materialistic clutter she craved. He'd tried denying Miriam before, but she'd caused such an almighty stink that it wasn't worth the trouble. Maybe she was testing him, though—

Ian knew women did this to ascertain whether their man would stand his ground. Well, he didn't have the patience for her button-pushing, not any more.

Palming a beat on the steering wheel, he followed the endless centreline and cat's eyes, straining to see through his prescription lenses, his neck jutted out towards the windshield. Clustered spruce trees flitted past behind split-rail fences. The rain was thickening to sleet, teeming in the headlamps. It all made him feel depressed. The more he tried not to think of Miriam ... the more he thought of her.

She picked away at him all the time. Pick-pick-pick. Only this morning, she'd had another tiresome dig about his magic.

'Why don't you get a proper hobby?' she'd said, working her way through a tub of chocolate ice cream. 'You could do something manly instead of—of shuffling cards and making stupid coins vanish.'

'I like tricks,' he told her. 'What's wrong with tricks?'

'For God's sake, Ian, what're you like?'

'I liked magic when you married me, Miriam.'

'You're such a wet blanket.'

Pick-pick-pick.

Miriam didn't understand the buzz he got from well-executed tricks. Typically, she didn't appreciate the time and effort invested in getting the sleight of hand just right. Why would she? She couldn't even appreciate the time and effort it took to earn the money she drew so much pleasure in frittering away. In an attempt to please her—was that even possible?—he sometimes tried to involve her in the magic, but she complained and disliked the rigmarole of the following instruction. She found the process awkward, time-consuming, and embarrassing besides—and although he persevered, she just wasn't interested. She'd forget which card she'd picked or ruin an illusion because she couldn't concentrate, and Ian knew this was direct to needle him rather than any genuine failure on her part.

He dipped his beams as another lorry hurtled past, sluicing rainwater across the windscreen in its wake. The wipers lunged back and forth. He slipped his thumb and index finger beneath his glasses, rubbed at his eyes.

They no longer even socialised together. On increasingly rare evenings, Ian ventured out with friends. He was obliged to ask Miriam along, of course, aware she always refused. She'd tell him to go and have a good time, and the next day he'd endure the silent treatment and the full force of petulance as if he'd wantonly abandoned her to go out boozing.

Thankfully they'd never had children—kids would've only complicated matters further. Miriam had never revealed a maternal side, and judging by the infrequency of their coupling, motherhood wasn't a priority. Perhaps she simply didn't want a family with *him*.

Ian's eyes went to the rear-view mirror, finding only darkness there. Coming down through the gears, he pulled off the main road, following a makeshift track into the trees, loose stones clanking against the manifold. The headlamps found a small, pale animal as it scampered across his path and the startled incandescent eyes of another. The Jag jounced along the rutted way a little farther before Ian doused the lights and shut off the engine, silencing Dire Straits mid-song.

He listened to the faint sounds of the engine cooling before alighting from the car, raising his collar against the cold. The sleet had petered out. Glistening silver birches swayed in the chill breeze. Stream water whispered somewhere close by. The winter sky held a gibbous moon and was dappled with stars. He heard the faraway engines of a descending plane. He plucked off his glasses and went at them with a handkerchief, his breath forming in little clouds. Amber orbs of distorted light identified the town, several miles in the distance.

Ian examined the lenses and slipped them back on. As he blinked, so the town's far-off glow sharpened into focus. He stepped around to the boot, lifted it open, and stared inside at the heavyset form wrapped in the Kashan rug. A hundred per cent wool it was. Hand knotted.

'You always hated magic,' he said. 'But you'll be part of my greatest ever trick, Miriam, dearest.'

Ian withdrew the shovel, eased down the boot, and strode purposefully into the woods, about to perform the ultimate disappearing act.

Hard Shoulders In The Sky

For several years now, it's been my intention to make a written record of this. An affair which came to pass in 2012 it burdens me yet, despite the time elapsed. I doubt that writing it down will ease the regret, but perhaps transcribing it from memory to paper will have a cathartic effect. Perhaps it will put an end to the nightmares.

Amanda's trouble was first brought to my attention by her older brother, Greg. I'd attended secondary school with him, where we'd run in the same circles and were once fairly good friends.

When we met again many years later, I didn't recognise him at first. Our fortieth birthdays were bearing down when he turned up at my office unannounced. He'd lost most of his sandy hair while retaining the lean build that helped him excel at most sports in school. After I made us coffee, he indicated the photograph on my desk of me and my wife, which started us talking. As it turned out, Greg had married the year after I had.

'Kids?' I asked him.

'One girl,' he said. 'She's seven. You?'

'We've a little boy,' I told him. 'Couple of years younger.'

'Time certainly flies, huh?' He drank some coffee. 'You've fared better in the hair-loss department,' he said, carefully replacing the cup and touching his balding pate.

'Ah, but you're slimmer, so we'll call it even.' I patted my stomach. 'Alright, what can I do for you, Greg?'

He shrugged and looked away. 'My sister's been having

problems,' he said. 'I've thought about trying to get her some help for a while now. Anyway, I bumped into someone from school a few weeks back, and he mentioned you do this for a living. Bit of a surprise, really.' He smiled. 'I figured it'd be better talking to a familiar face than dealing with a stranger, right? So, I looked you up, and, well, here I am.'

'Okay, I'm listening.'

'Do you remember my sister, Dave?' he asked.

'Vaguely,' I told him, which was the truth.

I'd seen Amanda at Greg's parents' house two or three times. I recalled her as a freckly teenager, flitting in and out of her room, peeping and giggling around doorways, no doubt excited by a house full of older boys. She'd just wanted to be part of the fun, I think, typical of a girl that age.

Greg stood and stepped across to the window, regarding autumnal West London, lightly brushing the arm of his navy suit. 'I love her, but I can't seem to help her through this.' He turned and looked at me with worry in his eyes. 'Would you talk to her?'

I observed him from behind my desk. 'What exactly is the trouble?'

'She lost her husband in a plane crash back in 2009.' He stared again through the blind. 'She's been plagued by it ever since. She doesn't sleep, hardly talks to anyone ... It's consuming her from the inside.'

'That's terrible,' I said. 'I'm so sorry to hear that.'

'You'll remember the flight, no doubt. Air France 447. A commercial flight from Rio de Janeiro to Charles de Gaulle International in Paris.'

That rang a bell: it was an infamous case. The news channels were full of it when it happened. 'The airbus?'

He nodded and shrugged. 'She can't get it out of her head.'

I made an appointment for Amanda to come in later that week and did some brushing up on the flight in question. The A330 airbus had crashed over the Atlantic in the darkness of 1 June 2009, killing all 228 souls onboard (216 passengers and 12 cabin crew). What was termed the worst accident in French aviation history was initially all the more unsettling by the plane's apparent disappearance. No distress calls had been received from AF447, and neither the French nor the Brazilians had any idea why or where it met its fate.

Fifty bodies were eventually recovered from the ocean in June 2009 by the Brazilian Air Force, some of which were identified, although attempts to find the wreckage were unsuccessful, even after a French nuclear submarine searched for the black boxes with Naval listening equipment. Indeed, it would be 2011 before the flight recorders were recovered using autonomous underwater vehicles. When investigators heard the recordings captured that fateful night, it began to shed light on a terrible but avoidable tragedy.

Reading about it gave me a chill. Imagining the fate of those lost, the scale of the search, it was hard not to feel a degree of sympathy.

Greg dropped Amanda off on a Tuesday afternoon and left us together. In her mid-thirties, retaining the mousy features of her youth, brown hair in a dishevelled tress, she sat across the desk, pale and subdued in a rumpled turquoise dress that almost matched her sea-blue eyes. Dark crescents beneath those eyes testified that she hadn't slept peacefully in some time. I saw nothing of the giggling, exuberant girl I'd witnessed in her parents' house.

'Thanks for coming in,' I said. 'Would you like anything,

Amanda, before we start? Something to drink?'

She shook her head. 'I didn't want to come, but my brother insisted.'

'That's okay. You're here now. Greg thought I might be able to help you with your troubles. Would you like to talk about the accident?'

'I can't stop thinking about it,' she told me.

'Your husband died on the flight. That must have been terribly difficult for you.'

She nodded meekly but offered nothing more. She peered around the office uncomfortably as if apprehensive of some hidden threat.

'Why don't you tell me about him?' I said.

She flinched then, presumably at the sound of a plane coming in towards Heathrow. It was common to hear them throughout the day.

'Tom was wonderful,' she finally said. 'Tender-hearted. He always loved travelling, flying especially. His work took him all over.'

'What did he do?'

'He was a motivational speaker.'

I sat forward. 'Is it specifically how Tom died that troubles you, Amanda?'

She didn't answer, just sat there picking at a chewed fingernail.

'Amanda?'

She looked up at me as if she hadn't heard. I asked the question again.

'I thought it'd be easier to deal with once they found the plane.'

'And it wasn't?'

She still appeared tense, so I took it as a positive sign that she was talking at all. 'Once they located those flight recorders they were looking for,' she said, 'I thought I'd at least know what happened. I thought I could try to go on with life. But I ... I can't.'

'Can you tell me why not?'

She bit her lip, like a frightened young girl with a secret. The day suddenly brightened, casting us in shadowed slats from the blind. The ring on her finger shone as she spun it absently, turning it easily as if she'd lost weight. 'I keep imagining what it must've been like for him. For all of them. He didn't deserve to die like that.'

'Reports suggested that the passengers probably didn't know much of what was happening,' I offered, hoping to ease her burden. 'It said they were killed on impact, that they didn't suffer.'

She looked at me as if I were naïve.

'That thing came down at more than ten thousand feet per minute. How could they not know what was happening? They were flying through storms before it fell into the sea. There was turbulence. They would have known.'

She wasn't about to be swayed on this, and I have to say I agreed with her. It struck me as unlikely the passengers could be unaware of impending death—or at least that something was dangerously wrong. The airbus crashed due to an aerodynamic stall: ice had gathered on something called the 'pitot tubes', depriving airspeed sensors of the air pressure required to provide accurate information. Eventually, the automatic pilot relinquished control back to the crew, but without valid data from cockpit computers, Co-pilot Bonin—the youngest and most inexperienced of the three—had lifted the airbus's nose continually, causing a loss of airspeed, whereupon a stall sent it plummeting. By the time the most senior pilot, Captain Dubois, had been roused from sleep, the situation was hopeless.

It's worth noting, however, that before the plane stalled, the pilot could've dipped its nose rather than raising it—the action required to stabilise the situation. At no time did the A330 actually fail, although its malfunctioning computers left pilots unsure which readings were trustworthy—which, I suppose, amounts to the same thing.

'I don't even know what happened in his final moments,' Amanda said. 'When they eventually found the plane, thousands of feet down, parts of it were intact ... Over a hundred bodies were still strapped in the seats. Tom wasn't one of them.'

I adjusted myself in the chair, somewhat disturbed by this grim image. 'He wouldn't have wanted you to grieve forever, Amanda,' I told her. 'It's been years since the accident.'

'Whenever I close my eyes, I see the cabin lights going out, see the plane hurtling into the ocean, coming apart, sinking to the bottom. I imagine those poor people trapped inside, their hair floating up in the water. I see Tom down there in the depths, rotting. I think about him being gradually eaten away by ...'

I brought a hand across my mouth, staring at her. I hadn't really appreciated how much this woman had been affected by the loss. She sounded truly haunted by the disaster. I wondered if she had any history of depression, if she was, for some reason, disposed to letting negative experiences get on top of her.

It seemed I needed to come at this from a different angle, though I wasn't sure what that might be.

'Do you travel by plane?' I asked.

'I'll never step on an aeroplane again.' She shook her head at the thought. 'Not now, not after what happened.'

'Have you ever had an unpleasant experience while flying?'

She thought about it, then shook her head again.

'You know statistically it's safer than driving?'

'There are more cars on the roads than planes in the air.' She whispered this as if it were something she'd considered many times, perhaps lying alone in bed, staring at the ceiling in the small hours. 'If something goes wrong, I'd sooner take my chances in a car. There aren't any hard shoulders in the sky.'

'No,' I conceded. 'I suppose that's true.'

'They hit the sea in the dark ...'

'You can't keep torturing yourself like this, Amanda. People are killed in accidents every day. Sometimes nobody's to blame, and there's nothing we can do but try to stop the same thing from happening again. That's why investigators don't give up until they find the flight recorders, even when it takes years. You must understand that Tom is at peace, that any pain he suffered has long since passed. It's time to move on with your life.'

'That's what my brother says.'

'He's right. Losing loved ones in such a dramatic manner is bound to hurt relatives and friends. Ultimately we carry on because there's nothing else we *can* do.'

I arranged another appointment for her, though I was doubtful she'd ever leave those events behind. My doubts were reinforced when I looked out of my office window following that first conversation. I watched Greg escort her across the leaf-strewn car park. Amanda suddenly stopped, looking up at the overcast sky. At first, I didn't realise what had seized her attention—and then the plane came into view. Bound for Heathrow, its engines roared as the undercarriage passed overhead. Greg tried to guide her towards the car, but Amanda stared after the plane until it landed, shoulders hunched, small feet rooted to the tarmac. The sight reminded me of that frightened little girl again, and I didn't need a degree to know what she was thinking about.

Later that night, during our evening meal, my wife commented more than once that I seemed miles away. Was there anything wrong? I told her I was fine and smiled falsely but remained preoccupied with the day's events. Part of me wanted to discuss Amanda's case with her because I couldn't stop thinking about it, but I didn't say anything. After we'd finished the dishes, my wife said she was going upstairs to take a shower. With our black Lab curled on the settee beside me, I opened the laptop and found online a documentary recounting the chain of events concerning Air France 447.

It covered the whole disaster, from the pilots' initial witnessing of St Elmo's fire, through the escalating confusion and ending, of course, with the fatal plunge. There was mention of the excessive reliability on airliners' computers and autopilot functions. The documentary brought into question the modern pilot's capability and expertise. For instance, should something so unexpected occur that the technically sophisticated aircraft relinquished control—were pilots sufficiently skilled to manage the situation? I watched the professionals discuss the case. I heard the pilots' exchanges from that night as they became resigned to the certainty that they—and everybody else—were heading for the ocean. Dropping like a stone, as one contributor described it.

After the ground-proximity warning system sensed the ocean below, the pilots exchanged their last words.

Co-pilot Robert: 'What do you think? What do you think? What should we do?'

Captain Dubois: 'Go on, pull up!'

Co-pilot Bonin: 'Fuck, we're going to crash! This can't be true!'

*****

Greg came back three days later. In jeans and a cut-sleeve shirt, he looked pale and tired, somewhat like his sister had the day I'd spoken with her. I could tell that something was wrong.

'She's dead,' he said.

I felt my scalp prickle. 'Dead ...?'

'I just wanted to say, you know, thanks for trying with her.'

I stood up. 'What happened?'

He shook his head. His bottom lip was going and I could see he was fighting back the tears. He looked at the ceiling, and his Adam's apple moved. 'She opened her veins with a razor in the bath.'

'I'm so sorry, Greg.' It sounded pathetic, but I didn't know what else to tell him. After all those years of learning and studying, all of a sudden, I felt useless, as if I'd failed him, failed his sister.

'I think she just wanted to be with her husband again,' he said, nodding his head. 'Yeah, I think that's it.'

I was about to go to him when he turned and walked from the room without another word. I stood there stunned, looking at the empty doorway. Was he too emotionally overcome to talk to me? I wondered. Was he judging my abilities as a psychiatrist? Should I have been judging them myself?

Overhead, another plane descended into Heathrow.

*****

If I learned anything from Amanda's case, it was that you can't always make sound judgements where someone's mental state is concerned. Regardless of training or experience, it's not an exact science. It taught me not to make assumptions about the severity or nature of a patient's illness. This is undoubtedly a mistake I made to assume her suffering was less severe than it was. I could have made a greater effort to ease her burden, to convince her I could help. In all honesty, I never once suspected she'd take her own life, despite her restive disposition, despite her reaction to the landing plane. Despite the things she said.

I didn't recognise the signs. That was a failing on my part. And Amanda didn't foresee any salvation in me, which I suppose was another failing. Had she done, she surely wouldn't have taken such drastic action. Now I listen more closely when patients talk to me. I try harder to ease their troubles, to provide a solution if I can. I watch closely for any indication that suffering is outweighing the will to survive. I have Amanda to thank for that.

I think about AF447 a lot. I also dwell on those terrible images: the landing gear at the bottom of the sea, the flight recorder submerged in silt, the huge tailfin surrounded by salvagers. Mostly I contemplate what it must have been like for Amanda's husband; and all the others, of course. I imagine them up there in the night sky, isolated above the vast ocean, hundreds of strangers about to share one experience, the last they would ever know. So many dreams and plans and hopes for the future, each snuffed out after a few minutes of manic terror. I think about the accident every time I hear planes coming in above my office, a daily reminder.

The nightmare began shortly after Amanda's death. Always the same. In sleep, I see the wrecked airbus at the ocean's bottom, the passengers still strapped in the seats, staring at me. Some have shocked expressions, some seem perfectly calm. Large portions of their faces are gone, pale skulls showing beneath the tattered skin. Their hair floats above them like deep-sea plants.

I haven't flown since.

Among The Living

Three months after the combined funeral, when we called unannounced at his house in the country, we were surprised how far Tony had let things slide. He slumped down on the sofa as we filed into the living room behind him, exchanging glances. Unwashed highball glasses, plastic meal-for-one dishes, and empty Foster's cans cluttered every surface. The TV turned low, displayed some sort of archaeological dig, workers unearthing and analysing artefacts from beneath the ground.

'Hey, mate,' Vinnie said, picking his way through debris on the laminate floor. 'How you been doing?'

Dustin stood by the net-curtained window beside Tony's beloved red and white Stratocaster, its strings untouched since the accident. He slotted his hands in the pockets of his worn biker jacket, looking as uneasy as we all felt.

Greasy-haired and thin, like a castaway, Tony was an image of abject misery. 'I can't live without them,' he said, holding his forehead with one hand, his eyes tightly closed. 'I think about it all the time ... and I can't go on without them.' He wore blue denim shorts, flip-flops, and a stained T-shirt. He hadn't shaved in weeks, perhaps months. Because he'd always been clean-cut, polished even, and the house pristine, the disarray was particularly unsettling.

Vinnie cleared strewn clothes from the sofa, sat next to him. 'I know it feels that way now,' he began, 'but we'll help you through this the best we can; you know we will.'

'I'm forty-six,' Tony said, shutting off the TV with the remote. His eyes, wide and glaring in his emaciated face, gave him the glassy look of the permanently bereaved. 'Forty-six and I had to bury my family. What are you going to do about that, Vinnie?' He looked at the three of us in turn. 'Tell me, what're any of you gonna do?'

'We'll help you get the place back in order,' Vinnie stated, indicating the mess, trying to sound more assertive than he likely felt. 'Or if there's anything else ... Like sorting out Lorraine and Kyra's things, we'll help with that too. Only if you want, you understand.'

'You think I should get rid of their things,' Tony mumbled as if the idea were abhorrent. 'Get shot of the memories and get on with life?'

'Of course not,' Dustin said, scratching at his shorn blond hair. 'No. Nothing's gonna happen until you're good an' ready. We're just saying, you know, we're here to help. We know how hopeless it must feel. But you're not alone, mate, no matter how much it seems that way.'

Tony glared at him through bedraggled strings of hair. 'Save your platitudes. None of it's going to help me.' He stared into his lap. 'Nothing's going to help.'

'Are the meds doing any good?' Dustin asked, followed by an awkward silence. He touched one of the guitar's tuning pegs.

'I can't even tell,' Tony said with a kind of cynical sneer. 'Today, I'll feel one way; the next day, I feel something else. Drowsy. A little spaced out, maybe. I can't tell.'

'Have you considered going back to work?' Vinnie asked, pressing his fingertips together. 'Listen, I know it's a big step, but, well, maybe it's what you need to get things moving again.'

'The job's gone,' Tony moaned, bereft and shaking his head, sounding like a hopeless drunk. 'Bloody Lloyds. It's all gone. They told me they couldn't keep it open, so I told them to stick it.'

And it was clear that the bank, the career he'd spent years cultivating, meant nothing to him any more.

*****

At the end of July, Tony lost his wife and teenage daughter in a rail accident. Lorraine and Kyra had been visiting Lorraine's brother in the north of England, and travelling home, their train derailed due to a faulty set of points. All nine carriages collapsed down an embankment, broken and twisted every which way.

As his closest friends, we tried to be there for Tony as much as possible but grew increasingly aware he wasn't coping with the loss. We knew it was a devastating blow, of course, we did—but really had no idea how someone should endure such a cruel tragedy. Tony had been raised solely by his father, who'd died a couple of years prior, and as he had no siblings, we felt it our duty to stand by him. But as the weeks passed after the funeral, despite our efforts, he seemed to withdraw more and more into himself. Often, when we'd phone him about paying a visit, he made excuses to put us off. This was something he'd never done before the accident.

*****

We went for a beer after leaving Tony's, the order of the day for trying to iron out problems. The Plough isn't far from where Dustin lives and pretty handy for the rest of us too. We sat at a booth table, each obviously wondering how we could help our friend navigate his ocean of grief.

'Must be something we can do,' Dustin said, picking at the label on his Newcastle Brown.

'He's getting worse,' Vinnie added. (Vinnie had a wife and two

323

young boys, so was perhaps most able to relate to Tony's plight.) 'Things go on like this, God, he'll end up beyond help. You hear of these situations, right? People who just check out and throw in the towel.'

'Tony won't chuck in the towel,' Dustin ventured, eyeing us warily. 'Will he?'

'I'm not so sure,' Vinnie said, tapping the tabletop. 'He's drinking far too much, and that's on top of medication. Looks like shit. He's quit the bank. I mean, that was his *livelihood*, right? Good money? If he doesn't have the job, how does he plan to support himself?'

We contemplated this as autumn rain fell, the night dark and miserable. In a gloomy mood, we drank more than we should've, perhaps just for the company. Coming up with answers wasn't easy, that was for sure. Had we an inkling what lay ahead, though, we might've tried harder to help Tony.

*****

The four of us had been friends since secondary school (primary in Vinnie and Tony's case) and became increasingly close through our late teens and twenties. Borne along by youthful exuberance, we had great times on the fly with Dustin's various motorbikes and Vinnie's old-beater cars, taking camping trips that were really an ill-disguised reason to drink, listen to music, and smoke a little grass. At weekends, before his employment with the bank, we'd hit the town and watch the pub band Tony played in.

We'd stood in the Crichton Memorial Church in kilts and jackets and watched Tony and Lorraine marry. Lorraine was made up like a doll, very beautiful. Best man Vinnie, who was given to practical jokes, had served Tony a prolonged ribbing, revisiting embarrassing episodes and memorable adventures we'd shared over the years.

Vinnie spoke for us all when he raised a glass and toasted how perfect Lorraine was for Tony, how she shone a light into his life.

The newlyweds honeymooned for two weeks in Indonesia, the Raja Ampat Islands, an archipelago comprising Waigeo, Misool, Salawati, Batanta, and hundreds more minor islands besides. Tony, a keen photographer, returned with a multitude of snaps: a paradisal collection of forested backdrops, jade waters and famous reefs. He and Lorraine had travelled extensively, meeting locals, trying unusual cuisine, scuba diving, and learning of the indigenous customs and traditions throughout different regions.

'They got practices over there you wouldn't believe,' Tony told us once, flipping sizzling burgers in his back garden. The summer sun was ablaze, but for a second, his expression darkened as if something had stalked across his grave.

'Oh yeah?' Vinnie had asked from his sun lounger, draining a Heineken. 'Like what?'

Tony appeared ready to divulge something, then only shook his head. 'They're just not the same as us,' he said, glancing off at Lorraine, busy pruning her rosebushes. 'It's hard to say without ... without sounding disrespectful to their ways—which I don't want to do. I guess they must just look at life differently.'

Over successive years we got to know Lorraine pretty well. She was into outdoor activities, mainly cycling and hillwalking and kayaking, and Tony shared those interests, often enjoying the excursions as picture-taking opportunities. When Lorraine fell pregnant, she and Tony were ecstatic, and as close friends, we were part of their joy. Little Kyra was born about a week before Christmas, healthy and happy, and that year's celebrations were such that, to this day, they remain clear in our memories. Sometimes it's hard to believe they aren't here any more.

*****

A week after our previous visit, Vinnie drove us back to Tony's, an attractive limestone house that Lorraine used to decorate with window-box flowers in summer. Without her and Kyra there, however, we worried that the isolation, idyllic as it was, might be making Tony's situation worse. Again we hadn't phoned ahead in case he told us not to come.

Vinnie parked behind Tony's Audi in the drive.

Inside, the house was in worse shape than before and had begun to smell stale, so we rolled our sleeves and cleaned up without a word. We washed dishes, aired rooms, and dumped accumulated trash in black bags. Tony, still in cut-offs and a nondescript T-shirt, occupied the sofa as we busied ourselves around him. Bearded and miserable, he looked as if he hadn't eaten or slept properly in God knows how long. A plethora of honeymoon photographs were spread across the glass table before him, depicting images of Indonesia's various exotic locations. Lorraine, bronzed and lithe, smiled excitedly in many, wearing wide-brimmed hats and sarong skirts full of life. Set among the arrayed photographs was a near-empty bottle of Jack Daniel's and crystal glass. There were also books positioned here and there. *Indonesia: People and Histories; A Look at Modern Indonesia; Southeast Asia's Largest Nation; Indonesia, the Essential Guide to Customs and Culture.*

Although he found little food in the kitchen, Dustin, chef by trade, set about rustling something up. Vinnie convinced Tony to shower and shave and get into clean clothes. Tony clearly wasn't keen but had no fight in him, either.

He reappeared a short time later, still gaunt and tired-looking but shaved and in a fresh shirt and jeans. On the sofa, tray on his lap, straggly hair brushed back, he picked at scrambled eggs and beans, washing it over with sips of tea.

'Been reliving old memories?' Vinnie asked, indicating the scattered photos and books on the table.

Tony chewed slowly, gripping his fork and staring. 'We bought these books before the honeymoon,' he said solemnly. 'Read them on the plane, fourteen damned hours in the sky.'

'Why've you dug them out again?' Dustin asked.

He contemplated this. 'There's something I remembered seeing in one. Something I think might help me get past this ...'

'Yeah?' Vinnie prompted, looking at the books, interested. 'And what's that?'

'I don't want to discuss it just yet,' Tony told him.

Tony didn't look at us, but we eyed each other, wondering at the implicit meaning in what he'd said. It was a curious admission, all of a sudden. A strange turnaround that didn't necessarily make much sense. Was he finally accepting what had happened? Was he now willing to forge ahead with his life? Certainly, we hoped so. But just what had he been reading in those books?

*****

Because he'd always been so together, so grounded, it was heart-breaking to watch when Tony collapsed at the funeral. Personable, intelligent and funny, he had built a promising career and landed himself a fine family. So, when he had to be almost dragged from the white coffins in their open graves after it began to rain and get dark, it was new ground for us all. Seeing him that way, yelling and in tears, was like observing a different man, an individual so overborne by life's indifferent twists that we barely knew him. Yet we weren't entitled to judge his actions or responses. The guy had suffered a terrible loss, after all, a catastrophe far beyond our comprehension.

*****

The following Friday, after work, saw us drinking in the Plough. Its interior was decorated with spray-can webs and ghoulish props for the upcoming Halloween. Red glass bowls with tealight candles adorned the tables, creating an intimate, séance-like ambience. A mummy statue stood by the door, legs bound, bandaged hands crossed at its chest. We were in good spirits, tipsy, even managing a few laughs, feeling that maybe Tony was improving or at least inching along.

'I was thinking ...' Dustin paused over a mouthful of hamburger he'd ordered from the bar, '... it's strange how things happen, isn't it?'

We waited for him to elaborate.

He swallowed and laid the half-eaten burger on his plate. 'It's like, here you've got Lorraine and Kyra on this train, right?' Dustin made a fin shape with his hand and cut through the air, representing motion. 'Tony's not even travelling on the thing, but because it's faulty—the line or points or whatever—his life's been ruined too.'

'Are you saying he'd be better off if he hadn't met Lorraine?' Vinnie asked.

'No, no,' Dustin said, wiping his lips with a napkin. 'Just the opposite. I'm saying it's sometimes impossible to avoid tragedy, no matter how careful we are. That life brings it right along to you anyway.'

'We keep telling him everything'll be okay,' Vinnie said, his face partially lit by fluttering red candlelight. 'It's what you have to say, of course, it is. But if anything like that happened to my wife and kids ...

man, I don't reckon I'd be able to handle it.'

This depressing thought gave us pause. A gaggle of hen-night lasses, all succulent legs and sparkly tops, screamed and laughed at the bar. We were silent until Vinnie said something that snared our attention:

'Isn't it Lorraine's birthday around now?'

Dustin frowned. 'Is it?'

'I'm pretty sure. Remember the party Tony had for her a couple of years ago? It was a few days before Halloween, right?'

'Yeah,' Dustin agreed, pointing a finger. 'He was gonna make it fancy dress, changed his mind, last minute.'

'Maybe it's today,' Vinnie said thoughtfully, looking at us. 'D'you think we should head out there? It's probably not the time for him to be alone. I mean, he seemed to be making a little progress, didn't he? Be a shame to let this set him back again.'

'Yeah.' Dustin nodded, still pointing. 'He probably reckons nobody's even remembered. That no one cares.'

'All right, drink up, men,' Vinnie said decidedly, glancing towards the darkening street and reaching for his mobile. 'I'll phone a cab.'

*****

When Tony answered the door, he was smiling, which made us do likewise. His long hair had been oiled neatly back over his head. In jeans and a black Santana T-shirt, he appeared fairly together as he preceded us to the living room, where we immediately noticed random streaks of mud and dirt across the laminate floor. A pile of soiled garments was loosely stacked in the corner—what looked like a navy boiler suit, mud-caked work boots, and padded gloves. The photographs and books remained there on the table, possibly since our last visit.

'You been gardening or something, mate?' Vinnie asked, studying the boot-prints on the floor.

'Something much better,' Tony told us.

'You feeling okay?' Dustin asked warily.

'Better than I've felt in a long time,' he confirmed, still smiling. But the smile was strange, not like Tony at all.

'I want to show you guys something,' he said, opening one of the larger books from the coffee table. 'Okay. Have you ever heard of the Toraja people?' He looked at us in turn and, of course, we shook our heads. 'Their country stretches hundreds of miles across the mountainous interior of Sulawesi,' he said, flipping through pages. 'It's basically a widespread land of hills and scattered villages, connected by little more than dirt tracks. Lorraine and I heard of the Toraja folk when we were over there, and recently I've been thinking about them a great deal.'

'What do they do?' Vinnie asked, peering at the open book that Tony handed him.

'They have a festival every three years,' Tony explained as we inched closer. The book's pages were large and displayed many photographs, which had been taken in forested surroundings, depicting people native to the land. 'They exhume their loved ones from their coffins. Then they clean and dress them. They keep them in a state of preservation, you see. Isn't that a radical idea? Isn't it amazing how different the world's cultures are?'

Vinnie positioned the book, so we could view it. The glossy photographs were nothing short of bizarre. They showed these Toraja people in what, at a glance, appeared to be average family snaps; but positioned among the healthy, living folk were ... upright corpses. Worse still, these dead individuals had been attired in fresh clothes—jackets, bright tropical shirts, sunglasses—as if attending a perfectly normal gathering. As if they could enjoy life like everybody else. Long-expired women wore necklaces and dresses. In one picture, the corpse had a smouldering cigarette in its mouth.

'Don't you see?' Tony was saying. 'Look how ... how at *ease* they are with their loved ones. I mean, this is absolutely normal to them.' He pointed emphatically at the book as if it held the answers to all his problems. 'Just look at the pictures; it's only a matter of—of culture, of upbringing, right?'

Vinnie flipped the page, revealing a picture of a young man combing the hair of an upright, suited male corpse. Next to this dead person, clutching a bouquet of flowers, was presumably his dead wife. In yet another photo, a man hoisted a swaddled dead infant for the camera. These bodies were old, decades old, desiccated over many years, barely held together by the brownish tissue covering their bones. Jesus, they looked like Mother in her fruit-cellar chair at the climactic end of *Psycho*. Vinnie again flipped the page and we saw a withered corpse dressed in what appeared to be a Nazi uniform. And another dead guy in a Hawaiian shirt. Vinnie had seen enough and closed and dropped the book as if it were rotten, something to be feared.

'Why the hell are you showing us this?' Dustin demanded. 'Christ, Tony, it's an insult to the dead.'

'That's your conditioning talking,' Tony said adamantly. 'I don't have to be separated from them, don't you see?'

'What're you babbling about?' Vinnie snapped and, looking down around himself, asked, 'Tony, what's with all the mud tracked across your floor?'

Tony's smile remained unsettling, like he'd borrowed it from someone else, like it didn't quite fit his face properly. He rolled his eyes as if we were all stupid. 'Haven't you understood what I'm telling you? I don't have to be away from my family any more. If I want them here, I can *have* them here ...'

We regarded each other.

'What do you mean?' Dustin asked, smirking, but only from nervousness.

'Come with me,' our friend told us, motioning with his hand. 'This way.'

He crossed towards closed double doors, which had brass handles and small panes of translucent glass. The doors let into the dining room. He opened them fully and stood aside like a tour guide.

Lorraine and Kyra were seated at the candle-lit dining table.

What remained of them.

Eerily canted, Lorraine's body was dressed in a black evening gown and delicate multi-chain necklace, the brittle remnants of thick locks messily framing an eyeless skull. Kyra's remains he'd dressed in a marshmallow-pink frock. Candlelight touched wild filaments of the corpse's straw-like hair. Its jaw hung hideously as if waiting to be fed. They didn't have quite the aged aspect of the Toraja dead, probably a matter of time or preservation, but they looked like hell, just the same.

Dustin, brought up short, made a weird little sound in his throat.

'Tony ... what the hell have you done?' Vinnie's words were choked with disbelief as he recoiled.

'It's Lorraine's birthday today,' Tony said, sounding strangely proud. 'And a birthday's always worth celebrating.'

They stared towards us—at us—vacant and dead, as if wondering what they were doing back here, above ground, among the living.

*****

We're heading up to the hospital tomorrow. Vinnie's collecting us outside the Plough in the afternoon. We have to try, don't we? Perhaps the professionals can help Tony more than we could. In light of our efforts, it seems they can't do any worse. Maybe each of us would benefit from a little treatment up there, considering what we saw that day.

The Priest

When the morning news reported that ongoing tensions between East and West had escalated from concerning to dangerous, and heated rhetoric included a threat of nuclear weapons, Father Coleman's first thought was *We don't deserve this planet.* Despite always believing in the back of his mind its inevitability, the idea of impending holocaust turned his blood cold. The horrors Man was willing to inflict on itself never failed to depress him, so after digesting this portentous update, he had promptly left the presbytery and walked briskly through London's West End, bound for his favourite café, experiencing an overwhelming compulsion to be among others.

Clusters of protesters were congregated around Westminster as he passed, toting placards and banners demanding peace and displaying anti-nuclear logos. *No to nukes,* the banners read. *Never again.* These demonstrators, teenagers to the elderly, were shadowed by stoic police officers observing their progression. One inspired individual near the front had come guised as the Grim Reaper, complete with ghoulish face paint and what he, Father Coleman, hoped was an artificial scythe. He allowed himself a wry smile: he admired their conviction to stand up and be heard, to march, but knew that if matters truly slipped off the rails, no amount of shouting in the street would make a difference. Seemed there was always some pending emergency nowadays: viruses, climate change, food shortages. More than enough to be getting on with, surely, without pointing nuclear warheads at each other.

He often made the entire journey on foot, but the day's early heat and periodic complaints from an old rugby injury decided him against it. A quick ride on the Underground then, trying to think about anything but looming nuclear conflict. What occupied his thoughts, as they inevitably did while he was on the Tube, were photographs he'd seen of civilians sheltering down here in the Blitz, sleeping on platforms and walkways, while Luftwaffe bomber aircraft shelled from above. During his short trip, a round-eyed youngster with rich, blue irises fixated on him from a stroller, sucking at its fingers, and he pondered what state the world would be in by the time this kid reached adulthood.

In the café at Marylebone Lane, he watched the waitress wending between tables. He hadn't seen her here before. Her accent was Polish, he thought, judging by their brief exchange when he ordered tea. She wasn't beautiful, not in any traditional sense, but certainly attractive, so much so that he found himself entranced. Her long dyed hair, secured in a tail, was the deep red of communion wine, hanging against the pristine white of her blouse. It shone alluringly, enflamed in afternoon sunlight spilling through the café's plate-glass windows. She wore too a clinging black skirt, tights, and flat sling-back shoes, which carried her soundlessly. She reminded him a little of Meryl Streep in *The Bridges of Madison County,* one of his favourite movies.

His attention went with her as she passed, for no longer did he berate himself for looking, for appreciating. These simple pleasures— desires from which he'd abstained since entering the priesthood— beckoned with sustained urgency. He'd given his best years to the Roman Catholic Church, but of late, he struggled to remember why. The calling he'd responded to years prior felt like a distant memory. Increasingly he was haunted by the passage of time and chances missed—regrets common in life's long journey—but in his case, such regrets proved harder to bear because they were self-inflicted. Indeed, he'd come to despise the physical solitude of his vocation.

He rotated his cup on its saucer and sampled the Darjeeling tea. Not sweet enough, not quite, so he spooned in another sugar, stirred, finishing the ritual with a double tinkle. By the counter, the tall waitress slipped through a doorway, so his attention turned to the canvas print decorating the wall opposite his table: a couple on their wedding day standing in front of a church.

From here, his gaze shifted outside to the shimmering street, where people absorbed the summer weather. Plump grey pigeons strutted among shoppers, pecking the ground for discarded morsels. A heavyset tattooed man and swarthy woman sat outside a restaurant across the way, each in shorts and a T-shirt, their eyes protected behind dark wraparound sunglasses. A little girl, their daughter, Father Coleman presumed, tottered beside them, her small cherry-red shoes skipping over flagstones which reflected the sun's glare. Her sleeveless dress was buttercup yellow, this girl, her blonde hair a mass of sausage curls, and he found himself smiling as she wandered happily with a balloon in her hand, a cartoon tiger grinning from the inflated foil material. His smile faltered, though: he will never have what this couple has. His chosen province had necessitated he forgo certain entitlements, and this was what he contemplated as he drank his tea and watched the girl with the tiger balloon.

When the waitress reappeared carrying a jug of ice water, their gazes connected briefly, sending a current pulsing within him, a series of welcome blips across the plateau of his emotional monitor. She looked mid-to-late thirties, a few years younger than him, with strong cheekbones and a prominent nose, her fingernails painted the same dark red as her hair. As she passed, the suggestion of a smile played across her full lips. He was about to return the smile, but already she was by, leaving him a heady breath of something delicate and clean, so he sipped his tea and wondered what people saw when they looked at him.

Another waitress stood working a shiny-fronted espresso machine, pushing buttons, moving levers, eliciting hisses and gurgles, and he marvelled that coffee preparation had become so refined. His knee injury complained quietly again, so he rubbed at it in gentle circles.

His attention returned outside, through the glass, snagged by a commotion in the street: a barefoot man shuffled around out there with a sandwich board over him. The man's straggly hair and beard, coupled with the sinewy, naked upper body, put Father Coleman in mind of Defoe's *Robinson Crusoe*, a book he read twice in his youth. The sandwich board asked HAVE YOU BEEN SAVED BY JESUS?

'Are you a sinner?' the scruffy man called to those around him, frail arms extended like a decrepit cabaret singer. 'Will the Lord welcome *you* into Heaven when Armageddon comes?'

Passers-by afforded him room, quickening pace, shunning his advance and snickering as if his mental state was contagious as if he were trussed not in a sandwich board but a straightjacket. A large scowling seagull, backing up on webbed feet, cawed at the man. The girl with the tiger balloon stared, one eye squinting under sunlight, weight canted; then she looked at Mother as if for an explanation, who only reached out and brought the child closer. A trio of teenage boys captured the man's sermon with mobile phones as he entreated them to heed his words, but they merely laughed and shouted obscenities. Father Coleman felt perhaps he should do something and set down his cup. But then he only looked on, as did his fellow patrons.

That poor sod out there probably has more faith than I do, he thought, feeling urged to discard his collar, feeling no longer worthy of it, an impostor, like a soldier decorated with medals from a battle he's never seen.

His belief had begun to wane lately, gradually inched aside by the carnal longing for the warmth of another, by the revelation that, where the priesthood was concerned, sacrifices would ultimately outweigh any gain. He felt this despite his acceptance that personal gain should not be a factor. He felt disappointed in himself. After his initial undertaking to become a priest—regular participation in mass, developing a relationship with his parish's clergy, seminary school, studying philosophy at the undergraduate level, college graduation and five further years before ordainment—after everything he had achieved ... his conviction, his *foundation,* proved unsound.

Today's society deemed the Church dated and archaic, and he had some understanding why people thought this. One need only watch the news any random day to appreciate the spiralling ugliness in the world. Atrocities came to hand-over-fist, each worse than the last. Mankind did not learn, heeding neither lesson nor guidance from reminders like Auschwitz and its huge glass containers, teeming with effects from the millions gassed and discarded in pits. It didn't learn from Japanese Kamikaze pilots trained to attack warships in suicidal dives. It didn't learn from children screaming because their skin was burned by napalm. It did not learn from the obliteration of Hiroshima and Nagasaki by Little Boy and Fat Man, thousands vaporised by these terrible weapons. Instead, it created and stockpiled more missiles capable of even greater devastation.

And faith? He almost chuckled. Well, there were no guarantees of anything; and this, ironically, was the only guarantee.

A television on the wall played the News. It showed by turns further footage of amassed missiles and fearsomely serried ranks of Russian and Chinese soldiers. The American President spoke from the White House before the female newsreader came back on-screen, looking decidedly unsettled, Father Coleman thought. Why could not world leaders realise that their countries, their lands, were here long before them and would remain long after they're gone? That they were but custodians and the planet wasn't theirs to destroy?

He shook his head, wondering what was wrong with people, why the compulsion to hurt was so common in the world. But this compulsion had always been around, Coleman knew. It could be traced as far back as civilisation, could it not? For evidence, one need only look at the Romans—a part of history he had studied in depth. People were aware the Romans had crucified Jesus, but many didn't know they'd actually crucified thousands of others. And often, the practice was much more basic than that depicted on television. For example, unfortunates were indeed left to perish on upright crosses, but sometimes the Romans would tie or nail individuals to X-shaped crosses and simply lean them against a wall to die. Slaves, disgraced soldiers, Christians, and political activists were subjected to this brutal death, often after suffering unspeakable injuries before being mounted. The condemned would often first undergo flogging, leaving him weak, bleeding, and in pain; then, he was made to carry the crossbar of his own cross to the place of execution. In yet more severe cases, the Romans had been known to cut off body parts prior to leaving a crucified man to die for hours and days.

Such an end, he believed, was too painful to imagine.

The restroom door opened, revealing an absurdly obese gentleman in an oversized suit. Inclined backwards, craning his posture to support the huge mass of his body, the laboured task of walking to his seat seemed an ordeal. The buttons of his pinstripe shirt were ready to give, his face glazed in perspiration. At his table, he slumped down and took a moment to compose himself, breathing, before wedging a napkin between neck-fat and collar and pushing a croissant into his mouth.

Fans whirred quietly overhead with minimal effect. Father Coleman was thankful then that the establishment door was propped open with a brick, inviting in the street's bustle. He withdrew a handkerchief from his trousers, softly blotting his forehead and cheeks. His undershirt clung to his spine coolly. His black suit stored heat, cooking him, and sitting still was a struggle.

He removed his round spectacles and breathed on them, buffing the lenses with a small satiny cloth. Doing so, he was reminded of a grainy black-and-white photograph he once encountered in a book on the Holocaust. Initially, he'd thought the picture depicted numberless pairs of glasses left atop a large mound of earth. That's how it had looked. Many of the round lenses caught the light, reflecting whitely, but mostly the lenses were dark, and it was their thin frames which reflected light. Then, on closer scrutiny, he learned there was, in fact, no mound of earth, and the photograph's reality, its awful truth, became clear: the picture's entire content was eyeglasses. Everything. A jumbled mass of eerie sightless eyes. Thousands upon thousands, who could tell how many pairs?

What if such evil had been inflicted against him? he wondered, finishing his tea. What could he have done? What would his faith have accomplished?

He slipped the spectacles back on and focussed once more on the wall's large canvas print: a handsome just-married couple in a church doorway, confetti suspended around them like gameshow prize winners, the bride in white, hands hidden by her bouquet, black hair pinned up in a fetching chignon. Her captured expression of delight reminded him of the dazzle-smile women hung on dentist surgery walls. He studied the intricate craftsmanship of the church—the high-tiered entranceway, the stained-glass windows—and the image evoked a familiar pang of separation: for him, the canvas comprised two mutually exclusive components.

These thoughts brought to mind a Scandinavian girlfriend he'd known as a teenager, before the priesthood, before he became someone else. He closed his eyes, shutting out the café, summoning memories, transported back decades to a massage he'd never forgotten. They were lying on the bed in his studio flat, the '94 World Cup final on television, Brazil versus Italy, played in California, right through to a shootout. Due to the summer heat, he was wearing only shorts, and this girl—Astrid was her name—this girl Astrid was kneading the muscles around his shoulders, her nails snaking and trailing his spine, her closed intimate fists pressing up and down his body. He recalled the wondrous unpredictability of those fingertips, those thumbs, the electrifying spontaneity of the experience. He wished he could relive it all, for real. Wished he could be that teenage boy again.

Father Coleman opened his eyes.

Across the floor, the fat man licked his fingertips. Outside, two male police officers had arrived in cut-sleeved shirts and peaked caps. They steered away the bearded individual with the sandwich board in short order, pigeons flapping around his dirty, bare feet. Had the authorities been summoned to a disturbance? he wondered. Or to assist someone vulnerable? Perhaps they hadn't been summoned at all.

The young girl in the buttercup dress was now contentedly perched on her mother's lap, knocking those cherry shoes together. The mother had removed her own sunglasses and daubed protective cream around her daughter's face. She put a spot on the tip of the little girl's nose, drawing a giggle, the grinning cartoon tiger spinning and bobbing slowly.

They reminded him of the mother and young daughter who were travelling to Disneyland in Los Angeles when their ill-starred flight was commandeered and plunged into a New York skyscraper. Curiously, he often thought of this four-year-old, Juliana, whom he had once seen on a television documentary about the 9/11 atrocity. The sole picture offered of Juliana had shown an incredibly happy, smiling child. Father Coleman imagined her on the plane, giddy, antsy, her short legs swinging clear of the cabin floor. All well until the brutalities began. He imagined the girl's mother, Ruth, soothing the child, assuring her everything would be fine, likely repeating this mantra until they simply aren't there any more. Sometimes he tried to reconcile how their day had surely begun—little Juliana careering around the house, spurred by the prospect of Goofy and his counterparts—with how it had surely ended, their last day, their only day.

He accepted there was no design, no master plan. Furthermore, he accepted that to label Man's self-inflicted ills and Nature's tragedies under 'God's mysterious ways' was as veritable a display of naivety as any, and nobody's naivety had been greater than his own. But still, it was difficult to accept because, for the most part, at his core, he remained a spiritual being—as one's spirituality surely cannot simply wink out like a dying ember. In truth, he no longer knew how he felt about these issues, no longer knew whether it even mattered.

He studied couples conversing across tables. He glanced sidelong at a young lady in a white and cerise hooped dress, like candy, as she stretched her arms and gathered her glossy hair in a loose tail before releasing it and forking her fingers through its flaxen length: this reflexive gesture resonated within him. He could not now fathom what had driven him to forsake his innate desires.

Outside, as the young girl tottered away with her parents, holding her mother's hand, merging among the crowds, he could still see the grinning foil tiger in the air long after they were gone.

The waitress with hair like sacramental wine approached his table again and cocked a hip. She smiled down at him, and the expression was blessedly genuine.

'Care for anything else, Father?'

He considered this long and hard before returning the smile. 'No, thank you,' he said.

He stood up, unfastened the clerical collar from his neck, and laid it there on the table. It was time to get on with life; indeed, long past it. Time to stop seeing negatives tainting every damned thing he looked at. He walked from the café out into the stir of bodies and sunshine, where he took a deep breath, pausing amid the crowds.

Suddenly, from far away—but ultimately too close—the sky was lit by incredible blinding light, followed by the most horrendously deafening blast and instantly searing heat. Rooftops were torn from buildings in the pulse of radiation. Windows exploded from fittings. As screaming erupted, he had time to realise that humanity had finally crossed a line, one from which it would not step back.

In the final firing of synapses and neurons, he was in that apartment again, cup final on television, summer warmth through open windows, Astrid's hands playing his muscles with the virtuosity of a musician.

And for him, at least, it was all over.

Gabriel's Mirror

When Gabriel Lambert arrived at Avalon House, the estate agent was already there. He'd been informed her name was Eileen Cuthbertson. As he stepped down from his Mitsubishi jeep, Gabriel was pleased to see she was not only young but hot. The tall brunette moved away from her Porsche, her svelte figure snug inside a two-piece navy suit. A red folder was tucked under one arm, and a small handbag adorned the other. She had the hip-sway thing down pat, walking as if flanked by bulb-flashing paparazzi. Her dark brown hair was pinned back, and her attractive face betrayed a business-like expression.

'Good afternoon, Mr Lambert,' she said, extending a hand.

'Afternoon,' Gabriel replied. 'So this is the place, huh?'

Eileen spun around, and they regarded the house. 'All set for the guided tour?'

Gabriel studied the property, catching her sweet perfume on the breeze. Avalon House crouched among overhanging trees, empty and unloved. It was an intriguing stone arrangement, with latticed dormer windows above and casements below, one of which revealed a FOR SALE sign behind the clouded glass. The place hadn't housed anybody in years: it was a scene of faded curtains, weathered window frames, and rampant weeds and foliage encroaching from every direction.

'You make the drive down here, okay?' she asked as they began towards the house.

'No problem,' Gabriel said, stealthily shifting his eyes to her hand and seeing no wedding ring. 'The roads were quiet.'

'Yo live in Edinburgh?'

'Living might be an exaggeration at the minute. A friend's letting me crash on his sofa for a while. My wife and I recently separated. We sold the house.'

'Oh,' said Eileen.

'So, I need somewhere quickly. I've landed a job down here, which starts at the end of the summer. To be square with you, the price of this place caught my eye the first time I saw it on your website. And it's only a mile from Blackwood—that's where I'll be teaching at the secondary school.'

'What do you teach?'

'History, though kids aren't much interested in history these days.'

They were standing right outside Avalon House, by the weed-choked walkway which snaked down to the red front door. The woodland shivered in the breeze.

'The price *is* very reasonable,' Eileen was saying. 'Even when taking into account, the place needs quite a bit of work.'

'Hasn't there been much interest?'

'Mr Lambert, I take it you're aware of what happened here three years ago?'

'With Jonathan Cathcart? I've heard something about it.'

She nodded. 'It's clearly maligned the house's saleability, but for someone willing to overlook what happened, this place would be a steal. It's quiet and peaceful, the rooms are a great size, and it has bags of potential.'

Gabriel knew something of the history, having heard it from his new employer at the school. Jonathan Cathcart, a self-employed electrician, had committed suicide here three years ago in the upstairs bathroom. A bit of a loner apparently, he'd lived in the house only two months before slashing his wrists with a steak knife at the age of forty-three. From what Gabriel understood, Cathcart had begun acting strangely during the weeks prior to his death. The locals said he swore something was *in* the house with him and that he'd claimed to hear footsteps upstairs in the middle of the night. Cathcart had no history of mental illness, and his sister—his only family when he died—couldn't understand why he'd kill himself. But the property's gory history actually dates back further. Five years before Cathcart bought Avalon House, it was home to the man who'd constructed it: a builder by the name of Alec Mackie. Like Jonathan Cathcart, Mackie had lived alone (he'd endured two divorces), and his life had also ended gruesomely, this time by a hunting rifle in the mouth.

Mackie was in his fifties when he blew his head apart in the kitchen. Blackwood's locals attested he'd displayed no prior signs of depression. Mackie's death was ascribed, by some, to his second divorce, a separation which saw his wife moving overseas with his two young daughters and a new lover. Was this reason enough for Mackie to swallow a bullet? Gabriel reckoned it was impossible to know.

'The house's past hasn't put you off?' Eileen asked as they headed down the walkway.

'Well, I don't wanna be imagining slashed wrists and gunshot deaths when I kick back after work. But I think I can live with it.'

She looked at him. 'So you know about Alec Mackie too?'

'Wasn't I supposed to know?'

'No, no, it's better you're aware of the facts, ghastly as they are.

Nobody else has even been inside this house since Cathcart killed himself. It really doesn't bother you?'

'Whatever was wrong with those men had nothing to do with the house,' Gabriel said, trying to sound braver than he felt. Of course, the history bothered him; people had topped themselves in the place. But the price was low, and he always prided himself in being able to nose out a bargain. Moreover, he liked the look of the estate agent and didn't want to appear cowardly by admitting misgivings.

'I don't buy into that kind of thing, anyway.'

Eileen slotted the key in the front door. 'What kind of thing, Mr Lambert?'

'Haunted houses and suchlike.'

She gave Gabriel a smile and pushed open the front door, and he stepped inside Avalon House for the first time.

They toured the rooms and Gabriel was pleased to find they were indeed a good size. Avalon's interior was in better shape than he'd expected. In the kitchen, he tried not to envisage Alec Mackie and the hunting rifle, but it was difficult not to. No signs remained of the grisly episode, of course, yet he felt a shiver ripple through him, nonetheless.

'Hard to believe what happened in here, isn't it?' he said.

Eileen wrinkled her nose. 'To be honest, I don't even like being in this room, nor the bathroom upstairs.'

'Is that where Jonathan Cathcart died?'

'It's pretty unsettling.'

'You must think I'm loopy, viewing this place.'

'It needs someone who can overlook the past,' she said, glancing around at the smooth covings. 'If you can, then the house is a great deal.'

'Who's actually selling it?' Gabriel asked. 'Who owns it now?'

'Jonathan Cathcart's sister, Vanessa. It was bequeathed to her after he died. She lives in London and doesn't have much interest in keeping hold of the place.'

Gabriel peered around. The house was coated with heavy dust, begging for a good clean—but what place wouldn't be after such a lengthy ownerless period? Two armchairs and a scratched coffee table remained in the lounge—most probably from Cathcart's time—but by and large, the place was sparsely furnished.

'Everything here is inclusive of the asking price,' Eileen said, pausing beneath the lounge's high ceiling. 'The furniture, the curtains, the fridge/freezer and cooker. The washing machine is brand new. Vanessa had it installed a few months ago. Also, if you want something removed, I'll arrange that, too.'

'This is all Cathcart's stuff?' Gabriel drew his hand over an armchair upholstered in red fabric, whereupon light dust became airborne.

Eileen nodded. 'Like I mentioned, if you want anything removed, I can arrange it for you.'

'Right.'

Gabriel shadowed her upstairs, treated to an eyeful of baby-smooth calves and shapely posterior as she sashayed back and forth. He wanted to reach out and caress her, but such salacious appetites had landed him in this position in the first place. He wondered again if she was single.

They briefly ventured inside the three bedrooms. Two were substantial, the one at the rear of the house rather small.

'Feel free to have a poke around,' Eileen said, squinting uneasily at the bathroom. 'I'll be downstairs if you need anything.'

Alone, Gabriel viewed the two larger bedrooms a second time. The one above Avalon's front door was spacious and caught the daylight. It was carpeted and comprised a walnut bureau in the corner and a large closet. The windowsill was peppered with dead flies. From here, he peered down upon his jeep and the estate agent's dark Porsche. Eileen suddenly emerged from the house, talking into a mobile phone, toeing a tussock of grass with her shoe.

'Very nice,' he said, admiring her curves.

July sunlight angled into the bedroom, highlighting the dust motes.

Was this Jonathan Cathcart's room? Gabriel wondered. Or maybe Alec Mackie's? He decided if he were going to move in here, he shouldn't dwell overlong on such things. Wasn't good to dwell, not when past owners had the habit of inflicting violent deaths on themselves.

He stepped out to the hall. In the bathroom, where Jonathan Cathcart had slashed his wrists, Gabriel stared down at the tub and couldn't help but conjure the bloody scene. The room was pokey, with a light blue sink, bath and toilet. White tiles. Worn linoleum floor. Again, no residual signs of violent death, he was glad to note.

He entered the smallest bedroom next. The floor was bare wooden boards, slightly uneven. Nothing in here but a full-length ornate mirror on the far wall. It was gilded in an intricate gold frame and shaped at the top like a snake's head. Gabriel stepped in front of it, studying the reflection of his body. He touched the glass with a fingertip, scoring the mantle of dust there.

The long mirror certainly appeared antique, and Gabriel found it secured firmly to the wall. Had Alec Mackie ever viewed himself here and considered blowing his head off? Had Jonathan Cathcart stood in this very spot and considered opening his veins?

'You might actually be worth a few quid,' he informed the mirror appraisingly. 'Everything inclusive of the asking price.' He smiled. 'I guess that makes you mine.'

Hands in his jeans, Gabriel sauntered to the bedroom door and gave the room a last cursory glance. As he made to leave, he thought he saw something move in his peripheral vision: a fleeting motion, nothing more. He glanced back towards the long mirror, where he sensed the movement had been, but nothing reflected in the dusty glass other than himself and the empty room.

*****

'I appreciate you taking time to show me around,' Gabriel said from his 4x4's window. He gunned the engine.

'You're very welcome.' Eileen clutched her folder to her bosom. 'You're really taken with it?'

His gaze shifted to Avalon's timbered gable. 'I think it's right for me at the moment. As I mentioned, I need a place fairly soon, and I don't much care for neighbours.'

'Well, there's none out here unless you count the hedgehogs.' She giggled. It was a childish sound, and Gabriel liked it a great deal.

'Listen, Eileen, I know this may be a little forward, but I was wondering if you were ... if you were *with* anyone, you know?'

She looked at him. 'You mean a boyfriend?'

'I suppose that's what I mean, yeah.'

'Not at the moment.'

'Would you fancy maybe going for a drink sometime?'

Eileen bit her lip. Gabriel saw a smile trying to escape.

'I don't think it'd be very professional, mixing business with pleasure.'

Gabriel nodded. 'What if I ask you again later when business is over?'

She shrugged. Now the smile was in full bloom. 'I suppose you'll just have to ask and see, won't you?'

Gabriel drove back to Edinburgh later the same day. The blue sky was clear, and he listened to Dr Hook, Aerosmith, and Guns n' Roses. As he clocked up the miles, he thought about Avalon House and its violent past. And he thought about Eileen.

At thirty-eight years old, Gabriel was besotted with women. He was besotted with golf, too, which ran a close second in his life, though it couldn't rival his preoccupation with the fairer sex. This preoccupation was the reason he'd been divorced and also the reason he'd been forced into finding a new school wherein to teach. He'd had affairs throughout his adult life.

When he was younger, one woman was never enough; this was something he'd discovered quickly, as soon as he'd begun dating. Too many different kinds mincing around to be satisfied with one. Different sizes, different smells, different faces. Different wants. It was the sheer variety which constituted his inability to be content with one. He'd lost track of the girlfriends he'd frittered away because he couldn't keep his hands off their enticing counterparts. And when a man could draw them in without too much effort, like Gabriel knew he could, straying became doubly hard to resist.

He indicated out and accelerated past an HGV lorry. The road ahead was clear.

Years ago, when he'd married Tracy, he thought it might quell the need to sample other women, but wedlock hadn't sated his appetites. If anything, being with Tracy every day had only underlined his failings: he simply couldn't be with the same person permanently.

Perhaps it was some sort of disorder, he thought. Sex addiction, or whatever it was called. Didn't Michael Douglas once have something similar? Can't-get-enough-ass syndrome. Satyriasis, that was it. Gabriel laughed as he accelerated into the open road.

In any case, he'd inevitably strayed from his marriage vows, as he knew he would. Still, mixing it up with a fellow teacher hadn't been the best move he'd ever made. Eventually, his affair with a female colleague had been laid bare, and the rector had promptly informed him that, should he leave quietly, he might keep his reputation intact and acquire a position in another school.

Therefore, Gabriel duly resigned from his teaching post last year and hasn't worked since. Now he was moving to Blackwood as a single man, where things were hopefully beginning to look up again.

*****

He met with his solicitor in Edinburgh two weeks later. Mr Hepburn's office occupied the third floor of a building on Frederick Street. Hepburn himself was a bald, middle-aged man attired in a double-breasted suit and garish tie. His glowing pate caught the overhead light with a such dazzling intensity that Gabriel wondered if the man buffed it every morning.

'No doubt you'll be glad to move in,' the solicitor said. 'Sleeping on a couch is hardly suitable accommodation.'

'Tell me about it,' Gabriel sighed. 'It's playing havoc with my back. Feel like I've aged ten years since the divorce.'

Hepburn smiled. 'Divorces can have that effect.'

'But I do want in quickly. I start teaching down there next month and really need to tidy the place up.'

'Far as I can see, the home report shows no viable reason why you shouldn't take the property.' He tapped a hefty document at his side. 'The asking price is certainly reasonable, although I don't know how you'll fare trying to sell it on, should you want to.'

'I've no intentions of moving again,' Gabriel said. 'Not for a long time, anyhow.'

'The house needs some TLC, but structurally it's sound enough. It's well built and will make a fine home with a little effort. There is something else I feel I should tell you, though.'

'Oh?'

'The old place has a bit of a murky past,' the solicitor continued, rolling on the castors of his chair. 'Two men've killed themselves there over the last ten-or-so years.'

'I'm well aware of the horror stories, Mr Hepburn.'

The bald man raised a hand. 'I wasn't sure whether to bring it up. As your solicitor, I thought I ought to.'

'Thanks anyway. So, where do we go from here?'

Hepburn scooted his chair forward. 'Okay. Immediate entry is available. Once payment is secured, you could have the keys by the end of this week. Go to the bank and request a banker's draft, which you can make out to me at this address.' He scratched down the details on a piece of paper and slid it across to Gabriel. 'Once that's done, drop it back here, and I'll get the ball rolling.' Hepburn stood and shook Gabriel's hand. 'I hope your new start in Blackwood is a pleasant one, Mr Lambert. It's a lovely little town down there.'

'After enduring a divorce,' Gabriel said, 'anything will be an improvement.'

Over the ensuing weeks, Gabriel moved into Avalon House and procured some new furniture. With the kitchen already equipped, he soon had the place in a liveable condition. He cleared weeds and tussocks of sprouting grass from around the house, filling multiple trash bags. This done, he still had time before the summer break ended and used it, familiarising himself with the town. To his pleasant surprise, he found it even had a golf course.

Blackwood was a homely little place, where people watched out for a neighbour, and nobody appeared to be on the make. Furthermore, it had enough females roaming about to keep him interested. The locals were friendly, although some gave him queer glares upon hearing he was the newcomer who'd acquired Avalon House. A few funny looks were to be expected; Gabriel didn't let it get to him because things would smooth out soon enough. He was starting over. He was here with a new job, a new home, and he felt as free as the gulls wheeling overhead. This was good enough for now.

*****

One Thursday afternoon, Gabriel was pacing the aisles of the local supermarket, picking up odds and ends. In the veg section, as he bagged some onions, he spotted a brown-haired girl in a floral skirt. She was squeezing a melon tentatively.

'Thought I recognized those calves,' he whispered to her.

'Mr Lambert,' Eileen said, sounding pleasantly shocked as she dropped the fruit into her basket.

'Gabriel, please. Only pupils call me mister, and that's only 'cause they have to.'

'How's the house?'

'Oh, I've been cleaning up. I'm getting there. The journey of a thousand miles starts with the first step and all that.'

Eileen appeared more youthful, with her hair unpinned. Its glossiness framed her heart-shaped face and augmented her allure. Her scarlet blouse was open at the chest, revealing an enticing swell and a wink of lace, and Gabriel held eye contact with her rigorously.

'How'd you feel about venturing for that drink sometime? Business is done and dusted, and you did tell me to ask again. So, here I am, asking.'

'Here you are.'

'You free Saturday?'

She glanced off down the aisle and back at him. 'What did you have in mind?'

'A drink, or a movie, maybe. Fun in general—fun's guaranteed. Lots of fun.'

She appeared unsure, so much so that Gabriel expected her to turn him down. But then the cheeky smile returned, and she said, 'Okay, Saturday. Let me give you my address.' And then she was rummaging in her leather handbag.

That evening, a mile from his new home, Gabriel partook of a pint of ale in the White Knight, the northernmost of Blackwood's two pubs. Locals stood talking along the wooden counter. Gabriel was seated in the corner, reading a *Guardian* someone had left, sneaking furtive glances at the buxom girl serving the punters.

After a time, he became aware of an elderly guy at the bar glancing at him repeatedly. The old man's face was heavily pocked and lined, his matted grey hair pasted greasily to his head, and his jeans and plaid shirt were rumpled and creased. Gabriel tried to ignore him, but the guy's ratty eyes kept squinting. Eventually, the man ambled over, a bottle of Coors in his hand.

'Mind if I join ya there, friend?'

Gabriel looked up at him. 'Do I know you?'

'No, don't suppose you do. Name's Crothers. Bill Crothers. Been in Blackwood as long as anyone.'

'I prefer to drink alone, Bill, if it's all the same to you.'

Crothers scraped out a chair and sat down. Gabriel bridled a little. The old man had the telltale nose of one who spends too much time in public houses, though right now, he seemed sober enough. His bad teeth were stones in a neglected graveyard.

'You're the fella moved into Avalon House.'

'That's right.'

'I thought it was you. Listen, I can tell yeh a few things concerning the men who lived there.'

'You're too late, Bill,' Gabriel told him brusquely. 'I already know the suicide stories. It's old news, so if you don't mind ...'

Crothers raised a gnarled finger and screwed up his face. 'Y'see, there you go, jumpin' the gun already. Folks ain't rightly sure those men did away with themselves.'

'It's really none of my concern what the folks think. I said I prefer to drink alone.'

'Police passed them off as suicides,' Crothers went on, crossing his skeletal legs. 'But I knew both men, Mackie *and* Cathcart, and I tell yeh they never killed themselves, no way. I knew Mackie well, and he wasn't no suicide risk, no sir. He was a strong man, in his head and in his heart.'

Gabriel supped his ale. 'You knew them?'

'Aye, 'specially Mackie. He'd drink with me in this very bar. Probably warmed that their seat of yours once upon a time. Well, let me tell yeh, there's goings-on the police didn't bother about, things maybe they *should've* bothered about.'

'Such as?'

Crothers relaxed a little. 'Such as Mackie paying tax on his motor the day before supposedly puttin' a rifle in his mouth. Why'd anyone do such a crazy thing?'

'He taxed his car?'

'The police knew he did it. And Cathcart—you know what Jonathan Cathcart did the same week they found 'im with slashed wrists? He put his watch in to be repaired.' Crothers raised his palm. 'Kid, you not. This old ticker his mother'd left him. The strap was broken if I recall right. This strike you like the actions of men fixin' to off themselves?'

Gabriel considered. 'I suppose not.'

'Mackie was spooked before he died, though.' Crothers swigged from his bottle, making an ugly slurping sound. 'I remember it clear as day. Was just after he returned from his holiday to Egypt. He'd bought this old mirror out there, see? Mackie was into old stuff, antiques n' things, and was always buying and selling. He had this big old gold mirror flown back from Egypt, and that's when he starts hearin' noises in the house.'

'Alec Mackie told you this, did he?'

'Swear it on ma dear mother's grave,' Crothers answered, fingering an X over his heart. 'Reckoned, there were footsteps in the room where he hung the mirror. Heard feet walkin' around in the little bedroom, he reckoned.' Crothers nodded emphatically. 'Sometimes sounded as if it were one person, other times like a whole troop.'

'You can't be serious,' Gabriel scoffed. 'Why didn't you tell the police this?'

'Did tell 'em. You think they'd listen to an old duck like me?' He shook his head. 'Those men *wanted* to suicide, and suicide's the way they went. Case closed. But Jon Cathcart, he told folks the same things afore he died. Walkin' sounds in the very same bedroom. That's common knowledge round here. You ask anyone; it's what folks tell ya. Besides, it's not likely two men'd kill themselves in the same house, is it?'

'I don't know,' Gabriel replied, shifting in his chair. A couple of people finished their drinks and left. A thick-furred dog watched him from the corner. 'The laws of chance would allow two suicides in the same house, even though it's unlikely.'

'Two suicides is one thing, sure enough. But for two men who folks swear weren't inclined that way? Two men sayin' noises were coming from the same bedroom?'

'If Mackie thought something was wrong with the mirror, why not turf the thing out, or sell it on?'

Crothers leaned back. Gabriel could see the old man had this angle sewn up, too. 'Last time I saw Alec Mackie was in this bar. He tells me he's gonna pull down the mirror and get rid of it, I swear. Said there was something about it that freaked him, though he never admitted what.'

'The mirror's still there,' Gabriel told him. 'It's fixed to the wall in one of the spare rooms.'

'Next, I hear, Mackie's missing half his head, and he's not hearing nothing no more. Few years later, Jon Cathcart's moved in, an' he's found with his wrists all cut up, just as dead as Mackie. You should watch yer step in there, mister.'

'Maybe I'll get rid of the mirror myself,' Gabriel said. 'Is it worth anything?'

Crothers batted a bony hand. 'Mackie never told me what he paid for it. Was pretty cagey about where he got it from, too. I ain't never laid eyes on the thing. Don't wanna see it, either. I'm saying only this. Two men've died in the house—died bloody deaths, mind—and that's where you're livin'.'

*****

That night, after dark, Gabriel heard the footsteps for the first time. He hadn't been near the bedroom since talking to Bill Crothers in the White Knight earlier. Truth be told, the lecherous old wretch had put the wind up him, and Gabriel was a little jittery about everything— the house, the suicides, the mirror.

He was in the lounge, staring out of the latticed window at the pines through the fading summer light when he heard steps from above. At first, it sounded like two feet, quick and scurrying, but soon the noises multiplied as if many feet were moving around up there.

Gabriel stood looking perplexedly up at the ceiling, a chill snaking down the muscled contours of his back. 'Someone's having me on,' he whispered. 'Someone's bloody having me *on*.'

He moved out to the foot of the stairs. He could now hear nothing, steps or otherwise, but it didn't matter. Those noises had been

359

unmistakable. He knew he should do the sensible thing and leave. Go find a constable to look the place over. Yet a part of him refused to be intimidated. He wasn't superstitious, and he wouldn't be made to act as if he were.

Gabriel eased open the cupboard beneath the stairs and slipped out one of his clubs from the golf bag. He clutched the 5-iron and felt a little safer. Thus armed, he started upstairs.

He hesitated in the hall outside the small bedroom, craning his neck, listening for the slightest movement, but the house was silent. Had he imagined the sounds? How could he have, when two other men had heard similar noises coming from the same bedroom?

He steeled himself and touched the doorknob, letting his fingers curl around it. Here goes. Nothing to fear. Only an empty bedroom with an eyesore of a mirror on the far wall.

He threw open the door and stood at the threshold, wielding the club like a psychotic golfer, peering cautiously inside, his heart going thud-thud-thud. He saw nothing unusual: the bedroom, the day's receding light, falling over bare floorboards. And his own ridiculous reflection framed in that damned mirror.

Gabriel lowered the club.

He edged to the closet and yanked it open, his heart still banging away. Nothing inside save for two wooden hangers. He wet his lips with his tongue.

He crossed the room to the mirror and studied his reflection; then, he looked down at the floor, scratching the nape of his neck. He touched the gilded frame and the glass and briefly wondered from which part of Egypt Mackie had acquired the thing. It was painful on the eye, no question, and he couldn't imagine why anyone would trouble to fly it in from abroad. No accounting for taste, was there?

Mackie never said what he paid for it. Was pretty cagey about where he got it from, too.

'Tomorrow,' Gabriel vowed, backing away from the glass. Decisively, he butted the floor twice with the 5-iron. 'Tomorrow, you're coming down. And that'll be an end to it.'

*****

Due to the humidity—at least this was what Gabriel told himself—it required considerable effort to fall asleep that night, but sometime after midnight, he drifted off. In the wee hours of Friday morning, he awoke, looking at the corniced ceiling. His watch said three-forty. Moonbeams played on the bedroom walls and shadows were deep. The air was heavy and warm, and sweat slicked his armpits; the bedcovers kicked to hell. As he lay there, the steps began again.

Gabriel squinted in the darkness, listening intently. Noises drifted from across the hall, from the small bedroom where the mirror hung on the wall. Like before, the steps increased gradually, as if more and more feet traversed the floorboards.

'What the hell ...?'

Gabriel pictured Alec Mackie positioning his hunting rifle in his mouth, and he imagined Cathcart sawing his wrists open with a steak knife. Suddenly it didn't feel such a good idea to be living in Avalon House, and neither a good idea to be alone in the dark.

He glanced across at the silvery length of the 5-iron, which leaned against the wall, within easy reach. He could burst into the little bedroom, sure this time to expose whoever was toying with him—but instead, he held his breath. He swallowed and palmed sleep from his eyes. Before long, the shuffling gradually subsided, like a reversal of what he'd heard. From many steps to fewer steps, and fewer steps still.

Then Gabriel heard nothing.

*****

Once astir on Friday morning, groggy and irritable from lack of sleep, Gabriel rose early and dressed in a crisp white shirt and jeans. He bought a hammer and crowbar from Granger's Industrial Supplies in Blackwood and laid them on the jeep's passenger seat while he rode back with the window down. By eleven o'clock, he was standing in the doorway to the small bedroom, a prying tool in either hand, staring at the mirror. He stepped into the room. Wind was brewing outside. It whipped around the gable and seeped in through the old window frame, the faded curtains wafting and stirring gently.

Gabriel took another few steps and halted a third of the way in, reluctant to approach the strange mirror. He looked around the room, at the dusty floor, at the curtains breathing softly.

'Right. I gotta do this, so I might as well get on with it.'

He made to step forward and paused when his eyes fell on the mirror again.

There was someone inside it, watching him.

The motionless figure was cloaked in a hooded black gown, which revealed only a pale, pointed chin. The mouth was an expressionless line, the lips colourless and tight. Gabriel could see nothing more of the cowled face. The figure's hands were together, hidden inside the gown's deep folds. The chilling spectre appeared distant as if the mirror was the gateway to another room, another dimension. Of his own reflection ... well, it was no longer there.

Impulsively, he whirled around, ready to bolt from the room, but the door slammed shut—*bang!*

He gaped at it for a moment, then slipped the hammer under one

362

arm and began yanking at the knob. It was locked and yielded not an inch.

'Come *on* ...!'

Gabriel checked frantically over his shoulder and saw the figure was now accompanied by another two. And they were moving towards him, towards the mirror's surface—towards the glass, which, if he was seeing right, was no longer a tangible reality.

He gripped the hammer's rubber handle again, clutching the crowbar tightly in his other hand, and felt the locked door against his back. The three figures became four, then five, and six. The foremost hooded form, the one Gabriel had seen first, was stepping through the mirror—*stepping through it!* The gown flowed slowly over the gilded frame like black treacle. Gabriel shook his head in disbelief.

The figure stepped down into the bedroom, and the one behind followed, and another followed him in turn. Gabriel watched them with wide-eyed amazement, awed by what he was seeing. The hooded forms began to fill the room, each one's mouth set in a stony grimace, their skin a curious blue-grey pallor. They kept coming from the mirror, one after another, fanning out in front of him in a semi-circle: ten cloaked figures standing like members of a Black Mass, the velvety material of their gowns luxuriant, catching the daylight with something akin to a panther's fur.

And they stared.

'Who ... who the hell *are* you?' Gabriel nervously glanced at the window. Could he throw himself through it? Would he survive the fall, the lacerations?

He was contemplating this when they moved on him. He brought the hammer to bear but to no avail. Soon he was lost beneath a mass of black, writhing, rat-like bodies.

His screams filled the house.

*****

The following day, on Saturday evening, Eileen sat in her living room watching the time pass: seven, seven-thirty, seven-forty-five, eight o'clock. She should've given him her number as well as the address in case something arose and he couldn't make it—which had apparently happened. She mentally gave herself a slap.

Where *was* he?

She ventured to the window and peered out at the summer evening for the third time, expecting to see his jeep rolling belatedly up the road. He'd be cheeky and apologetic, armed with a bunch of flowers. You'll never believe what happened, he'd say. And she'd pretend to be annoyed, even though she wasn't.

But Gabriel wasn't there. No jeep rolled up the road. Children played on bikes and kicked a football around in the park opposite her house. She'd spent ages getting ready and he wasn't going to show. But he'd been so keen. She couldn't really believe he would have backed out.

Maybe something had happened. Staring blankly through the blind at the street, she worried at a fingernail, considering Avalon House and its macabre history.

Maybe Gabriel was in trouble.

*****

Once off the main road from Blackwood, Eileen followed the winding track out to Avalon House. Waning sunlight filtered pleasantly through the pines, silhouetting their peaks against the sky. The weather was calm, and she told herself nothing could be wrong on such a perfect summer evening.

364

One rutted mile later, she drew the Porsche up outside Avalon's front façade, approaching with caution. She set the handbrake and got out. Gabriel's jeep was there, its flank and large tyres spattered with mud. The driver-side window was inched down marginally. Eileen squinted at the house's windows as she came to a halt: bright sunbeams played on the glass, and she could see nothing against the glare.

She moved down the walkway, knocked at the front door. She waited, then back-pedalled and looked upward, regarding the house again.

'Gabriel?'

Birdsong trilled around her, though the house remained quiet and tranquil. When she tried the front door, it swung open, revealing the hall and the flight of wooden stairs.

'Gabriel! Are you home?'

Nothing came back other than her words travelling hollowly around the place before dispersing into silence.

'It's Eileen. Are you home?'

The kitchen door was ajar. She went there, and the room was empty. A plate and a glass sat on the worktop by the sink. A busty blonde smiled seductively down from the calendar on the wall. Eileen left and stepped into the lounge.

'Gabriel?'

The lounge was empty, too. She soon ended up back in the poorly lit hall.

By the stairs, she placed her hand on the newel post—and quickly removed it, seeing the wood was carved distastefully into a dragon's head. The bannister and stairs stretched upward and to the left, beyond sight. 'Gabriel, if you're fooling around with me, I assure you I'm not in the least bit amused!'

She ascended the stairs, her movements drawing creaks from each successive riser. When she reached the top, she clutched the rail and took a few composing breaths.

'Gabriel?'

She checked the first bedroom. A pair of jeans lay on the bed and the duvet was crumpled and unmade. Curiously, a golf club leant against the wall. No sign of the man, though. She checked the next bedroom. This one was carpeted but unadorned. And unoccupied. Next, she came to the smallest bedroom.

Eileen tried the door. The latch clicked, and it opened inward with a groan.

She poked her head inside. There was nothing to see other than the large gold-framed mirror on the far wall, which reflected her violet frock. The room hadn't been altered since Alec Mackie died in the house ten years ago. It remained dusty and uninviting. She looked down at the floor, where she saw an iron crowbar and a claw hammer. She shivered and turned to leave the bedroom when she heard the closet door creak ever so slightly. It was ajar a few inches.

'Gabriel?' She began over there, her heeled shoes clumping on the floor. Within touching distance of the closet, Eileen reached out and closed her lacquered fingers around the handle. She pulled open the door—

—and her eyes bulged in her head.

'My God,' she whispered, reflexively moving away.

Gabriel was hanging from a beam inside the closet, his leather belt secured around his throat, supporting his suspended body. He was dressed in a white shirt and jeans, shoes dangling a foot clear of the floor. Coils of black hair fell across his face. His arms hung limply at his sides. His terrified glistening eyes stared ahead as if entreating someone for help, desperate for assistance that never came.

*****

Nightfall comes, and they watch from the windows of Avalon House, hooded and unseen in the dark. The police officers move around out front, plain-clothed and uniformed, talking animatedly with one another. The darkness is attenuated by headlights, and as the hour grows late, the throngs eventually decrease.

One car departs, followed by another, and soon a cortege of red lights is receding into the distance. They watch two men load the body bag into a van and slam the doors. One man bangs the vehicle's side twice with his hand. The ignition fires, and the van is leaving. Nearby, an officer assists a woman into a Porsche; he adjusts the hem of her violet dress so he can close the door. They watch everything from the upper latticed windows until the last car has driven away.

From there, they move back into the small bedroom, eleven monastic figures shifting through the night. They enter the mirror single file, each stepping in before the next proceeds. Finally, the last hooded form goes inside. The newest member, and his velvet gown, slide over the gilded frame and are gone. And so the glass reflects the room once more, reflecting the darkness. Again Avalon House is silent.

367